THE KINGDOM

Shades of Sir Walter Scott! This fat romantic swash-buckler is squarely in the tradition of the Waverly novels and all the more entertaining for it. Henderson has come up with a plot set in a marvelously exotic fairytale Jerusalem at the time of the 12th century Crusaders. His young Gallic hero, a favorite at the court of Queen Melisande and the protector of a wild witch-girl who lives in a ruined castle, loses his memory and becomes a mameluke (white slave), then a Moslem lord, then a fiery Islamic spiritual leader. Naturally there's a happy ending . . . any reader willing to totally suspend disbelief is in for a swell time.

Publishers Weekly

THE KINGDOM

L.W. HENDERSON

AVON
PUBLISHERS OF BARD, CAMELOT, DISCUS, EQUINOX AND FLARE BOOKS

THE KINGDOM is an original publication of Avon Books.
This work has never before appeared in book form.

AVON BOOKS
A division of
The Hearst Corporation
959 Eighth Avenue
New York, New York 10019

ISBN: 0-380-00000-8

First Avon Printing, May, 1974.

AVON TRADEMARK REG. U.S. PAT. OFF. AND
FOREIGN COUNTRIES, REGISTERED TRADEMARK—
MARCA REGISTRADA, HECHO EN CHICAGO, U.S.A.

Printed in the U.S.A.

NOTE

NOTE

The historical events narrated here occurred between the years 1150 and 1174 A.D. At that time, the Near East was torn between two conflicting ideologies—Christian and Moslem. This is the story, unrecorded by history, of a man who rose to extraordinary heights in both these worlds, and who found the means to reconcile their conflicting claims in himself—through honesty and love. If certain episodes strain our credulity, it should be noted that most of them—such as the surrender of the Sultan's bodyguard to the leader of the Assassins, and the self-immolation of the soldiers of the Old Man of the Mountain—are attested by contemporary records.

To Thornton Wilder
il miglior fabbro

JERUSALEM

DAMASCUS

MOUNT SINAI

EPILOGUE:

JERUSALEM

THE PILGRIMAGE

In the afternoon, the wind often changes to the south-west at Acre, blowing a cool seabreeze from the Mediterranean into the torrid streets of the town, which have sweltered all day under the ridge of Mount Carmel, severe sentinel of the Holy Land. "Come unto me," Carmel seems to say, "my way is a way of hardship; the paths on which I shall lead you are stony ways; beyond my shoulder lies the desert on which moulder the bones of many pilgrims; yet if you have faith there shall be sustenance enough, as there was for Elijah who was fed by ravens in my shadow, and at the end of your journey lies the Kingdom of God."

In the mid-twelfth century, a young man, his helmet of chain mail thrown back, and his fair hair blowing in the breeze, stood at the rail of a ship gliding into Acre harbour. The headland of Carmel stood out to the south, its slopes sheathed in the feathery silver of the olive groves, right down to the edges of the town, which rose proudly behind its battlements. So many towers, so many spires, Acre itself seemed to be the Celestial City. Chief port of the Kingdom of Jerusalem, Acre had grown rich on the pilgrim traffic in the bare half-century since the First Crusade of 1099 A.D. had conquered coastal Syria and established the Frankish Kingdom of Jerusalem.

There was nothing remarkable about this young man at the rail. Guy of Vienne, knight, aged twenty, was born to a small manor house with a dozen farms in the valley of the Vienne, which meanders through Poitou in western France, at that time in the domain of Henry Plantagenet of England.

Vienne! A gentle, pastoral land, tilled by a Gallic race of serfs who were tied to the soil by the iron law of the feudal system, under their Norman masters. Yet it was a system that seemed ordained by God: each serf served the lord of a manor, each lord served a baron or count, and counts served the King. And when the King summoned his vassals to defend Christ's Holy Sepulchre in Jerusalem against the infidels, the whole land rose and followed him.

That great Crusade was now over, but every year the custom was for younger sons of the manor houses to "take the Cross"—by which was meant service in the Holy Land to keep the infidels at bay. Guy, himself a second son, took twelve of his serfs with him and set out to serve the son of his Count, Amalric of Lusignan, who was already an important man in the Kingdom of Jerusalem. After all, his brother, Henry, was now lord of the manor of Vienne. Guy was not needed at home.

It had been a time of high excitement, "taking the Cross," in the little village of Vienne. In every farming family one younger son of a serf was chosen to accompany his master. Each peasant house was filled with the bustle of preparation, as the women folk made the chain mail suits, patiently sewing the iron rings on a leather jerkin, and signing each one with the mark of a cross.

Guy himself learned to use the sword, the lance, the battle axe, jousting daily in the courtyard of the Count's castle. The Senechal of the Count, like most senior officers, took a poor view of the young recruit's abilities, worked him over mercilessly, roared, cursed, and finally pronounced him fit to face the infidels.

Then came the ceremony of his knighting, the long night vigil in the cold, empty church at Poitou and finally in the morning before the whole congregation, the blessing of his spurs, the presentation of his sword to God, and—the vows: chastity, humility, obedience. Few in his age ever kept (or intended to keep) such vows. But he was one of the few. And when he arose that morning in the bone-cold church, he felt transfigured, giddy with the thought of a great work to do.

Perhaps that is why people looked at him twice when they saw him now. In his hauberk, or chain mail suit, under a linen surcoat, he looked very straight and tall, as though he did not know how to slouch or stoop. Like most young men of his time, he had matured early and even at twenty he carried himself well.

There was about him, perhaps in his Norman inheritance, a certain freshness, a cleaness, a candour, that gave him a special quality, as though he were not quite of the same stuff as his fellows—a distinction he bore as though it did not exist. Above all, it was the straight, blue eyes, that never dropped from the object of their gaze, that made people uneasy. This young man was looking for something out of this world, they said—he was one of God's fools.

"Acre, it seems, is a rich city," Guy said to a seaman beside him at the rail.

"Rich! You wouldn't believe it!" the brown levantine sailor replied. "You have not lived until you have seen Acre. Everything turns into money—they're making it faster than ducks lay eggs—golden eggs, master!"

A crowd was gathering and the sailor enjoyed his pedagogic role. "Look in the shops and your eyes will pop out of your heads! Gold, silks, perfumes—you will live like queens, ladies! And the girls, oh! oh! oh! Keep an eye on your codpieces, masters—they will buzz around you like flies at the honey pot—"

The eyes of this motley collection of pilgrims on the deck began to light up. It was not in these terms that the Pope had preached the Crusade throughout Europe. He had called on men to bleed and toil and die for the recovery of the True Cross. But now that it was recovered, and a Christian king ruled in Jerusalem, what harm was there in turning this pilgrimage to good account? Poor men in lambskin clothing, sitting on all their worldly goods, saw themselves suddenly rich; toil-worn widows, who had spent their legacies on a ship's passage to Syria, now fancied themselves in gowns and carriages.

"But we have nothing," Guy said. "We are all pilgrims."

"Does a knight travel empty-handed, master?" The sailor gave him a curious hard look.

The young man flushed a little under this scrutiny. "I have twelve men at arms and we are travelling to Jerusalem to serve the King."

"Then you are already rich—you have your travel money. I wish I had so much." The seaman kissed his fingers to his lips. "A lead groat makes a silver penny, and a silver penny makes a gold dinar—it is all how you invest it. I have known pilgrims who invested all their travel money at Acre and never got to Jerusalem at all!" He grew confidential, answering questions and giving advice with the aplomb of a banker surrounded by his ingenuous clients.

The ship had rounded the mole, under the Tower of Flies, and was now approaching the jetty on which stood a quivering mass of humanity, of every nation, every complexion, every type of garb, but mostly Eastern, with all the hectic pulsation of a Syrian crowd. Naked, brown boys bobbed in the water for coins; turbaned porters with little signs and bells canvassed the merits of this or that caravanserai for the night; money-changers, their desks strapped to their shoulders, offered competitive rates of exchange—even before the men and horses had been disembarked.

All military contingents were marshalled in a camp on the hill of Turon, a mile east of the city, by the little river Belus, which supplied it with water. The camp was controlled by the Knights Templars, a military Order of the Church that looked after the pilgrim traffic and the defense of the Kingdom. Guy's men were provided with tents and rations, in exchange for a large levy on his purse. Everywhere in the Kingdom, he noted, money counted a great deal. The Venetians had the levy of the port tax; the Genoese had the transport levy for the baggage waggons. The very Syrian rabble had their hands out at every turning, begging for coins. A strange land this, to be God's Kingdom.

But inside the camp, all was merry. Sergeant Berthold mustered his men—Yves, Robert, Bertrand, Balian, Geoffrey, Jean, Peter the tall and Peter the short, Hugh the farrier and Hugh the miller, and Hugh the groom,—only to find that many had lost pieces of their equipment, or stolen or hidden it from each other. Some had already sold buckler and dagger, and more than one water bottle was filled with wine. All were playful as children on holiday from school.

These were the serfs of Guy's village, bound to his service, as he was to the Count's. Boys his own age, they had grown up together, wrestling on the village green, hunting birds' eggs in the spring and rabbits in the fall. They followed Guy because they must, but also because they loved him with a devotion that was fully returned.

Guy threatened to punish the malefactors, thought better of it, talked to them roughly, cuffed them gently, and sent them to the camp kitchen for dinner with a "Good appetite!"

It was evening now and a mounted knight, wearing the white mantle of the Templars with the red cross on the left shoulder, invited him to dine at the Templars' Mess in Acre. Guy found Brigitte, his mare, still restive from her long confinement on shipboard and very ready to take the evening air. And so, in the twilight, they rode together down the hillside to Acre.

Guy glanced keenly at his companion. The Templar was middle-aged and heavily bearded like all Templar Knights, in contrast to the clean-shaven Franks, like Guy. He volunteered no information and seemed withdrawn into a life apart. Yet there was so much to know and to say that the younger man hazarded a question.

"Are we likely to see action on the way up to Jerusalem tomorrow?"

"Yes, sir, we are," was the laconic reply. It fairly made Guy's heart leap to think it would come so soon. He waited for the Templar to enlarge upon it, but no more seemed to be forthcoming. He prodded again.

"Is the country unquiet, then?"

After a pause, the Templar answered this. "We usually lose a few caravans at this time of year. It's part of the game."

The game! Guy was exhilarated, but also taken aback. "Is it safe, then, do you think, to take them? There are many old and sick among the company aboard our ship."

"All the same, we take them. They pay, don't they? If we did not take them we should lose the money. They must take their chance. Mind your head, sir, we are passing St. Anthony's Gate."

They followed the inside of the city wall, along a street lined with imposing houses of smooth-cut stone, with many a marble-pillared archway and cool, rich interior. In the carriage way, there was a mass of fine carriages, litters borne by black slaves, carrying men and women of Frankish race, yet wearing the silks and turbans of the East. To Guy it was as though he had entered Aladdin's cave.

He could not repress a further inquiry, "Does the Temple do big business, then?"

"All this is the Templars' Ward," his companion answered, as they rode side by side. "These shops, the gold merchants, the money exchange—the banking house itself, the largest in the East—all belong to the Temple. Without the Temple, there would be no Kingdom of Jerusalem."

It was the largest statement he had made up to now and, as they cantered into an imposing courtyard and dismounted, Guy risked a final prod. "And are you very rich, then?"

Their eyes met on this straight, for the first time. The Templar stared a cool moment, while the grooms took their horses away, before he said, "I, sir? I own the clothes I stand up in, no more. Will you go in?"

The Templars' Mess was a magnificent refectory of a size unknown to Guy before. At least seventy or eighty knights, mostly travellers like himself, ate around a semi-circular table that lined the walls. Servants in Syrian dress stood behind every third or fourth guest to wait on him and fill his flagon with wine. A great fire burned in the center of the room, on which a score of pigs were roasting. Never before had Guy seen such a profusion of good things, with sweetmeats, cakes and jellies he thought fit only for fine ladies. Each of the guests ate from his own plate, wiping it clean with the flat, unleavened Syrian bread, before having it refilled. The very plates were pewter, embossed with the Templars' cross, while he was used to eating off a plain wooden platter at home.

At the table opposite, a knight of Provence was quarrelling with two knights of Normandy over the distribution of fiefs. Now that the entire coast of Syria was secured by the lords of the West, the scramble was on for possession of fiefs, the lands which each lord handed over to his vassal knights, in return for their oaths of fealty and military service. There had been skirmishing lately, Guy learned, between men of the Count of Tripoli and the Prince of Galilee, and only the mediation of young King Baldwin III of Jerusalem had restored peace on their borders.

"Norman pigs!" shouted the Provençal, between gulps of the harsh, red Syrian wine. "Pig Normans! Where were you when our Count Raymond captured the Holy City?"

"Not Raymond! Godfrey! Godfrey of Bouillon took the Holy City; everyone knows that!"

The Provençal, now drunk, went on, impervious to the Norman knights' protests. "You are like ticks on a man's flesh! You crawl into his bed and tickle his wife after he has brought her home! My father went over the walls with Count Raymond himself. With his own hand he slew sixty of the heathen in the Church of the Holy Sepulchre. He followed the good Count to Tripoli and fought the siege there for eight years. I was born in the County of Tripoli.

Now you interlopers think, because you take the Cross, you can come and settle on our land. Vermin!"

Guy turned away from the brawlers. His eyes sought the head table on a raised dais at the end of the hall. Here, the Chapter of the Temple ate together in seclusion. They were God's warriors, who served no liege lord. Surely, thought Guy, they were above this sordid squabbling. As he looked, his eyes unwavering met another stare, returned. It was a slightly older man, very dark, very magnetic, who was looking at him. The stare remained unbroken until a steward, carrying a flaming pudding on a tray, came between. Several times Guy asked the dark man's identity; at last the steward told him. It was Gerard of Ridfort, Master of the Temple.

At his own table, Guy found himself the center of interest when he said his liege lord was the Count of Lusignan, and that he came to serve with his son, Amalric of Lusignan. Amalric was the right hand of Humphrey of Toron, he was told, and Humphrey was King Baldwin's commander in chief, with the title of Constable. Some said Humphrey was aging and that Amalric would soon be Constable in his place. "You will be a great man in the Kingdom!" they assured him with bibulous flattery.

"That is, if King Baldwin wins!" one commented drily.

"Are the Saracens so dangerous, then?" Guy queried.

A guffaw of coarse laughter greeted this question. Many knights, the more drunken ones, found it so funny they laid down their heads and beat their hands on the table.

"The Queen is dangerous, not the Saracens," explained one who carried his wine better. "It is not the war with the infidel we are fighting now. It is the war between mother and son. Melisende is Queen in her own right. She ruled even Fulk, her husband, and went to bed with the guard of honor! But now Fulk is dead and his son Baldwin is King. Yet still Melisende will not give up the crown. The whole Kingdom is divided. It is a rotten business, with marches and counter-marches, as they take each other's castles. Fortunately, I'm out of it. I sold my lands to a Genoese. I'm on my way home to Picardy."

Guy understood very little of all this. "Will the King and his Constable be in Jerusalem, then," he asked, "if they are at war with the Queen?"

"Oh, yes. Like all family affairs, it is a war but not a war. You'll have to watch yourself up there. Remember, you're a King's man. Don't have any truck with the Queen's men, unless you want to wind up with a dagger between your shoulder blades."

Guy's head was hurting him and he left early. Mounting his mare, he made his way alone back through St. Anthony's Gate and out into the countryside. The moon had risen and flooded all the land with a clear, white light. He could see the ships, fluttering the flags of many nations, in the harbour. The city lay in darkness, save for the watch-fires on the towers. And, to the southwest, the dark outline of Mount Carmel rose blackly against the glitter of the moon-reflecting sea.

Guy returned to the military encampment and found his tent. His groom was waiting up patiently for him. Good Hugh, a peasant boy from one of his father's farms, just the same age as himself—his mother had been Guy's own wet-nurse, they had played together on the village green—was in distant Syria because his master claimed this service from his serfs.

"What, Hugh—still up?"

"Yes, master. I wanted to know about tomorrow. The camp marshal says they are moving us out at dawn in the pilgrim convoy. Will you stay with us or ride ahead?"

"I shall ride with you. Make sure they have a waggon for our baggage and let no one else poach on it. I've paid enough for it! I'll wear full mail. It is an open road through Saracen country. And see that you get your sleep."

"Yes, master. Will you not turn in?"

"No, I'll ride awhile in the moonlight to get some air. My head isn't well. Goodnight, Hugh."

"But, master—"

"Goodnight, Hugh!" Guy patted his groom's shoulder and rode away.

The coastal road led southward, past the camp on the Belus River, toward the compelling height of Mount Carmel. Letting the reins slacken, Guy rode on in the moonlight, as in a dream. The mare stumbled occasionally for there were rockfalls across the road, which wound around the seaward slope of the mountain, commanding an awesome view of the moonlit coast, hundreds of feet below. On a grassy headland, Guy stopped and dismounted, looping the reins over a tree branch. He advanced to the edge of the precipice. It seemed as though all the countries of the world, silent and asleep, were at his command.

Alone, with no one to watch him, he stepped momentarily out of his skin. How often he had fancied his arrival in the Holy Land! It had seemed to him as though, defying the laws of time and space, he were approaching the heavenly coast, suspended somewhere between the ancient elm woods of Vienne and the golden, cloud-capped towers of the sunrise. Of course, he had always known this journey would not be easy. There, on the threshold of the eastern light, he would meet Apollyon, the Spirit of Darkness. They would grapple together, and what chance would he, the unlearned countryman, have against the ancient evil of the world? Yet somehow, he knew not how, the enemy would yield. Hosannas sounded in his ears, he knelt to kiss the ground of the promised land.

"How simple I am," he reflected. "It is a good thing they cannot read my thoughts, these clever ones, who knew how to turn the Cross to advantage. Perhaps this is how I shall be someday. And yet, there is something they have missed, something I may yet find—"

The hosannas still sounded faintly in the cold night wind, above the breaking sea. Secure in his conscious isolation from the world, the countryman from Poitou knelt on Elijah's holy mountain and, holding his sword before him, renewed his vow. "I swear—I shall find it!" he said aloud. Then he mounted his mare and rode placidly back to camp. But what he was looking for he could not easily have explained.

The caravan to Jerusalem left at dawn. Never was there a dingier, more quixotic company than these pilgrims—rounded up in their hostels and caravanserais for the journey to Jerusalem (round-trip payable in advance to the Order of the Temple). For better than a mile, they stretched along the highway, a human migration of Europe's misery and want, in search of hearts' ease in Outremer, the land across the sea. From peasants' wattled huts they came, gnarled and bent after years behind the plough—from the dark, fetid shops of the artisans, where they had spent a lifetime tooling leather and hammering on brass—men with thick wrists and broad thumbs from the village smithy—maids, red-armed and calloused on the knees from many a palace scullery—here were the offscourings of taverns, brothels and the lairs of thieves—men and women fleeing the law, a nagging mate, a bad debt. Here they were, cast up on this alien shore, ragged, unwashed, old, sick, lame, blind, hoping, groping, praying for the greatest of miracles—to be born again into the Kingdom of the Lord Jesus Christ.

"Into line! Into line!" The Templar Turcopoles, half-caste mercenaries, riding up and down the flanks of the caravan, slashed at the stragglers with their whips, and made way for the more fortunate travellers to move up to the front—carriages (rented by the Temple) with families of wealthy burghers, seeing the world for the first time—scape-grace sons of the castle and the manor, mounted on hired nags—heiresses in litters, carried by Nubian slaves (also hired), travelling in search of husbands—all accompanied by their servants, dogs, parakeets, pushing, elbowing for the best places in the parade—all bound for God's Holy City.

"Will you ride with us?" A knight's patrol moved up the line to reconnoitre the way, and Guy readily accepted the invitation extended by his friend the taciturn Templar, leaving Hugh and his men to accompany the baggage wagon. In the dawn, the air was deliciously pure and fresh with the aseptic taste of the desert, but as the day wore on the sun grew oppressive, reflecting off the silicate rock in the Nazareth hills with a blinding shimmer. Guy had awakened feeling feverish, with a singing in his head. Everytime he rose and fell in the saddle, his whole being seemed to crack asunder. But he said nothing to his companions.

Three hours out on the Nazareth road, a messenger rode up to them from the hills ahead, covered in his own cloud of powdery, white dust. "My lords," he shouted, "I bring you news from my master, William, Prince of Galilee. There are Saracens in the Plain of Jezreel, beyond Nazareth. They are looking for a shipment of gold seized by men of the Count of Tripoli and my lord of Galilee has given them passage through this territory. As you know, we are at war with the Count of Tripoli also. My lord of Galilee regrets it will not be possible to give you his protection. Turn back, my lords, turn back."

The knights sat their horses astounded, without motion, except for a flighty Byzantine, who began to lisp excitedly. "Oh, what shall we do? Think of all the poor people! Think of my money bags!" And he galloped back in the direction of the caravan.

Cursing, the Templar called to him in vain. As he had feared, the Byzantine had thrown the entire caravan into confusion. Some, especially the well-to-do, made a great outcry and demanded to return at once. One immensely rich and ugly old lady, who rode in a curtained litter, carried by two horses, fore and aft, descended and waved her stick at the Templar. "Save me!" she screeched. "I'll be raped by the Saracens!" And she began running up and down the lines, crying "Rape! Rape!"

The bulk of the pilgrims, most of whom were on foot, accompanied by their donkeys and carts drawn by oxen, begged to continue. Food and water were short and any delay would work hardship. At last the Templar sorted things out. Those who wished, including the Byzantine knight and the principal candidate for rape, returned to Acre under escort. The remainder continued, while the knights patrolled ahead.

The patrol split into pairs, and Guy rode in silence be-

side his taciturn friend. About noon, the reflected heat
rose from the ground in quivering waves; Guy's mail grew
as hot as a fiery furnace and he envied the Templar the
silk burnoose, a loose Arab robe which he wore over his
armour. They were in the Nazareth hills now, low, rocky
and desolate, until a defile, opening onto the Plain of
Jezreel, dazzled their eyes with a vision of young wheat
fields, rippling smooth and flat, like the breakers of a vast
green sea. To the south rose the strange, dome-like outline
of Mount Tabor, the mountain of the Transfiguration. But
there was no time to study it. Down below, at the foot of
the hillside, there was a movement of many men fording a
stream. Even at this distance, their black armour glinted
in the sunlight. Saracens.

Dismounting and leading their horses on foot, they descended the hillside, where scrub and cacti in a narrow
gully provided cover. Now it was easy to see the enemy in
great numbers, perhaps one hundred strong, carrying
several heavy chests across the stream. They had recovered the booty. Also, riding bound as prisoners, were two
Frankish knights, evidently men of the Count of Tripoli.
From the direction of the movement, the Saracens were
headed eastward and they would be across the border into
the territory of the Sultan of Damascus before the pilgrim
caravan reached Nazareth.

For several moments Guy and his companion watched
the careful, beetle-like movements of the Saracens' contingent fording the stream. For Guy, the moment of confrontation was one of extreme exaltation. Here was the
gaping mouth of hell, here the dark legions—strange that
they looked so small, so natural, almost, he had thought,
so *human!* Surely it was for this he had come, to throw
himself, a living sacrifice upon them, no matter how
many, even though fear lodged in the pit of his stomach,
making his mouth dry and his arm nerveless.

Guy had risen, in his excitement, and the Templar laid
a warning hand on his arm, drawing him down again.
"Not yet, lad," was all he said. Not yet! To the young
man, not to act seemed like a betrayal of all the vows.

Only slowly, as he watched the black helmets reach the other side of the stream and gallop away in the direction of Damascus, did understanding break upon him that by his inaction the caravan was saved.

His head was now throbbing with a blinding fury, as though a wild beast had clawed its way into his brain. They found their horses and returned to the defile, reaching Nazareth just after the caravan drew up in the courtyard of the Convent of the Annunciation. There was a great flurry of dismounting, as each of the pilgrim groups sought the shelter of the cloisters to rest in the shade. Guy rode into the courtyard like a man distraught. The heat, the beast in his head, the conflict of conscience, proved too much for him. He pitched from the saddle to the pavement unconscious.

When he awoke, it was evening. A fire blazed on the ground at his feet, and he lay on a straw mattress with his head propped on a roll of bedding. Someone was laying cold compresses on his forehead, changing the cloths and wringing them out in a basin of cold water. He could see now it was a girl, a very beggarly girl, dressed like a Syrian. Beside her, sitting on his haunches, was an old Arab, heavily lined and dark, with intense, compelling eyes. The Arab was also very ragged and dirty and he seemed to be mixing something in a bowl, using a pestle which he took from a small basket. He spoke excellent French, but with an Arab accent, that Guy had now learned to recognize.

"I will give him the potion, but only if I have the lord's permission. I will not be taken for a poisoner."

"No, no potion, no potion!" It was Hugh who spoke, standing beside him, twisting and untwisting his hands in an agony of indecision.

"What is it, Hugh?" said Guy, still very faint.

"Sir, this is an infidel doctor, or says he is a doctor, he was with the caravan. He wants to cure you, but I said no potion, after all, he is only an infidel."

"Perhaps I have only had a touch of the sun," Guy intervened.

"Not the sun. Brain fever," commented the Arab with

decision. "Only an antidote will cure you. Besides, you have a concussion of the skull."

Indeed, his head felt very bad. He became aware again of the grateful coolness of the compresses, and the soft hands of the Syrian girl. Perhaps the old man's daughter, he wondered?

"Who are you?" Guy looked at the Arab directly.

Again his look was returned, almost as though there were some understanding between them.

"My name is Barac. I am a Syrian. It is true I am what you call an infidel. But I am a good doctor. We have better doctors here than the Franks."

The directness pleased Guy. He would trust him.

"It's all right, Hugh," he said. "Do as the doctor orders. But take me up to Jerusalem."

The potion, consisting of herbs and poppies, mixed with oil from a small phial in the Arab's basket, was put on his tongue. The taste was terrifyingly strong and Guy felt himself swimming again into unconsciousness.

He completed the journey travelling in the baggage wagon. A straw mat was laid under him, and a canvas canopy was erected over his head to keep out the sun. The jolting was atrocious, and he would have died of the pain in his head if the Syrian girl had not been there beside him to hold his head in her lap. Occasionally, he saw the figure of the Syrian doctor, following the wagon mounted on a donkey. But most of the time he passed in grateful oblivion.

At Jerusalem, the caravan stopped at the Templars' Hospice outside St. Stephen's Gate. Hugh and his men carried Guy in and laid him on a bed in the infirmary. The doctor and the Syrian girl had disappeared.

"Did you pay them?" asked Guy.

"No, master, I did not. After all, how do we know he was a real doctor, so dirty and heathen and all? Besides, he said himself, he wanted no money."

"Did he now!" This was a new idea for Guy. "Anyhow, he may be no doctor, but my head feels a lot better. I'll be up tomorrow."

The next day, Guy was himself again, a little weak from his experience, but blissfully forgetful of his non-encounter with the Saracens. Even the recollection of the old Syrian doctor and his daughter had faded from his mind. All he could recall was the strange, compelling eyes of the one, and the soft, brown hands of the other.

Leaving the hospice alone and on foot, he set out to find the headquarters of the King Constable, taking with him a letter from his liege lord, the Count of Lusignan, to his son, Amalric. St. Stephen's Gate had been open since early morning and was jammed with people, accompanied by bullocks and donkeys piled high with produce, for this was market day.

In the fifty years since the first Crusade, Jerusalem had been largely rebuilt by the Franks. Like all medieval cities, the streets were narrow, paved with stone and rising in stairs from level to level, so there was no wheeled traffic. Many of the walls belonged to great public buildings, basilicas, convents, chapter houses, armories and palaces; all these buildings were supported by flying buttresses, thrown across the street and resting on houses or pillars on the other side and sometimes they were utilized as supports for overhead passageways. All the buttresses and archways employed the sharp, pointed Saracen arch, unknown in Europe at the time, which gave the streets a strange, oriental flavor.

Turning to the right, inside the Gate, Guy followed St. Stephen Street toward the King's Palace and frequently passersby had to flatten themselves against the walls to permit the passage of Frankish ladies in their litters, supported by pages wearing doublets of yellow and crimson. Occasionally, a jewelled hand drew back the curtain of one of these litters and Guy found himself looking into the pale face of a lady with long unbound hair, wearing a dress of white samite and cloth of gold.

At the walls of the Church of Holy Sepulchre, the street joined the most famous of all Jerusalem's streets, the *Via Dolorosa*, the Way of the Cross. This narrow passageway, not more than a mile long, wound up the gentle incline of

Mount Calvary, until it reached the Church of the Holy Sepulchre. Almost its entire length was filled throughout the daylight hours with processions of pilgrims, barefoot, carrying candles, searching everywhere for relics of the True Christ.

"Buy! Buy!" The merchants of relics canvassed the crowds, each with his tray filled with true, authenticated mementos of the Passion. So many yards of the "seamless garment" were hawked in Jerusalem's streets in the early years of the twelfth century that the original garment would have been many miles long! A credulous age, and yet—something very real had happened here to start all this.

"Is it really Calvary?" asked Guy of a poor, passing friar. The man, in his tattered monk's cowl, looked at Guy with narrowed eyes. Finally the monk took his measure large, for he replied, "All the world is Calvary, my son, and Christ dies there every day. Go in peace."

Guy pushed his way through the crowd as quickly as he could and took the first exit into Palmer Street and the fresh air again. The sound of bells greeted him very close by, so that his head rang with the deep, sonorous clamour. For he knew, without asking, that he stood on the threshold of the Church of the Holy Sepulchre, enclosing the very rock of Calvary and the tomb of the Saviour.

The great south portal stood open before him, but Guy did not enter the Church of the Holy Sepulchre that day. The words "not yet" echoed in his mind, from where he did not recall, but he quite simply took direction from them. His journey, he seemed to grasp, was like one of those mazes with many hazards which must be crossed safely, before winning through to the goal. This hazard he would leave to another day. And, giving a coin to the first blind beggar, he crossed himself and passed on.

The Palace of the King lay in Patriarch Street, directly across from the Church of the Holy Sepulchre. A few inquiries brought Guy to the guardroom of the Lord Constable, where he asked for the Constable's aide-de-camp, Amalric of Lusignan. No one was very sure when Amalric would be accessible. The guards were mainly "poulains," half-caste soldiers, men with swarthy skins and narrow, and laughing—or was it mocking?—eyes.

"If you hunt with the owl, you must come out by night," the sergeant said flippantly, a quip his subordinates seemed to find funny. The gist of it was that Amalric and his friends slept by day and caroused by night. If my lord wished to wait he was welcome, but the wait was likely to be long. Guy waited.

About seven o'clock in the evening, he received a summons to dinner in the Constable's mess. The luxury of the interior was overwhelming to a new arrival from dark and gloomy Europe. His first impression of the East was one of glittering—reflections of torches in mirrors of polished steel, incrustations of light on mosaic walls, scintillations of glass and mother of pearl in inlaid tables and chairs.

Amalric, a fat, oafish man in his mid-thirties, seemed genuinely glad to see his countryman. "Well, well," he chattered, "you've become quite the man. The gosling has turned into a goose!"

Guy ignored the quip and handed Amalric the letter from the Count, his father, but the letter was dropped unread. His host seemed more concerned with his friends, greeting this one and that one at the tables. All were lordlings like himself, overfed and overdressed, though none, thought Guy, looked quite as foolish. No peacock was more splendidly arrayed than Amalric of Lusignan in his Eastern incarnation. He was in pale beige burnoose, sewn with golden cord at the seams, over a tunic of cloth of gold, fastened by a belt of Arab workmanship studded with jewels. On his feet were soft, leather shoes with toes so long that the upturned points had to be caught back to his ankles with little chains; and on his head, a turban of many colored silks wound in strands like a rainbow. Nowhere, except for a dagger at his waist, was there a sign that he was a Frankish knight in a field of war.

Over dinner, Amalric talked of his favorite subject. "How much gold have you brought with you?"

"No gold, only silver for the expenses of my men," replied Guy. Good God, he thought, the man thinks of nothing else. Even one of his front teeth is made of gold.

"Well men are worth money out here." Amalric dipped his hands into rose water and dried them on a napkin offered to him by a black slave. "There is a terrible shortage of men, as you'll find out. How many did you say you had?"

"Twelve men-at-arms."

"Not many. But every little counts. There are not more than five hundred knights in the Kingdom, with maybe five thousand men-at-arms, and, of course, all these filthy poulains. The Knights of the Temple and the Knights of the Hospital are growing stronger every day. And they're no friends of ours, you see."

Guy did not see, but he let him talk on. So this is what the East is like, he thought. Turbans and pointed shoes and gold in the mouth. Black slaves and rosewater. Carpets on the floor instead of straw. Money instead of honest trade. Poulains got by Frankish fathers on infidel mothers. Miscegnation.

"Now this quarrel with the Queen only makes things worse." Amalric was attacking a pheasant whole with his bare hands. "You can't trust these southerners. All the knights and lords with fiefs in the south are Queen's men, because they know they will lose their fiefs if the King is crowned. His Majesty,"—here the voice dropped to the confidential,—"has promised me a rich fief in the south near Nablus—"

But Guy was not listening. He had an abstracted air, as though looking for something he had mislaid and feared lost.

That night, after dinner, there was gaming in the knights' mess. Amalric was an avid player of dice and rolled them with a practiced hand. He and his friends, all with fat wallets, their hair perfumed and their hands beringed, knelt on the carpet in a circle. In the light of the torches, their faces were lit with avarice, as the piles of gold changed hands. But luck was not with Amalric tonight. His gold pieces were exhausted and his promissory notes refused. He had been drinking steadily.

Desperate, he turned to Guy. "Where is the money you brought with you?" he demanded thickly.

"The strong box is in the guard house at the hospice," replied Guy warily. "It is locked for the night."

"Never mind. You have twelve men-at-arms, you say? Are they all strong men, young in years?"

"They are the best men in the seigneury of Vienne."

"Then they are worth at least a hundred dinars each out here!" exclaimed Amalric in a transport of delight. He turned to the others in triumph. "There, you see! I have property worth twelve hundred dinars to put in the game! Give me the dice!"

But Guy was at his ear. "No, my lord. These men are flesh and blood. They are mine. They cannot be played for in a game of dice."

Amalric was beside himself. "And why not? Your serfs are property like anything else. You do whatever you want with them; you buy them, sell them, work them, flog them, and you have taken their wives and sisters to bed, I warrant, whenever it pleased you. So why not play for them in a game of dice?"

Guy said nothing. The rage he felt was murderous. His serfs, to be gambled away at a throw of the dice by this drunken tosspot! It was too much. He would no longer do vassal service to such a man. He would be free. As he left the room, he heard a low whistle among the players, as they turned back to their game, leaving Amalric of Lusignan out of the circle.

He rushed headlong down the stairs and out into the bright, star-filled night. He knew what he was doing was dangerous and against all law and custom. But he trusted that a way would be opened to him and the thought filled him with elation.

"I am playing for pretty high stakes, myself," he muttered under his breath.

CHAPTER TWO

THE LEPER

On the Feast of St. Anne, Queen Melisende went to Mass in the Church of the Holy Sepulchre. She was received at the south portal by the Patriarch and the Canons, all vested in white. The royal party entered the circular ambulatory, in the centre of which lay the tomb of Christ, and turned eastward through the great Crusader archway into the choir of the canons, coming to a stop at the stone of unction, commemorating Christ's embalmment before burial.

At once, the church filled up with the people of the Court, the townsfolk and the sisters of the adjoining convent. So great was the crowd that the heat, in late July, became oppressive, and many of the ladies in the Queen's entourage were fanning themselves with their ostrich fans. The white-bearded Patriarch took his place on the throne behind the High Altar, looking very small and frail below the great mosaic picture of Christ, bearing the Cross in His left hand, holding Adam with His right, leading majestically to Heaven with a giant stride, His left foot raised, His right still planted on the earth.

The choir chanted the Kyrie eleison ... "Lord have

mercy." "Lord have mercy," responded Melisende in a
firm voice. She was a fine looking woman, even in her late
forties, with the high cheekbones and taut skin of her Armenian mother. Only half-Frank, she followed the eastern
customs of dress and manners, as did all the ladies of her
court, so that in their robes and jewels they resembled a
covey of birds of paradise. But beneath her finery, Melisende was also a woman with a steel will, which the
world had tempered but not broken. Was she not the
rightful Queen? Was she not obeyed? Was the defense of
the Kingdom not in good hands? To all this she could answer yes. But it was nothing to her now. All was dust and
ashes because of a child who lay dying in her apartments
at the Palace. Why had God sent her this affliction? Oh,
she knew, she knew.

Now the voices of the congregation were raised in the
Confiteor. "I confess to Almighty God that I have sinned
exceedingly in thought, in word, and deed, through my
fault, through my fault, through my most grievous fault
..." Here Melisende struck herself three times on the
breast. She had sinned against her husband and against
both her sons.

Brought up by her mother in the Armenian way, she
and her three sisters had always felt as strangers among
the Franks. One by one, they had been married off to brut-
ish men of war, because it was good policy for the Kingdom. The Kingdom! The Kingdom! Why had the Franks
ever founded this accursed Kingdom of Jerusalem, if it
was only going to devour its own children by marriage
and war? And the seeds of hatred were planted in her
breast.

She had sinned against her dead husband, Fulk. How
could she be expected to love a dwarfish, middle-aged
man, just because the Kingdom needed his money and his
men? No wonder she kept her own room, and opened her
door at night to other lovers! Ah, Hugh le Puiset, he was
the only one to whom she gave her heart. And what had
they done to him? He had been stabbed by a lackey of
King Fulk in an alley at night. No matter that the lackey

was tortured to death before her eyes, protesting Fulk's innocence to the last!

She had sinned against both her sons. Baldwin, the eldest, was weak and pleasure-loving. She had kept him from the throne. A King in name only, he sulked and caroused with his courtiers, while she ruled. Now the country was divided between the followers of mother and son. Men on both sides would die—and all because of her pride.

She had sinned against Amaury, her youngest. He had been her darling, her love child (was he really Fulk's?), and she could not bear to see him wedded to that slut of a girl, Agnes of Courtenay. She had got the proof she needed and exposed her to all the world as a common whore! But did Amaury thank her? Not a bit. He repudiated his wife and went off to court a princess in Byzantium.

Well, at least she had sent the hoyden, Agnes, packing, and taken away her only son by Amaury, little prince Baldwin. The boy was the image of his father, an angel of heaven, her own grandchild, her flesh and blood. She had kept him at the Palace and watched over his every footstep. And then he was struck down by this—hush. The word must not be spoken!

She lost herself in prayer. "Blessed Virgin, save him. Punish me. I am the sinful woman, the harlot, the jezebel. Let the judgement fall on me, but spare the little one. Intercede for him, O Mary, full of Grace, the Lord is with thee, blessed art thou among women and blessed is the fruit of thy womb . . ."

The Patriarch gave the blessing. "May Almighty God bless you, the Father, the Son, and the Holy Spirit." But Melisende remained a long time kneeling in prayer beside the Stone of Unction. She rose, shaken by grief, supported by her ladies.

Just at that moment, an altercation broke out between a Syrian and a Greek in the ambulatory by the south portal. Descending the narrow stairway from the Chapel of Calvary, the Syrian chased the Greek, shouting curses at him for desecrating the sanctuary. Each of the Christian denominations had its own altar there, its own prayer carpet, its own site for the True Cross. If a member of one denomination walked over the carpet of another denomination, there was always trouble. Caught by the Syrian, the Greek raised a dagger, just as the Queen came upon the scene. At the same moment, a young man, who had been walking around the ambulatory, neatly disarmed the Greek and tumbled him to the ground. It was Guy.

The fracas was over in a minute and both the combatants fled. Guy's quickness had impressed Melisende.

"Well done," she said, looking at Guy with admiration. Melisende always had an eye for a likely young man, and this one had an amazing resemblance to Hugh le Puiset. "Where did you learn your *coup de main*, Sir—?"

"Guy of Vienne," he answered, looking quietly at Melisende with his steady eyes. "That trick was taught me by the senechal of the Count of Poitou."

"So, you are from Poitou. Then you must be in the service of Amalric of Lusignan?"

"I was, madam. I have left him."

"Left? Does a knight leave his lord's service so easily?"

"If his lord is unworthy . . ."

"And are you the judge of that? Have a care, young man. You have made yourself a dangerous enemy. And yet I like a man who sets a high value on his service. So Amalric of Lusignan is unworthy!" She laughed her low, throaty laugh. "Tell me, Sir Guy, am I worthy of that *coup de main* and those beautiful eyes?"

Guy blushed scarlet and dropped his eyes. Yet he had seen his way open to him. "I am your servant, madam," he replied quietly.

"Agreed, then!" Melisende was in high good humour. "You need have no fears of Amalric here. His writ does not run in Jerusalem, and in Jerusalem I am Queen. Have you any men with you? We need men."

"I have twelve men-at-arms," Guy answered.

"A windfall for me, then. Report to my Constable,

Manasses of Hierges, and he will appoint you and your men to the Household guard. Your arm, sir."

And with Melisende, the Queen, on his arm, Guy emerged into the blazing July sunshine.

The Citadel occupied by the Queen stood by the Bethlehem Gate, at the top of David Street. It was a powerful fortress, enclosing in its walls a central courtyard of great proportions. Around the inner walls were ranged the stables, the granaries, the storehouses, the kitchens, and the barracks where the Household Guard was lodged. The barracks were comfortable quarters, recessed in the walls, connected along the courtyard by a covered walk. Here the men-at-arms lounged at their ease, polishing their weapons and playing at checkers, until summoned by the Constable for guard duty or daily exercise in the yard. Guy's men, in their new uniforms bearing the Royal insignia, were well pleased with their step up in the world, and little thought how they owed it to their master's *coup de main* and level eyes.

The Queen and the Court kept their state in the Tower of David, built into the northwest corner of the Citadel and separated from the courtyard by a curtain wall enclosing a garden of orange trees. It was a gloomy tower, said to be built by Herod, and its stones stood four feet high and eight or nine feet long. In its Great Hall were held the morning levees, at which the Queen appeared publicly to receive guests and hear petitions, seated on a throne of tesselated wood, inlaid with silver, ivory and mother of pearl. The trumpets sounded from the galleries around the hall, hung with banners. Below, all space swirled in color, flags, canopies, turbans, robes, faces shouting "Long live the Queen!"

Guy was ill-at-ease the first time he took his place on the dais at the Queen's left hand, for Melisende tended to keep Guy beside her. If people supposed much from this—and they did—they were wrong. Melisende herself had no illusions about what life held for her. Sometimes she looked into his grave eyes amused, as though she said,

"Ah, you are mine, you know, but you are also free because you are you. Be kind to me; I am an old woman and I have great griefs and I shall never ask you for anything!" But, of course, no such words were ever spoken.

Guy won many friends, however, because he was trusting and innocent; the intrigues of the Court passed him by unnoticed, and he was pitied for his want of observance, but, at the same time, above reproach. Even the little Arab dragoman who kept the Court records, sitting cross-legged on the dais, under the weight of his enormous turban, like a beetle under a toadstool, took him under his "protection", explaining the intricacies of Court etiquette, in his absurd falsetto.

As for the ladies in waiting—dusky and graceful in their oriental gowns, cut so low as to seem positively provocative to him as they sat on cushions around the Queen's feet and chattered among themselves—Guy could not keep his eyes off them. Sometimes his glance was returned, but he quickly averted his eyes. For him, the women of the East were still the daughters of Belial!

The Constable Manasses, who stood at the right hand of the throne, was a large, powerful, battle-scarred man, who commanded the army of the Queen. Guy liked him instantly, but he had to bear the veteran's scorn for his easy rise in Royal favour. He need not have worried for Manasses was a shrewd judge of men. He engaged the new favorite at sword play in the courtyard, noted the strength of his arm and the sureness of his eye, and drew his own conclusions. He took Guy in hand, and trained him in tactics for fighting the Saracens.

"Are they as good fighters as we?" asked Guy, between fencing bouts in the courtyard.

"Good? Better, my lad, get that through your head! The Arab is a clean, tireless, merciless foe, who never gives up, wears you down, and saves his strength for the kill. And they will kill us all someday, unless we learn to fight them by their own rules—that is, without mercy and without quarter! The only good Moslem is a dead Moslem!"

By far the most interesting man at Court was the historian, William of Tyre. A politician turned Archbishop, he combined the roles of adviser to the Queen, tutor to the young prince Baldwin, and chronicler of the Crusades. His study in the south-west corner of the Tower was a retreat from the world, filled with musty books, ancient maps, and even a telescope for stargazing.

Initially, the telescope brought Guy into the philosopher's hideaway. Of Arabic origin, it brought the stars no closer, but its plain glass, set with crossed hairs, could be trained on a star and its declination and right ascension calculated on a pair of setting circles. Guy was soon able to install the settings to the old man's delight, and they passed many an evening tracking the planets by the ancient star maps of Ptolemy.

Sometimes, when they had tired of looking at the sky, Guy would question the archbishop. "How can God enroll such wicked men under the banner of His Kingdom?"

"Do not disturb yourself about God, my boy," the old man replied, "He has put up with the folly of men ever since the fall of Adam. But even wicked men can cleanse themselves of sin by defending Christ's Holy Sepulchre."

"But is our cause just?"

The Archbishop appeared a little shocked. "You must remember that we are His Chosen People. Many of us are wayward, wicked, blasphemous even, but He has given His blood upon the True Cross to redeem every one of us. That is why we cannot abandon His Holy Sepulchre to desecration by the unbelievers."

"And would they—the unbelievers—really desecrate it?"

"They have! They did! That was how it all began!" He appeared a little distracted, and roamed about his study, picking out books at random as he talked. "How soon men forget. Men come here to fight for God's Kingdom and forget what they came for. Only we historians remember the truth. Look here, it is set down in my own chronicle how one hundred and fifty years ago, the Caliph al-Hakim, the accursed, declared himself God and burned down the Holy Sepulchre in Jerusalem. From that day on

God's people have been persecuted in this land and every
relic of the Passion has been defiled. Even the True Cross
was urinated on by the infidels. And you ask me if our
cause is just!"

There were times when the Queen sat in the garden under the orange trees, while William of Tyre taught his
lessons to the young prince. His pupil was a wonderfully
serious boy, as children often are when they are unwell.
At seven, he was small for his age, with very white skin
and pale eyes. In his short tunic, emblazoned with the
Crown of Jerusalem in gold thread, the hood thrown back,
and his blond hair cut close around his head, he looked
like the angel sent to Tobias.

The boy was especially delighted when Guy was sent
for, to give some advice about the planting of the fruit
trees and the making of a small fountain. Guy was clever
about these things, and had once made an ornamental garden in Vienne which was the delight of his mother.

"I should have been an engineer, not a soldier," he
grinned ruefully.

"You look much more handsome as a soldier," replied
Melisende. The blood rose to his face, and he cursed his
propensity for coloring so easily.

From the beginning, the boy attached himself to "Master Guy," as he called him. Guy responded by calling him
"Master Baldwin."

"Master Guy, my grandma says you know how to
throw a man over your shoulder with one hand. Could
you teach me to do that?"

"I think I could," Guy replied.

They practiced it several times on the lawn and, to his
surprise, Guy found that the child picked up the technique
quite easily. It only remained for him to play victim and
to tumble on the grass over and over again, to shouts of
glee, "I threw him! I threw him!"

Melisende was pathetically grateful for anything done
for the child. He had never been allowed out of the Cit-

adel, because he was thought to be unwell, and because it was not considered to be good policy to show him, an invalid, to the people.

"Have you never seen the country, Master Baldwin?"

"Never. Could I?"

"If I teach you to ride. Tomorrow you shall practice on my horse. She is a good quiet mare. Her name is Brigitte and you must bring some sugar for her. But remember, the reason for these lessons is a secret!"

A month later, after autumn was come and the days were cooler, Guy rode out the gate of the Citadel on a borrowed horse, leading Brigitte by the reins. Just beside the Bethlehem Gate and inside the city walls, a window of the Tower of David overlooked the garden of the Patriarch's palace. Guy passed beneath this window where the Prince was waiting. By standing up in the stirrups, he was just able to lift him down and into Brigitte's saddle. He placed a rough cloak about the boy's shoulders and adjusted the thongs on his feet. Then they set out at a canter through the city gate and down the road to Jaffa.

It was a glorious day. Dark clouds scudded over the horizon, and the hills of Judea looked purple in the distance. The road ran past many farms and vineyards, with well-cultivated lands, rising in terraces up the hillsides. Each terrace bore its garland of green trees, heavy with fruit. Guy bought some apples from a farmer and they stopped to talk to the smiling, toothless old man. He complained about the "terrible labour" of his life, especially the never-ending work of repairing the revetting walls of his terraces, due to the erosion in the spring. In the end, Guy suggested a trough of half-shell, terra-cotta tiles along the tops of the walls to catch the run-off of the water. The old peasant scratched his head and promised to "think about that", and pressed more apples on them, but they laughed, shook their heads and rode on.

Often, the prince and Guy talked about the True Cross.

"Do you think, Master Guy, that the True Cross which

Patriarch Fulcher keeps locked up in the Church of the Holy Sepulchre is really it?"

"Why not, after all?"

"Well, after all it has been through! I mean, how can we be sure? The infidels had it before we captured it—and it has been lost so many times—and before that it lay buried in the earth for hundreds of years. How can we be sure?"

"Does there *have* to be a True Cross?"

"Of course—somewhere!"

"Why, Master Baldwin?"

"Well, I look at it this way. The cross I wear, the cross on your coat, the cross in the church at home, all these crosses are copies of the True Cross. So there must *be* a True Cross somewhere or all the other crosses are false, too, and there was no redemption. I don't believe that, do you, Master Guy?"

"No, I do not."

"Then you do believe it is the True Cross? Because Our Lord would not give us a false one, would He?"

"He would make it true for us."

"How? Tell me."

"I was just thinking that, in the same way as the Host on the altar is bread one moment and then it becomes the body of Our Lord for us, so the True Cross, no matter what happened to it, or where it comes from, or what it is made of, probably becomes the True Cross for us also."

"Oh, yes, Master Guy, that's how it must be. Thank you, thank you for telling me. I feel much happier now."

The afternoon turned hot and they stopped at a waterfall to drink and cool their faces in the spray. Beside the fall there was a wayside cross with a crudely carved image of the Saviour hanging on it. Suddenly, the boy took his friend by the hand and said, "Master Guy, will you swear to be my friend for life?"

"Of course."

"Let's swear it, then, by this cross."

Each one kissed the wood of the cross, after he took his oath.

The Prince's absence had not gone unnoticed. The wanderers were greeted by a furious Constable and a terrified Queen. Patiently, Guy tried to explain but it was Baldwin who put matters right.

"I made Master Guy do it," he announced calmly. "I told him I wanted to see my country and now I've seen it and I'm glad. So you don't need to cut his head off after all."

Later that night, Melisende had a long talk with Guy alone. She talked to him as her confidant and told him all that was in her heart. Baldwin was dying of an unmentionable disease. It was a secret known only to a few, the Constable, the boy's father and herself. On no account must the name of the disease be spoken. Fortunately, there was nothing, as yet, to be seen. A loss of feeling in the feet, in the hands, the nose, the ears and parts of the body, that was all. The rest would come later. "Soon," Melisende's voice broke, "he will rot before our eyes like a stinking carrion!"

Leprosy. Guy should have guessed it. Thereafter, on his walks through the city, he began to notice certain hooded figures, especially on the streets leading from the Postern of Lazarus to the covered market called Malquinsinat Street (Evil Smelling Street). Each of these figures wore a long gown and hood, with large overshoes and gloves, and kept to the windward side of the street. Clack, clack, clack, went a wooden clapper, warning all people that a leper approached. No disease was more dreaded, because of its terrible nature and because there was no cure.

The main food market was on Malquinsinat Street. Here, one day, Guy watched one of the hooded figures buying some wine. The leper held out a wooden mug, tied to his waist with a cord, to receive the wine which was poured directly into the mug, so that he did not touch the bottle. He paid for it by placing a coin from his purse in a bowl of vinegar on the merchant's counter.

"Where are you from?" asked Guy. But there was no

reply. Perhaps this leper did not speak French. Perhaps he
did not speak.

"He is from the leprosarium at the Postern of Lazarus,"
the shopkeeper said. "They should be locked up, poor devils!"

Immediately Guy set out for the leprosarium. His knock
at the door was answered by a very old nun. Guy asked if
the Mother Superior was at home.

"The Mother Superior does not live here," the nun replied. "You must ask at the Convent in Bethany. We are
only poor lay sisters here." The door began to close.

"Wait," said Guy, "it is you I want to see. May I come
in?"

"That is not allowed," answered the nun. "Unless . . .
you . . ."

"Yes, yes," Guy said hastily, "that's it. That's why I
must talk to you."

He was admitted to a dark stone building, with dirty,
unswept floors, opening out at the back into a walled garden. All around the walls of the garden were small straw
huts, shaped like beehives, with a wooden door and window at one side. In each of these a leper lived. He received his regular rations in a basket which was hung
from the limb of a tree or on a post.

Many of the lepers lay on the ground before their huts.
Their hoods were thrown off and their gowns were
bunched up above their knees so that they could crawl
around or propel themselves on little platforms equipped
with rollers. Some had no feet left at all, only gaping
stumps, black with flies, below the knee. Others were missing hands or parts of their face. One grinned at Guy as
though he was glad to see him, until Guy realized that it
was only the grin of a skull—all lips and cheeks had been
eaten away.

"Sister," stammered Guy, "is there nothing you can do,
nothing at all?"

"We do everything we can, sir. The rest is up to God."

"But, I mean, is there no cure, if you began early
enough, before . . ."

"We cannot cure them. We can only care for them."

"Can you always tell, for sure . . . that is, if you were to come and look at someone for me, could you be certain . . ."

"I cannot leave this place, sir," answered the nun quietly. She lifted up the long sleeves of her habit and revealed a pair of hands, suppurating with pus and decay.

On entering his quarters at the Citadel one night, he found an old Arab waiting quietly for him, squatting on his haunches inside the main gate.

"I let him in, sir," explained Hugh apologetically. "He said you would remember him."

It was Barac. The Syrian bowed low.

"I have something very personal to say to you, master. It is necessary to see you alone."

"Of course. Come with me."

Guy lived, along with other knights of the Household, on the second floor of South Tower, just over the warehouse. The Syrian followed him up the circular staircase. Guy closed the door behind them and asked his guest to sit down. They faced each other across a small writing table beside the bed.

"I should thank you first for what you did for me," Guy began.

"You are better, then? That's right. Keep out of the sun, avoid native foods, and above all, do not think too much. Your illness is of the mind." He tapped his head significantly. Guy let this pass. Barac went on.

"Now it is I who need your help, master. My daughter is in trouble. We live in the Syrian quarter, east of St. Stephen's Gate, near the Postern of the Magdalene. My cousin has a shop there—dry goods, embroidery, brocades from Damascus. A week ago the sergeant of our quarter came into the shop—you know how it is, a sergeant is appointed to oversee each quarter—my cousin pays him a 'tax' to keep the shop open because he has no license,— you know, we are not Syrian Orthodox, we are Moslems, sir, and we do not qualify for a license. The sergeant who came in talked to my daughter who helps in the shop and tried to take her away, but she would not go with him, so he became angry and he has told my cousin he will not accept the 'tax' any more and that he will cancel the license. Then two days ago he took my daughter away."

Guy asked for the name of the sergeant, the place he lived and the unit in which he served. Since it was a sergeant he had to deal with, he did not need to go himself. He called Hugh, and gave him a written message, ordering the sergeant to surrender the girl. He also gave Hugh (but quietly, so that the Syrian did not see it), a small bag of money to take with him, to make sure the sergeant kept quiet. Then he turned back once more to Barac. An idea had struck him.

"You are a doctor, Barac. And I remember you told me once that the doctors among your people are better than our doctors."

The Syrian did not dispute this. Instead he fixed his penetrating eyes on the speaker and let him continue.

"What is leprosy, Barac?"

"It is a curse of God."

"Does that mean there is no cure for it?"

"If the afflicted is outside God's covenant—" Barac spread out his hands deprecatingly.

"And what is God's covenant?" pursued Guy.

"Islam—the people of the Book."

"Am I outside God's covenant, Barac?"

"But it is not of you, I think, we are speaking." The Syrian tried to deflect the argument.

"Would you—could you—cure me, Barac?" insisted Guy.

"But it is not you—"

"Barac, answer!"

"Master, I would do much for you."

Guy heaved a great breath. He felt as though he had won a tremendous point, his pulse quickened and excitement, a new hope, shone in his eyes.

"Barac," he said softly, "I, Guy of Vienne, command you to cure someone for me. Will you do it?"

"I will obey you, master."

After the Syrian left, Guy laid his plans. Arrangements must be made for Barac to see Baldwin as soon as possible. That might not be easy. To admit a Syrian, and a Moslem at that, to the Royal apartments . . . However, he would see that it was done. He owed it to the boy and also, he felt, to the Queen.

Shortly afterwards, Hugh returned, leading the Syrian girl. She was not tall, but dark and very delicate in her ragged, blue Syrian gown with a black apron over it, and a veil in her hair. But she wore the veil off her face, in the Frankish fashion. It was a beautiful face, oval and sunburnt, which set off the long black lashes as she kept her eyes fixed on the ground.

"Will you go back to your father, girl?" Guy asked. "It may not be safe for you to live in the city now. You have no permit. Can you do kitchen work?" The girl's nod was barely perceptible. "Is that yes? Then you can live with the maid-servants in the Citadel and work in the kitchen. I will have a pass made for you so you can come and go when you please. That is, if you wish it?" Again, the faintest indication of assent.

"Hugh will take you down," he said gently. "And, Hugh, you can let it be known if anyone gives this girl trouble, he will pay for it."

At that moment, the most embarrassing one Guy could remember, a cry escaped from the girl, as though she had been holding it back all this time and could contain it no longer. She threw herself on the ground and kissed his feet, kissing each foot separately, slowly, passionately. Transfixed with surprise, Guy was unable to move. Before he recovered, she had gone, her long, black hair concealing the tears on her face.

As soon as he could, he approached the Queen. She listened to him gravely and in silence.

Finally, she said, "What you say is of the greatest importance, of course. We must leave no stone unturned, but . . . This doctor, you say, is a Moslem? A magician, perhaps? He might put a spell on the little one, with his black arts. It could even be a plot by Damascus to kill the heir to the throne."

Patiently, Guy explained that it was he, Guy, who had sought the help of the Syrian doctor and that the doctor himself was unwilling.

Melisende was not convinced, but was clearly afraid to miss any chance of a cure. At last, she decided to call in the Constable. No step as important as this should be undertaken without him.

The Constable Manasses, a man of forty and a veteran of many campaigns against the Saracens (several times captured and escaped) was not one to countenance any dealings with the infidel. The plan was foolish at best, criminal at worst. But, in the face of the Queen's anxiety, he could not rule it out altogether. It was decided that Barac should be brought to the Citadel, that the interview should take place in the Queen's presence, and that no powders, liquids or potions should be administered to the child until they had been examined by those who could be trusted.

"Young fool," he muttered to Guy, as he left the conference.

Nevertheless, the Constable was thorough in his plans. A rendezvous by night was arranged with Barac at the house of a private citizen. From there, the Syrian emerged dressed in the robes of a Frankish doctor, with the exception of the skull cap which he refused to don, insisting on wearing his own turban instead. Since very many Franks, living in Jerusalem, also affected to wear the turban, it was decided to allow this eccentricity.

Entering the Citadel on a permit furnished by the Constable, he was taken at once to the Queen's apartments, which were off the balcony overlooking the Great Hall. The balcony was furnished with Persian rugs on the floor and over the railings, and lit with torches in iron brackets affixed to the stone wall. As soon as he arrived, a leather curtain was raised and the imperious figure of the Queen emerged. She stood beside Guy, facing the Syrian doctor.

"Is this the man?" Melisende asked.

Guy nodded.

"Let us go then."

They proceeded down the balcony to the end where they entered a little room in the corner of the tower, overlooking the garden. Baldwin, feverish, lay in a child's bed with a crucifix above his head. There were a few chests for clothes and toys in the room, no other furniture. Only Melisende and Guy were present at the interview.

The Syrian sat down at once on the bed and began talking to the boy in quiet, serious tones.

"You are tired tonight, little master. That is because you have been playing so hard today. It is good to play hard. You will play more when you are older, but not yet. You have tired yourself out with running and playing ball. That is a beautiful ball you have. It is a pity that you lost it. But, little master, what made you think it went into the well?"

The child's eyes grew wide. "But it did go in the well—did you see it?"

"No, I did not see it. You thought you saw it, but you did not. And you should not have climbed down the well to look for it. Does your grandam know you did that?"

Melisende gave a start. "What does he say—about the well? Sweet Jesu, child, you did not go into the well?"

"I—I—" stammered the boy.

"It is best to tell the whole story, little master," went on Barac smoothly. "Otherwise, how will you explain the scrape on your arm . . ." He lifted the sleeve of the boy's nightshirt and revealed a long contusion on his elbow.

Melisende held her breath. The boy was not abashed but delighted.

"How did you know?" he demanded.

"I know many things, little master," said Barac.

"Then do you know where my ball went?" asked the boy.

"It went in one of the tiles for the new fountain, standing beside the well. You will have it again tomorrow."

The boy asked, "Can you tell me things that are going to happen tomorrow and the day after tomorrow?"

"Yes, little master, I can tell you that you are going to wake up feeling much better tomorrow. And better still the day after, and the day after that."

"Oh good. You mean I'm going to get well?"

"You have spoken, little master," concluded the Syrian. He stood up. "I will see him again in three days' time. He will sleep now. You need have no fear."

And, bowing low, holding his hands palm outward, he backed out of the room escorted by Guy. A moment afterwards Guy returned with the ball in his hand. The boy was already asleep.

The next time the Syrian came, the scene was repeated. This time some of the tension in the air had relaxed. It was late at night and the boy was in bed, but he was in high spirits.

"I found my ball," he announced. "At least, Master Guy found it. It was just where you said it was. And I'm feeling better, too. Are you a doctor?"

"I am a sheikh, little master, that is what my people call a doctor. And I am going to help you get well. Give me your hand. Do you feel me take it?"

"No, master sheikh, I feel nothing."

The Syrian asked for a broach Melisende was wearing on her dress. With the pin, he pricked the boy's finger and squeezed out a drop of blood.

"Did you feel that, little master?" he asked.

"No, master sheikh."

"That is because there is an evil jinn in your body. This jinn has lost his home and he wants to live in your skin. He wants to squeeze you out of it. That's why you feel nothing. But I am going to draw the jinn out of your body and send him away to find another home."

Taking the boy's hand, Barac drew his palm across it, using a drawing, gathering, sucking motion, as though pulling something tangible, something with a resistant force in it, out of his finger ends. He did this several times. Throwing back the covers he did the same to the boy's feet. Finally, he moved to his head, drawing his hands up over the cheeks and temples toward the crown. As he did this, Barac repeated under his breath certain words in Arabic. "Allahu Akbar . . ."

When he finished, the child was asleep. Barac rose.

"I will see him in three days. Let those who disbelieve be confounded. He will be well." And bowing, as before, he left.

At the Queen's command, Constable Manasses was present during the next visit. Together with Melisende and Guy, he stood at the foot of the little bed and watched Barac talk to the boy. They spoke of many things, of books, of comets, of flying horses, of jinns.

"And your jinn, little master," said Barac, "is gone. I saw him flying over the town tonight. He found an old donkey tethered to a tree, and that's where he made his new home!"

"It's true," cried the boy enthusiastically. "I can feel! I can feel!"

The others looked doubtful. Then Barac proposed a game and asked the Constable to bandage the boy's eyes. Next Barac asked the Constable for something to put in Baldwin's hand. Puzzled, Manasses grudgingly reached in his purse and gave the child a coin.

"It's a gold piece!" Baldwin cried. "It's a big one. A whole dinar! Can I have it?"

"Of course, my lord," the Constable said, scowling.

Barac turned to Melisende. With trembling hands she took off the small crucifix she wore under her dress and handed it to Baldwin.

"Why, grandam, it's your own very special cross, the little one from Armenia, with the Saviour on it!"

"Oh God, oh God!" cried Melisende.

Barac turned to Guy, who put his own hand in Baldwin's.

"He has given me his hand," the boy crowed. "He is my own, my very best friend!"

Melisende threw herself in a passion of weeping onto the child's neck, pressing him to her heart again and

again. The Constable looked hard at Guy, with the faint
beginning of a smile, and nodded slowly. When they looked
around again, the Syrian was nowhere to be seen.

Before the end of the year, Guy of Vienne was appointed Master of the Household, and a Knight of the
Kingdom, with a fief including three villages and a castle
in the vicinity of Nablus.

CHAPTER THREE

THE GIRL IN THE TOWER

The winter rains came and with them the cold north wind that drives the bedouins on the desert to the shelter of their crooked black tents made of goat's hair. On Mount Lebanon, the giant cedars folded their boughs in order to shed the massive weight of the heavy snowfalls. In the valley of the Jordan, which marked the division of the Holy Land into two armed camps, Christian and Moslem, not a man or horse stirred. War was over until spring.

Castle Shechem stood on a spur from Mount Gerizim, overlooking the Vale of Shechem, a two-hour ride north from Jerusalem. It was not an imposing castle, Guy decided, the first time he rode up the pathway. Its deficiencies could be seen at a glance. The mountain behind the castle rose high above the battlements, laying it open to attack from the rear. An olive grove spilled down the lower slopes of the mountain right to the edge of the platform on which the keep stood. The platform fell away at the sides into a deep fosse, or ditch, while the front was defended by a small forecourt behind a crenellated wall and gatehouse. No, it was not an imposing castle, but he was master of it.

Surprisingly, the stout wooden gates were ajar but no one seemed to be within them. Guy tethered his horse in the gateway out of the rain, crossed the courtyard, and leapt up the rock-hewn steps to the entrance of the keep. An old woman was in the guardhouse, bent over a fire, stirring a cauldron. She spoke neither French nor Arabic but some dialect Guy had never heard before. He mounted the circular stairway in the tower at the right hand of the entrance. No one was in the Great Hall. All was dust and cobwebs, hanging in festoons from the gallery around the upper floor. The central hearthstone was cold and bare and looked as though it had not held a fire in a long time.

"The devil!" Guy said aloud, wiping the rain off his face with his sleeve. "I should have come down before. It's been deserted. They've all run away."

He caught sight of a movement in the gallery and, looking up, saw the tall figure of a girl leaning over the railing, looking at him fixedly. He had an impression of loose-flowing, tawny hair and a face both haunting and haunted. For a moment, neither spoke.

At last she said, "I suppose you're the new master?"

"Yes."

"The castellan, Messer Adhemar, is gone to the village. I asked him to leave the gate open for me. I wanted a chest I left behind. It's silly of me, but I can't seem to get it downstairs. You must forgive me, coming back like this."

His thoughts whirled. This must be the daughter of Sieur Everard, the last siegneur of Castle Shechem. It was rumored that he had a mad daughter who had been confined in a convent in Nablus. Sieur Everard had died in captivity in Aleppo and his death had so deranged his daughter that no man could either tame her or marry her. There was no other heir and, lacking a lord by inheritance or marriage, the fief had fallen vacant.

"Wait for me. I'll give a hand." He ran up the tower stairs to the gallery where he found the girl sitting on her small, wooden chest looking entirely self-composed. She was about eighteen, with an old-young face, that had on it a wide smile. Guy had an impression of fiery beauty, tragic, brave, but smiling.

"Why, you're soaking wet!" she said. "What a poor welcome for the lord and master. No servants to wait on him, light him a fire, and dry his clothes for him. It's all my fault, really. I dismissed all the servants a year ago when ... Messer Adhemar was waiting for new orders which never came."

Guy looked at her closely. Was she mocking him? He decided not, and yet there was something about her that cared nothing for the world and seemed to laugh at its foolishness. And what was the meaning of her careless appearance, the unbound hair, the rough, woolen dress girdled by a cord, the bare feet ... ?

"May I sit with you?" He threw his cloak over the railing and acted on his own suggestion. "I should have sent warning ahead of me, but I wanted to see how things were for myself. It's my first ..."

"Your first castle?" She seemed amused. "We had not expected so young a master."

"My brother is sieur of Vienne, in Poitou, and I served my lord the Count for two years before taking the Cross." She made him feel defensive, although she was a girl and younger than he. She looked as though she might have commanded the castle herself with all the zeal and ferocity of an old campaigner.

"And you," Guy said, "are you not living here any more?"

"Oh, no. I have no claim. They wanted to make a nun of me, but I am not made for the religious life. All those bells calling to matins and compline, in nasty, damp crypts like dungeons. I want to live in the fresh air and sunshine with the wild creatures which know no evil."

"But where ..."

"... do I live? I have a tower on the hill, not far from here, a ruined tower no one has used for ages, it's all falling in, but it's quite habitable really, and there is room for Adèle, that's my gazelle, and Bruno, my stag, and all the hares and partridges I free from the farmers' traps.

Oh, I hoped so hard you wouldn't mind. You see, it's all up to you now. It's your tower. Oh, please say it's all right."

She made her wild, incoherent request seem so natural, so simple, that only an inhuman wretch could deny her. In fact, before he had time to say anything, she took it as settled.

"If you'll help me down with the box, I'll strap it onto the back of Melissa, my donkey, and I won't ever bother you again."

He was about to say he would send it after her, but then he remembered the absence of servants and ended by carrying the box on his shoulder down to the entrance of the keep, where a white, sad-eyed donkey was tethered. He roped it to the donkey's back between her paniers, then he untied his own mare and lifted the girl, protesting, into the saddle.

"No, please, you mustn't. I shall be perfectly all right. Let me go!"

"You said it's my tower. Can't I see it? Which way, my lady?"

Guy led the mare, the girl, and the donkey with the box out of his castle gate. After rounding the spur they climbed a hairpin track that zigzagged up the mountainside. There, at the top of the first hill, at a distance of perhaps a mile, stood a lonely, round watchtower, its crumbled top outlined against the rainy sky.

Finally, they entered a stone-fenced yard, filled with ducks, geese, and smaller creatures in pens and cages. In one of the pens, roofed with rushes, he saw the tiny, delicate face of a gazelle looking out. After dismounting, the girl opened the pen to lead out a doe not more than two feet high, with slender legs and polished, ivory hooves. "My soul," she murmured gathering the animal into her arms, "my other self." The doe answered by burying her face in the girl's breast.

After untying the box, he offered to take it inside.

"But you needn't," she grew flustered, "you mustn't—"

"You promised to show me my tower."

The box was on his shoulder and it would have been unkind to keep him waiting. They entered a mud-floored room with a well in the center and a hearth to one side. The smoke, having no exit, had blackened all the walls and the timbers overhead. Around the inside of the circular walls was a stone stairway, without a railing, mounting to the next floor. Guy began the ascent.

"Stop. No, really, I won't have you carry it any farther—" Tears of rage appeared in her eyes.

Guy emerged into what seemed to be the girl's bedroom, with a pallet of rushes laid on the floor, a table piled with trinkets, a small candelabra, but for a lady's room oddly enough, no mirror. Birds had entered the arrow slits around the room and nested in the rafters. A portion of the wall adjoining the roof was missing and the hole stuffed with straw. He set the box down carefully beside the narrow, virginal bed.

"And do you live here alone?" he asked, amazed.

"Do you think I cannot?" she defied him. "I am as able as any man to live as I please. Besides, no one will bother me. They call me the witch of Shechem already. Someday I shall be a hag with a tall hat and a broomstick on which I shall ride over the mountain by the light of the full moon."

He noted the stairway continuing upward to a trap door in the roof. "And will you take off from up here?" he teased. She followed him up onto the roof in angry silence. The top of the tower was surrounded by a wall of broken embrasures, from which many of the merlons had fallen out, and in one place the wall itself had crumbled away, leaving a gaping hole that was visible in the bedroom below.

The rain had momentarily ceased and, through clouds, there were glimpses of sunshine. The nearer landscape was still brown, with many outcroppings of slate and shale, for it was a treeless country except for the oak forests in the valley. But it breathed a sweet and lonely kind of peace, poised, as it were, on the edge of eternity.

The couple leaned against an embrasure in silence, he engrossed by curiosity, she by wounded pride.

"I suppose you have a name," he said at last.

"I am Alice," she replied indifferently.

"I am Guy." After another silence he went on. "I know about your father. He was a very brave man. The Constable Manasses told me about him. They fought together before Aleppo. It was very ill-luck that he was captured."

"Do you know the citadel at Aleppo?" She spoke looking straight ahead. "It is very deep, with dungeons one hundred feet below ground. Some men have been kept there for ten years. The Saracens kill them a little at a time, beginning with the eyes. It is true. A man who was with my father, and who was ransomed, saw him die. They took the eyes first . . ."

"Don't, Alice . . ."

"They sent the eyes to me in a basket of lettuce, with the ransom note. But we could not pay. We have always been poor."

"Look, Alice, you must come away from here. No woman can live alone like this. It's madness. I won't let you. You shall have your old room back at Castle Shechem. I'll get you a lady-in-waiting, maid servants, anything you like. I won't bother you. The fact is, I'll be away most of the time. You shall take charge of everything for me."

She looked at him as though it was his sanity that was in question. "And what will my guardians say about that? I am a ward of the Crown, you know, as it is a Royal fief."

"They will appoint me a guardian, if you prefer."

"You?" Her broad mouth curved slightly into an ironic smile. "I am sure you would make me an excellent guardian. But I have nothing to do with any man, or any woman either, for that matter. I am free. Up here I feel free. I need no one. No one at all. Please remember that."

Guy rode back to the Castle in a sort of trance. Nothing like this had ever happened to him before. It was outside his comprehension. The girl was probably starving, selling off a few trinkets to some Jew in Nablus from time to time; she couldn't possibly go on like that. Besides, there was the danger of attack in that lonely tower, and how could he protect her, so far away? Of course, she was mad, that explained it, but it was a fine sort of madness, and he admired the furious look on her face when she told him she didn't need him. But she did need him, by God's blood, she did. And what was he to do now?

With the coming of spring, Guy was more frequently at Castle Shechem. By permission of the Queen's Constable, he removed his men-at-arms from the Household Guard and installed them in the Castle. He obtained servants in the village and the interior of the great hall was swept and scrubbed and strewn with fresh rushes. And there were long conferences with the castellan, Messer Adhemar, in his little room over the gate house.

Messer Adhemar was a short, massive man, of swarthy complexion, with broken teeth and gold rings in his ears. His parentage was mixed Syrian and French and he spoke both languages with utter impartiality. After twenty years of service, he had lost several masters, but the habit of loyalty was deeply ingrained in him. He gave advice when needed and obeyed orders without question. Guy knew at once he could trust him.

"All I can tell you, sir, is that this girl will cause you trouble. She was always a wild thing, running barefoot on the hills. A good girl, mind you. She loved her father—too much perhaps. Sieur Everard was a hard man. He fought like a tiger, but he had a weakness for that child. A love-child, sir, she grew up without a mother. It is said Sieur Everard killed his wife long ago because she was unfaithful to him. A dark story. That was before my time. I served him ten years. He was a good master, but he was away too much. He neglected his lands. Now you must be firm with these peasants, sir—"

The fief of Shechem was divided among three villages, comprising perhaps one thousand families. They were, for the most part, Samaritan Jews, who had inhabited the

land for two thousand years. Mainly shepherds, their
flocks roved the hills for many miles on Mount Gerizim,
their holy mountain. In the Vale of Shechem, some had
farms and market gardens and took the produce to market in Nablus. But they were a self-sufficient people, living
apart, and asking nothing of the world but to be left alone.
Tithes were hard to collect, for they hid their wool and
grain, and they avoided service on the Castle lands so that
these fields were fallen into neglect.

"You must be very firm, sir," the castellan said again.
"These people understand only force. There is a whipping
post in the village square, which can be put to use whenever you please, sir."

Guy called a meeting of all the mukhtars, the headmen
of the villages. Instead of summoning them to the Castle,
the meeting was held in the square of Shechem Village, a
departure from custom that made Messer Adhemar raise
his eyebrows, but he never dreamed of contradicting his
master. On the appointed day, which dawned with all the
golden freshness of spring, the square was alive with the
nodding turbans, green, blue and saffron, of the villagers,
many of whom had come from the most distant parts of
the Vale.

The mukhtars, flurried by the order for an open-air
meeting, were at a loss to know how to provide for it
properly. The village police, consisting of youths with
staves, cleared a place before the tavern, and brought out a
very old and battered wicker armchair (the only chair in
the entire village) for the lord to sit on. A scribe spread his
mat alongside, with his ink and quills, while the mukhtars
in their bright turbans, and lambskin robes, grouped themselves around the vacant chair and discussed the situation
with one another. Firmness was needed, all agreed. The
new lord was young, they said, and inexperienced. He
must be made to understand that the people had special
rights. Even the Moslems respected the Samaritans as a
people under God. They could not do unclean work, or be
drafted for military service. Firmness, they agreed, was
essential.

If they had expected a clatter of Frankish horsemen, flourishing swords, they were surprised. Three men rode into the square and dismounted. They hitched their horses to the whipping post. Messer Adhemar laid his hand on the post, and said, "Take my word for it, sir, a touch of the whip and they will do your bidding." Leaving Hugh to tend the horses, Guy and his castellan advanced alone and on foot through the throng, which opened before them.

"Salaam aleikum," said Guy to the Chief Priest, the Haccohen Hagadol. "Salaam aleikum," he repeated to each of the mukhtars. Bowing low and touching their foreheads, they replied in their own Samaritan tongue, "Shalom, shalom." There was another unexpected deviation from custom, as Guy refused to occupy the chair until each of the mukhtars and the Priest had been provided with a rug on which to sit. This done, the meeting was opened.

Guy spoke first. "Men of Shechem, you have a great land, an ancient land, a holy land. I come to rule it justly. The laws of your council, the Cohanim, will be upheld. If any man has a grievance against another, let him go before the Cohanim. If any man has a grievance against me, let him appear before me in the sight of the Cohanim. I will give him justice. For your law shall be my law, and my law shall be your law, and the law shall be above us both."

There was a movement among the crowd as Guy's speech was translated by the castellan. No one was more astounded at his words than Messer Adhemar. The mukhtars looked at one another uncertainly. Guy continued.

"For justice there is a price that all must pay. In the absence of your late lord, your tithes have not been collected. Your forced service has not been done on the Castle fields. Answer me now: is it your will that these tithes be paid and this service done?"

Messer Adhemar nearly choked at the unprecedented question. The mukhtars were at a loss how to reply. But the crowd cried loudly, "No tithes! No forced service!"

"Then I propose to you a new system. If you do not

pay tithes, you shall pay money. This means you shall own
your land and pay me taxes only. And if you do service
on my lands, I shall pay you money, at a fair rate to
which the Cohanim shall agree. So those who hold lands
or flocks shall be the owners. And those who labour for
me shall be paid wages as free men and not as forced service. Is this your will?"

Again the mukhtars searched one another's eyes, astonished. A new day had dawned in Shechem and this time
the crowd howled its assent. It fell silent again as Guy
raised his hand.

"Let the mukhtars consult on what I have proposed."

It wasn't necessary. The crowd pushed forward, seized
Guy's chair and raised it on their shoulders. Shouting and
cheering, they carried him to where his horse was tethered. He mounted and grinned a little slyly at Messer Adhemar, as they rode away.

"Well done, sir!" The honest castellan tried to give his
loyal assent. "A good strategy for these people, who are a
special people and who love money. They will work for
you now."

"I have thought about it for a long time," replied Guy,
"and I would like to try it someday on my own estates in
Vienne. It may be my brother will not agree. But I am
sure that in time to come, perhaps in a hundred years, this
is how it will be."

Messer Adhemar scratched his head. "Maybe so in a
hundred years, right now it will take time to survey the
land and draw up the deeds and I still think I can get the
best results by flogging them, if I may, sir."

"You may have your way now, Messer Adhemar, but I
will have my way in the end."

The villagers of Shechem soon became accustomed to
the sight of their new lord riding around the farms and
cottages, and stopping to talk with each of his serfs.
Sometimes, he offered a peasant advice about tilling his
land, or he called over a pretty daughter of the house to
pinch her cheek and make her blush.

The ancient custom of the 'droit de seigneur,' that gave

the lord the right to any maid in his villages, was dreaded
by all the mothers. Guy knew this, and he amused himself
by teasing the village girls. Whenever he saw a maid that
appealed to him, he stopped and whispered to her while
her mother trembled. Once he found three pretty maids in
the stocks which Messer Adhemar had set up in the village. He was informed that they had been caught picking
cherries on his estate. Of course, he set them free, but not
before he had kissed each one soundly on the lips. When
the mothers of Shechem saw that they had nothing more
to fear from their young master's playful molestations,
they became his strongest supporters, and even boasted
about the inroads he made among their daughters.

The men in the three villages, tended to be fatalistic.
After all, lords come and go, but a countryman's work
goes on forever. Messer Adhemar soon had the whole
male population at work, sweating and groaning, to repair
the ruin of the lord's estates. There were some angry mut-
terings when the first laggards were seized, stripped and
tied to the whipping post in the village square. Sergeant
Berthold was dispatched from the Castle, armed with a
bull's pizzle, to administer justice. He was always very
conscientious where he thought his master's interests were
concerned, and there were few laggards after that. Actually, it was well understood in the village that a reprieve
from summary justice could be had by making a direct ap-
peal to the Castle. But, in practice, the mukhtars never
permitted any appeals. They were well-satisfied to have
the zealous young sergeant keep order for them. After all,
it was easier that way. And so Shechem and its sister villages continued in their ancient, somnolent ways.

As soon as he could, Guy despatched masons and car-
penters to repair the watchtower on the hill. Alice refused
them admittance and they returned rebuffed. After that,
Guy discovered that on certain days the girl was in the
habit of leaving the tower in early morning to spend the
day on the hills, returning only at dark. On one of these
days, after she had left, the workmen were dispatched
again. They set fresh stones in the wall and retimbered the

roof, sealing it with beeswax. Alice, on her return, raged
all night against Guy, weeping bitter tears into her pillow.
Afterward, she kept the iron shutter in the door locked
and fastened the key to the cord about her waist. In future, her privacy would be inviolable.

"You must give up this mad project of yours," the
Queen said to Guy one day, toward the end of March. She
was walking with him in the Citadel garden. The new
fountain had been finished and it played prettily among
the tubs of Damascus roses surrounding it.

"What project do you mean, ma'am?" asked Guy.

"You think I don't know that you have been to the
Treasury and tried to get the dowry of this girl, Everard's
daughter, assigned to her? Naturally, as she is my ward,
they referred the matter for my approval."

"And you gave it?"

"Of course not. What right has she to her dowry? She
had already refused two offers of marriage."

"If you had been in her place, would you have accepted
these offers?" A look was exchanged between them. Guy
knew his ground.

"Perhaps not," said Melisende, after a pause. "But she
should have taken the veil. The dower was promised to
the convent in Nablus."

"Some people are not made to wear bonds, either of
matrimony or of religion."

"What nonsense you talk. She is a wild, unbiddable girl,
and, I am told, possibly a witch. She will only bring you
harm. Oh Guy, Guy, why are you throwing yourself away
on her? Lie with the girl if you want. But remember, a
gentleman does not marry for love. You could marry a
princess. Though I'd much rather you'd stay as you are."

"Then I shall stay as I am, since it pleases you."

"And you will give her up?"

"Alice? Why she won't even speak to me. That's why I
want her dower for her. She'll take nothing from me."

"What she needs is someone to rule her. You could do

it, if you were her guardian. But I shan't let that happen."

"Then you will give her the dower?"

"Of course not! Why should I?"

It was always the same. This was the Queen's game, to force him to force her, so she could have the pleasure of yielding to him. He must play the game.

"Because I wish it," he said.

Melisende made a gesture of mock submission. "Then I have no choice, have I?" Suddenly, she became serious, grasping his arm. "But you will be careful, Guy? You know how much you mean to us, to the boy and to me?"

Guy rewarded her with one of his steady smiles.

It was no use. Alice would neither receive his letters nor open the door to him when he called on her. At last, he hit upon a stratagem. He deposited the entire dower sum, which had been entrusted to him, for her, by the Treasury, with a certain money broker in Nablus. He knew that Alice was in the habit of calling on this broker to pawn a few things about once a month. His instructions to the broker were to advise his client that the Treasury had placed the sum in trust for her, and not to mention Guy's name at all.

He had done everything a man could do. Surely now he could forget his little witch girl on the hill. But he could not. He felt there was some evil on the hill, an evil that was not of her but around her. He had his bed moved from the seigneurial room at the front of the Castle and placed it in one of the small tower rooms at the back, where he could watch the tower on the hill. Sleepless, he stared into the dark, thinking.

It wasn't that he cared for her, he assured himself. What bothered him was her loneliness. He wondered about the stories he had heard of spells cast on the farmers' sheep, of witch fires playing over the old tower at night. He didn't believe any of it, of course, but with a girl like that, anything seemed possible.

No, no, she was not a witch, of that he was sure. He knew by the very openness of her face and the way her mouth turned up at the corners, an honest mouth, a warm mouth. Not that she was exactly beautiful. She was strange, strange; there was a provocation in her firm full body and her splendid eyes. She was strong-headed and she needed to be ruled, the Queen had said. But how?

He remembered a beautiful falcon he had once had, a gift of his father long ago in Vienne. He had trained her himself, letting her off the chain for short periods, and whistling for her. When she came back, he gave her food from his own hand. At last the proud bird was given her freedom, but she continued to come when he called, she nestled in his jacket with just her small, iridescent head showing. He had often kissed her, pressing his lips into the soft, downy feathers . . .

Damn it all, wasn't he the master here? Were his wishes not obeyed by everyone? Ask Messer Adhemar, he would soon tell you! But alas, Messer Adhemar could do nothing for him in this case. And, God knows, he asked very little. All he wanted was to watch over her, to protect her, to provide for her. A proud girl like that could not be kept on a chain. She was too magnificent. And her mouth was soft and warm . . .

But she would not come when he called.

In the tower on the hill, Alice, awake, also thought about her old home, and the man who had taken it from her, and the change this had brought into her life. She harbored no bitterness, of that she was sure. The past was dead. It was a guilty past and the guilt had been paid for. Her happiness was not tied to any man or woman. Men and women could not be trusted, she knew that. Even her father had killed the one he loved because she had betrayed him and all his life he had fled that memory. Now the ghost was stilled. With God's own creatures she was at peace. They were Eden; they were the world before the Fall; they were innocent even when they killed. She would be like them, a child of nature, a stranger to man.

Then this blundering male had come, taking possession of everything, talking about *his* tower, *his* land, *his* rights.

He could leave nothing alone, but had to be prying, mending, talking, until he had destroyed all the defences she had built up around her. Of course, to be just, it was not his fault. He might have ordered her away; he had every right. From what she had heard, he was well-liked in the villages. When she thought of him in the abstract, he was good, trustworthy, even likable. But when he appeared to her in person, he was, after all, a man, imposing himself on her by his very presence, his way of standing too close to her, and looking at her with his unwavering eyes.

Fortunately, the gift of the Queen's dower had come to save her. Now she would pay him for his tower and he would have to give her a deed for it, and then he would have no right to interfere in her life again. She wondered if he would come to collect the payment himself. He might send his bailiff and, perhaps, his men-at-arms. That would be hateful. But perhaps he would come himself. He was a gentleman. Then she would have the opportunity of explaining to him how she owed him nothing at all. Yes, that's how she hoped it would be.

In April, the hillsides and the Vale of Shechem were alight with flowers, the wild narcissus, anemone, flax and asphodel. It was the time the Samaritan people celebrated the Passover on Mount Gerizim. For seven days, there was a general movement of all the principal families, taking their tents and huts to the top of the mountain. With them went donkeys loaded with fuel for the ovens, and sheep for the sacrifice.

The Haccohen Hagadol made a ceremonious visit to the Castle before the event. "We wish to inform my lord," he told Guy, speaking French painfully, "that a tent will be set up for you on the mountain on the night of the Passover, and that all the men and women of Shechem pray you to do them honour by your presence."

Guy accepted with pleasure, saying quickly, "Your Reverence, there is only one thing that would add to my pleasure and that is for you to extend your invitation to the former mistress of this place, the lady who lives on the hill. I would like you to make this invitation to her in person."

The Priest hedged. "My lord's wish is my own. But the lady may not eat with us. Such is our law."

"Then she will eat with me in my tent. But you will make the invitation yourself."

The old man bowed. "My lord's wish is my wish." With a sigh, he set out on his long walk up the mountainside.

The sun was already going down on the last day before the Passover when Guy returned from his weekly visit to Jerusalem. Together with Hugh and two of his men-at-arms, he climbed the mountain on foot. The whole of the Cohanim, seventy-five priests in all, wearing white turbans, white robes, and carrying staves, received him and conducted him to his tent. Inside, they had set up his old wicker chair (it had become "his" for all ceremonious occasions) and a table of sweetmeats, since, explained the Priest, a non-Samaritan could not touch the Paschal meal. "Now it is time," he said. "Will it please my lord to come?"

The scene on the mountaintop was solemn and beautiful in the extreme. Bare except for the desert flowers, the land fell away on two sides, eastward toward the valley of the Jordan, lying in the blue shadow of the mountain, and westward, where the setting sun lay on the horizon of the sea, washing all the country with luminous light. It was like the ending of the world's first day when God saw that it was good.

And there, sitting high on a boulder overlooking the western expanse, Guy saw in silhouette the slim, erect figure of a girl. His heart gave a leap. She had come. He ran to her at once.

"You must come down," he cried, "they're going to begin." And he held up his arms to receive her. Alice hesitated, took a step downward and slipped inadvertently into his arms. He released her at once but felt pleased and a bit elated. They walked together to the site of the altar, which was set up on the highest part of the mountain. The whole Samaritan nation was gathered there in two groups, the priests on one side and the people on the other.

"May it please my lord and lady to know," said the Chief Priest, "that you are standing on the true Bethel, the house of God. In fact, God who is exalted revealed it through Moses, on whom let there be peace. This is the place where our lord Abraham, on whom let there be peace, pitched his tent. Here he remained and settled down, and God who is exalted appeared to him, and conversed with him, and set upon him the seal of the circumcision, giving him and his seed the land forever."

"Here's the homily, aimed straight at me," Guy whispered to Alice.

The sun had almost sunk below the horizon. A tremulous silence filled the air, and the Chief Priest approached the altar, which was set in a long trench below the level of the ground. At one end was the tannur, the oven ready to receive the sacrifice, at the other end stood the slayers, clothed in white. Only a weak bleating from the sheep broke the stillness.

At that moment the sun dropped from sight, and the Haccohen Hagadol shrieked the command, "Shattu attu!" Then, everything happened very fast. The knives were drawn across the throats of the sacrifice, the blood was collected in pots and mixed with hyssop, and the doors of the huts and the tent poles were smeared with it. The sheep, after cleaning, were committed to the tannur, and for a space of three hours, everyone relaxed.

Guy retired to his tent and received the priests and elders. His men had brought up a chest filled with presents, and each of his guests left the tent well-gratified. Small coins were scattered to the children who clamored about the door. Alice sat in the corner on a heap of cushions and wondered at Guy's way with his people.

The Haccohen Hagadol started to leave but Guy stopped him. "Your Reverence," he said, "I would learn something about your religion."

"I am at my lord's command," the Priest replied.

"You say that God deeded this land to Abraham and

his descendants?" The mukhtars and elders were listening intently.

"It is written in the Scriptures."

"Who are Abraham's children? What does the Scripture say?"

"That God said, 'This is my covenant between me and thee and thy seed after thee.' " the Priest said.

"And is Abraham's seed your nation only or is it many nations? See that you tell me exactly what the Scripture says."

"It is written—'a father of many nations have I made thee.' "

"Then the covenant God made with Abraham is also with me and with my nation and the land is deeded to all true believers."

The old Priest bowed his head. Never before had he been put down by Scripture, and before his own people, too. He felt a holy rage in his heart, which he could barely disguise. He replied, "We do not deny it. What is it your prophet says?—we render unto Caesar the things which are Caesar's. But you only hold your power by the will of God. If ever you prove unworthy, the power shall be taken from you."

The Priest looked proudly, even arrogantly at him; the look boded a bitter feud between them.

When the tent was cleared of people, Guy ordered his men-at-arms to close the entrance, and he filled a plate with food which he shared with Alice, sitting on the ground. The time seemed propitious, and Alice told him about the dower money and her plan to pay for the land deed to the tower.

"So, you see, I shall not be a charge on you any more," she announced triumphantly. "Haven't I done well? That should show you that I can manage perfectly by myself."

But the effect on Guy was not what she had anticipated. He glowered at his food and gave no consent to the proposal to sell the tower land.

"You forget," he said at last, "this tower of yours is a defensive position. In time of war, it may be necessary to fortify it, in order to watch the roads over the mountain and prevent an attack on the Castle from the rear. I can't agree to let it go."

"But that's so unreasonable," Alice blinked back her tears. "When you need it, you shall have it. I'm not your enemy. But meanwhile it should be mine, not yours."

"Yours or mine, what difference does it make?" Guy replied. "The truth is you shouldn't be there at all. It isn't safe for you. Anything could happen. With summer, there may be Saracen raids."

She looked at him baffled. That's the way it would always be, she supposed. He was still a man. Men could never be fair or treat a woman equally. She hated him at that moment, but said nothing about it.

Instead, she changed the subject. "You put down the Chief Priest very cleverly. He won't like that, you know, and I'd advise you to keep a watch on him. My father used to say that he had a nasty, waspish temper and never forgot a slight. But what puzzles me is what you meant by 'making a covenant with God' for this land. This isn't how the transaction is usually done, you know. The Jews of Jerusalem claimed their Zion was the true Holy Mountain, and the Samaritans claimed it was Mount Gerizim. The Romans took it away from both of them by right of the divine Caesar. The Moslems conquered all in the name of Muhammad. And now Guy of Vienne is lord of Shechem by virtue of—what? You never did tell me how you made your covenant with God."

Guy listened to her tirade with lowered eyes. He felt the whiplash of her words as keenly as if he had been bound to the whipping post himself. Perhaps what hurt him most was the fact that she scorned him enough to inflict it. Especially since, in his heart, he believed she was right. From the beginning, he had rejected the materialism of those who had created "God's Kingdom." But he had hardly acted differently himself. He had acquired land, become wealthy, had even desired this proud and magnificent girl for himself. Was it for this he had taken the vows, after the long night vigil, in the cold chapel before

dawn? He wished he could tell her that, he wished he
could see clearly through his confusion, and call to her,
"Wait for me! I was lost awhile, but I found my way back
to you. Let's be friends!" But it could not be like that; she
did not see him as one of her kind. He was less, oh, much
less than the wild creatures she loved, because their love
was not of the flesh and their possession was not of this
world. She was the sort of girl who lived on a plane so
high, he somewhat ruefully reflected, that to be worthy of
her was to lose her.

At midnight, the Samaritans opened the tannur and distributed the flesh of the sacrifice to the entire community.
Men, women and children attacked the flesh, tearing it
with their hands and eating hastily, in memory of the children of Israel on leaving Egypt—"and ye shall eat it in
haste," says the Scripture, "it is the Lord's Passover."

After that there were celebrations and dancing until
dawn. The light was just breaking in the east when Guy
left his tent, with Alice and his men, and began to descend
the mountain. Where the paths divided to the Castle and
the tower, he sent his men homeward and accompanied
Alice alone.

For a while they walked in silence. Then Guy stopped.

"Please, Alice, I must tell you something. Can't we stop
here?" They sat on a grassy slope, white with asphodel.

"I'm sorry about what I said," Guy began. "You can
have the tower. I'll have the deed drawn up at once. I
don't care about the price. Let the bailiff settle it at your
valuation."

Alice relaxed a little. She leaned back luxuriantly. "My
own tower," she said. "Thank you, Guy." It was the first
time she had ever used his name. Emboldened, he went
on.

"I only want you to promise me something. If ever . . ."

"There you go. Conditions again. I tell you I won't have
conditions!"

"Just that you'll come back to the Castle awhile. For
the summer. I'll make it lawful and decent, as I promised.
Only say you'll come."

"But I don't want to."

"Say it for me."

"Why?" She was exasperated. "Why, why, why?"

He was lying beside her and reached over, placing his far hand across her on the ground.

"Because I love you."

He was not touching her. But she felt the imminence of his whole body over her. She was trapped, just as the wild creatures were trapped by cruel men. Her entire being revolted.

Barely audibly, she whispered, "Get up."

He did not move.

Then, "I hate you," she said clearly.

Slowly, in stunned silence, he removed his imprisoning arm. At once, she jumped up and ran. Moments later he followed, calling her. But she gained the tower first and slammed down the shutter, bolting it from within. He beat on the iron without avail. He had lost.

Guy walked homeward, in the slowly breaking day, and tried to take stock of the situation. It was worse, far worse than anyone knew. Danger was abroad and there was nothing he could do now to save the witch girl on the hill. He must look to himself. On reaching the Castle, he summoned the castellan. "Messer Adhemar," he said, "I want all the roads into Shechem patrolled daily. Put a man at each crossing from dawn to sunset to stop all strangers. I was set upon yesterday at Jacob's Ford, on my way from Jerusalem. Someone is trying to kill me."

CHAPTER FOUR

THE GRAND MASTER

On Easter Sunday the bells of the Church of the Holy Sepulchre rang out with more than usual clangor. Not only the great bell in the big tower, but the bells in all the domes as well as the sanctus bell that normally rang only at solemn high mass. Shutters were thrown open and questioning faces appeared; people in the town shouted the news across from balcony to balcony; costermongers, who had just learned it from urchins that roved the bazaars, broadcast it in their stentorian cries—the King had been crowned!

A strange, hurried, furtive coronation it was, without warning or panoply, attended by only a few witnesses, lords and knights of the King's court, but a proper, legal coronation none the less, in which Patriarch Fulcher (under duress, it was said) placed the crown with trembling hands on the head of the young, red-bearded Baldwin III. The King was visibly nervous and uneasy. It pained him to flout his mother, the Queen, this way, but his courtiers would have it so. "Long live the King!" the knights shouted, unsheathing their swords and flashing them upward toward the painting of Christ Triumphant over the altar.

The aged Patriarch shivered at the martial display, so unseemly in the holy place. Many years ago, he had crowned Melisende with the same royal crown, and the Queen still lived. He owed the endowment of many a convent and chapter house to Melisende, truly a faithful daughter of the Church for all her sins, and this was how he repaid her, by crowning her son despite her. He would never have done it but for the squad of armed men that appeared at his palace door that morning. "God forgive me," murmured the rheumy-eyed old man, as the *Te Deum* burst from the choir and the grim-faced, military assembly marched from the church.

In the Citadel, a few streets away, Melisende sat in the window embrasure of her tower room and heard the bells. She, too, knew their meaning, though no one had dared to tell her. Her son, bashful and ashamed, had come to her the night before. "I cannot help it, Mother," he had said, pursing his soft, weak mouth in embarrassment, "the barons insist I must be King."

"They don't care a fig for you," she had told him tartly. "It's for themselves they want it. They came out here for land and they think you'll let them grab it. My way has been too peaceful for them. They want war, but war, my son, is a two-edged sword. If you let them, they'll lose you this Kingdom.

"What are we, after all, but a few castaways on an alien shore? We have built ourselves cities, castles, churches, but we cannot defend them always. The enemy are like the sands of the sea, there is no end to them. And we cannot look to our own people to send help forever. They will tire in the end and leave us, and we will be alone. When that day comes you will remember what I said, and what you think now is the babbling of a foolish old woman will seem wisdom to you then."

But maternal advice is wasted once the bird is flown. Baldwin would go the way of all the men of his family, seeking worldly acclaim, conquests, a rich marriage—all illusions. Melisende, looking out the window, sighed. She thought of her wasted life, the loss of all she had loved— even the young Prince, for whom her other son, Amaury, cared nothing.

The child had not been well lately. The high hopes of last autumn, when the Syrian doctor had come, were dwindling. It is true he was in good spirits; his malady seemed to have been arrested. But the mystery remained. The boy claimed, in all apparent honesty, that the feeling was restored to his hands and feet. But it was significant that this power was only recovered when the Syrian was actually present. When he was absent, these claims, valiantly maintained by the child, were patently false. The doctor was now an infrequent visitor. Business, of what kind he never revealed, kept him away. How could you ever trust these people?

Nevertheless, she was not a woman to succumb easily. She would fight for her rights. Quickly she rose, summoned the members of her household. The Constable Manasses was ordered to issue a proclamation to the people, asserting the rightful claim of Melisende, eldest daughter of Baldwin II, to the throne of Jerusalem. A convocation of all barons, knights and vassals of the Crown was called to uphold the rightful authority of the Queen. And a double guard was ordered on the gate of the Citadel.

These were treacherous days in Jerusalem. No armed man knew for sure who was with him and who was against him. There were so many brawls and murders between the King's faction and the Queen's faction that the Patriarch had to call for a curfew from sunset to dawn. And still, in the morning, the sergeants had to direct their work crews with barrows to pick up the corpses left lying in the alleys and tavern yards.

As Master of the Household, Guy remained at his post in the Citadel, travelling only infrequently to Castle Shechem. It was about this time that he first felt the shadow that was to fall across his steps. Wherever he went (and he usually travelled alone), there seemed to be some-one following him. Often, this shadow proved to be harm-less, though once or twice he was challenged by several armed men with masked faces. Each time he extricated himself with a good show of sword-play followed by a quick retreat into the warren of alleys between the houses.

Late on an evening, never to be forgotten in his life, when he was in the vicinity of the Temple, in the southeast quarter of the city, he sensed palpable danger. Actually, he had not wanted to walk in this quarter at all, but he was forced into it by the tactics of his pursuers. Slipping through the empty sheds of the cattle market, he emerged at the base of the high, stone wall, known to the Jews as the "Wall of Wailing." Here, in former times, they had bewailed the destruction of the first temple built by Solomon. Above the wall, on the great plateau of Mount Moriah, stood the castle of the Templars, a sanctuary for-bidden to all but members of the Order.

It was there at the Wall of Wailing that his attackers closed in. Looking for a way of escape, Guy sidled along the passageway between the cattle sheds and the Wall, leading to the postern of the Tannery. The shadows, two or perhaps three, with drawn swords, lurked in the sheds opposite, moving along with him. As they drew closer, Guy desperately sought a vantage point from which to fight. The stones behind his back were huge boulders, said to be the foundations of the original Temple. One of these, under an overhanging rock, seemed to be recessed somewhat and to offer a niche where he could not be at-tacked by more than one man at a time. He stepped inside the niche and found himself wedged against a ventilation grille of heavy iron bars at the back. Leaning on the bars, the grille suddenly swung inward unexpectedly and he tumbled into a pitch-black hole.

Down, down he fell into the pit to be agreeably sur-prised when he landed on straw. Straw was everywhere, also the smell of dung, and the sound far off of the stamp-ing and snuffling of horses. These, then, were the stables of Solomon, now used by the Templars for their chargers.

It was said these stables could hold ten thousand horses, although the Knights of the Temple did not number more than a thousand in the Holy Land. Most of the stalls, therefore, were empty. A cat brushed against him, evidently hunting rats. Feeling for the wall, Guy made his way into a central corridor of enormous length, built of rough-hewn stone, the roof barrel-vaulted and resting on piers of giant size (the stones of the original Temple upended). The central corridor was cross-cut by many other corridors, each so long that an arrow could not be shot from one end to the other. At intervals a small oil lamp, hung by chains, flickered in the distance.

Guy's predicament was acute. To be discovered in the Templars' vaults where they kept, besides their horses, all their stores of grain, arms and, it was rumored, untold wealth, was extremely dangerous. A veil of secrecy surrounded the Templars and all they did; to penetrate the veil was to court death. Nor would his position in the Queen's Household serve him here. The Temple was not answerable to the Crown and, in fact, disputed its power at every turn. The best course would be to find a way out that would not attract attention.

He began to run, past the horse stalls, up the great stone stairway leading to the next level of the building. The corridor led on upward, lit now by flaring torches on the wall. On the right, he looked into the giant refectory hall where the Knights ate their communal meals. Groups of servitors drowsed among the rushes on the floor and cats lurked under the tables looking for scraps. He took an exit on the left of the corridor, leading into the public baths, now dark and deserted. The baths consisted of a deep pool that drained into the ancient sewers laid by the Romans. There was no way out on the main floor, but, leaping up a circular stairway in the corner, he reached a balcony that circled the room and opened onto a small passage. This was opposite the dormitories where the Knights, fully-clothed, their arms beside them, lay sleeping under the bright lights of a central candelabrum.

Which way now? Guy dared not return to the main cor-

ridors and found an exit by climbing a ladder at the end
of the passage. It led to a trap door in the ceiling and into
an attic. The building was exceptional in having a steeply
pitched roof and he saw then that the dark was alive with
eyes—more cats. The creatures ran everywhere, hissing
and spitting at his intrusion. Slowly and carefully he
crossed the roof, walking on the joists to avoid making any
noise. Somewhere there must be an opening to the outside.
But there was none.

Instead, he found a panel in the floor of the attic dis-
placed and a light emanating from the room below. The
panel was part of a coffered ceiling and looked directly
down, through a deep sleeve, into the hall of the consistory, where a meeting was now in progress. The aperture
was small, circumscribed by the sleeve, and opened on one
end of the room only, but what he could see made his
heart falter and the hair of his head rise from the scalp. It
appeared to be an altar, having lighted candles on it, but,
in the place of a cross, there was instead the graven image
of a large cat.

Although he felt that many persons were in this room
only one appeared within his frame of vision. It was a
man robed entirely in white, with a woolen mantle about
his shoulders and on his head a white skull-cap, fringed
round with a black halo of short, curly hair. He faced
away from the viewer, so that his features were not dis-
cernible. However, to Guy there was something strangely
familiar about him, either in the wiry suppleness of his
body, or the intensity that emanated from his gestures. He
appeared to be receiving a postulant seeking admission to
the Order.

In the background the voices of many persons unseen
chanted a sort of litany in a two-part antiphonal style.

"You must entirely renounce your own will—"
"And entirely submit to that of another—"
"You must fast when you are hungry—"
"Keep watch when you are weary—"
"Thirst when you would drink—"

The words, indistinct and lost in the vastness of the hall, had a mournful sound, like a requiem for the dead. Indeed, there was an odor of death about this proceeding that was overwhelming.

The Receiver spoke now, in a gentle but vibrant voice. "And do you still wish, all the days of your life, to be the servant of this Order?"

Another voice, hoarse, like someone near death, replied. "Yes, sir, if God pleases."

"Learn, then, to obey by doing as you are bidden."

Now, something began to occur which was entirely outside Guy's vision. It seemed as if there were a movement of many persons; something heavy, like a piece of timber, was dragged across the floor; there were whispered commands; a sound as of spitting and curses. Several times a word was spoken in a harsh guttural, "Deny! Deny!" Again, Guy could not tell why, the hair lifted perceptibly from his scalp. And all the while the Receiver stood watching the scene with gently folded hands. After what seemed an interminable time, he spoke again.

"Has this man passed the tests?"

A chorus of voices replied, harshly and breathing heavily, as though after a great ordeal, "Sir, he has."

"Come, then," said the Receiver softly, "let him receive from me the kiss of peace."

And the man in white below him passed out of sight. Again there was a hiatus, during which some unseen ritual took place in utter silence. Guy wished to hear, to see, to know no more. Something had occurred which was beyond his understanding, something that both fascinated and repelled him. His limbs were trembling and his whole body was bathed in sweat. He must find a way out of this place. His only chance was to go back down the ladder. He decided to risk it rather than be trapped as a spy. But when he opened the trap door he saw the body of a man swinging from a rope that was part of the mechanism of the extension ladder. The man could not have been hanging more than a few minutes for he was still dancing on air.

Instantly, Guy severed the rope with his sword and the man dropped to the floor. In another moment, Guy was beside him, loosening the knot, massaging the swollen cords in his neck, trying to make him speak. He was a hardy-looking man of perhaps thirty-five, with a constitution that a few minutes of hanging could not easily break. But he didn't seem to welcome this intervention.

"I wish to God I had not been born," he gasped.

"Why, brother?" Guy asked.

"I denied—I denied—"

"What did you deny?"

"Don't you know?"

"No, what did you deny?"

"I thought everyone knew in this place—don't you know? Haven't you denied, too? Am I the only one—" With a long wail, the man siezed Guy by the throat and began to throttle him.

Guy could hear the pounding of running feet, many people crowded around them; the man was lifted up and taken away and torches were thrust into Guy's face. He was asked a torrent of questions he could not answer, inevitably his hands were bound, he was led down innumerable corridors and steps to a small cell into which he was roughly thrust. The iron door clanged behind him. He was a prisoner.

How many minutes or hours passed he did not know, when the door opened again and two Turcopole guards, half-caste mercenaries, addressed them peremptorily.

"You must come with us. The Master wants to see you."

More winding corridors, leading this time into what was once the Mosque of Aksa, built by the first caliphs of Islam. Vast open spaces, dimly lit, flagged with colored marbles and carpeted with heavy rugs, lay under a dome supported by hundreds of marble columns. Stone walls subdivided the space into guard-rooms and ante-chambers, filled with armed Turcopoles and black Nubian slaves, many of them sleeping. They came to a walled-in chapel, formerly the retiring room of the caliph.

The doors were flung open and the prisoner summarily thrown to his knees on the stone floor. Guy was in a small, bare room, full of shadows, with a curved recess at the back where the 'mihrab' stood, the marble niche facing Mecca. Around and above it, the gilt inscription still proclaimed the glory of God, the Merciful, the Compassionate, glittering in the light of a single candle on the table.

"Gently, brothers, gently," a voice spoke from behind a table. It was the voice he had heard in the consistory. A man in white arose from the shadows and came forward into the light, a man of dark complexion, with short-cut hair and beard and blazing, magnetic eyes—the same man Guy had seen before in the mess at Acre, Gerard of Ridfort, Master of the Temple. He was as thin and sharp as a tempered blade, yet, like a blade, he seemed ever to be bending, twisting, yielding, so he could better thrust home. And in the crook of his arm he carried a great white cat.

"Master," replied one of the guards, "this is the spy. He has most probably seen—"

"Most improbably," interrupted the Master. "Unbind him at once. He is our guest. Bring forward a chair. A cup of water, perhaps?"

He poured from a carafe and handed the cup to Guy. At a nod, the guards were dismissed, and the Master sat down behind the table, softly stroking the cat and half-smiling, looked at Guy.

"I have been expecting your arrival for some time. You are well-known to me, Sir Guy, and I have formed a certain opinion about you. A high opinion, I might say—oh, don't protest. I have invited you tonight because I have chosen you. My instinct never fails me about this."

"But I was not invited in, I fell in," Guy said.

"Nevertheless, you were invited," responded the Master smilingly. "You must know that you have been watched for some time. You have enemies, but not all those who followed you were murderers; some were guardian angels sent by me."

"And the men who were after me tonight—?"

"Were my angels, driving you to me."

Guy felt a shiver of nameless fear, such as all men experience when they venture onto unknown ground. He had lost his bearings and the familiar world was far away.

"Then why was I arrested?" he asked.

"The brothers were over-zealous. They thought you had attacked one of them."

"That man had been hanged."

"And you rescued him, so he has told us. You acted well to save his life. We thank you."

"He wanted to die. He said he had denied something."

"Denied what?"

"I don't know. I thought perhaps you could tell me."

"There is so much we deny in our Order. We who have been chosen for this way of salvation have denied everything. When you enter these portals, you put the world behind you. Here you will see a different kind of human being, knights dwelling together in brotherly love, meekness and frugality, eating sparingly, touching liquor not at all, abominating dice, and the snares of women, all for the sake of the Order.

"Look about you. See these rough walls, this marble, this gold. We care nothing for these things. We use them and cast them aside. Similarly, we take no care of the body. The knight of this Order does not comb himself, does not wash often, does not perfume his body. He wears his clothes until they fall off him.

"Fighting is the sole business of our lives. A knight of this Order fights to the death because he knows he will never be ransomed. And, just as the body must be kept under control, the mind must be kept single, pure and undefiled. Singleness of mind means that each man who gives his life to this order has no further thought but to live by the Rule."

He said these things quietly, but with complete authority. Guy, against his will, was drawn to him but was at a loss to understand the things he had witnessed—the hanged man, the scene in the consistory, the cats.

"What do you call your cat?" Guy asked.

"Her name is Baphomet," the Master replied, stroking her. "No doubt a corruption of Bastet, the cat goddess of the ancient Egyptians, and Mahomet, the Prophet of Islam."

"Is she, then, an evil goddess?"

"Dear boy," the Master replied, "you are still caught up in these tautologies of good and evil. You must learn to throw off these spiritual bonds. What is good? What is evil? They are interchangeable, depending on your situation. For example, your good is the evil of the Sultan. The Sultan's good is your evil."

"Do you mean there is no difference between good and evil?"

"I mean—and even your village *curé* at Vienne will not contradict me—that good is necessary for evil, and evil for good.

"Is God, then, also evil?"

"God is the author of evil in the sense that the corruption of the world is ordained by Him, as a means for carrying out the design of the universe."

"And the Order—to which aspect does it belong?"

"The Order is above good and evil. We have abandoned the illusions of ordinary men, so that for us there is no inner conflict, only the peace that comes from servitude to the Rule."

Guy took this in slowly, for his mind was not accustomed to such calisthenics. But beyond the paradoxes, which the Master flashed before him like a juggler's shining balls, he caught a glimpse of a higher concept—the concept of man as an instrument of God. For a moment, his whole being rose with the exhilaration of this thought that he might be the chosen instrument to establish the Kingdom of God on earth!

Then a swift depression seized him. He was not, could never be worthy of becoming such an exalted being. "You are mistaken, Master Gerard," he said, "you have chosen the wrong man."

"I am never mistaken. The time is not yet, but one day you will come to me of your own accord, and I shall receive you with the kiss of peace." He savored this in silence. After a pause, he went on, "You are in considerable danger and I shall not always be able to give you my protection. You must beware of this necromancer with whom you are consorting, a Syrian by the name of Barac. He is our enemy and will bring great harm upon us all. It is my duty to warn you."

Guy thought of all that was in jeopardy, the Prince's recovery, and the future of the Kingdom. But he said nothing. He only wanted to be away from this place and the man with the magnetic eyes. He needed to think and, if possible, to recover his bearings. "Thank you Master Gerard," he said, rising.

The Master held him only a moment. "You should not come here again. It will be noticed by others. If you need me, send a message and we will meet in the Temple Church." Then the doors swung open for him, moved by unseen hands. He was free again. The man with the cat remained looking after him for a long time.

After the attack at Jacob's Ford, Guy took Hugh with him, mounted on his own horse, whenever he rode to Castle Shechem. They retraced the scene, in an effort to establish exactly how it happened. A grove of oak trees lined the stream at the narrow crossing point and their over-hanging branches made an excellent concealment for a man to drop from, "like the Devil's Familiar," as Guy put it.

"He landed on your back, then?" Hugh enquired.

"And held on for dear life! I don't think he is used to riding a horse."

"Then he couldn't use his knife?"

"Exactly. I half turned and grasped his hand with the knife in it, holding it at arm's length, so— Then, as we reached the other side, I directed Brigitte into the trees

and ducked, so— And the branches, passing low, swept
him away. Brigitte was frightened, though, and carried me
on several lengths before I could dismount. When I got
back to the ford, there was no sign of my Familiar."

On their return to Castle Shechem, a deputation of villagers stood before the gate. There were shouts of "The
assassin! We have the assassin!" At the top of the steps to
the keep, the three mukhtars stood importantly in their
red turbans, like figures in a frieze, and the family of the
accused knelt wailing. Guy had a presentiment of a deeper
mystery, and this was only the beginning—like a miracle
play, in which these were the tumblers and jugglers who
performed before the play began.

In the guard room, astir with men at arms, Messer Adhemar had taken charge. Guy was led to the rear wall
where the unfortunate wretch hung. The manacles on his
wrists were fastened to the stones above his head. He was
battered and bruised from beating, his clothes torn, his
ugly satyr face a portrait of hopeless suffering. At a glance
Guy recognized him.

"This is the man," he said. "Who is he?"

"A poor goatherd, sir. The village people brought him
because he was absent from the mountain during the Passover. They found him several days later hiding in his
shed."

"Has he confessed?"

"No, sir. He says nothing. He is very stubborn."

"But why does he want to murder me?"

The castellan translated, but there was no response.

"What harm have I ever done him?"

Still silence.

"Ask who sent him, then?"

Silence again.

"Shall I put him to the question, sir?" Messer Adhemar
asked.

"I must know the answer," said Guy, troubled.

"Very well, sir." Messer Adhemar was prepared. He
took a white-hot poker from the fire, and held it before
the wretch's face; so close that his eyeballs reflected the

glow, and the hair of his head lifted from the heat. "The lord will know who sent you. You must answer him. Do you understand?"

There was no reply. Slowly, deliberately, the castellan laid the fiery iron on the man's face, just below his right ear. A terrible scream rent the room, and those nearest could smell the burning flesh. Still, he did not answer. Messer Adhemar sighed.

"It is a stubborn case, sir. He is under some great fear. If you will put him in my charge for the night, I will bring you the answer in the morning."

"Very well, then."

Messer Adhemar lifted a stone in the floor by the large iron ring, revealing a narrow flight of steps going down into a watery pit. At an order from him, the prisoner's manacles were struck off and he was dragged to the edge of the pit. But it was unnecessary to go any farther. The miserable creature evidently thought he was being flung into his grave, and his fear overcame him. He dropped to the floor babbling incoherently. Messer Adhemar put his ear down. He nodded.

"He is talking," he said with satisfaction and began to translate: "A man at the inn in Nablus gave you money—a single gold piece! Is that all, filthy dog?—Five gold pieces, that's better.—What sort of man?—a Frank, a great lord! His name?—Doesn't know.—His rank?—A king's man! How do you know, filthy excrement?—Because of the trappings on his horse outside. Very well, keep talking and I may not skewer you and eat you for supper after all.—What did he look like, this lord?—Very rich, very fat, go on. His clothes?—Silk burnoose, silk turban, chains on his shoes—"

Guy spoke up. "Ask him if he had a gold tooth."

Messer Adhemar relayed the question and had an affirmative answer.

"Amalric!" exclaimed Guy. So that was it. Guy's desertion had not been forgotten. He had known he would have to reckon with it someday. It was true he owed Amalric his service since Amalric was the son of Guy's leige-lord. In

Poitou he would be called to trial for desertion. In Jerusalem, Guy had become a lord himself and his allegience was to the Queen while Amalric had allied himself to the King. This was even further ground for disagreement and sooner or later, it must come to open war.

Guy left the guard house and spoke to the mukhtars waiting outside. "This man is guilty," he said. "If I turn him over to you, what does your law require?"

"He must die," said the chief mukhtar. "Our people will stone him in the field of blood."

The prisoner's family, mother, wife and children, lay prostrate on the steps, overcome with horror and fear. Only the old mother raised her head, wrinkled like a dried plum, her white hair wrapped in the black kerchief of the widow. Wordlessly, she looked at Guy and held out one gnarled hand in supplication. She knew what she asked was impossible and yet, being a mother, she asked. At that moment, Guy thought of his own mother far away in Poitou, of how she might never see him again and of how she had promised to pray for the intercession of the Blessed Virgin for him, every day.

"Release him to his family," he told Messer Adhemar. "He has been punished enough. And see to it there is no lynching. That is an ugly crowd outside the gate. They are afraid and they want to prove their loyalty at the expense of this wretch."

After that, there were no more attacks in the village. But the people remained uneasy. It was summer now, the traditional season for Saracen raids. They might come in small groups of three or four horsemen, crossing the deep cleft in the Jordan Valley, to carry off a small herd of sheep or goats. Or sometimes they might come in an army, burning and pillaging, taking away the women and children as slaves. For their defence, the villagers looked to the lord and his men-at-arms. With no more than twelve men, besides his castellan, Guy could not do much. He saw now why the shortage of men in the Kingdom was so acute.

Added to the Saracen threat were the witchfires on the

hills at night. Many villagers came to Guy to report these and they all blamed them on the 'witch-woman' in the tower. Some said they had seen her dancing around the fires in the nighttime and conjuring evil spirits. Descriptions of the fires varied but all agreed that they flared up quickly and went out as fast, sometimes a dozen times in succession.

Messer Adhemar insisted that Guy alone had saved the girl from being burned as a witch. Everyone knew of his preference for her and that she had refused him. This, too, fanned the people's fury. The idea that the young lord could not have her, if he wanted her, seemed incomprehensible, an affront to the natural order of things. The women of the village were especially indignant as they talked about it at the washing pool. Pounding their clothes with rocks, they asked what right had she to refuse him? Was he not master? Did he not have the '*droit de seigneur*' to any woman he chose? They all agreed that the girl should be punished. If he would not do it, they would.

"I warn you, sir," Messer Adhemar told him, "the Lady Alice is in danger. Let a child be born in the village with six fingers on one hand and the lid will blow off. They'll blame it on witchcraft and nothing you can do will save her."

In early May, the King left Jerusalem. The convocation of lords and knights had ended badly, with brawling and sword fights that even the pleas of the Patriarch had been unable to quell. The lords with estates in the south declared for the Queen, including the great fiefs of Jaffa, Ascalon, Oultrejourdain, and the city of Jerusalem itself; those in the north, Galilee, Acre, Tripoli, and Antioch, declared for the King.

In his philosopher's hideaway, William of Tyre recorded these events in his great history of the Crusades. The young Master of the Household often called upon him for his opinion. "How can those," Guy asked, "who came all the way across the sea to defend the Kingdom against the infidel, now take up arms against one another?"

The Archbishop replied sadly, "It has happened even as the Scripture foretold. For Our Lord Himself said: 'Think not that I am come to send peace on earth. I came not to send peace but a sword. I am come to set a man at variance with his father, and the daughter against her mother, and the daughter-in-law against her mother-in-law. And a man's foes shall be those of his own household.' And so it has come to pass."

Meanwhile an army was forming at Acre led by the King and his Constable, Humphrey of Toron, ready to march on Jerusalem. The Queen consulted her Constable, the lords and the city fathers. In a crisis like this, Melisende was at her best, a commanding figure of great dignity. She addressed them all in the Great Hall.

"My lords, we are, by the grace of God, in this holy city, Queen of the Latins. We are the defender of the Holy Sepulchre. We have with us the True Cross. All we ask is that you fulfill your oaths. From you, Hugh of Jaffa, we are due fifty knights. From Maurice of Oultrejourdain, forty-five knights. From Hugh of Ramleh, forty knights. The Master of the Hospital is bound for one hundred knights. The city burghers of Jerusalem for sixty knights—my lords, will you fulfill your oaths?"

A roar of assent went up from the Hall. But the Constable Manasses was not entirely pleased. "By denuding the countryside of troops," he said, "we are virtually making a siege inevitable. Jerusalem, with its large population, cannot stand a siege of any length. The water supply is inadequate and the hot season is just beginning. Besides, where is our relief to come from? Everything depends on the Temple. How will Master Gerard move?" But the Master sent no delegate to the council.

To Guy, who looked for a pattern in all things, it seemed as though the finger of God was pointing at him. Perhaps there was a reason, after all, that he had been "chosen" by the Master. He sent him a message asking for an interview. The reply came back at once: "Light a candle to St. John of Damascus at vespers tonight."

The angelus bell was already ringing when Guy walked

down David Street toward the Temple Church. It came over him now how sadly the city was changed. In the past year, he had grown fond of the old stone alleyways, with their many arches and festoons of flowering vines hanging down from the rooftop gardens. It had been a city of peace and now, alas, the peace was shattered.

Troops were everywhere, pitching camp in the gardens of the great houses and knocking on the doors of reluctant citizens to requisition lodgings. Saddest of all were the herds of silent, frightened country people, crowding into the cattle market with all their animals and belongings. For them, war meant the loss of everything, murder and raping if they stayed outside the walls, starvation and suffering if they took refuge within.

The Temple Church, a glorious octagonal building of blue Persian tile stood in the midst of a great enclosure called 'the Haram' on the top of Mount Moriah. This was surmounted by a golden dome, called the 'Dome of the Rock'. It was built by the first Caliphs of Islam to enshrine the rock, from which Mahomet ascended into heaven, mounted on his horse.

A flight of many steps around the octagon led to the portal. Inside, the walls and floor were faced with slabs of blue marble. Marble, too, were the twelve monolithic pillars that supported the dome, around the drum of which a scrollwork in gold proclaimed the motto of the Templars: "Not unto us, O Lord, not unto us, but unto Thy Name give the glory." The lights of many altars flickered around the octagonal walls, and Guy lit a taper before the shrine of St. John Damascene. He lit the taper from the oil lamp suspended over the altar. While he did this, one of the cowled monks in sandals approached him.

"Would you like to see the church?" He would know that voice, those penetrating eyes, anywhere. He nodded his assent. The monk lit a taper himself and led the way to a gate of intricate ironwork at the side of the altar steps. With the words, "Follow me," he disappeared down a winding flight of stairs, cut in the original stone of Mount Moriah. They led to a small cave under the dome

of the rock. Setting his taper down, the monk threw back
the hood of his cowl and smiled at Guy with his familiar,
insidious scrutiny.

"We shall not be overheard here," he said. And, indeed,
the chanting monks above sounded very far off. Master
Gerard had a liking for theatrical effects, which seemed to
invest their interviews with a more than ordinary signifi-
cance. Guy realized that the meeting was momentous and
was afraid that his purpose might have been misunderstood. They sat on a slab of rock.

"Master Gerard," Guy ventured, "I do not come, as
perhaps you think—"

"You don't come for yourself." The intervention was
encouraging.

"Exactly. We feel—that is, the whole Court feels—that
you should declare yourself or the city will be destroyed.
If you will act with us, we can defend the city. Otherwise—"

"And they have sent you here to teach me my duty?"
The tone had a patronizing note that nettled.

"No, Master Gerard. I speak for myself. I came to this
country to defend the Holy City. I expected the Master of
the Temple to do the same."

The dark man came near to striking him, but withdrew
his hand after barely grazing his cheek. "You have temerity, truly. Who gives me lessons? The second son of a
small manor house in Poitou! A petty lordling of the
Crown by virtue of the Queen's favor only, which is to be
bought with smiles and kissing! A boy who has yet to
break his lance in the lists of Our Lord!

"Do you know to whom you speak? The Grand Master
of this Order has authority over the lives and souls—yes,
souls!—of five thousand knights, not only in this country
but in France, in England, in Spain, in the lands of our
lord the Pope, and in the Holy Roman Empire. What the
Master bids any one of these knights to do, he does,
asking no further questions, no matter how dangerous,
how blasphemous, how obscene! And this is the man you

instruct! I would take this from no one but—" The storm had spent itself, however. More gently he went on.

"You must understand, dear boy, that there are greater things at stake than you know. But you should begin to have a glimmering. We of the Temple have no business with these dynastic wars. Our duty is elsewhere. We have the Kingdom of God to defend. Within a few days, I shall take my knights into the field to meet the true enemy, the sons of Beelzebub, who have thrown down their gauntlet to us. Will you be with us?"

Once again, this speech touched a hidden doubt about his mission. Had he lost his way, Guy asked himself, enmeshed in other loyalties and possessions? His thoughts took a new tack. "Master Gerard, you are right. I am nothing, nobody. I dare not talk to you except by your favor. But I have found out something which may be important. It was not the Syrian Barac who tried to kill me. It was Amalric of Lusignan, deputy of the King's Constable. I don't believe Barac is evil. He cured me, and he had cured the King's son."

"How—cured? Can the Devil cast out devils?"

The mystery of the cure lurked in these words of Scripture like a hidden scorpion. Barac had cured the leper Prince—could that be the Devil's doing? And the cure, repeated often, did not last. Could that be God's will?

Thoughtfully Guy asked, "What do you know of Barac?"

"That he is the Prince of Devils, a master of spies, and that he is conspiring the ruin of everything. He is in league with the Saracens and he is in league with Amalric, and he is faithless to both. He is a man who must rule or destroy the world. But I am drawing the net on him tight. Very soon, perhaps tomorrow, I shall close it. And then *I* shall cast out devils!"

"And what will become of the leper boy?" Guy cried. "He needs him. He will die without him!"

The Master smiled his enigmatic smile. "Better that one innocent should die, than that the Prince of Devils should live."

Guy was appalled. He knew that he had been right to distrust this man. And yet he had been attracted to him. Why? There was something between them, a love-hate that united them. They were like riders, side by side, but their horses were pulling in different directions.

"There is no use then, Master Gerard," said Guy, getting up.

"Do not be hasty, dear boy," replied the other. "Go if you must. But you will come back." They began to ascend the stairway out of the cave. "You should keep an eye open," continued the Master, "if you return to Castle Shechem. Your friend Amalric may be conjuring up the devil himself. Take care—"

The monks had concluded their vespers and were putting out the lights on the altar. Worshippers streamed out of the church and down the steps into the Haram. Guy, troubled by what he had heard, left deep in thought and when he roused himself and looked around, the man in the monk's cowl was gone.

Failure weighed heavily on him as he walked back to the Citadel, jostled by the unwonted fracas in the twilight streets. The Queen, the leper boy, Alice—he had failed them all. Most of all, he had failed to discern God's purpose. The awareness that is the beginning of wisdom came on him—that we do not control our lives, because we are part of a vast plan of events that has a pattern so much greater than we can see.

He entered the courtyard to the sound of hammering in the forge, as horses were shoed and the armorers worked on swords and lances. Lights were carried to and fro and the bustle of unusual preparations surged around him. Among the crowd, he discerned the slim figure of a girl, Barac's daughter. For some time, she had been assigned the duty of cleaning the officers' rooms in the tower. Now he wanted to speak to her but could not even recall her name. He strode after her and laid a hand on her shoulder. She stopped as if transfixed and turned slowly, looking up at him.

"My lord?"

"Please, I want to speak with you. Come to my room."

She followed him up the stairs to the top floor where he lived and stood mute, her eyes downcast, as he locked the door.

"What is your name, child?" he asked.

"My lord, your servant's name is Yasmin."

"Where is your father, Yasmin?"

"Is he needed? Is it for—"

"No, no. Just tell me what I ask. Is he in Jerusalem?"

"I cannot tell, my lord."

"You mean you don't know, or you mustn't tell?"

"I cannot tell."

There were mysteries, too many mysteries about these people. This man came and went through their lives like smoke. They would leave a message at his cousin's shop and sometimes Barac would be there, ready to serve any request. At other times, he was as invisible as if he had never existed. Guy did not have the feeling that the Syrian meant him any harm. On the contrary, he felt a special sympathy between them. Yet he had to consider the possibility that he had gained access to the Citadel to make maps of fortifications or cause any amount of mischief. Perhaps his spies had told him about the boy's ball in the well, that day, and the whole miracle had been a fraud—!

"My lord is very sad tonight." The girl was still standing before him, and her voice came like a trickle of cool water over his remembrance. He looked at her in surprise, to find that she cared about him, and recalling her action in this room many months ago, he blushed again. He saw her meek, doe-like look under the dark lashes intent upon him, and he thought of Master Gerard and his net. No, he should not have her.

"Not sad, Yasmin," he replied. "But afraid—for you. "It is not safe for you here any more."

The soft, almond eyes moistened. "My lord is sending me away?" she said, looking at the ground, her hands folded before her.

He went to her and placed his arm about her shoulders,

feeling her body tremble under his hand. "It is for your sake, child. There is war, you know—" But she was weeping. Gently, he tried to dry her tears with the sleeve of his rough linen surcoat.

"How have I displeased my lord? I have served him as he bade me do, cleaning and sweeping for him and I asked nothing. I mended his clothes and he did not notice. Each day I left a flower in his room and he did not see, but I was content. Why does he send me away now?"

"Yasmin!" All this was something new, recognizable in retrospect, but revelationary now. He had to tell her the truth. "Yasmin, listen to me. Your father is in danger, and you with him. There is a man in Jerusalem who has spread a net under your feet, and one day soon, perhaps tomorrow, he will close the net and there is nothing more I can do for you. Now, do you see? I am trying, once more, to help you. Go, Yasmin. Tell your father, if you will, but go!"

She looked up at him over her shoulder. "It is not through my fault?"

"It is not."

"And I may come again, if God wills?"

"If God wills."

She turned, facing him closely. "I will go then."

After a moment, he tried to think of something to say. "You may need horses. Do not stay in the Kingdom. It will be best to go to your own people. Perhaps Damascus—"

But she was not listening. She was watching his lips and thinking her own thoughts. At last she said, "Before I go, may I kiss my lord?"

He was astonished but not displeased by her request. He placed his arms about her, but she stiffened instantly.

"Listen to me, my lord. I am a Moslem girl. It is forbidden to me to do this, or even to uncover my face before my lord, except as I am his bondslave and as he commands it."

"My bondslave?"

"I, myself, saw the money paid out by his servant, ten gold pieces, to the sergeant for me."

"Ah," he remembered, "yes."

She placed the tips of her fingers on his shoulders. "And he does command it?" she asked.

It was, he thought, a ritual of her people, yet a ritual in which she believed, and he began to believe in it, too, so that they were both carried away by it and not by their own volition. The vows were forgotten.

"I command it," he said.

She reached up and placed her kiss upon his lips and he did not reply with his own, but he supported her body with his hands until she had completed it. Then he gathered her to him entirely. Again and again he tasted the sweet fullness of her mouth, prolonging his pleasure until it held no more secrets for him. Now it was he who demanded more of her, and she yielded to him unquestioningly, anticipating his desires and fulfilling them beyond obedience.

All their loving, the gradual awakening of their need for each other and its fulfillment, was accomplished without a word. He uncovered her pure, firm virginity with a sort of awed wonder that anything so frail and perfect could be his, could need him and make him feel so complete. He laid her on the bed and kissed the fine line of her throat, as slender as the stalk of a flower; he caressed the small, unripe breasts and felt them swell under his hand.

And she? She felt as though the heavens themselves had opened into her lap. She caressed him, marvelling at the thick, blond hair, the astonishing whiteness of the flesh, the unutterable strangeness of the man who was now her own. And she knew it had to be. For it is written in the Koran: man carries his fate hung like a stone about his neck—even as she carried his weight now upon her.

Darkness fell, and the activity in the yard died down; the torches were put out; and soon only the cry of the watch was heard echoing from tower to tower along the walls, as the night hours slipped away. On the bed, in the top chamber of the south tower, Yasmin lay awake beside

the sleeping figure of the man she called her lord. It grew
cold after midnight in the Judean hills, even in May, and
she drew the single blanket over his nakedness, rising to
put on her dress. Then she lay down beside him again,
lying with her head cupped in her hand, watching him.

It would be hard to explore her thoughts for they were
obscure, even to herself. She was a child of her own people, living in an occupied land, among the hated for-
eigners. The gulf between herself and the Frankish conquerors was as great as the contrast on the pillow between
her black locks and his fairness. If she was to be Jael to
his Sisera, of the biblical story, now was the time for her
to drive the nail into his temples while he slept, exhausted
from loving her. But such a thought was far from her. She
hated the Franks with all the fanaticism of womankind
and of Islam. But not this one. Why she made this exception was not a question for her. He was excepted. It began
the night she had held his head in her lap, as they travelled in the wagon to Jerusalem. He was not then a con-
queror, he was helpless in her hands and she had loved
him. Later, when he purchased her and made her his
slave, even though he neglected her, she loved him still.
God sent these things and it was our duty to submit to the
chains He forges. Praise be to God.

She must go now; there was much to do, many people
to warn. She rose and put on the Moslem veil she wore as
a shawl. Day was breaking and it would be possible to slip
out the gates as soon as they were opened. Then she could
cross the city and find her father while there was still
time. She would fetch the horses from their hiding place
and reach the scouts in the mountains before nighttime.
Fire signals on the hill tops would do the rest of the work.

Softly she slid the bolt in the door, but hesitated and
looked back. Returning to the bedside, she bent a moment
over the sleeper, smoothing the hair back from his face.
Then she imprinted the faintest kiss on his mouth. "My
dear lord," she whispered.

CHAPTER FIVE

FIRE AND SWORD

Aaron, the goatherd, looked at the sun and measured the length of the shadow of the thorn bushes. Noon. He put the ram's horn to his lips and called together his flock. The leader came quickly enough, for this always meant a few dried figs from her master's pocket; the others followed more langorously. Together they descended the precipitous slope of Mount Gerizim toward the stony outcroppings at the base of the sandstone cliffs. Here Aaron found the shelter of an old shed in the shadow of the rock, where he awaited his wife's daily visit.

He was in good spirits today, despite his customary lamentations. The white scar below his ear was nearly healed, though painful to touch, and the bruises over most of his body had subsided to a dull ache. Below him, the flat roofs of Shechem village baked in the sun. Few people were abroad, mostly little knots of men at the tavern and women at the well, discussing their calamities. And their calamities were very great.

In a pastoral land, the loss of a whole flock of hundreds of sheep is like an act of God. That's what the mukhtar said it was, and Aaron turned it over and over in his mind. An act of God. It filled him with awe to think that anything so vast, so overwhelming could come to pass because of him. The more he thought about it, the more it drove him to a single inexorable conclusion. For one glorious moment, Aaron was God.

Actually, he had not meant to do anything so grand. All he wanted was gold. Just before the Passover, the King's officer at Nablus had given him five gold pieces to make the attack on the young lord at Jacob's Ford. When the attack failed, he went back to Nablus for new instructions. This time the King's officer had given him another five gold pieces (they were buried with the first five under the floor of this very shed) and a little vial of poison. His instructions had been explicit. All he had to do was to take a lamb to the Castle as a gift offering. While there, he was to stand near the well and drop the vial into it. This plan was much better than the first. Unfortunately, by this time he had been missed from the Passover feast and the Chief Mukhtar had had him arrested before he could put the new plan into effect.

Now, after his agony in the lord's dungeon, everything was changed. It was incredible that his life had been spared. For this, he was his master's creature, almost pathetically anxious to please, obey, and kiss the ground before him. The young lord could do no wrong. It was the Chief Mukhtar who was to blame for everything—it was he who had delivered him up to the torturers, it was he who had led the lynching mob from which he had narrowly escaped.

Fortunately, he had managed to keep the small vial of poison. It had been easy to pass the sheep pens one dark night and empty the vial in the drinking trough for the Mukhtar's sheep. How could he have known that a rain squall—so unusual at this time of year—would come in the night and carry the poison through the gutters to all the other flocks as well? Anyway, the village deserved to suffer for what it had done to him. He was glad to have had his revenge.

Now he caught sight of Sarah laboring up the hill,

with his dinner bag and a wine skin over her shoulder. How bowed she was, like an old woman already, and only fifteen years married! She climbed with her head down, as though she had something on her mind. On arrival, she crawled in the low entrance and flopped down against the wall in silence. Aaron seized the dinner bag and drew out the unleavened bread, goat's cheese and olives. He also took a swig at the wineskin. They were not accustomed to conversation.

Today, however, after she had gotten back her breath, Sarah volunteered a statement. "Fifteen more sheep died this morning. All Levi's. Most others are like to die." Then, after a pause, as though this were not the chief reason for speaking, she added, "Everyone's blood is up."

"What is the use of that?" Aaron was irascible. "They must bear it. It is the will of God."

"They say it is a curse, rather."

"Good! I curse them again!"

"They say it is the witch-woman's curse. The Chief Priest told them."

He gaped at this. "The witch woman! What has she to do with it?" He was thoroughly aroused now. He felt cheated of his revenge. Well, they should not get away with it. "They have been punished by God. They must submit, damn them, they must submit!"

There was a very long silence. One would suppose there was nothing left to say. But before she left, Sarah added, "They say they're going to burn her."

"Burn her?" He was listening now with every fiber of his being.

"Tomorrow is the sabbath. So it will be the day after, in the evening. We are all to bring straw to fire the tower. The Chief Priest says it is the law."

Aaron turned this over. The witch woman was protected by the lord of the Castle, everyone knew that. If anyone touched his woman, he would be very angry. He would seize as many men in the village as he pleased and deliver them up to his torturers. That was the way of lords. Unless, of course, Aaron turned informer. A plea-

surable vision then rose before his eyes. He saw the Chief
Mukhtar disgraced, forced to walk through the village at
the tail end of a cart of soldiers carrying whips; while he,
Aaron, wearing the red, pointed turban of the Mukhtar,
stood on the Castle steps to receive a bag of gold as his
reward.

"Well, if she's guilty, she deserves punishment," he
threw out, adding casually, "Mind the goats this afternoon. I've business."

"You're not going back to Nablus?" countered Sarah.

"Be silent, woman! What is it to you where I go? A
man's business is his own." And he flung himself out of the
hut. Sarah looked reflectively after him until he reached
the foot of the hill, where he took the path running behind
the village toward the Castle. As soon as he was out of
sight, she felt along the floor of the hut for a loose stone.
Finding one, she looked beneath and took out ten gold
pieces, and knotted them into the corner of her kerchief.

The siege began at the end of May. The King set up his
banner on the Mount of Olives, across the Kedron valley
from Jerusalem, and the colored tents and pavilions prolif-
erated down its slopes like spring flowers after rain. The
armies of the Count of Tripoli, the Prince of Antioch and
the Prince of Galilee took up their positions before the
principal gates, and the trumpeters blew their trumpets,
marshalling the troops. At first, there was a festive air
about it all, with much coming and going of embassies between the camps, and receptions in the royal marquee.
Every morning, hunting parties sallied forth, ranging over
the countryside with dogs and hawks, to return at evening
with the kill. After dark, banquets were held on silken carpets spread on the sand, while native musicians played the
harp and rebeek under the stars.

But, under cover the business of war was going inexorably forward. Out of sight, the engineers were readying
the assault machines, to be trundled up to the walls at the
appropriate time. The largest of these, the mangonel, was

capable of flinging a half-ton weight against the fortifications.

When the mangonel appeared before the Gate of Jehoshephat, facing the King's tent, the King's men greeted her with whoops and hollas, and a sigh went up from the defenders as they thought of all the grief that must ensue. The archers along the walls tightened their bows and feathered their arrows with burning rags, filling the sky with flame in an attempt to set the mangonel afire, but her cables and timbers had been soaked in water and would not burn. Then the singing of the twisted cables announced the release of the great catapult; the air reverberated with the sound and everyone's heart stopped. The mangonel lurched and spat forth barrels of flaming tar that poured over the defenders and drove them from the walls in a dance of mortal frenzy.

Immediately, scaling ladders were set up and the King's men swarmed over the parapet, making a concerted rush to open the gate. Reinforcements arrived on the battlements, swords came into play, cutting off the hands and arms that clung to the top of the scaling ladders. The King's men who were already inside found themselves cut off. It was too late to lay hands on the winches operating the portcullis. For a moment, there was a breathing space, a time for men to stop, to hear the confessions of the dying, to carry out the dead. Then it began all over again.

The Holy City lived on, from moment to moment, from day to day. The scene at the Gate of Jehoshephat was reenacted at the Gate of David, at St. Stephen's Gate, at the Zion Gate. The defenders had no rest, and, as time went on, they began to have no hope. All the buildings in the vicinity of the walls were soon burned out, adding to the host of refugees encamped on the grounds of the Hospital. And, although the Hospital made a daily distribution of bread, there was not enough to go around.

The Queen no longer went out. She fell on her knees at the *prie-dieu* in her room and for the ten thousandth time confessed her sin, which like most sins was a sin of pride, pride in her own will and in the justice of her cause. The world had used her unjustly and she would not submit to injustice. And because she would not submit, the injustice was multiplied and visited on the heads of her people, and the city of God was laid waste. Now, at last, understanding began to break upon her. Perhaps, after all, wrongs had their own purpose. A loveless marriage, a lover murdered, a son's disloyalty—perhaps even enormities like these had their place in God's plan. "Thy Kingdom come, Thy will be done, on earth as it is in heaven," she wept.

In the courtyard of the Citadel, unusual activity was centered around a crude brick kiln which had been erected under the direction of a man, stripped to the waist, his face and body streaked with sweat and charcoal, as he helped his crew fire the ovens. The Prince was watching intently, primed with questions.

"How will it work, Master Guy?"

Guy looked at the Prince and marvelled that the boy could not feel the heat even at close quarters. "Not so close, Master Baldwin," he said. "It's quite simple, really. I melt down the limestone rocks we use in repairing the walls. When mixed with water it makes a burning hot liquid we call milk of lime. Poured in the casques here, we can fire it from our slings and the casques will break on the enemy's mangonel. The more they pour water on it, the faster it will burn."

"And burn up the sling and the cables and the people and all," the Prince said merrily. "What a good idea. If I were King, I'd make you Constable."

The oven doors were opened and a crowd gathered around as the word spread that the lime in the pans, stirred by two men with long ladles through the open door, was "cooked." This was indeed a dish to set before a King, and the nearest they would get to a miracle. Spirits rose, and applause broke out.

Now the tricky task began of drawing off the pans and pouring the molten liquid into the casques, which had been specially bonded with wire to prevent premature breaking. Wagons and horses stood by to transport the "devil's brew" to the batteries of slingers along the walls.

The fastidious appearance of the Court dragoman, dwarfed by his enormous turban, seemed almost incongruous, as he sought insistently to get Guy's attention. "My lord—my lord—" he called, falsetto, above the heads of the crowd, "there is someone to speak with you. It is one of your serfs." The latter word caught Guy up; he turned and stared. The quavering figure of Aaron the goatherd was in front of him, hanging limply, held up by two stalwart men at arms.

The dragoman handed him a bit of paper, written in French, and signed by Messer Adhemar. "Sir," it read, "come at once if you can. There will be two horses waiting with Sergeant Berthold at Jacob's Ford. The goatherd knows the way." That was all.

"We took it from the serf," explained the dragoman, "when he was captured."

"Is it bad news, Master Guy?" enquired the boy. "May I hear it?"

Guy nodded and led the way into an empty guardroom, where the prisoner could be interrogated.

"You say he was captured?" Guy came to the point at once.

"He entered the city as a spy," the dragoman volunteered importantly. "He was turned over to the sergeants by the sisters of the Convent of Zion. They found him lurking in the crypt of their convent."

"So," Guy turned to Aaron with new interest, "you know a way into the city?"

When this was translated by the dragoman, the goatherd related his adventure, how he had followed the route known to the goatmen in the Vale of Kedron (friends of his, for all goatmen are a fraternity) from ancient times, leading under the walls through the sewers built by the Romans.

"And could we return by the same route?" Guy asked.

The answer, accompanied by vigorous nods, was affirmative.

Quickly, methodically, Guy made his decisions. The escape route must be used the same night—the goatherd must lead them safely through, if need be, at dagger's point so there be no betrayal—he and Hugh must follow in bedouin disguise—the dragoman could help procure the robes—and they must proceed on foot with all speed to Jacob's Ford, a ten hours' journey. He gave the orders; the little Arab secretary left, mincing, on his errand; the goatherd was led away for safekeeping to a cell.

"Master Guy," said the Prince with a hint of reproach in his voice when they found themselves alone together, "does this mean I'll never see you again?"

"No, it does not," Guy answered with heat. "We are friends, aren't we—for life? I swore it! But you'll be all right—you'll see."

"Oh," the boy protested. "I don't care about myself. It doesn't matter, after all, if I don't get well. But I must do something about the Kingdom. It's all wrong, you see, this fighting among ourselves. Oh, Master Guy, sometimes I have a dream, and I am being carried in a litter, because I cannot walk, and the royal standard is flying over the litter, and the True Cross is carried before me and all men look to me to give the commands, and I cannot give them because I am blind and deaf and dumb. Oh, it is a terrible dream and I awake crying. Perhaps, if you are with me, Master Guy, you will know what must be done. Because, you see, we both care about it, don't we,—the True Cross, I mean—and there are not enough who care—"

Guy's eyes were full of tears. He wrapped his friend in a crushing embrace and said simply, "I swear it. When you need me, I shall come." But after they parted, he added under his breath, "if I am allowed to live." Dark circles ringed his eyes, and he wore a peculiar heavy-lidded expression, haunted by guilt. Only Guy of Vienne would die of guilt—because he was no longer chaste.

At that moment, the Constable came up to congratulate Guy on the success of the quicklime device. Already, one of the enemy's mangonels had been destroyed; the sound of cheering came distantly from somewhere along the walls. Guy's heart lifted again and he chose this as an opportune time to explain his errand and obtain the Constable's consent. The grizzled, old man listened, rubbed his chin, and said, "You are God's fool, boy, but go—"

That evening, three bedouins knocked at the door of the sisters of Zion at the Second Station of the Cross, near the Gate of Jehoshephat. The leader doffed his kaffieh, or headcloth, and threw open his burnoose to reveal a full coat of mail emblazoned with the Queen's crest. "Sister," he said politely, "don't mistrust us. I am Master of the Queen's Household and these are my friends. But we must visit the cellars in your crypt on the Queen's business."

"Blessed be the great Mother of God!" exclaimed the sister in a fright, for she recognized the third member of the group as the man who, earlier that day, had been arrested in their convent. However, by the light of a lantern she led her nocturnal visitors down the stone steps under the convent to a level that was once a Roman street. Through the centuries, Jerusalem had become a layered city; each civilization built its city above the preceeding one at levels of ten to fifteen feet apart.

The light of the lantern revealed the cobblestones and sidewalks of the Roman street, and even the game of noughts and crosses scratched in with knives by soldiers on the very spot where, men believed, Christ took up His cross. One of these flat stones was loose and Aaron quickly lifted it, to reveal below a horizontal tunnel of terracotta tile, about three feet in diameter. This was an ancient Roman sewer, no longer used, but so dark and fetid that even the flame of the lantern would not burn in it. The three "bedouins" dropped inside, bade the sister goodnight, and replaced the stone above their heads.

Creeping along the tunnel was painfully slow, for much of the sewer was filled up with dirt, the carcasses of animals and massive stones. But fortunately, it was the dry season and there was no seepage of water. A couple of hundred yards to the eastward, the tunnel fell rapidly, passing under the Herodian wall and descending with the slope of Mount Moriah to the floor of the Kedron valley. Here it was necessary, at times, for travellers to crawl along on their knees and elbows. At least two hours passed before the tunnel levelled out and they emerged from the mouth in a bush of prickly cacti beside the dry bed of the brook Kedron.

Pleased to find themselves behind the King's forward lines, Guy and his groom looked at each other's sorry appearance and laughed aloud. They adjusted their torn and tattered clothes as best they could, wrapping the headcloths around their faces and securing the black goatshair robes so that no glint of arms or armor might appear. Aaron, their guide, was jubilant, too, at having proved his good faith. He found stout staves for them all and, like the Wise Men, they set off along the sunken bed of the river, skirting the walls of the city. It was a clear, moonless night, and once they left the watchfires of the encampments behind them, they were able to abandon the river bed and strike northward into the hills.

The dawn was a hallowed time for Alice. She liked to greet it on the high land overlooking Shechem, when the world was in darkness and the valley was awash with mist. The world was clean and pure, as it was when the Lord first walked in the Garden in the cool of the day, and she walked alone with Him.

But not entirely alone, for she had Adele beside her. The gazelle grazed only at dawn and drank once a day from the tarns formed by the spring rain. As soon as the sun was up, the tiny doe pointed her delicate face, white and fawn nostrils quivering, into the dawn wind. From that moment, she seemed to take her leave of the earth and to live only in the air, skimming over the ground with leaps and bounds, as she celebrated her glorious freedom. At these times, Alice herself hardly breathed and Adele became her disembodied soul.

Later, the mists dissolved, the morning light whitened and hardened, and the heat drove the wanderers to the shelter of the wadis between the sandstone rocks. Here the doe's coloration, with dark and light stripes on her flanks, blended so perfectly with the stony landscape that she literally vanished from sight, only to reappear, surprised and curious, at a call from her mistress, nuzzling her nose in her hand.

But, when parted from her "other self", Alice had much company from the wild creatures she visited every day. She knew their homes and called on each in turn—under a rock here, in a cranny there, out of a moss-covered hole in the ground, little pairs of eyes were watching for her arrival. She brought eggs for the mongoose that lived in the stump of the dead cedar tree, and grain for the sand grouse whose nest was in the dusty ground. Even the little golden hamster blinking in the unaccustomed light, came up from its subterranean galleries for its quota of sunflower seeds.

On this particular day, however, there was a strange uneasiness among the wild creatures; they poked out their heads, sitting up very still as if listening, and hardly touched their food at all. And all at once, they began scurrying away, some into their holes and those which had no hiding place hopping through the grass and across the bare open spaces, almost like a mass migration. The movement was all to the northward, while from faraway in the south came the sound of a horn and a faint rumbling like thunder.

Adele materialized out of nowhere, her head held high, nostril quivering. "What is it?" Alice cried. "What do you hear?" The doe, all at once, leaped in the air and began to run, from rock to rock up the wadi for the open hill above. Alice followed, growing frantic with the general fear, and cutting her feet on the sharp rocks. Then she saw it, high over the mountain, like a black planet slowly wheeling through the sky. A falcon. Now understanding broke upon her; she recognized the hunting horn and the baying of the greyhounds still out of sight. The doe was making for the safety of the tower, but this was at least two miles away, over uneven country, without cover of any kind. "Run, Adele, run," cried Alice, knowing she could not possibly keep up. Then, swifter than a falling star, the falcon plunged. Its aim was unerring; only by a frantic twist of the head the doe managed to avoid being blinded, but a strip of flesh was torn from her shoulder as she ran on.

Now the hunt came into view, a line of horsemen spread out along the horizon, gradually encircling the quarry and cutting off her escape. Again and again the falcon dived; each time the gazelle barely avoided blinding, but she was weak from loss of blood now, confused and wandering in a circle. At last Alice caught up with her, her own sides heaving and her dress torn; she lifted the timid, dazed creature in her arms and ran on. Once more there was a rush of wings, and for a moment Alice thought the hooked, toothed bill was about to tear her own eyes out—when a shrill whistle sounded close by; the bird sheered away and came to rest on the wrist of a huntsman who rode alongside.

The hunter was dressed in the richest of leather jerkins, fastened with gold hooks, with a turban of silk on his head. His hands were gloved, with gold rings over the gloves, and from his right wrist dangled a golden chain, that he fastened to the falcon's leg. With his other hand he reached into a satchel suspended over his shoulder and took out a large piece of livid meat which he fed to the bird.

"Be careful." He waved at Alice. "Make for the tower while I call off the cursed dogs." He turned away shouting, "Back! Back!" to the beaters who wheeled around with their dogs, each leashed on a silken cord, keeping perfect time with the horses. Only the golden huntsman, attended by his groom, accompanied the running, stumbling girl until she reached the tower, still holding the blood-soaked doe, in her arms.

He dismounted and, unfastening the falcon from his wrist, handed the bird over to his groom. At a sign from him the groom withdrew and the huntsman followed Alice into the tower. At once she collapsed, sobbing, into his arms. "There, there, my poor girl, you'll be all right now." He instinctively struck a paternal note, divining her fear of men. Although not twice her age, he comforted her as a father, while still allowing his hand to wander over her bare shoulder and arm, under the torn dress.

"You must take care of your little creature," he said, "this is the hunting season, you know. I do my best to curb the filthy custom but habits are hard to change. I shall protect you in future, have no fear. Now dry your eyes, my child. You see, you are perfectly safe with me."

He was indeed a golden-mouthed comforter—even his smile flashed a glint of gold—and his soft words brought her into something very like dependence on him. "You will protect me, then?" she stammered. "I am alone in the world and Adele has no one but me."

"And now you both have me," her self-appointed protector said importantly. "But is it true—that you have no one? The lord of the castle—?"

"He is nothing to me," Alice said, her eyes still brimming with tears of terror. Her look had turned to one of gratitude.

"Ah, then you are safe enough. You cannot trust these hot young men. Let me advise you," his voice dropped to a confidential whisper, "whenever you are in need, call on me and I will come. My camp is not far away, and my men will watch for your signal."

Her understanding lagged. "But what signal shall I give?"

"Let me show you something wonderful." He took from an inside pocket of his jerkin a little box, containing a quantity of black powder. "This, my dear, is Chinese fire. I had it the other day from a traveller to Damascus. Empty it on the ground and light it with a slow-burning wick, from a candle perhaps. Be careful not to stand too near. It will glow with a marvellous light. My men will see it for it rises to a tremendous height. And, presto! like the slave of the lamp—I shall be at your side!" He closed the box with a snap and pressed it into her hand.

"You have been so good to me," she murmured.

"Nonsense, my child," he responded gallantly. "It is no more than my duty to a damsel in distress!" He kissed her hand with elaborate ceremony. "Take care of your beloved creature." And, once more, flashing his glittering smile, he bowed himself out the door.

Alice listened while the hooves of the horses faded into silence and wearily closed the door. She sank to her knees beside the little bleeding doe and slowly began to clean and bind the savage wounds, tearing off strips of her dress to make bandages. "My soul," she murmured, "you are safe at last. Sleep, sleep in my lap. No one will hurt you." She began to sing an old lullaby she had learned as a child.

Toward evening, the same day, the three bedouins stopped a distance away from Jacob's Ford and climbed the hills above the river, where they joined a fourth bedouin, a goatherd with his flock. Together they sat on the ground and gazed intently into the trees overhanging the river. A great deal of activity was taking place under these trees, and the sound of men and horses rose clearly on the evening air, with occasional shouts in a foreign tongue.

"Saracens!" exclaimed Guy. The strange goatherd picked up the word and nodded vigorously. By signs, and broken Frankish phrases, he indicated that a hundred men had been camping there. Sometimes, he said, two or three scouts rode up into the hills and lit fires. Bright fires of many colors. When the scouts found a castle unmanned or a village undefended, they sent up a signal, and the Saracens attacked. Many villages had been burned, many prisoners taken. Only the goatmen were left unmolested, the stranger told them, gloating.

The first stars came out and still the bedouins sat on the hillside. One would say they were statues, carved out of the black, basalt rocks that littered the valley. No one could guess they were poised to make a break for the river as soon as night fell, while the fourth was held prisoner lest he give them away.

Suddenly, the strange goatmen pointed up the valley to the northward. For a few instants, the sky reflected a bright red glare that slowly died away. A signal, thought Guy. He calculated the distance, gauging the source of the

light across several intervening hills at perhaps ten miles
away. Shechem. Agitated, he rose and began to run
toward the river. He must reach the horses on the other
side before the Saracens began to cross. Hugh accompanied him and, after a struggle with his conscience, Aaron
followed.

All was in confusion beside the river. The Saracens had
clearly seen the signal too and were in the process of sad-
dling horses, donning arms and putting out fires. It was
quite dark under the trees and the three bedouins had little difficulty in reaching the ford. A guard challenged
them and they answered "Salaam aleikum" and went on
picking their way with their staves across the stones in the
shallows.

A few minutes later, they had reached the other side.
As Guy, who was in front, scrambled up the bank he
heard a rustle in the tree overhead and, remembering his
previous experience here, instinctively ducked. But he received a challenge in French.

"Who goes there?"

"Guy of Vienne."

The challenger jumped to the ground and was transformed into a very anxious Berthold. "Sir," he expostu-
lated, as Guy threw off his bedouin disguise and Hugh followed suit, "I thought you'd never get through the infidels
and all. I have horses for you both in the bushes here.
There's trouble in the village. They're all up in arms. Messer Adhemar has talked to them but he can't quiet them.
The Priest has stirred them up. Will you mount my stallion, sir? He's the fastest."

The three Franks mounted, but nothing could persuade
Aaron ever to ride pillion again in his life. He took to his
heels and the others gave him no more thought, but
spurred their horses on. Twenty minutes later, they clattered through Shechem village, and found all in darkness.
Not a man, woman or child was in the deserted streets.
Doors swung open on their hinges as though the houses
had been abandoned in haste. This was troubling, uncanny.

Was it the Saracens they feared, or was the Devil himself at their heels?

Beyond the village the whole valley spread out before them, white in the moonlight. The Castle with the great, greyish bulk of Mount Gerizim behind it, leapt up in front of them.

The mountainside was alight with small, spurting ugly flames, moving quickly to and fro. The riders drew nearer, and saw hundreds of people huddled in a black shadowy mass in the sheepfold about half way up the mountain's slope above the Castle on the upper edge of the olive grove. Beyond them, the slope was bare up to the tower and small groups were running forward carrying torches and bundles of straw which they piled around the tower. Some threw brands, like blazing spears through the air. They landed on the roof, igniting it. Great sheets of flame arose, illuminating the round stone walls like a bright beacon pointing toward heaven.

"Oh, God in Heaven," cried Guy, "is she inside?" Not a sign of life could be seen in the tower. They rode up into the olive grove where Guy reined in. They had perhaps ten minutes before the Saracens would arrive. The Castle must be alerted and on no account must the garrison leave it to come to his aid. He sent Berthold to the Castle with this message.

Berthold was greatly distressed. "May I not come back to you, master?" he pleaded.

"No one must leave the Castle walls. Those are my orders. Sound the alarm." Berthold obeyed.

"Pray God she has got away," Guy muttered to himself, and then to Hugh, "Wait for me here."

The people of Shechem fell back in utter silence when Guy rode out among them. Their silence was the most ominous thing about them, for this was not a frenzied mob, it was a mob possessed by an evil spirit. The burning of the witch was a revenge, but it was more than that: it was a rite whereby the evil forces that had blighted their sheep, and taken their land, and deprived them of their inheritance, could be exorcised. If someone had to suffer, who better than this child of the ungodly, the foreigner, the enemy of God's elect?

The old Priest was there, moving among his people like a tattered bird of ill-omen, but Guy did not reprove him. He rode straight into the yard and drove out all those with brands, riding them down and slashing at them with his whip until the yard was cleared. Then he dismounted, looping the reins over the gatepost. "Alice!" he called. "Alice! Alice!" But there was no answer, only the crackling of flames which were now funneled through the tall shaft of the tower. If she was inside, there was only one way out and that was through the door, since all the windows were no more than arrow slits. Guy hammered on the fiery hot iron shutter, calling again and again. But no reply.

It was a movement in the crowd, a scarcely audible sigh from hundreds of bodies packed close together, that alerted him to what had happened. Following their gaze, he ran out of the yard and looked back at the top of the tower. There, silhouetted blackly against the leaping white flames, stood the figure of the girl on the parapet, her own dress and hair aflame, holding in her arms the struggling, fear-crazed doe.

"Wait! Wait!" called Guy, running forward, but he was too late. She had leaped, committing her body to the air, and landed, herself a blazing brand, on the earth of the yard. In a moment Guy was at her side, smothering the flames with his hands. The doe lay still, partly under her, with a broken neck. The girl's body never moved, but her lips twitched slightly and a faint breathing stirred the charred hair across her face. She was hideously burned.

"Hugh!" called Guy, but the groom was already there. Together they lifted the broken body, moving it as gently as possible. Guy snatched a rolled up blanket from the saddle of his horse and with that they made a sort of stretcher and carried it toward the sheepfold. All the way he kept talking to her, begging her to try to live, without reply. Either she was gone, or had no wish to come back.

A blast on a trumpet, distant but shrill, echoing through the hills with a menacing reverberation, appraised them of their plight. The Saracens had arrived and were already laying siege to the Castle. Perhaps they had expected to find the gates unguarded, but in this they were disappointed. A steady humming rose from the walls and battlements as every man within drew his bow and let fly his feathered arrows at the assailants. The scene, watched from the sheepfold, was trance-like in its movements, the black-helmeted Saracens encircling the walls and endeavoring to put up ladders, the defenders pouring down fire on them from above, men running, horses plunging—all etched in black and white in the light of the moon.

"We are too late," Hugh said in despair.

"We wouldn't be too late if it hadn't been for the signal fire." Guy was bitter. "What villain lit that fire—?"

"Someone who knew there was trouble here—"

"And hoped to draw the garrison out. That's it, a Saracen plot. They've caught us in a trap."

"Is there nothing we can do, master?"

"Wait, wait. Maybe there is." Guy's mind was working fast. "Soon they will concentrate at the gatehouse and try to force the gate. If we move down under cover of the olive trees, we may reach the rear wall unseen. Then we can work our way round to the front—"

"But we are only two, master. If we carry her, who is to stand them off?"

"You'll carry her in and I'll stand them off."

Unexpectedly, a voice beside them spoke. "No one," Alice said "must carry me. Save yourselves. I have betrayed you. I deserve to die."

"Betrayed?" Guy was thunderstruck. "You mean—"

"I lit the signal fire."

"But why—why—?"

"Because I trusted where I should not, and I did not trust where I should. Oh God, let me die. I am vile, vile. I deserve to be punished."

Guy tried to lift her in his arms but she fell back speechless. He leaned over and kissed her forehead. It was as though he was in a dream. And part of the dream was that he should take off the ring on his smallest finger and place it on one of the fingers of her hand. Did she know he had done this? He could not tell, but about her mouth there hovered the faintest shadow of a smile. This he took, with all the firmness of faith, as consent. "Come," he said abruptly to Hugh, "we must go. We will carry her as far as we can."

Hugh, almost tenderly, lifted the unconscious girl over his shoulder, and Guy preceded them, his sword drawn, as they skirted the wall of the Castle. No black helmets along the back—none along the side—and Guy began, almost improbably, to hope. How he was going to gain access to the keep, he had no idea, but with the wild confidence of youth, he trusted himself to the event.

All the activity was centered now before the gatehouse at the front. A battering ram was in action, consisting of the trunk of a large tree, swung by short chains fastened along its length. The commands in Arabic were interspersed with the thundering thud of wood on iron and the cracking of the masonry of the gatehouse. It would not last long. Meanwhile, the forecourt inside the gate was strongly manned and the defenders kept up a steady fire of rocks and arrows upon the besiegers' heads.

Just at the corner, where the side wall of the forecourt abutted the keep, Guy saw his opportunity. Three Saracens had propped up a scaling ladder; two were holding it and the third preparing to mount. The latter, having his back turned, took the full thrust of Guy's sword between the shoulders. When the blade was withdrawn, he fell from the ladder helplessly, like a puppet whose strings have been cut, and rolled down into the ditch beside the Castle wall.

Guy now faced the other two: one, a huge man with a massive, curved scimitar; the other, his squire, carrying a short, two-edged blade. He tried, dark as it was in the shadow of the wall, to size up his opponents. In daylight, he would have no chance at all, he knew, against the giant whose blade was tempered Damascus steel and could shatter his own untempered weapon at a blow. But in the dark, he could move faster and confuse the bigger man with his agility. This he did now, dodging back and forth under the ladder, so that the scimitar fell and fell again on air and finally, stuck fast in a wooden upright of the ladder.

When this happened, Guy whirled about to face the squire, a thin, spidery man who fought two-handed, with sword and dagger, like a tarantula. This left his body unguarded, however, and when Guy thrust with his longer blade, its point found the chink between corselet and helmet. It was a lucky blow, not fatal, but sufficient to cause such a suffusion of blood that the squire dropped to his knees and crawled away into the dark.

It was man to man now, against the giant with the scimitar. The Saracen was a superb swordsman, cutting and slashing so that the broad, shining blade, single-edged and curved-tipped, seemed like a thing alive. The air itself sang and hissed, as the blows rained about his head, and Guy knew he could not keep dodging around the ladder much longer. Then, his quick eye noticed something. The Saracen's hands were bare, with one forefinger hooked over the right cross-piece of his scimitar; this was the secret of his unerring blows and Guy kept his eyes fixed on that forefinger as though his life depended on it. As soon as the hand was at rest, he aimed his own blow, a single downward cut with the edge of his blade, and the finger was severed. The scimitar fell to the ground, clattering on the stones like a dead thing, now that its life-source was cut off.

"Quick, Hugh," Guy called. "Take her up the ladder. I'll follow." Then, astonishing Hugh, he added, "Remember, Hugh,—she is my betrothed!"

All this was clearly observed from the Castle walls. There were helping hands to take the girl over the top and carry her into the keep. Guy drew in a breath of enormous relief, only now realizing the full, incredible miracle he had accomplished. He had saved her!

It remained only to save himself. Rage and pain had

combined to turn his adversary into a raving animal. Unable to wield the scimitar left-handedly, the black-mailed giant had drawn his dagger and hurled himself forward. Guy had one foot on the ladder and turned to ward off the blow. He succeeded and then raced for the top. The unexpected thing was the behavior of the ladder itself. It shuddered and heaved up in the air like a cobra lifting its head to strike. The giant had picked up the whole ladder, with Guy on top, and was about to fling it down into the ditch.

In that moment, Guy saw his end and he knew why it had come. He had broken his vows. He had not been chaste, he had not been humble, he had not been obedient to his mission. He was no longer worthy to be an instrument of God. The whole world spun around his head, the battering ram at the gate, the flaming tower, the moon in the sky . . . Then it all disappeared.

DAMASCUS

CHAPTER SIX

THE MAMELUKE

Ibn ed Daya, the old warrior and Governor of Aleppo, attended Friday prayers regularly at the Great Mosque in the Street of Souks. Even in winter he stood in the open courtyard, under an icy drizzle, without seeking the shelter of the colonnades. Fine drops of rain ran down his puffy, bloated face and gathered on the tip of the grizzled, square-cut beard. One must show these modern upstarts and heretics the true rigor of the old faith, he reflected to himself as he performed the obeisances of two rekkas.

Like his master Nur-ed-Din, the Sultan of Damascus, he showed a stern implacable zeal against the barbarians of the West. He had nothing but contempt for the soft, heretical Syrians who espoused the new mystical doctrines of the Ishmaelites, the spawn of Satan, who were in league with the Christians themselves (may God condemn them to everlasting torment!).

The aged Imam in his black robe, leaning heavily on his saber of office (always carried in territory conquered by the True Faith), was intoning the Fatiha. "In the name of God, the Merciful, the Compassionate—" His muffled voice droned on, "Praise be to God, Lord of Worlds, the

Compassionate, full of mercy, King of the Judgment Day—"

The Governor wished the Imam would hurry up. He was cold and his war wound was throbbing in his thigh after so many prostrations. In addition, he was uneasy about the security of his position. Armed guards were stationed at intervals of fifteen paces all along the top of the colonnades surrounding the prayer floor, their bows strung at the ready. They had received a special dispensation from making the prostrations themselves, in order to keep an eye on the crowd. Even their presence did not make him feel safe. He knew how fanatic the Ishmaelites were and, in the service of their own Imam, they would risk instant death.

"Peace be on you and the mercy of God." At last it was over. The icy rain in the open courtyard began to turn to snow. The Governor was glad when his horse was brought and he could take his departure through the sullen populace. His attendant, a fair-haired, bearded mameluke with a scar on his left cheek, helped him into the saddle. He was getting old, he, who used to leap on the backs of the wild Kurdish horses in Mesopotamia and break them single-handed, now needed help from his slave. The procession moved off, the Wali, his fiercely mustachioed Police Chief and his men in front, his personal bodyguard to the right and left, and the mameluke walking by his saddle slightly to the rear.

How the old woman got through the police lines, he did not know, but suddenly, there she was, prostrate on the cobblestones. Her grey hairs were awry under her shawl; her right hand, crushed by the hooves of the horses, was still clutching a bit of paper. A dreadful hush had fallen over the crowd, and the Governor sensed the need for a politic gesture.

"Hand me this woman's petition," he ordered the mameluke, who sprang to obey. The Governor unfolded the paper in silence and studied it impassively. Trusting that no one would guess its contents he folded it again and handed it back to the mameluke. "Arrest this woman!" he said.

The Wali's men went into action, turning about, this way and that, roughing up the spectators. But the old woman had disappeared. The mameluke looked at the paper in his hand and saw that it contained the sign of the Evil Eye. Instantly, he leaped forward into the crowd and, after a moment, emerged dragging a skinny, wild-eyed youth by the arm.

"This is the culprit," he said.

"Mameluke dog!" shouted the Wali, who was furious at being outsmarted by a slave, "we are looking for a woman, not a man!"

"This is your woman," replied the mameluke with laconic satisfaction, and he wrenched off the youth's jubbeh. Under the long sleeves appeared the pulp of a bloody hand; inside the breast was a shawl and attached to it were two false locks of grey hair.

The youth spat defiantly. "God is great," he cried, "and Ali is His vice-regent on earth!" Instantly, he was bound with cords and dragged off by the Wali's men to the grim forecourt of the castle on the hill. As the iron portcullis rang down, the Wali dismounted and saluted the Governor.

"I apologise to the Emir for this incident," he stammered.

The Governor dismounted, and said somewhat stiffly, "Take this wretch to the dungeon and question him. He may have something to tell us."

Then he placed a hand on the shoulder of the panting mameluke who, having no mount, had had to run all the way through the souks after his master. "Well done, al-Adil," he said.

"But how did you know this youth was the culprit?" asked the Governor later that night. The mameluke attended him, removing his kaba of chain mail, and replacing it with a loose, damask farajeyeh, lined with warm wool against the cold winter night. "What I mean is—why this youth more than any other? Was there some special sign?"

The mameluke brought a brazier and placed it near his master's special divan. The glowing coals illumined his face like a portrait of the young David attending upon Saul—his fair hair and beard like an aureate halo about his head, his eyes downcast in submission, and the jagged scar on his left temple a tale untold. He filled his master's cup before answering. "There is a sign for all things, O Emir," he said at last. "A cause and effect which links the world together, so that it produces a perfectly running 'engine', as we would say in the Roumi tongue."

Ibn ed Daya settled himself on the divan and drank deeply. He enjoyed these talks with his young mameluke, who like all his class was a white slave. The slave pleased him especially because he was a hostage for his own son, held in the Frankish castle of Banyas. He treated him well, taught him Arabic, and loved him like another son.

"And what is the link which led to this one youth out of ten thousand?" he pursued.

"Evil," replied the mameluke simply, "is a traceable substance, which leaves its mark wherever it goes, just as quicksilver leaves its traces in the human body. He who gives the Evil Eye has the evil in his own eye."

"In the eye of the Ishmaelite?" The Governor grew more interested. "How could you tell—?"

"I have seen these eyes before, O Emir. They are the fanatic eyes of a man who serves not God, but the Devil rather in the place of God. They burn—they burn—"

"So you knew him by his eyes! Truly, the dervishes of the Ishmaelites are fanatics, for they claim to be a Chosen People, through whom God acts to save or to destroy the world. They kill all who oppose them and they have no fear of death themselves. Can you understand that?"

"I can understand that God would choose a man or a people as His instrument. But the Devil may do the same."

The Governor nodded. "I am a soldier. I obey the Commander of the Faithful. It is necessary for all men to obey, for otherwise there is chaos. But I do not know what is right, what is wrong. I speak only for your ears. I have studied the works of these accursed dervishes, and I see in them no light. The world is still the same—a world in which the wicked flourish, and the noble are trampled underfoot."

The Governor held out his cup to be refilled. The mameluke knew that he was thinking of his son, young Ibn ed Daya. Did young Ibn ed Daya still live? The Governor had offered the return of the slave, al-Adil, in exchange for him—a handsome offer since the mameluke was believed to be of high degree. Only the Governor knew his origin, which he kept a close secret. But there had been no reply to his offer and the old man lived on in dread and hope.

"If Ibn ed Daya is dead—" he began, but did not finish. For then al-Adil, whom he had rescued from the slave market, and to whom he had given a robe of honor and a decent name—al-Adil must also die. And now, strangely, it seemed to him as though he would be losing his son twice over. Distracted by the thought, he drank deeply and said, "There *is* no right or wrong. There is only forgetfulness."

"Then what makes you dislike the Ishmaelites?" al-Adil asked.

"Because they wish to destroy the world and build it new. Only a Saviour can do that."

"And is there a Saviour among the Ishmaelites?"

"An Imam. The Ishmaelites believe that only the descendants of Ali, son-in-law of the Prophet, on whom let there be peace, are the true Imams. Some say the seed of the Prophet died out with the Seventh Imam, Ishmael, remaining hidden from sight and only to be revealed through God's pleasure."

"And has he been revealed?"

"Behold God's Chosen One, Rashid Ali, whom they call the Old Man of the Mountain!"

"He who lives in Masyaf? Is he an Imam?"

"Already he has proclaimed the Resurrection, the ending of the Law of the Prophet, on whom let there be peace, and the beginning of a new law, under which all things are permitted. In Masyaf, men have taken their sisters and daughters to wife, women wear men's clothes, and the dervishes dance themselves to death!"

"Can all this happen—and there is no revelation?"

"No revelation! No revelation! I tell you no revelation!" The Governor had become very drunk and he began to cry like a child. "There is only the grape. Give me the grape—"

"O Emir, the jug is empty," replied al-Adil. "Shall I refill it?"

At that moment, a fracas erupted in the hall outside and the door was unceremoniously flung open. The Wali struggling with two of the Governor's personal bodyguards, entered the room.

"Hands off me, dogs!" he cried. "My business is with the Emir—"

"Admit the Wali," ordered the Governor, adding, "Forgive the attention to duty. I had given commands that I was not to be disturbed."

The police chief advanced into the room, his short black tunic somewhat disarranged and his turban awry. He bowed, touching his fingers to his lips and bending to place them on the floor. "I kiss the dust before Your Excellency. What I have to say is for your ears alone—" He looked doubtfully at al-Adil.

"The mameluke is my cup-bearer," replied the Governor thickly. "I must have my cup—"

"O Emir," replied the Wali sharply, "the dervish has spoken!" There was a moment's silence.

"Well," said Ibn ed Daya finally, "has he given us the names of the conspirators?"

"He has given us a name."

"Only one? There are many conspirators. You must heat the irons again, O Wali! You must screw the rack more taut—"

"The name on the lips of the Ishmaelite is a name in ten thousand, O Emir!" The Wali looked away in embarrassment. "It is a name beside which other names pale as the moon before the sun—"

"What name, O Wali?" roared the Governor.

The Wali bowed again to the ground, not daring to look up. "It is best that Your Excellency should hear it from the lips of the Ishmaelite himself. Let not evil tidings fall from my mouth—"

"My son!" The Governor had risen from the divan, his empurpled face working slowly, as he stared before him with bulging eyes. "You are speaking of my son?"

"Will it please the Emir to speak with the dervish?"

Like a blind man, the Governor staggered forward, the mameluke supporting him, as the doors were held open, and the small party, with Ibn ed Daya at its head, proceeded into the corridor and down the spiral stairway of the tower.

The Citadel of Aleppo was built on a rock which dominated the Syrian countryside like a giant sentinel. Inside the living rock, a whole city had been hollowed out, with barracks, storerooms, granaries, armories, and in the lowest part—the dungeons. The galleries leading downward were built on a steep incline around the central shaft and the tramp of mailed feet on the solid rock echoed dully, as the Governor's party, led by two torch bearers, descended into the depths.

"This way, Excellency." The Wali led his master obsequiously past rows of iron cages in which wild animals that once were men, some on all fours, clung to the bars, staring and babbling. In the central pit of the shaft, the Wali's torturers stood at attention beside fires where the irons were heated; in their hands was an array of pinchers, hammers and skewers all designed to extract the information their master required.

In the midst of this lay the Ishmaelite, naked on the floor, slippery with blood and sweat, a barely recognizable remnant of the youth with the blazing eyes. What inner strength sustained him against the worst that fiendish minds could devise none could guess—except for the young mameluke. For a moment their eyes met—the culprit, now close to death, and his captor, still in the flush of life.

"What do you know that I do not know?" the mameluke's eyes seemed to ask.

"My secret is not for your asking!" the dark, bloodshot eyes of the Ishmaelite seemed to answer.

At the Governor's arrival the torturers sprang to their posts, the guards stiffened, the Wali became more voluble in his triumph. The Governor stood in the midst of the curious, leering crowd, a shadow of his former self, drained of all authority and power by the dread of what was to be revealed.

"Speak!" said the Governor softly, as though addressing an honored guest. "You knew something of young Ibn ed Daya—"

The eyes glowed momentarily in the mangled face. The voice was thin but surprisingly clear through the torn and swollen lips. "Yes," said the Ishmaelite, "he was my friend."

"Was—?"

"We were at Banyas together. We were both sent on the same mission to the Roumis. I carried the gold. Ibn carried the plans of the city and Citadel of Aleppo." Again the eyes glowed briefly. A stir of horror passed through the spectators. "You may do what you like to me now for your days are numbered, O Emir, even as the hairs in the beard of the Prophet."

"But my son—" stammered the Governor.

"—is a faithful servant of the Hidden Imam, revealed to us by God on the Day of the Resurrection, may he be rewarded in Paradise. We were scholars together at the madresseh, Ibn and I. Oh, he never brought me to his home—I was too, how do you say, unconventional. But he was also unconventional in his heart. Know this, O Emir. Your son scorned you and your kind utterly, utterly. Pretending to believe in the Law and the Prophet, in fact you believe in nothing, you have given yourself up to deceit, and the true imamate of God has been usurped by men of blood and greed and lust. But your son was not like

you. He believed with us, the elect of God, that all men
are brothers and he was ready to die in this belief."

"And did he—die?" The Governor brought out the
words in painful gasps.

"The elect never die. They come from Paradise and
they return to Paradise. I myself have been to Paradise
many times. I brought Ibn with me. We ate of the
hashish, the divine seeds of regeneration, and we walked
together in the garden; the fountains splashed wine and
rosewater on our faces; the maidens, beautiful as new
moons in the sky, played to us on their zithers; and we
tasted the everlasting joys."

The Governor was near the end of his self-command.
He tottered slightly on his feet, so that the Wali and the
others smirked, thinking him drunk, but he was, in fact,
cold sober now, only very faint from fear. In order to disguise his weakness, he bent down on his haunches,
touching his hands to the floor to keep them steady, and
he spoke to the dying man in a low voice, audible only to
themselves.

"Do not play with me, Ishmaelite," he said. "If you
have hated me, I never bore you any hatred. What has
happened is not my will, but the will of God. Be plain—be
plain—"

"O Emir," came the soft reply, "I also did not hate. We
who act on the divine command are above hatred. We
only despise you, as the Angel Gabriel despises a worm.
We tread on you and on your kind as unworthy to encum-
ber the Kingdom of the Most High. You with your power,
your armies, your riches—what are you now? A poor
creature, crushed utterly under the just retribution for the
wrongs you have inflicted on God's elect. And this is how
He, the Lord of Worlds, has brought you low—by sending
your own son into the camp of the Roumis, the Unbelievers, in order to deliver you up to them. So may your do-
minion end and the reign begin of the Most High Imam,
the descendant of Ali, the Vice-Regent of God, may His
name be exalted!"

"Never!" The Governor stood up, strengthened by an

access of rage. "Never shall I believe my son capable of such treachery! It is a lie, Ishmaelite, said to spite me. You shall die with a lie on your lips!"

But the voice of the man, faint with death, still rang clear. "Your son gave the plans to the Citadel of Aleppo into the hands of the Lord Constable of Jerusalem in my presence. The Roumis know your dispositions and weaknesses, the location of the armories, the secret passages under the walls, all that is needful to capture and destroy the seat of your power. Willing hands are waiting to open the gates, to stab your commanders. There is none you can trust. Those to whom the Evil Eye is given are past help. It is a mercy of God, to prepare you for death!"

"My son—where is he now?" asked the Governor hoarsely.

"He is in Paradise. The Lord Constable granted us safe conduct out of his territory, but his aide, Amalric of Lusignan, was a perfidious traitor who took us to the castle of Banyas as prisoners. When he received your offer to exchange the mameluke here for your son, he set me free instead, and put your son to the sword. Your son died a true believer, with the cry of 'Ali!' on his lips. See, he gave me his ring before death—"

The Ishmaelite held out his mangled hand and the Governor saw his son's ring among the shreds of flesh. It was too much. Throwing back his head, he struck his own face and wailed, "Ai Yiee! There is no refuge but in God! May He deliver me from the evil of this day!"

At a sign from the Wali, an executioner held a scimitar poised over the neck of the Ishmaelite. "Is it your Excellency's pleasure that he should die?" the Wali asked ingratiatingly. But in his grief, the old man was past hearing. After waiting in vain for a reply, the Wali turned quietly to the executioner and made a sign. The Ishmaelite saw it and cried loudly, "Ali!" before the sword fell.

Then the Wali, remembering his discomfiture the previous afternoon, glanced scathingly at the mameluke who stood beside his master, supporting his weight. "O Emir," said the Wali in his most unctuous tones, "What shall now be done with the hostage for your son?"

The Governor seemed not to understand. He continued to lean on the mameluke's arm as he made his way back to the stairway. "What son?" he mumbled. "I have no son. I shall die childless—"

"The hostage, O Emir! His life is forfeit!"

At last the Governor seemed to notice the slave at his side. He looked at him, but without recognition. "He is no son of mine!" he declared. "I do not have a traitor for a son! All traitors should die!" And he continued to ascend the ramp looking neither to right nor to left.

At once, the mameluke was seized by the Wali's men, the robe of honor torn off his back, his arms bound to his sides with cords. The executioner cleaned the blood off his sword and stood ready, the sweat glistening on his naked arms. For a few moments the Wali delayed in order to savor his triumph. The delay cost him his revenge.

Before he could nod to the executioner, the voice of the Governor was heard again from above, near the exit to the dungeon. "The slave, al-Adil," he said, "should be sold in the slave market to the highest bidder. He is of no service to me any more." And with that, the broken old man passed out of sight.

There was usually an hour or so between the first and second showings in the slave market in Damascus. The first showing was confined to female slaves, and was attended by a crowd of better-class customers: ladies purchasing maids, nurses and personal attendants, and gentlemen on the lookout for a desirable addition to the harem. The second showing put only male slaves on the block, mainly for use as common laborers. This sale was usually attended only by the overseers of households, rather than by people of quality.

The large compound of the slave market, or khan, opened off the main thoroughfare of the Street Called Strait. In the shadow of the gateway, there were stone mastabah benches on which the vendors set out the refreshments and the customers stopped to sip their ices and talk. Two portly gentlemen in long jubbehs, of royal blue, with high Court turbans, could be overheard in passing.

"May God preserve you, O servant of the Grand Eunuch!"

"May God grant your prayer, O Master of the Royal Table!"

"Very poor merchandise today, I'm afraid. There is no quality at these auctions any more. Now, if they would bring prices down, I might be interested—"

"A little girl with dark eyes, perhaps—?"

"Don't make me laugh. Maids for the royal kitchens, that's all. But we are not prepared to pay their prices—"

"—unless the right thing comes along—"

"—with the proper qualifications—"

"—like the one with breasts like rosebuds—?"

"Stop! You'll kill me with laughing!"

The voices trailed away among the chattering crowds.

The khan, or merchants' warehouse, was built against an ancient Roman colonnade. It consisted of three stories where the merchants had their auction rooms. But on a warm day like this, the sale was conducted in the open, on a platform erected at the back of the courtyard.

The agents for the various merchants took up their places on the stage, sitting cross-legged on small mats, their rolls of documents with ink horns and quills, beside them. They looked idly over the crowd, agreeing, with much shaking of heads, that business had fallen off. It was the war, no doubt, especially since the news from Aleppo, that caused the wealthier citizens to put their money in gold and diamonds and divest themselves of bulky property.

"These auctions have become a farce," complained one agent. "My master reserves the best now for private sale. To put it up before this rabble is to cast pearls before swine!"

"Wait a moment. Look there. That litter just inside the gate, in the shadows. That's the third day running it has been there. Who do you suppose—?"

"You mean, a *lady's* litter at the male auction? How indecent!"

"These Court ladies are grown very bold—"

"Do you think she will buy?"

"She does not bid. Only watches."

"How indecent!"

By now the slaves had been brought out of the khan for the next showing. They were herded onto the platform in groups guarded by the overseers, armed with whips, a bedraggled crowd, old, young and maimed. The slaves were heavily weighed-down with arm and leg irons, but each stood alone on the block when prodded by the overseer behind. All were naked.

The sale progressed slowly, the exasperation of the agents matched by the apathy of the crowd. There was even some jeering when an elderly Jew was auctioned off for three groats. The Jew had lost both his feet and swung to and fro on crutches, like a chicken trussed up in a poulterer's shop, ready for the killing. The auctioneer assured the crowd that he could write—but what was the value of that? A schoolmaster bought him to copy out lessons.

Eventually, the mameluke, al-Adil, took his place on the block. He stood very still, his head a little on one side and his eyes fixed on some point above the rooftops, so that you might almost think he was listening to a distant bird. Extremely emaciated, his rib cage stood out in sharp relief and his large, well-proportioned limbs and loins were rawboned. He wore his left arm in a sling. Only the full beard, tawny and fierce, gave his scarecrow figure an oddly majestic look. A few murmurs of approval greeted his appearance, but there was a marked reluctance to begin the bidding. Mamelukes were notoriously bad buys, being generally unbiddable, either rebellious or despairing.

"Come, masters, what will you give for a fine mameluke—young, strong, lusty—he will be an addition to any household," the agent attempted to drum up interest. "A Roumi as proud as Lucifer, but broken, masters, well-broken—excellent physique," (here the agent ran his hand over the muscular body, turning it this way and that to show its advantages), "ideal for work in your fields, on your threshing floor, or on your tread mill. Or breed him, masters—see, what a stallion!—you will get back your investment tenfold."

Guffaws. The agent blustered. "Nonsense! These barbarians are mettlesome creatures. Take my advice, masters, put the bit between his teeth, and you'll be able to drive him as much as you desire. Your bids, masters, your bids!"

But there were none. In truth, there was something intimidating about the mameluke, a sort of quiet fierceness that none of these good, fat bourgeois felt like challenging. One old peasant at last bid three dinars and asked if the mameluke could plough, and then it turned out he wanted to put him in the traces, not behind the handle bars!

"Certainly, master, certainly!" responded the agent amiably, "harness him and whip him and he'll plough you a hectare in the twinkling of an eye! But surely he is worth more than the price of an ox! What more am I bid, masters?"

At this moment, a large black eunuch, armed with a scimitar, made his way from the back and approached the platform. A whispered colloquy took place and the agent became instantly obsequious. "Masters," he announced, "the mameluke is withdrawn from sale!"

Instant sensation. Heads turned this way and that, to stare at the mameluke who was handed over to the black eunuch and led away, wrapped in a dirty jubbeh hastily thrown over his nakedness by the agent. The litter at the gate had now disappeared. The gossip rose to fever pitch, as the agent sat down with a smile of satisfaction and entered the sum of one hundred gold dinars in his books.

Three days later, the Chief Eunuch, Mesroor, in the Ishmaili Palace, made his way to the slave quarters with an important message. The palace was a small but sumptuous establishment, befitting the embassy of an independent sovereign vassal to the Court of the Sultan of Damascus. Located in a quiet side street, it attracted little attention, no doubt intentionally, for there were many nocturnal visits by unknown persons to its modest door. As a 'house of propaganda' belonging to the Ishmaeli sect the place was under constant police surveillance.

Mesroor entered the slave barracks with the authority of a master. During the prolonged absences of the lord, he bore on his finger the seal-ring of his master, giving him authority to act in his name, and he was entitled to carry the lord's steel scimitar, a privilege he never forebore to exercise.

"Salaam!" murmured the slaves, rising respectfully at his appearance. He proceeded down the corridor of low, ribbed vaulting overlooking the courtyard, as far as the infirmary, a single cell at the end. He went inside, closing the door behind him.

On a pallet of straw, laid on the floor, he found the mameluke slave, al-Adil, lying on his back, resting his head on his forearm and staring through the iron bars of the small, high window, at the tops of the cypress trees in the garden, outlined against the blue sky.

"You are comfortable this morning, I hope?" the eunuch inquired with heavy irony. The attention given to this particular slave, not to mention the absurd price paid for him, excited both his jealousy and his curiosity. For three days there had been a constant succession of professional attendants into the infirmary waiting on the almost inert mameluke slave. His finger had been cauterized, his beard and hair trimmed, his body massaged and oiled. Clad now in the garb of the house slaves, consisting of wide pantaloons of the finest white linen and a small sleeveless red vest, fastened with gold lacing across his bare chest, the mameluke seemed a new man. But he had still not lost his dreamy, indifferent air. Nor did he answer the eunuch.

"Surely you will be pleased to know that your mistress has sent for you," Mesroor said sarcastically. "Now that you have been made presentable, you must make your obeisance at the feet of her, who is to you as the moon is to the tides, as the salt lick is to the wild antelope of the desert. Stand up and I will teach you the obeisance."

Obediently the mameluke rose and stood unsteadily on
his feet. He was still very weak, for the doctor had
prescribed a restricted diet, until his stomach was accustomed to more nourishing foods. Furthermore, he was feverish with the inflammation of the gangrene caused by
the irons on his leg.

"You will follow me to the audience hall," the eunuch
said, "and there you will wait by the door on the lowest
level of the floor. The mistress will enter at the top level.
On her appearance you will prostrate yourself on the
floor, kissing the dust three times. When you are commanded to approach, you will crawl forward on your
belly, propelling yourself with your hands. On no account
must you raise your face from the floor unless you are
bidden. Do you understand?"

"Yes," replied the mameluke simply, "I shall make obeisance to this lady to express my thanks for the kindness
she has done me. But I shall not crawl."

The lips of the eunuch curled. "Come," he said.

On leaving the cell, they traversed the hall and went out
into the courtyard of the palace. Enclosed on three sides
by a covered arcade, the open space in the center was like
a sun-filled forest glade, shaded by tall cypresses, and
bright with colored lanterns suspended on long cords from
the arches of the arcades. At the foot of the trees grew
soft green mosses and anemones among the flag stones,
splashed with the spray from several fountains which were
set in basins of tesselated marble.

The fourth wall of the courtyard was a noble house
front of colored marbles, inset in the center with a massive liwan, or recess, under an arabic arch encrusted on all
its inner surfaces with reflecting glass and mother of pearl.

The audience hall was cool and bare with the austerity
of marble. The floor rose in three levels like ascending terraces. At the rear of the top level, a raised divan dominated the room. Sunlight filtered through marble fretwork
windows on one side; other walls were hung with shields
and trophies.

Mesroor took up his position at the entrance, holding

his scimitar horizontally in both hands, as though to bar the way in or out. The minutes slipped by and the mameluke stood in the center of the lower floor uneasily, as though on the threshold of a new adventure, perhaps of a whole new life. Never had he known such a luxurious peace as in this lofty chamber.

His glance rose to the tesselated ceiling, encrusted with the names of God in gold; he admired the damask drapes, the chests inlaid with elephants in ivory and peacocks in lapis lazuli. Somewhere in the garden outside, a bird sang—a long-drawn out fluting that floated through the windows and came to rest in the room like a fallen blossom.

Suddenly, there was a rustling and two black eunuchs, bearing scimitars in their hands, parted the beaded curtains beside the throne and took up their position on either side. At a sign from Mesroor, the mameluke flung himself to the floor and pressed his face to the cold marble. Steps approached, soft-slippered, dainty. They halted a moment on the top level, then slowly descended to the middle level, and then to the lower level and came to rest directly before him. Raising his face slightly, he could see two red sandals, and a pair of delicate, dark feet, with henna-colored toe nails.

"What is your name, mameluke?" came a voice, tiny, gentle, like running water.

"My name is al-Adil, mistress," he replied, without raising his face.

"A good name," she pursued. "It is one of the ninety-nine names of God, whose perfection be extolled." After a pause, she added, "Do you know my name?"

"I do not, mistress."

"My name is Yasmin. Does that mean anything to you?"

"No, mistress."

"Come, look on me, mameluke," she ordered, with a flash of fire, as she raised the veil from her face. He obeyed and saw a small, slender girl, with a dusky, oval face, looking down at him out of puzzled, dark-lashed

eyes. "In the name of God, the Compassionate, the Merciful, say if you know me."

"I would to God I did know you, lady," he answered,
still humbly kneeling, as though imploring her forgiveness.
"You see . . . I have lost my memory."

With an imperious gesture, she commanded the slaves
to withdraw. Directly the doors were shut and they were
alone together, the Princess bent forward and took the
mameluke's face between her hands, and, to his infinite astonishment, kissed him full on the mouth.

CHAPTER SEVEN

YASMIN

Spring comes suddenly to Damascus, as though the land had emerged from a trance. The sun grows yellower, the grass is full of tiny flowers, people congregate like clouds of midges in the market place, the merchants roll up their shutters, the muezzins in all the minarets shout their call to prayer with lingering gladness on the long-drawn-out syllables—"Allahu-u-u Akhba-a-a-r!"

Beside the Rashid Ali Palace, an orchard descended in terraces toward the Barada river. From this slope it was possible to see as far as the farthest limit of the oasis where the desert begins. The slave al-Adil was sitting alone in the orchard, his back against the gnarled trunk of an apple tree, a sheaf of parchments in his lap. From time to time, he picked up one of the fallen pages, which were each ornately illuminated with the name of God in letters of gold across the top: "In the name of God, the Compassionate, the Merciful . . ." He was reading the Koran.

If it was strange that a slave should pass the day like this, taking his ease in the cool of the orchard, it was not stranger than his puzzlement before the word of God as revealed to his Prophet. Somewhere he had learned all this before, in another life, but it came back to him now in another guise, with all the wonder of a new revelation.

He returned again and again to sura 6:74. "The guidance of God is the only guidance. We are commanded to surrender ourselves to the Lord of Creation, to pray and to keep from evil. Before Him you shall all be assembled." Had he not done this? Had he not followed whither the Lord had led him, striving only to battle for the right, and to overwhelm the wrong? But what was right and what was wrong? This was the puzzle he could not solve, for life was like a many-sided gem—every way you turned it, it flashed with different fires, some pure white, others vivid red and green and black—yet it was the same stone.

All winter long, through his illness, the Princess had tended him, sending him doctors to cure the gangrene in his leg, providing him books to read and delicacies to eat. Yet she had never spoken to him again after the day she had so wantonly kissed him. Was she ashamed of her forwardness? He could not tell.

In the days that followed his slow recovery he waited, somewhere between dread and hope, for the expected summons. But it never came. Was it right that he dreamed of this slavery almost with longing, almost loving the bonds that bound him to his mistress, the mistress with the dark eyes and the tiny mouth he wanted, yes, wanted to kiss? At times he felt a dull anger that she had awakened this longing in him, only to cast him aside. He often weighed the possibility of escape, but could not finally make up his mind.

It would be easy enough. He still slept alone in his little cell in the infirmary. There was never a guard. No one contradicted him when he wished to sit in the orchard. The wall was easy enough to vault. Indeed, it was strange that all was made so easy for him—a slave who was given no orders, whom the slave master ignored, for whom all doors opened, almost as though he were under some special dispensation. Was this the sign he was given?

His eyes sought the parchment again, tracing with pain-

ful eagerness the scripted involutions of sura 6:79. "It is
God who splits the seed and the fruit stone. He brings
forth the living from the dead, and the dead from the living. Such is God. How, then, can you turn away from Him
. . . He sends down water from the sky, and with it brings
forth the buds of every plant . . . Behold their fruits when
they ripen. Surely in these there are signs for true believers . . . Momentous signs have come to you from your
Lord. He that sees them shall have much gain, but he who
is blind to them shall lose much indeed . . ."

Al-Adil dropped the parchment with an involuntary cry.
He would try it—he would test the Sign! He would walk
boldly through the garden gate into the slave quarters and,
leaving the Book under his pillow, he would pick up his
few belongings, his turban, his sandals, his cloak, and pass
along the corridors, into the courtyard, and out by the
front gate.

No one stopped him. In the distance, behind a pillar of
the colonnade overlooking the courtyard, he thought he
saw the figure of Mesroor the eunuch, watching. But the
figure made no move to follow him. The porter sitting
outside his lodge gave him a surly look but did not stir.
Even the two guards armed with swords and daggers,
standing on either side of the gateway, stirred uneasily as
though undecided whether to bar his way or salute him,
but did nothing. It was the Sign.

When al-Adil cried out, after coming to his resolution in
the orchard, another figure which he did not see also
stirred uneasily, in the loggia on the palace roof. Lying on
cushions on the terrace floor, under the shadow of the
projecting roof, behind the moucharabie, a beaded wooden
screen, the Princess kept her watch. Each day, when the
mameluke took his ease in the orchard, she watched him,
a prey to conflicting thoughts.

At times she sent her maids away, so that she could
weep in peace, for she dreaded their pitying glances. They
could not know what she alone knew—that this was no
ordinary slave, but the man to whom she was bound for
life. What was worse, even he did not know it, having lost

all memory of his former life. How could she bear this knowledge, unless he gave her some sign—if not of recognition, at least of desire?

Day after day, she fought the struggle within her. She would reach for the bell to summon him. After all, had she not the right? He was gentle, he was kind, he would do whatever she asked of him. But it would not be the same as it was in the Tower of David, beside the Bethlehem Gate, in the years gone by. He was older now, sterner in appearance, even greying a little at the temples after his terrible ordeal. Perhaps he would no longer choose her of his own free will. And if he should ever recover his memory—how would he judge her if she had used him as a slave? She would rather die than undergo his censure. And each time she reached for the bell, it dropped from her hand unrung.

When she saw him rise, therefore, and walk purposefully out of the palace gate, she knew her hour had come. She had given the strictest orders that no restraint was to be placed on him; he was to do as he pleased, go where he liked. She had done this in order that he might be free to act as he chose. Only so could she justify herself to him. But what if he chose freedom?

The day waned and night closed in over the watcher on the loggia and still she never left her post. She refused all food and the pleas of her maids to retire; she tore her silk dresses to shreds and stained the cushions with her tears; but in the end her patience was rewarded. Toward the third hour of the night, al-Adil reentered the gate of the Rashid Ali palace and saluted the night watchman just as though he were on official business for his mistress. As usual, no one stopped him. The Sign was complete for both of them.

In the morning, Mesroor came to his mistress to make his report. The previous afternoon, at one hour before the Evening Prayer, the slave al-Adil left the palace unbidden. Though he could not follow him personally, he had sent one of the hashishin—the Chosen Ones to do this. (The Princess frowned darkly at this and Mesroor hastened on). The hashishi reported he had followed the slave through the souks as far as the Umayyad Mosque. There the slave had stopped in the outer court during the Evening Prayer, but later entered the covered Mosque and sat on the carpet under one of the pillars to listen to a sheikh expound the Scripture to his followers. The slave al-Adil was the last to leave and he engaged the sheikh a long time in questions, which the hashishi could not overhear. Afterwards, the slave passed an hour alone in the darkened mosque, praying before the mirhab stone. ("Praying?" interjected the Princess, astonished. "According to the hashishi, he performed the prostrations for five rekkas," replied Mesroor.) After that, he reported with a peculiar relish, the slave al-Adil resorted to the thieves' market where he sold his sandals for two lead groats, and he proceeded from there to a tavern of ill-repute, where he gambled and drank the rest of the evening with "common men of his own type." At closing time, the slave al-Adil was "ejected" from the tavern and made his way "drunkenly" back to the palace. Such was the hashishi's report.

To Mesroor's astonishment, the news seemed to please the Princess greatly. "May God approve you, Mesroor," she said, "but in future you are not to have the mameluke followed, by the hashishi or by anyone else. Nor is any word of this to pass your lips or the lips of the hashishi. What you have told me is to be forgotten as though it has not been!"

"On the head be your commands, mistress," replied Mesroor.

Later in the day, the Princess decided to meet al-Adil in privacy. As soon as he took his accustomed place in the orchard, she asked for her parasol, and announced that she would take a walk. Followed by only one maid, she slipped into the orchard and along the inner wall. (Why did she fear to be seen by Mesroor who she knew was watching from the loggia? She had no reason to fear. She was mistress and could talk to her slaves as she pleased. Yet she kept to the inner wall.)

As soon as al-Adil saw her, he jumped up and walked toward her. She hastened forward and caught his hand to prevent him kneeling, (it tortured her conscience to see him do this). He stood smiling down at her and holding her hand in his.

"May the Lord restore you to health!" said the Princess, not daring to withdraw her hand until he released it.

"Thanks to you, mistress I am better," he replied.

"And do you have no sandals when you go outside?" she asked, trying to cover her confusion.

"O mistress, look on me with the eye of mercy. I sold them to obtain a mug of beer."

The Princess was taken aback by his honesty. "You should have told me you wanted beer. It would have been provided. See that it is done, Fatima," she said, turning to her maid. Then to the mameluke again, "You have been through a great ordeal, I know. Is there anything else you require for your health?"

"Yes, mistress," replied al-Adil smiling slightly, and still holding her hand mercilessly in his.

"Then speak that it may be given," she said faintly.

"I would like a horse."

For a moment the Princess was stricken by some new terror. What could this mean? A joke? A new bid to escape? Then she remembered him riding up every day with a clatter of hooves and a holla, into the courtyard in Jerusalem, scattering the chickens and the maids in all directions. Of course he would want a horse! How stupid she was!

"I'm sorry," she stammered, "I am a foolish woman—I did not think—" After a pause she went on in growing confusion, "But how do you mean—in what way—?"

He came to her rescue. "As your groom, mistress." And, taking pity on her, he released her hand.

"Of course!" She looked up at him gratefully. He had made things easy. She felt better already, as though she was reaching some kind of understanding with him. In her relief, she permitted herself a little archness.

"And will there be anything else, sir?" she asked.

"Yes."

The boldness of the bare word, from which the obligatory 'mistress' was conspicuously absent, shocked them both. After a long silence the mameluke said, in a lowered voice, "I wish you to ride with me."

The words were spoken and they changed everything forever. She would not have thought that he could have found a way to say so much, so simply. It was bold, but she welcomed that, for it took from her the burden of setting forth their new relationship. It was also gentle, for it drew a discretion over their declaration of love.

She lowered her eyes before him, for he was looking at her steadily in that way of his which no woman could endure, and she answered simply, "Inshallah—if it be God's will!"

Usually they took their horses on the mountain road which led westward toward the Great Rift Valley. The first hour out was the best, especially early in the day. Al-Adil liked to leave the stables before breakfast, just as the morning star arose in the east. To please him, the Princess filled the saddle bags with oranges and nuts and a flask of sherbet packed in mountain snow. When they reached the promontory overlooking the city, at the hour when the light was just enough to tell a black thread from a white, and the muezzins were crying from all the minarets, they dismounted and stood hand in hand and recited the morning prayer together.

Damascus lay before them like a casket of jewels, the domes of all its khans and souks shimmering as the sun glinted on the glass skylights; the roofs of the Sultan's palace gleaming with gold-leaf; and brooding over all, the dull onyx-colored stones of the Umayyad Mosque so old that already it seemed to belong to the beginning of the world . . . a casket of jewels spilled out on the lap of the desert to the glory of God.

"God is most great!" intoned the muezzins, "I believe there is no God but God. I believe Muhammad is His Prophet!"

And the two solitary figures on the promontory answered, "Guide us in the straight path, the path of those whom You have favored, not of those who have incurred Your wrath, nor of those who have gone astray."

Then they broke out the breakfast and ate it seated on the ground, while all the birds began to sing in the carob trees. A cool wind blew in from the desert and al-Adil opened his travelling cloak to admit the slight form of the girl to his shelter and warmth. She laid her head on his shoulder and asked herself if her happiness could last. "Inshallah!" she repeated beneath her breath.

Al-Adil also felt he was himself again for the first time in all his years of captivity. How long was it? He had lost count of years since his accident, after which he had had to make terms with a new life. But now at last he had come into his own. There was a rightness about it all—the sense of adventure, the feel of his horse between his legs as he rode upward into the mountains; the nearness of the slim girl by his side, so near that when their horses passed in a narrow defile his thigh pressed against hers—all this, he felt, had been his before.

Sometimes they rode far into the mountains, for al-Adil had a wish to see the Great Rift, which divided the Holy Land into two halves, east and west, Moslem and Christian. This was wild and savage country, among narrow gorges, and between giant cliffs of layered sandstone, honeycombed with caves, the lairs of brigands. Yasmin was as fearless as himself, and rode her mare bareback, holding on by the long black mane. Al-Adil preferred a saddle with stirrups, in which he stood up and sang war songs in the Roumi tongue, which amazed the peasants as they galloped by.

He was an imposing sight, for he had grown heavier with the years, and stood a head taller than most Arabs, his fair hair streaming in the wind, his scimitar held on high, and singing like an avenging angel. This terrifying appearance stood them in good stead one day when they fell in with a company of merchants, making their way back to Damascus laden with the profits of their trade in

Jerusalem. Merchants always were free to cross the frontiers in time of truce, but they ran the risk of pillage from lawless bands on both sides.

The merchants were huddled, with their asses and coffers of gold, at a small spring in a narrow defile where they had stopped to drink. Before them in the road was a large rock, that had been rolled down from above to block their passage. The rock in place, the brigands attacked. Al-Adil, riding up from the opposite direction, took in the scene in an instant. Waving Yasmin back, he advanced alone to the fallen rock and in a stentorian voice, which echoed along the defile like thunder, he ordered the brigands to come out. They did.

Two and then three ragged men, with hungry looks and bows slung across their shoulders, scrambled down the rocks, cowed but still menacing. Al-Adil demanded their business and they told him they had not eaten for a week. Turning to the merchants he asked if it were not God's law that every man should give to another's need. Trembling, they admitted the obligation. The slave had become the arbiter. At his command, the merchants opened their coffers and took out fifty pieces of silver—enough to feed five men for a week. After handing the money over to the brigands, al-Adil bade them fly from his sword at the peril of their lives. Again they obeyed.

The merchants, greatly relieved, came forward and kissed his hand, which he negligently allowed them to do, as if he were a great emir, instead of a groom in the Rashid Ali palace. (Slyly, he looked back to see if Yasmin had seen it.) Then the chief of the caravan trotted up on his mule and flung open his coffer, begging al-Adil to take his fill of the gold—for in this way great brigands were paid for their protection against little brigands.

But al-Adil had no wish for it. He picked up a single coin and turned it over and over in his hand. It was a gold dinar bearing the impress "Melisende: *dei gratia: regina: Jerusalem.*"

"My lord, my lord," said the merchant anxiously, "you shall have as much as you like. Take your fill."

But al-Adil wanted only this single gold piece which he slipped into the pocket in his belt. "Tell me, masters," he said, "what news can you give me of the Queen of the unbelievers, is she well?"

Glad to get off so lightly, they eagerly answered his questions. The Queen, he learned, had surrendered the Kingdom to her son and retired to the convent in Nablus. King Baldwin had married a Byzantine princess, Queen Theodora Comnena, who led him a dog's life. The leper prince had been set aside from the succession. The Kingdom was run by the new avaricious Constable Amalric of Lusignan. "May God curse all unbelievers," exclaimed the chief merchant, spitting.

"May God approve your words," replied al-Adil.

Later, they saw the Great Rift, coming upon it toward evening, when the valley lay in darkness, under the great shadow of Mount Lebanon to the west. The snows still lingered on the peak of the holy mountain, and its crown of dark cedars was tipped with fire as the sun went down behind it. Although it was becoming dusk, al-Adil insisted on descending the twisting trail to the floor of the valley, which lay flat and treeless, once a rich farmland, but now deserted by the inhabitants who had been carried off by opposing armies encamped on the hills on either side.

Deep in the valley, ghostly in the light of the rising moon, lay a great wilderness of stones of massive size. It was the Temple of Baal that had become the Temple of Jupiter Heliopolitan after the coming of the Romans. It had been decorated with many lofty domes and pillars and cornices—now all fallen into ruin. Only the bats flew at evening among its roofless, echoing chambers and bedouins built their fires where the holy of holies once stood.

If Yasmin had any compunctions about the hour and the place, they vanished before al-Adil's declared desire to spend the night in the ruins. Immediately, she set about gathering rushes from the banks of the stream that ran beside the walls, laying them for his bed on the temple floor. On the rushes he spread his cloak and drew her down by his side. Alone at last, they embraced as they had longed to do—as they had once done in a past only Yasmin remembered.

But after a time, al-Adil fell silent, as he reflected on the mysteries of which he knew nothing. It was these black moods of his she feared the most, when he brooded alone.

Who was he really, he pondered? Almost as if in answer to Yasmin's anxiety, he burst out, "Are Seljuk princesses in the habit of buying themselves rude, barbarian lovers!"

"But you were not a rude barbarian," she objected, smiling.

"What I mean is—what were you doing there at all?" he insisted.

"In the slave market? I was about my father's business."

"Which was—"

"My father is a very great man. Someday you will meet him. He thinks highly of you. I have heard him say you may be useful to us."

"Is that why you bought me?"

"I only did what I had to do for your sake. Now, stop fretting. Besides, you are perfectly free."

"Free!" His answer was faintly bitter. "I am still your slave."

She put her finger tips on his lips. "Don't say that word. It is better, so you are safe."

"But I have no wish to be safe!"

"What would you be, then?"

"Perhaps—one of the Chosen Ones?"

She shivered and, instead of answering, closed his mouth with a kiss.

That night, they were awakened by loud voices and the tramping of mailed feet on the terrace of the sacrificial courtyard, below the sanctuary where they were hidden. Looking down, they spied a party of Crusaders, sitting around a camp fire among the fallen pillars in the open. They were roasting a pig they had taken from some peasant in the course of a night patrol. Al-Adil listened with curiosity to the coarse Roumi voices, cursing and laughing.

"You know," said one, "I could swear by the Blessed

Virgin I saw a paynim girl gathering rushes hereabout at twilight. I'm willing to bet two groats she's still in the ruins. I heard some horses neigh nearby, too. Let's have a search. Remember if we find her, I have her first. Then you can toss up for your turns."

Al-Adil's blood turned to fire and a vein of anger throbbed in his forehead. He would gladly have taken on all of them together, dirty, lecherous barbarians! But Yasmin managed to restrain him. They made their getaway where the horses were tethered, and they regained the Syrian mountains before daylight. But even after, al-Adil could not hear of the barbarians of the west without a throbbing in his forehead.

Intimate meetings between them however, were necessarily rare and fleeting. The Rashid Ali palace was filled with eyes—there were eyes behind the moucharabie overlooking the courtyard, eyes behind the beaded curtains in the audience hall, the reception rooms, the corridors, eyes in the hay loft in the stables. And there was Mesroor. Wherever the Princess went, he was there, obsequious in his salaams, impassive, ubiquitous. No one served her as devotedly as the eunuch, yet never before had she felt his presence such a burden.

It was a sign of the trouble in her conscience that she could bear none of these eyes, these presences that surrounded her now. She kept to her apartments, attended only by her old nurse, Fatima, to whom she confided everything. It was Fatima who acted as go-between, taking her mistress' food tray to the kitchen, through the service yard at the back of the palace, where the slave, al-Adil, might by chance be sitting, mending a stirrup. And if he looked up and said quietly, "Tell your mistress I will ride with her tomorrow," she would bear the joyful news back to the room at the top of the palace. But if he said nothing, but only saluted her and turned away—her heart pained her, for she knew the grief of her mistress.

One day Fatima accosted him in a motherly fashion, for she had grown sons herself. "You are thoughtless, mameluke," she said, "you know how my mistress hangs on your neck, awaiting only a sign from you, and you do not give it. Why do you play her false this way?"

"I do not play her false, little mother," al-Adil smiled. We must not meet too often. It is not safe. Besides, when she wants me she can send for me."

"Oh, you are perverse. You know my mistress will not send. She would rather die than send! Let me tell her you wish to see her."

"How? I cannot see her in the stables, and I am certain we are followed when we ride out—"

"I will show you a secret stair. Come this evening after dark and wait by the slaves' entrance. I will guide you in."

And so began their evening visits, which gladdened Yasmin and banished the dark shadows from her mind as long as her lover was with her. It was her pleasure to wait on him, to make up to him for the unjust yoke she had placed upon his neck. She changed his clothes, she massaged his body, she missed no opportunity to give him pleasure. He rewarded her with loving so passionate it took her breath away.

But the shadows remained. As usual, after he had fallen asleep, she lay awake and the spectres rose before her. How could she tell him the truth? How could he understand it? Would he reject her utterly if he knew it? For he was too simple, too straightforward for her devious ways. They were not like that, these Western men. They wanted to love a woman-goddess who could do no wrong. But Eastern women were not goddesses. They served their men like slaves, and then did devious things behind their backs.

Already, she felt, he had begun to suspect her, and it had cooled his ardor. Of course, she knew that one loves more than the other. Long ago, when they first met, she had known this. He was the master then, but it was only his nature to be kind that had led him to choose her, he had not really loved her at all, he had merely exercised his rights.

And now, how far he was from her, even though lying

by her side—his lost self was hidden behind a veil of amnesia, and his present self was chafing at the bit. He was not born to be a slave. She must free him, he would never forgive her if she did not. But how could she do that, without losing him forever?

So the night hours slipped away, and when the day star rose, she would gently massage his feet, waking him submissively like an Eastern wife, and he would open his eyes smiling, and let her continue until the sky grew flushed and she was frightened lest he not be able to get away in time. Then he would leap up, kiss her, and be gone.

But there were other days when he gave no sign. Fatima would pass him several times, waiting for his nod, but he only wished her good day.

"O mameluke," she would plead, "what shall I tell my mistress?"

"Did she send for me?" he would ask inexorably.

"Mameluke, you know she does not send!"

"Then you must bid her good evening."

And he would pass through the palace gate (the porter had been warned to let him come and go at will) in the direction of the tavern in the lower town.

On these occasions, Yasmin felt her heart within her fail. She would not weep, nor complain, nor show anger. She was like one swimming in a dark stream, weighed down by a heavy stone about her neck—and the stone was her conscience. She faulted her lover not at all. He was blameless in her eyes and beyond reproach. It was for her own duplicity she was being punished.

Then, when Fatima saw how desperate she was, she would bring the water bowl, the pipe charged with hashish; carefully she would measure out the red dust, fill the pipe with it, and light it, striking the flame from a flint. When the hashish was burning hotly, she would pass the tube to her mistress and let her draw in the sweet smoke, through the cooling water, inhaling it deeply.

Yasmin took the hashish easily, from long habit. In fact, it was only the arrival of al-Adil in her life that changed this habit and made her desist. For he lived in a different world. Not for him these soaring dreams, emptying life of all meaning, and lifting it to the heights of vertigo. And yet with him she experienced something of the same emportment, a sense of floating above the world borne up by his arms, but in blissful security, without the terror of the descent to the real.

But when his arms were not there to lift her, she had to call the efreet. He usually came after the third pipe. Yasmin feared him dreadfully while she waited, but once he had carried her off and she was utterly in his power, she abandoned herself to him. Only the efreet understood her, she felt, and asked no questions.

Like all efreets, he was of monstrous size and very black, so that he enveloped her in a sort of darkness, when he lifted her up in his arms. Against the night sky he was scarcely visible, only his teeth shone like constellations, and his eyes flashed like falling stars when he blinked. But his body and the night wind were like one as he swept her away.

He set her down in Kurdistan. She saw her dear mother again, spinning and singing as she used to do outside their house in Mosul. That was long before their wanderings began and all the visits to the villages up and down the country bringing the Good News of the Revelation. Her mother was still young and fresh, the fear had not scarred her face with lines during the long persecution, and she did not yet know the horror of the cavalry charge, the flashing scimitars of the Caliph's horsemen, and death on the cobblestones of Baghdad.

Her mother smiled over her spinning wheel, as though the world was all still before them and she stroked her daughter's hair when Yasmin kissed her hand. "Peace be on you, daughter," she said. "You are well and look so fine, you must be a great lady now."

"Yes, Mother."

"And is your father well?"

"He is Imam now, Mother. After the persecution, we fled to Jerusalem and brought the Good News to many. And now there are thousands in the land of the Roumis

and in Syria who are ready to rise. And the King of
Jerusalem is afraid, and the Sultan in Damascus is afraid,
and the Caliph in Baghdad is afraid. We have established
the Kingdom in Masyaf and father is Prince."

Still the mother nodded and smiled, as though all were
just as she expected. "And are you in love, daughter?" she
asked.

"Yes, Mother," Yasmin bowed her head.

The smiling spinner stopped her wheel and bent her lips
to her daughter's ear. "Whomever you love, daughter,"
she whispered, "cleave to him, for all else passes and there
is only love."

Yasmin's soul was filled with joy by this encounter, and
she wept tears of happiness on the efreet's shoulder as he
gathered her up. But afterwards her elation turned to terror, as the journey grew wilder and stormier. The night
wind blew with hurricane force and lightning rent the sky
with jagged forks which descended upon Masyaf. And
when she found herself in the Courts of Paradise on top
of the holy mountain, all was blackened and blasted, the
fountains ran with blood, not wine, and the dervishes dancing in their white robes were all skeletons, dancing a
dance of death. Frantically, she searched for her father
among the ruins, calling, but he did not come.

Sobbing, she pleaded with the efreet to take her home
but he was inexorable. On he carried her, into immense
reaches of time and space, over white landscapes like the
moon, all utterly dead; only meteors whirled by and died;
and gigantic shadows moved across the constellations, putting them out one by one, so that the universe around
them grew very dark and cold, and Yasmin heard her father's voice calling down the wind, "There is no God!"

In the morning she was violently ill and the doctor who
came blamed the hashish for it and forbade her to take
any more for several weeks. But Yasmin remembered everything that had happened to her and her soul was sick
to death. She lay inert, refused all food, and turned her
face to the wall. "Let me die, only let me die!" she said.

Fatima went to the service yard and found al-Adil in

the stables. "Mameluke," she said gently but firmly as she
might to one of her own sons, "now you listen to me. My
mistress is ill and wants to die. The doctors can do nothing
for her. You are to come to her tonight and you are to
love her. Do you hear me?"

"I will come," replied al-Adil, taken aback.

After that his visits began again, and Yasmin mended
quickly. He gave no explanation for his absence, but he
told her he loved her and she believed him because his
word was sacred to her, even as his name, al-Adil, meant
"blameless," or "one whose testimony is to be believed."
And, indeed, as he kissed her through her long black hair,
he believed it himself.

Summer came to Damascus with its fierce desert heat,
drying up the mountain streams, so that even the Barada
ran foul and sluggish, the fountains ceased to play, the
trees in the orchard wilted, and the song birds fell silent.
The heat had an ugly effect on men's tempers, especially
during the month of Ramadan, when no food or drink
passed their lips from dawn until dark, and some even refused to swallow their spittle. Ramadan soured the disposition, released the bile into the stomach, and caused evil
humors to rise to the brain.

So it was with Mesroor. The obese, black eunuch had
brooded long on the evils of the world. All men were
wicked, all men transgressed His Holy Law, especially in
matters of lust, even in the house of His Chosen One. It
was intolerable! Was it not written: "If any of your
women commit fornication . . . confine them to their
houses until they suffer death"? So be it.

Mesroor lovingly contemplated the moment when he
would confront the lascivious woman, the red harlot, with
her sins. He stood before her one morning in her tiring
room, as her women were brushing her hair, and she applied kohl to her eyes, making herself falsely beautiful
for—. He had the words ready, his pendulous lips and
fleshy jowls were impatient to spit them forth.

"Your lover," he said, "your lover will not save you

now. You shall listen to me. Truly, I am a slave. But I am also responsible to the master of this house for its honor and decency. And when the mistress of the house itself, its purest ray, its finest jewel, is defiled, I must speak out. For it is written: 'Women are enjoined to turn their eyes away from temptation and to preserve their chastity—' "

The Princess covered her ears with both hands. "Silence!" she cried, "I will not hear you!"

Inexorably Mesroor went on, his voice rising in a chant, " '—to cover their beauty, to draw veils over their bosoms, and not to reveal themselves to any except their husbands, their fathers, their sons, their brothers, their women servants—' "

Spitefully, the Princess completed the sura of the Koran for him: " '—and their men servants who have lost their manhood!' "

Mesroor received the slight with great dignity. "I have never complained against the wisdom of God. His will be done! But for the adulterer and the adulteress there shall be no mercy. It is written: 'As for him who had the greater share in it, his punishment shall be terrible indeed.' "

"What nonsense you are talking, old man," retorted the Princess, dismissing her maids with an impatient gesture. When they left she went on with passionate intensity, "How dare you speak to me so, Mesroor? By what right—"

"By the duty I owe to this house, may it be preserved against your disobedience!"

"And what do you mean by disobedience?"

"The same as was laid against Potiphar's wife, 'she sought to seduce her servant.' "

"But I am no man's wife. How then can I be disobedient?"

"It is written: 'Good women are obedient. They guard their unseen parts—' "

The Princess flung her cosmetic box at him. It struck the eunuch just above one eye, and blood began to trickle freely down the broad planes of his face. The immense body shook with the indignity, the fatty breasts trembled and the rolls of bare flesh glistened with sweat. But he controlled his rage. He would not lay a finger on the godless woman, whose punishment must come from on high. Not so the other party in guilt, the fornicator, the defiler.

"And if I do not listen to you—?" she defied him.

"The Truth, whose perfection be extolled and whose name be exalted, must be known."

"Indeed. And who will believe you?"

"It is written: 'If any of your women commit fornication four witnesses shall be called in against them.' The hashishin will testify against you."

Yasmin faltered. He had set the spies on her! She must not betray any weakness. Quickly, she steeled herself to be very cool. Her hope lay in being able to discredit him. Taking a bold line, she said, "Mesroor, you should leave the hashish alone. You and your spies are having too many lustful dreams. I shall overlook it this time. If it happens again—"

"If it happens again," retorted Mesroor, "the slave shall be given up to the knife."

She leaped to her feet. "The knife!" she exclaimed.

Mesroor closed his eyes, beatifically contemplating the longed-for consummation of his desires. "The slave, al-Adil, shall lose his manhood," he said in a sort of ecstasy.

Yasmin became like a woman distraught. "You are mad!" she gasped. "You are sick! You must be locked up! Guards! Help!"

Four guards entered the room. But they were not of the household slaves. They were hashishin, dressed in the long white seamless robes of the dervishes. They wore tall, white hats and carried scimitars, and their eyes were dilated with hashish.

Mesroor smiled amiably. "I have given instructions that the hashishin are to watch over your safety. Have no fear, mistress. You will be well-protected. Now I will send your women back to you." And, followed by the hashishin, he withdrew.

Yasmin discussed the matter at length with Fatima. She must warn al-Adil to escape. Yasmin thought he should go to Masyaf and throw himself at the mercy of her father. Only the Imam could save him now and her father would do anything for her sake. She wrote a note for him, giving directions, signals and passwords necessary for him to reach the holy mountain.

But al-Adil would not go. Quietly, he told Fatima he would visit the Princess that night as usual. The nurse wrung her hands and begged him on her knees, for her mistress' sake, to be gone. He only smiled. "You forget," he said, "I am a mameluke. A mameluke is supposed never to quit his post!"

And sure enough, about the third hour of the night, Yasmin heard his step on the secret stair which led to the private chapel in her apartments, just behind the mihrab stone. Long ago, her father had shown her this stair, with instructions to tell it to none. Yasmin fell into al-Adil's arms weeping.

"Oh my love, my life, my lord," she sobbed, "I have been so afraid! You must not come here. I have brought you only danger. Leave me, leave me."

But he would not. She struggled against his kisses, as she had never done before, but love was too strong for her and she yielded to him in the end, begging his forgiveness. For after all, was it not the Night of Destiny, the twenty-sixth of Ramadan, "a night better than a thousand months," says the sura? "On this night the angels and the Spirit by the Lord's leave come down with His decrees. That night is peace till break of day."

In the morning, when the thought of his danger came back to her, he kissed the puckers of worry away from her forehead. "Rest easy," he said, "all will be well."

"But Mesroor will see!" she exclaimed.

"Mesroor *has* seen," he replied.

"You mean—"

"I knew he would be waiting on the stair, and I left him with his own knife in his side."

She was astounded. He solved everything, this man, he

was defendant, judge and executioner. Yet he was like his name, "blameless," unstained by any blood. And she wondered at him.

She went with him to the stair to look, for they must remove the body, she said. But there was no body, only a few drops of blood on the steps. No doubt the hashishin had rescued him, alive or dead. This presented a new complication, but the Princess met it with her accustomed spirit. She sent for Mesroor. High and low they called him, but he was nowhere to be found. Then she summoned the four hashishin.

"Mesroor has gone?" she enquired sweetly.

"He has gone," they replied.

"Probably to Masyaf?"

"Probably to Masyaf."

"It is well. In the meantime, and in the absence of my father, you will obey me. On your head be my commands!"

"On the head," they replied, kissing their fingers and touching the floor.

About three weeks later, the Imam arrived. He came quietly, as usual, in the nighttime, with few attendants, riding swift horses. They clattered into the courtyard, after the double gates were opened, and suddenly the palace was filled with shouts, as torches were brought by running slaves, and the household assembled, the men and slaves in the courtyard, the Princess behind her moucharabie.

The Imam, a tall, dark man, his beard streaked with grey, mounted the steps of the liwan and cast his flashing eyes on the groom who came forward to take his horse.

"Is this the slave called al-Adil?" he inquired of another figure that loomed beside him in the shadow. It was Mesroor, looking very feeble and frightened, the whites of his eyes rolling in his head.

"It is, O Protector of the just."

The Imam bade the mameluke approach and al-Adil bent respectfully before him. For a moment, as each looked into the eyes of the other, al-Adil felt that he had done this somewhere before, in another life. The effect was heightened when the Imam laid his hand upon the mameluke's head and said, not unkindly, "Peace be on you, my son. Have you a touch of the sun?"

"Master?"

"Or is it concussion again, as it was at Nazareth?"

"I know not your meaning, master."

"You have a perversity about falling on your head, young man. This time you shall pay for your cure. Does the name Barac mean nothing to you?"

"Nothing, master. You see, I have—"

"You have lost your memory. I know. Perhaps, if it is the will of God, it shall be restored to you again. In the meantime, al-Adil, I have news for you. Know that God, whose perfection be extolled and whose name be exalted, is the doer of whatever He wills."

And, turning to his attendants, he commanded, "Bring me my robe of honor." When it was brought, he asked al-Adil to put it on. "Good, very good, it suits you well," he commented with sardonic amusement as the slaves clothed the mameluke in a damask robe, fastened with a jewel-studded belt.

The household was clustered around them, under flaring torches in the shadowy courtyard. It was as though they were witnesses to a fairy tale. "Now listen to me, my children," began the Imam. "This young man, who is known to me, is no slave but a man of high degree, one chosen by God. He has lost his recollection due to a grievous injury and until God wills that it should be restored to him, I have been appointed custodian of his rights. He is, therefore, my vassal, and I invest him with my fiefs of Rusafa, Khawabi and Ulayqa and the castles and rents thereof, in token of which I accept his fealty."

Hidden springs of memory prompted al-Adil to do what was expected of him. He knelt again before the Imam, pressing the palms of his hands together and placing them between the hands of the Imam as he swore the oath of allegiance. When he had done this he rose and the Imam embraced him, kissing him on both cheeks and saluting him as Emir.

"I have yet another announcement to make," said the old man, with almost malevolent humor. "The Emir will doubtless recall, when his senses are restored to him, his erstwhile betrothal to my daughter, the Princess Yasmin. It will please him, therefore, to know that the marriage contract will now be drawn up and it may be consummated at the first moment assigned by the astrologers. The Emir will no doubt be pleased to accept your good wishes."

The Imam stepped into the shadows, watching with a sort of dark pleasure as each of the household took their places, in order of precedence, to present their respects to the new Emir. Al-Adil accepted their wondering obeisance with a grave and unperturbed courtesy, giving to each his hand to kiss, and answering a word of kindness. Last of all came the household slaves, among them Fatima, who wept as she bent over his hand and whispered, "Oh, my lord, be kind to my mistress."

"Of course, Fatima, tell your mistress that I shall send for her at the first moment permitted by the astrologers."

The obese body of the slave Mesroor lay stretched out on the steps of the palace. The Imam came forward, saying with a mordant wit, "Mesroor is my most faithful slave. None has guarded the honor of his mistress with more vigilance than he. I give him now to you as the defender of her honor and yours."

"Rise, Mesroor," said al-Adil, smiling slightly.

But the eunuch did not move. He lay blubbering with fear and clutching his side, that was swathed in heavy bandages. "O Master," he croaked, "I am ill and near to death. Only give me leave to go."

Al-Adil ordered him taken to the infirmary.

Later that night, when they were alone in the new apartments which were hurriedly prepared for him, al-Adil turned to his benefactor and thanked him with his simple candor. "Why you have done this for me I do not know, my lord, but, inshallah, I will honor my oath to you for it."

"I have done what had to be done to save you, my son," answered the Imam. "I owe you this—never mind why. But let me be plain with you. My daugher loves you with a love akin to worship. In her eyes you can do no wrong. See that you do not deceive her. All that matters to me is my daughter's happiness. I love her more than anything in this world. She is my sun, my moon, my stars—I had almost said my God. For her sake, therefore, I am going to exalt you. You shall live a charmed life, no man shall dare to touch a hair of your head, as long as you honor your marriage vow. Oh, I do not forbid you to take other wives, or concubines. Yasmin will submit to your will in everything. But you shall give her pre-eminence in your affections, that is all I ask. That—and a son. For you are called to a great destiny. I have also chosen you for this because I believe you worthy. You have a quality I prize above all others—you are a fool. Don't protest! I mean no disrespect. You are foolish enough to be trusted, al-Adil, and in a world of knaves that is the supreme tribute that can be paid to folly. You are pure in heart, no matter what your sins, and this is purest madness for any man unless he is supremely powerful. I am going to give you that power."

He spoke matter-of-factly, almost prosaically, as though mentioning household matters beyond dispute. But his eyes took on that burning fanaticism which sets the world alight. "Today I am the most powerful man in the world, not because of the strength of my armies, but because all men fear me. From the farthest Himalayas to the Pyrenees, the seeds of my Imamate have been sown and have sprouted shoots, green as the color of Islam, and at a sign from me all this bounteous harvest shall be gathered up and laid at my feet by my faithful ones." He paused a moment, then resumed with heightened ecstasy. "All this shall be yours. My Imamate must be passed on. I have no heirs, except my daughter. Even as the Prophet, on whom let there be peace, willed his Imamate to his son-in-law, Ali, on whom let there be peace, so I shall pass the same power, descended through many Imams, to you. You shall rule an empire vaster than any man before you; your name shall be mentioned in the Friday Prayers in every mosque from the land of China to the land of Spain, and men shall hail you as God's Vice-Regent on earth—"

"Stop!" said al-Adil quietly. "I have no wish for all that. I will keep our bargain and be faithful to your daughter—no more!"

Slowly the old man took in al-Adil's words and he began to emerge from his ecstatic trance. He stared at the younger man with glazed eyes. "You refuse?" he asked, stupefied. "You refuse to be God?"

CHAPTER EIGHT

IMAM-TO-BE

The following letters passed between the east wing and the west wing of the palace in Damascus late that summer:

"To the Emir al-Adil and my dear lord. In the name of God. I hope I do not weary you with these letters. Now that we may not meet until the night of consummation—a whole month! It is gracious of you to write me each morning. Tell me all that you do. We are all business here with the making of my wedding dress. Three women are working night and day and we still fear we may not be done in a month's time. It requires ten yards of damask, six of silk, and eight of the finest gossamer. Then the jewels are to be sewn on individually, at least one hundred diamonds, three score pearls and as many rubies, or perhaps sapphires . . . I had started on a magnificent red gown but suddenly I remembered you liked blue, so I stopped the women at once until I asked you. I want it to be so pleasing to you for the night I am presented. My love and peace be on you."

"To the Princess Yasmin. In the name of God. I rise
early each morning and take my horse to the mountains for
about two hours. It is glorious but I miss you beside me.
On my return I go to the bath. Sometimes I talk with
Master Sa'di, the Master of the Dervishes. He is very wise
but I do not understand a word he says. Then I see the
secretaries. Both are very clever but I do not like the
older one. He has a squint and I do not think he shows
me all the correspondence from Masyaf. There is much
busines to transact—the treaties with the Sultan, the provisions for the new castles, and the daily court. I do my
best. But the business of the hashishin is beyond me.
They all come to kiss my ring, but they tell me nothing
of their employment. I wish I had your advice. My love,
Peace be on you."

"To my beloved lord. In the name of God. The secretary
Hafiz should be sent back to Masyaf if you do not like
him. He cannot be dismissed because he is privy to our
counsels. I saw you ride home this morning. You looked
so handsome. Please answer about the dress as I must look
for new damask if it is your wish. You do not mention
what you do in the evenings. My love and peace be on you."

"To the Princess Yasmin. In the name of God. I miss
you very much. There are so many things I cannot understand. Why can we not meet now that the marriage contract has been signed, when we met so often before? At
least let me come to see you by the secret stair. Let your
dress be any color. As soon as you have been presented to
me I shall take it off anyway! If you must know, I go each
night to the tavern, but incognito. My friends think I am
just an officer of the palace guard. I met three or four
knights of the Sultan's army on my first visit. They had
a private room in the gallery overlooking the floor. There

was a dancing girl who performed very well. Someone on
the floor insulted her. I struck him on the mouth and
instantly all his friends attacked me. The knights in the
gallery saw it and leaped down onto the floor for my
defense. They were armed with swords and made quick
work. Afterwards they invited me to the gallery. Now
I go there all the time. Sometimes we play chess and
one of them, whose name is Salah ed Din, is very clever
and courteous when I beat him. Please answer me at once
if I may use the secret stair. My love. Peace be on you."

"To my beloved lord. In the name of God. Do not ask
me about the stair. Of course you may use it if you wish.
It is a matter for your decision alone. The reason it is
different now is that we are different. A slave may look
on his mistress' face, but a free man may not visit his wife
before the night of consummation. That is the Law. You
may decide for yourself whether you will abide by the Law
or not. I do not have to make such a decision since you
are my law. Why do you feel you must rescue every
maiden in distress? Especially a dancing girl, who I am
sure is used to insults, else why is she there? Since you
have told me so much, why do you not tell me if she kissed
you for your gallantry? I am glad you have friends. But be
careful, my beloved. You do not understand our ways yet
and great princes do not visit taverns in disguise as they
did in the days of Haroun al Rashid. Remember, the Sultan's knights may be enemies to us or else police spies.
I do not want my dress to be "any color." I want it to be
as you desire. A Moslem husband is expected to be a
despot! My love and peace be on you."

"To the Princess Yasmin. In the name of God. Yes, she
kissed me. How do women know all these things? Salah
invited her and she came to the private gallery. Did you

*think I cared? I wanted you all the more at that moment.
I will not hear a word against Salah—he is my ideal. However, I will take care, as you say. What I mean about the
Law is—why is there a law for slaves and a law for free
men? Is not God's Law the same for all? Very well, let the
dress be blue. I can see that as a Moslem husband I lack
a certain brutality. However, I shall do my best to be
despotic. As a start, let me see you! Please answer. My
love. Peace be on you."*

*"To my beloved lord. In the name of God. You did not
ride out this morning. Why? What is wrong? Are you all
right? The servants say you were hurt yesterday. Do not
keep me in suspense. Answer at once. My love. Peace be
on you."*

*"To the Princess Yasmin. In the name of God. It is
nothing. I wrenched my back in a fall from the saddle
yesterday when my horse stumbled. I am in the bath now
and a huge negress is massaging me. She is very rough
and it is hard to write while she works on my back.
Another thing about the Law. I think your father, the
Imam, has dispensed the Law for all Ishmaelites. If that
is so, why must I abide by it? Ouch! I must get rid of this
negress, she is a brute. I miss your hands on my body.
Why do you not answer me about tonight? My love.
Peace be on you."*

*"To my beloved lord. In the name of God. I knew it. I
knew you were not well. I am sure you do not tell me
everything. How dare that negress slave hurt you! She
should be whipped. I will send the doctor to you at once.
Do not forbid him—for my sake. About the Law—there*

*is much you do not understand. Master Sa'di says the out-
ward forms of the Law are for the unitiated, but for the
initiates there is another Law, the Qa-im which is called
the Resurrection. Although you are heir of the Imam, you
are still uninitiated. Even I, who have taken the first steps
of the initiation, am not yet one of the Chosen. That is
why we must still obey the Law. Of course, if I thought
you really meant it about coming tonight, I would not
disobey you. But I do not think you mean it. Besides, I
have a headache. It is an old complaint. Master Sa'di pre-
scribes hashish for it, and I told you what that does to me.
I am afraid of the efreet! My love. Peace be on you."*

*"To the Princess Yasmin. In the name of God. I am
horrified. Why did you not tell me about your headaches?
I do not like you to take hashish. It worries me greatly.
Let Master Sa'di dispense the Law as he pleases. He
should leave my wife alone. I do not like these hashishin,
as you know. They do not speak straight, they pretend to
kiss my ring but they do not show me their hearts. I have
made up my mind. I will come tonight. Await me. My
love. Peace be on you."*

*"To the Emir. In the name of God. Your word is my
command. Peace be on you."*

*"To the Princess. In the name of God. You do not
approve! I can tell, because you did not add your love.
I do not understand. I become lost in your Law and your
dispensations. However, I have changed my mind. I will
sleep alone. But I am jealous of the efreet. My love. Peace
be on you."*

"To the Emir and my beloved lord. In the name of God. Do not fear the efreet. I have banished him from my room. Only my head gets very bad at night. I wish you were with me. But I obey you in all things. My love and peace be with you."

"To the Princess. In the name of God. Fatima tells me you are in great pain because the hashish has been withdrawn. Why did you not tell me you needed it. I did not mean to forbid it—you must not take me literally. How long has the efreet had this hold on you? I told Fatima to give you as much as you need but not enough to bring the efreet. My love. Peace be on you."

"To the Emir and my beloved lord. In the name of God. You are angry about the hashish. I promise you I shall not let it come between us. I shall take no more than you will allow. Do not be jealous of the efreet. He will never enter your marriage bed. I promise! How splendid you are to wish to keep the Law! I will do anything to make up to you for any pleasure you have lost. I promise! I promise! My love. Peace be on you."

The Emir ordered three horses saddled and the saddle bags filled with provisions for several days. He took with him two retainers, an old man who knew the road well, and his son, and on a day in early autumn he set out for the north and the Jebel Bahra. Travelling as most Ishmaelites did in disguise, he wore no insignia of rank and he wrapped his kaffiyeh across his face, fastening one end into the agal around the head, so that only his blue eyes marked him out as a stranger.

It should not be thought that al-Adil was running away.

He made this very clear to Yasmin when he bade her goodbye on the secret stair. As soon as she understood his wish to visit his new possessions—"to come into my own," as he put it—she agreed. She wanted him to feel he "belonged" to her and to her people. After all, it was still nearly a month before the consummation of the wedding. But she wept on parting and she made no difficulty when he arbitrarily lifted her veil and kissed her. It was dark on the stair, so perhaps the Law was satisfied.

He was glad to reach the great plain and the wheat fields, grey under autumn skies. He felt alone here and better able to think out his situation. He was not running away, especially not from Yasmin. He saw her wherever he looked—in the graceful shape of a willow bending in the wind, in the faces of the late desert flowers by the wayside. He wanted her with a physical pain, which left no doubt he loved her. But a part of him remained aloof from his love, watchful and observant.

As long as they were in the Sultan's territory, the three horsemen remained in disguise, eating in vile roadside hostelries and sleeping by their horses on the ground at night. But once they rode under the rugged cliffs of the Jebel Bahra, the retainers broke out the Imam's colors, green and white, on their bridles. They threw a white lambskin cloak over their master's shoulders and they replaced his stained kaffiyeh with a white turban. The Emir had "come into his own."

The mountain villages, poised on the edge of space, their tumbled houses of white adobe and red tiles clinging to the sparse earth like eagles' nests, welcomed him as a savior. In each village square the mukhtars awaited him, standing before the assembled populace and bearing offerings of bread and salt. After years of persecution, pillaged by the Sultan's men, driven to the mountains, the Ishmaelites had been given a protector. Al-Adil bore with him a rescript appointing him military governor of the Ishmaeli territories.

But he was more than that. In the first village he entered, his heart stood still as the entire assembly prostrated themselves on the ground. Already the word of his succession had been published abroad. He was the heir, God's Chosen, the True Imam to be. It was several moments before he summoned the presence of mind to raise his hand. "God is great!" he said. They rose and answered with one voice, "And the seed of Ali is His Vice Regent on earth!"

He had short talks with the mukhtars and the small contingents of the Imam's soldiers who were posted in the villages. He ordered new dispositions of troops, the building of stronger road blocks, and the rationing of food supplies. Everywhere he was obeyed with alacrity and gladness. Instinctively, he warmed to it, and gave new courage and confidence to the people who had now become "his" people.

In each village, the Emir was led to the mosque, usually a simple unroofed enclosure, and the preacher presented the Scripture to him to read. The Emir mounted the rostrum and recited the Fatiyeh: "In the name of God, the Compassionate, the Merciful, King of the Judgment Day—" Over the heads of the assembly, he saw in the distance range after range of the Jebel peaks, each crowned with its village, mosque, and here and there the towers of a castle. This was his land.

The castles were few and far between, small, primitive structures, mostly carved out of living rock, but for that reason well-nigh impregnable. The new master took formal possession of Rusafa, Khawabi and Ulayqa, confirming in each case the resident governor. Finding the garrisons unmanned, he gave orders for the impressment of peasants for their defense. This had always been difficult for the governors to enforce, for the peasantry shunned military service, but when the Emir proclaimed the order, he was obeyed without question.

He also freed large numbers of prisoners on the grounds that in troubled times he needed their services. One of these, Abdulla, a peasant of about thirty, dark, swarthy and taciturn, was lodged in the dungeon of Ulayqa for the murder of another peasant who had insulted his honor. Unable to pay the blood money to the

family of his victim, Abdulla was sentenced to die. The
Emir reprieved him, paying the blood money on his be-
half, and made him his personal bodyguard. He had an in-
fallible sense of how to attract loyalty to himself. Abdulla
proved to be no exception.

Most bodyguards were slaves and Abdulla prided himself on his status as a free man. This, he felt, gave him the
right to give his master advice when needed. "This man is
untrustworthy," he would say "he owes too much money."
"That man cannot keep a secret, he has a young concu-
bine," and so on. Of his own life he said nothing. He was
known to have a wife and two or three small children who
followed him when he moved from place to place, but
they were never introduced to the Emir's court.

Completely illiterate, Abdulla, nevertheless, knew a
large part of the Koran by heart, as well as most sayings
of the Prophet, on which the law was based. This proved
to be invaluable to al-Adil when he was called to sit in
judgment. Standing just behind his left ear, the bodyguard would bend low and softly ask, "Is he guilty or innocent, master?" If the verdict were guilty, Abdulla would
tell him, in a whisper, the appropriate sentence.

Abdulla's sentences were invariably harsh—he knew his
people and what they expected. Thieves lost their right
hands, liars their tongues, and traitors their heads. But
sometimes, when it concerned a woman, perhaps an unfaithful wife, who was condemned to death by suffocation,
al-Adil suspended or mitigated the sentence.

More troublesome to the new Emir were the large numbers of pilgrims who came on foot across the mountains
seeking cures. He did not know what to do with these
crowds of sick or lame, some on stretchers, who waited
patiently through the night for him to appear at the castle
gate. They were humble and inoffensive and sought only
to touch his robe as he went by. He was shocked by their
superstition and forbade this, but still they came expecting
a miracle. Then it happened.

At Rusafa the Emir set up his court, awaiting permission from the Imam to proceed to Masyaf. Soon he was

besieged by these hordes of miracle seekers who pitched their tents in the town square outside the castle gates. One morning, the sight so angered al-Adil that he ordered his soldiers to clear the square. Instantly, beating with the flat of their swords, the soldiers drove everyone back—all except a young child in a basket abandoned by its mother in the melee. It was a boy of about two and a half years, his face blue and his eyes turned up, from whom all breath seemed to have departed. At once, a tremendous silence fell on the crowd; not a man, not a soldier moved. Al-Adil was baffled. Turning slightly, he said to Abdulla, "What must I do?"

Abdulla's instinct in these matters was sure. He had agreed with his master's desire to avoid the confrontation; he had, in fact long ago urged the Emir to "send this rabble packing." But now the confrontation had come, he knew equally well it could not be shirked. With perfect confidence he looked the Emir in the eye and replied, "You must cure him, master."

"But how?" Al-Adil felt his heart falter.

"As God wills, master. You may blow into his mouth; it helps sometimes."

Appalled at his predicament, al-Adil knelt down beside the basket. He picked the child up and placed his mouth to the boy's, blowing rhythmically three or four times, he contracted and released his hands each time. The tiny cheeks distended, the eyelids fluttered and the eyes came into focus. Seeing the big stranger with the blue eyes and the golden mane bending over him, the child leaped up and ran terrified to his mother.

Al-Adil was never allowed to forget this incident. Word of it reverberated throughout the Ishmaeli territory like a thunder clap. Men trembled visibly before him and women fainted if he looked upon them. Suddenly a great gulf seemed to widen out between him and the people he had come to call his own. Now they expected the impossible of him. He refused to see any more petitioners and the crowds obediently dispersed. Then he discovered that his servants were selling the water in which he washed his hands for protection against the Evil Eye. He beat the servants until he was breathless and afterwards wept in the privacy of his room.

Abdulla found him, his shoulders shaking, his head leaning against the wall. The bodyguard placed a hand on his arm with rough compassion. "Do not grieve, master," he said. "It is the will of God."

"How could they do it?" al-Adil groaned.

"The servants? They did wrong to sell the bottles. But they did no wrong to believe."

"You mean they really believed—"

"Certainly. After all, you did cure the child."

"But Abdulla, you know yourself, you told me how to do it."

"You did it, master."

"But how could I? Nothing like this ever happened to me before!"

"Before, master, you had not been chosen."

Al-Adil slowly turned and looked Abdulla in the face. "You mean—you mean you, yourself, believe—"

Without reply, the bodyguard opened the front of his jubbeh and revealed a small skin of water, tied around his neck with a cord. Was this, al-Adil thought, what Abdulla meant by the will of God? Was he being used in some way by a power greater than himself? Perhaps, after all, in one way or another, we are all carriers of God's will.

One morning, he received a message, brought from Masyaf, ordering him to return to his embassy in Damascus. The Imam had heard of his remarkable success, congratulated him upon it, and forthwith banished him from his realm. Al-Adil smiled. The old man was jealous. So be it. His time would come; he was the Imam-to-be.

As the Jebel Bahra faded into the distance behind him, the Emir rode homeward deep in thought. He must not refuse his destiny, whatever it was to be, and he felt a curious elation at the prospect of immersing himself in the destiny of an entire people. Perhaps, after all, the Ishmaelites *were* God's elect. Still a small part of himself remained detached, watching the unrolling of events as though at a miracle-play.

Sa'di, the Master of the Dervishes, lay on his prayer mat, propped up by cushions, smoking a pipe of hashish, in the empty dancing hall. He wore a seamless robe of fine white wool, with the flared sleeves and skirt especially designed for the sacred dance, although he rarely danced himself any more. He was over fifty years of age and his beard was snow white, but the hair on his head still was a vigorous black. His face displayed the fine structure of his skull, the high cheek bones and the thin frontal bone, in sharp relief. Only the eyes moved, following the lazy buzzing of a late autumn fly as it crawled over the letters of gold on the ceiling spelling out the ninety-nine names of God.

Sa'di was an ascetic. He travelled from place to place in the manner of the dervishes, and usually found a place of refuge in a monastic community where he could pursue his contemplation in peace. As a teacher of the Ishmaeli doctrine, he trained the young dervishes who were sent to him from Masyaf, expounding the esoteric principles and supervising the spiritual exercises necessary for their entry into the brotherhood of hashishin.

The Rashid Ali palace housed a dozen of these novices. Behind the novices' cells, lay the madresseh, or school of dervishes, under a single domed roof above the main dancing floor. It was here that the Master sat alone each morning in the hour before the dance. He liked to give himself up to meditation, so that his spirit was purified of all imperfection before the dancing began. Only when the spirit burned clear would it be possible for him to take the leap which led to ecstasy. But alas, the flame, lately, always contained some worldly dross which sullied it before the first step could be taken.

This had not been so when he was young. He relived those early years in memory—the thrill, the excitement of a new doctrine, which swept among the young like a wildfire on the steppes. To throw off the old ways, the crooked

dealings of the politicians, the sham morality of the religious sheikhs—to be free, really and truly free—that was
the doctrine of the new Imam, Rashid Ali of Masyaf.

How wonderful it felt then, to be liberated from obedience to the law of men, so that each man could be himself, live as he pleased, dress as a beggar, grow his hair,
love without restrictions or restraint—yes, that was the
key to the whole doctrine: God had suspended the law so
that all men could live by love.

At least that was the doctrine as Rashid Ali taught it at
Masyaf in those early days. He had revealed himself as
the True Imam who comes direct from God, who *is* God
living among men, so that the law of men means nothing
and only the Imam's will is law. Dervishes came from all
parts of Islam to learn the new doctrine and write down
the Imam's revelations—revelations which came to him
under the influence of the divine drug—the hashish.

Soon the Dervishes all began taking the drug and they
became known as the hashishin. The Imam sent his dervishes to the east into the land of the Huns; to the south,
as far as al-Yemen; to the west, where frontiers of Islam
crossed Africa into Europe. Everywhere they found con-
verts, especially among the poor and oppressed. Soon the
Ishmaelites were to be found in every household, in every
mosque, in the court of the Sultan himself. The millennium
seemed to be at hand.

Instead, the Ishmaelites were faced with savage repres-
sion. The powers in the world united to stamp out the
heresy. Hundreds were crucified, thousands imprisoned.
Sa'di learned what it was to live in hiding, eating berries
from brambles by the wayside, begging a cup of water
from householders who chased him from their doors. Yet
even this he could bear, for the sake of the ineffable
teaching. It was the assassinations that sickened him in the
end.

For some reason he could never understand, the King-
dom of God could never be realized on earth until the
Kingdom of man was destroyed. Or so the Imam said.
One after another, the enemies of the Imam were marked

down for death. The hashishin were expertly trained in this grisly work, they could pass through impregnable walls, they could find their victims anywhere, no one was safe against them. Such was the law of the Imam. But it was a law of death, not a law of life. That was the mystery.

Was the Imam wrong? Sa'di avoided that thought with exquisite care. Instead, he dwelt on the idea of another Imam who should appear in the fullness of time to "lead his people in the path that was right and not in the path of error." He wondered what his Sign would be ... was he waiting for a stranger to Islam, a man without a past, but with the simplicity of a child? Perhaps that was what all Islam waited for—a simpleton of God, who should be guided by him, Master Sa'di!

The Master of the Dervishes was smiling a little as a novice approached and whispered in his ear.

"Well, well," said the Master, "admit him. Do not keep my pupil waiting."

The novice admitted the pupil who was al-Adil, returned from the Jebel Bahra, to ask after Master Sa'di. Al-Adil liked to keep up the fiction that he was a postulant, sitting at the feet of the Master, a fiction that flattered and gratified the old man.

The novice had removed the Emir's cloak, replacing it with the white wool robe of the dervishes; he strapped on the dancing slippers with the hard, flat toes and placed the ascetic skullcap on the Emir's head.

Al-Adil bowed, touching his right hand to his head, then to his heart. Silently, he sat down in the cross-legged posture of the pupil facing the Master. For a long time no word was exchanged; only a fly buzzed erratically in the late autumn sunshine. The Master pulled a few times on his pipe and then put it aside.

"You are restless today, my son," he said at last, although al-Adil had scarcely moved. "Only in perfect stillness can the spirit find release."

"I am sorry, master," replied al-Adil.

"Perhaps if you tell what is troubling you, your spirit can be liberated."

"My trouble, Master—is myself. Who am I, after all—if I knew that, I would be at peace. This cursed memory of mine—I struggle with it, I plead with it. I creep up on it and try to surprise it—but it tells me nothing. Nothing but a ridiculous tale of a man without a country—you know it all, I've told you everything. But why does the story begin in the middle, with no beginning? Before that, there must have been another life that haunts my sleep. But when I wake, it is gone like quicksilver. How can I be at peace if I don't know who I really should be?"

"And what is he called, this 'I' you speak of?"

"I—why, I am al-Adil!"

"And when al-Adil looks in a mirror, what does he see—a great Emir, heir of the Imam, God's vice-regent on earth, whose nod is life and death? Lies! Does he see a slave, naked, in chains, sold in the slave khan for a hundred pieces of gold? More lies! Al-Adil is not this."

After some moments of silence, his pupil asked softly, "What then am I, Master?"

The master said, "For half my life I sought to unite myself with God. I looked in my mirror and said, "Who is this worm called Sa'di?" I rejected him, I cast him off as a snake casts off its skin.

"Then one day, during the scared dance, I received my illumination. I saw the terms 'I' and 'God' were a denial of the unity of God. I ceased from that moment to think of myself apart from God. When I danced, God danced. Now I am no more. I have vanished."

After another long pause his pupil spoke again. "And when you look in the mirror now, what do you see—nothing?"

"Everything!"

"Can a man, then, become—can he be—?"

"Be silent! A great dervish, al-Hallaj, once uttered the words which you would thoughtlessly say. For this he was crucified."

His pupil thought a while, then asked, "What did al-Hallaj say?"

"Hallaj said:

'I am He whom I love and He whom I love is I,
We are two spirits dwelling in one body:
If thou seest me thou seest Him,
And if thou seest Him, thou seest us both.' "

"And for this he was crucified?"

"The world was not ready for God. That is why we are at war with the world."

"And who can overcome the world?"

"Only a man who is himself the Living God. Such are the True Imams. For many years they have been hidden from us, but now they will be revealed again. The springtime of the world returns when God is resurrected among His Creation . . ."

"Is it the time of Resurrection, Master?"

"The Resurrection is at hand. A new Imam shall arise who will replace the Law of Death with the Law of Life. And then—"

A gong sounded in the depths of the building. The Master faltered a moment, his attention fixed on the fly which was crawling across the gilt letters on the ceiling.

"And then?" prompted al-Adil.

But the room was filling rapidly with novices in their white robes, who took up places on the dancing floor with arms outstretched at intervals equally spaced between them, so that their fingers barely touched and they seemed to fill the entire floor space. A group of musicians sat down in the balcony and began to play on their reed flutes and drums. The air was charged with expectation, but no one moved, and still the drumming grew louder, and even Master Sa'di brought down his gaze from the ceiling and gazed over the hall with an air of wondering anticipation, and the drumming increased in volume until al-Adil, overcome with restlessness, stood up and took a few steps down onto the floor.

At that moment, first one, then another of the dervishes began to turn. They turned very slowly, rigidly upright like mechanical dolls, and the movement filled their skirts and their sleeves with air so that they stood out stiff and

board-like from their bodies. The only movement was
made by the feet, as one toe pushed the floor and the
other acted as the pivot. The eyes of the dervishes remained open, but they were unseeing, the pupils dilated
with hashish.

Now all the dervishes in the hall were turning—except
al-Adil. For a moment he looked uncertainly at the Master who gave him a little nod of encouragement, and then,
almost instinctively, without any clear intention, his body
began to turn. It was surprisingly easy. The drumming
faded and was succeeded by a rushing sound in his ears,
there was a moment of intense pain in his forehead and
then, suddenly—peace. A great peace in which he seemed
to float free of himself, a disembodied soul on its journey
to the Infinite.

Al-Adil was restless and could not sleep. By day he had
danced with the dervishes; that night he was found in the
Tavern of the Golden Cockerel, with his friends Salah and
Ishak, drinking beer. A struggle had begun in his soul between the claims of the world-to-be and the world-as-it-
was. It was his effort to reconcile the two that caused his
restlessness.

He sat in Salah's balcony above the tavern floor, with a
good view of Jullanar, the so-called "Pomegranate
Flower." His bodyguard, Abdullah, was sitting on the floor
watching the performance. He was dressed like his master
in a dirty jubbeh that gave no hint of badge or rank. Abdulla had his doubts about these nocturnal forays but did
not presume to question his master. He merely narrowed
his eyes and kept his hand on his dagger.

As she danced, the Pomegranate Flower turned herself
toward the balcony and loosened her dress so that her
breasts were shaken free by the rhythm of the dance. She
was beautiful and she knew it; her movements were as
graceful as the oriental willow; and her eyes—what said
the poet of her eyes? "God said to them, Be—and they
were, affecting men's hearts with the potency of wine."

Salah, to whom her attention was directed, was not

insensitive to her charms. A dark, intense young man, below average height, he was accustomed to attracting attention. On his simple, black soldier's tunic he wore no badge of rank, he carried no weapon except a dagger, no rings bejewelled his hands. Despite his simplicity, there was a royalty about him which made men (and women) look at him with awe, as though they could guess his destiny. And the dark young man reciprocated by smiling a little apologetically, as though to beg the world not to give away his secret.

Salah knew the eyes of the dancer were on him, but he pretended not to notice. Indeed he resorted to his favorite diversion—talking. When he talked, in his low, softly modulated voice, he made all things seem sweetly reasonable, even the most extreme. At the moment, he was praising the beauty of war. War for him was sweeter than love, and yet not entirely different from it, just another kind of ecstasy.

"That moment, when I had my sword at his throat," he was saying, "was the best in my life. He was not my enemy, he was my friend; he showed me the way to glory! 'Submit to Islam!' I cried. If he had submitted, I should have hated him, but he did not, he cried, 'I spit on your Prophet!' and I loved him for it and killed him with joy."

"Who was he, this infidel?" al-Adil asked.

"A Christian dog, peace be with him," replied Salah. "It was on one of my uncle Shirkuh's campaigns against the unbelievers. I tell you, I love these unbelievers because they give us the chance of glory. There is no glory in these bitter feuds among Moslems. The Danishmend Emirs against the atabegs of Aleppo, the Caliph of Baghdad against the Caliph of Cairo, the True Believers against the Ishmaelite heretics—there is no glory there! Only shame, shame to Islam!"

There was a burst of applause from the floor as the Pomegranate Flower completed her act, and she cast a triumphant look at the gallery. Salah, distracted from his thought, paused and threw a flower from the serving table

onto the tavern floor. "How beautiful she is," he said
abstractedly.

"What remedy, Salah, do you propose?" asked al-Adil.

"For beauty? A night in her arms!" laughed Salah.

"No, I mean for Islam."

"A jehad! A holy war—it is the only way," Salah replied quickly. "Then all our divisions will be healed. We
will unite under the single banner of Islam, and destroy
our enemies, even as the Prophet, on whom let there
be peace, destroyed the unbelievers at the battle of Badr.
Think of it! A united force of twenty million Moslems
from Samarkand to Castile—one Law, one Prophet, one
God!"

The lights were extinguished; men on the floor returned
to their cups; the dancer had disappeared. Al-Adil replied
to Salah, "But how are men to be united?"

"By brotherhood. Listen Ad'l," Salah said, using his favorite nickname, "we are not alone. We who believe God's
justice on earth, have many friends, if only we find them
and bring them together. We are a great brotherhood, the
Just Brotherhood, and when we act together, who can
stand against us? I have heard you say a hundred times
how you hate to see the strong oppress the weak—the
great emirs who swallow up the little emirs—the rich merchants who extort from the poor—the slave-masters who
fatten on human flesh—and all the while God's people are
being destroyed by these maggots. But we are not like
that—you and I and Ishak and ten thousand more—we
are not all maggots. A dozen times a day, my men come
to me and they say 'Master, only let us fight for a just
cause, and we will follow you to the ends of the earth!'
They are my Ikwan, my Brotherhood. And someday I
mean to lead my Moslem brothers into battle. That will be
the only battle worth fighting!" He looked shrewdly at al-
Adil. "Don't you agree, Ad'l?"

"Yes," replied al-Adil slowly, "I agree that all men
should be brothers. But you will have to kill many, first,
Salah. Is it worth that price?"

"Did the Prophet, on whom let there be peace, ask that

question at the battle of Badr? With three hundred he conquered a thousand! The belief is all."

"But if others believe differently—"

Salah grew flushed and angry. "One Law, one Prophet, one God!" he shouted, half rising.

His friend Ishak took him by the arm, forcing him back to his seat. "Calm yourself, Salah, we are friends. Aren't we, Ad'l?"

But al-Adil was looking elsewhere. Unobserved, the Pomegranate Flower had entered the balcony at the back and slipped down on to the divan beside Salah, taking his hand in the shadows, and whispering in his ear.

"Thank you," she said. "It is long since you have come to me, beloved."

She ran her fingers through his thick, black hair and leaned across his breast, looking up into his face. How could he resist her? He did not try. They kissed in the dark.

"I shall be waiting for you tonight," she said, stroking his cheek with the back of her hand.

"But I am with my friends."

"Bring your friends. We'll have a party together."

"Not I," said al-Adil. "That is—you see—well, I am to be married."

The others leaped up in astonishment.

"Why did you not tell us?"

"All the more reason to celebrate."

"Fill the cups. Kiss him, Jullenar!"

Embarrassed, al-Adil submitted to their raillery.

After the tavern closed, the three friends, somewhat tipsily, roamed together in search of the street of the Pomegranate Flower, followed at a short distance by al-Adil's faithful shadow, Abdulla. The city lay in utter darkness, lit only by the round, luminous orb of the moon, that bathed the narrow, twisted streets in a strong white light, picking out the rows of overhanging balconies and projecting windows with their fantastic ornaments and cupolas. The streets between their narrow walls were pitch black, and most men abroad at night employed a torch-bearer to light the way among the tethered donkeys, carts, slop-piles and sleeping ruffians. Salah and his friends employed no torch-bearer, however, for their errand was, if not irregular, at least out-of-bounds for officers in the Sultan's army.

The house of the Pomegranate Flower was enclosed in a forecourt, entered through a plain wooden door in the adobe wall. Standing back, Salah threw a handful of stones over the wall, so that they rattled on the ground in the inner court. After a long pause, there was a whistling sound, as though a rope had been thrown down from the top of the wall. Instead of a rope to climb, it was a noose with a slip-knot that fell neatly over Salah and Ishak who were standing close together. Al-Adil, warned by Abdulla, slipped outside the circle of the noose just in time. In an instant, four or five men leaped down from the wall and set upon their victims. Immediately, al-Adil noticed that they wore the white woolen robes of the hashishin.

"In the name of Ali!" he shouted. The assailants froze, knives poised in the air. Boldly, al-Adil strode forward and tore open his short, plain surcoat, displaying beneath a coat of mail, emblazoned with the arms of the Rashid Ali palace.

"These are my friends," he said, "I bid you release them!"

The hashishin bowed to the ground. "O, Emir, to hear is to obey!"

Struggling and protesting, the victims were freed and the attackers took to their heels. Ishak was particularly indignant.

"A trap!" he said. "He led us into a trap! These men are his assassins!"

"Peace, Ishak," replied Salah. "He has saved our lives. Ad'l is not to blame for this. I cannot say so much for the little Flower—"

They looked up at the silent house. By its very muteness it seemed to confess its guilt. Certainly, Jullenar would have looked out, unless she was part of the plot.

"But why—?" asked al-Adil of the echoing night.

"It is a blow against the Ikwan," said Salah, "not against any of us. They mean to destroy the Brotherhood before it destroys them. But we must not destroy one another, because we love one another, don't we, Ad'l?" And he threw wide his arms.

"Oh, Salah," said al-Adil sorrowfully, "I have not told you all. I am not just a soldier in The Ishmaeli Palace. I am the Imam-to-be—"

"No need—no need—I knew everything!" replied Salah. "My Brotherhood kept me informed! It helped me to know you better. From now on we must not be parted. Together we can save Islam. I want you to meet my uncle, Shirkuh. He is very clever man, a great general—you will have much to say to each other—"

Arm in arm, the friends passed along the silent street, leaving the dark house alone in the moonlight.

The day set by the astrologers for the union of al-Adil and Yasmin caused a stir in many streets and households of Damascus far removed from the Rashid Ali palace. In the Street of Confectioners, boys plied the bellows from early morning, as cooks thickened the treacle over their fires to make the kataif, or sweet pastries, furnished as a gift for the wedding tables. The apprentices kneaded the flour and water and rolled the pancakes thin as paper to be baked on copper trays. Then the chief chef added the treacle and honey, sesame oil and ambergris, and some even perfumed their concoctions with musk. "Who is the kataif for?" cried the passers by, smelling the sweet odors issuing from the shops, and this gave the confectioners the opportunity to pass on the news: "Didn't you know? Today the Ishmaeli Emir weds the Princess of Masyaf!"

In the early afternoon, after the siesta, the Princess Yasmin emerged from the portal of the Rashid Ali palace, surrounded by her ladies in waiting. She seemed paler than usual, though this might have been caused by the effect of her ice-blue dress that shimmered with silver thread, like sparkling hoar frost under an azure sky. To those who saw her, she was an enchanted Princess: smaller than the authentic standards of beauty required, her lips not so broad, her breasts not so full (she refused to use artifice as other ladies did), with a doe-like perfection that took one's breath away. So slender were her wrists which peeped out of the hanging scarves across her arms, so delicate was the neck with only a ribbon for ornament, so exquisite was the modelling of her head under the white turban supporting the marriage crown—she appeared too frail for mortal love. A burst of applause broke out in the street at her appearance. Then her ladies threw over her head—almost pretending to have forgotten it in time—the izar veil that covered her from crown to foot, but made of such a transparent tissue that one could still see her smile gently and a little shyly before she stepped into her litter.

The marriage procession set out: three litters at first, then more and more—for they kept stopping at houses along the way where they were joined by other ladies who had accepted the invitations to present the bride to her husband. Solemnly, the guests each kissed the bride on both cheeks—she leaned out of her litter and lifted her izar just enough for this—mounted their own litters, and took their place in the swaying, glittering, bedizened equipage that threaded the souks and narrow streets of the city. A horde of merry clowns from the Street of Sideshows danced eagerly in front of the procession, including one dwarf who carried an enormous plate on the end of a pole without once letting it fall. The guards of the Rashid Ali palace walked alongside the litters holding aloft their jewelled scimitars and behind came the emissaries of all the souks, bearing their wedding gifts, discreetly advertising their wares.

All afternoon the procession wended its way through the streets, growing a little longer all the time, until it arrived at the home of the bridegroom. Since the latter resided at the same palace as his bride, there was an air of fiction about all this, but color had been given to the ceremony by setting out at the east wing and ending at the west wing. Bright rugs hung from all the windows of the palace, and a carpet stretched all the way from the street to the Great Hall.

In the Hall the guests assembled: on the lower level, the commoners sat on the floor with their gifts before them, on the next level, the noble ladies reclined on divans placed against the walls, while on the topmost level, the Princess sat upon the throne, attended by her ladies-in-waiting. Eunuchs came and went, carrying trays of sherberts and candied fruits, while from behind a fret-work screen at the left side of the throne, an orchestra of lute players and singers entertained the guests.

Still the bridegroom did not come. The Emir al-Adil had left the palace early to join his friends, Lieutenants Salah and Ishak at the officers' mess. There he passed the time in company with the Sultan's officers at an entertainment of acrobats and mummers, especially engaged for the occasion. All the acts bore some ribald allusion to the imminent consummation of marriage and brought roars of laughter to the throng sitting on their heels in the mess hall, and some embarrassment to the guest of honor on his divan in the front rank. Al-Adil buried his blushes in the common cup which was passed from hand to hand—but sparingly, because it was recognized to be bad form for the bridegroom to drink too deeply.

At last the voices of the muezzins were heard crying the evening prayer and the company broke up, with Salah and Ishak and some of their men accompanying al-Adil to the Great Mosque. An autumn twilight, smoky and blue, had fallen on the streets, and soldiers of the Sultan accompanied the wedding party, carrying cressets, poles with cylindrical frames of iron at the top filled with flaming wood. The ancient courtyard of the Mosque was a pool of darkness, shut in by the grey walls of the colonnades on four sides, in the shadows of which the torchbearers stood, their cressets flaring. In the open prayer space, al-Adil and his friends repeated the prayers of two rekkas and listened to the exhortation of the preacher before taking their leave.

They proceeded through the darkened streets to the Ishmaeli palace, where the lights and female voices in the Great Hall announced the presence of the bride and her party. Standing in the courtyard, the Emir bade his friends goodbye.

"May God give you happiness!" said Salah, as they embraced.

"May God grant our reunion!" replied al-Adil.

Then, after making a gift of gold to the soldiers, the bridegroom leaped up the stairs of the west wing, to his apartments on the upper floor. The room was bright with candles, that cast a flickering glow on a scene of opulence: the floor was set with low tables of inlaid wood, each surrounded with cushions as for a banquet; the walls were hung with tapestries of gold-embroidered silk; and at the upper end there was a divan of alabaster, wide enough for two persons to sit upon, canopied over with red satin and surmounted by the arms of the Ishmaeli palace.

Waiting servants removed al-Adil's cloak and tunic and brought him the bridegroom's robe of honor, made of yellow gold like his hair and beard, so that it seemed like a marriage of the sun and moon. Impatiently, he sent for the overseer of the household. This was none other than Mesroor. Reprieved from shame, and reinstated in the Emir's favor, he proudly bore his master's summons to his mistress.

The bridegroom had sent for his bride. Yasmin rose swiftly, like a bird about to take flight. All the ladies rose with her. She mounted the stairs to the upper room, and there the company was taken by surprise. At the top stood the bridegroom, his arms outstretched to his bride. This was a breach with custom so great that everyone stood still in astonishment, except Yasmin, who continued to advance toward her husband. As she reached him, he caught her hand impetuously and knelt to kiss the tiny palm.

Out of what dim memory this alien act arose, no one could guess; only Yasmin knew, as she looked down, her eyes brimming, and she took from her bosom a white rose which ⸱he inserted into the folds of his turban. Then the vision faded; the knight of the rose melted into the

Saracen Emir, who took his place cross-legged on the divan while his wife, surrounded by her women and guests, stood demurely before him.

"Will it please my lord to look upon his bride?" asked the ladies in waiting.

Gravely he nodded, and the tire-women lifted off the long veil, the crown and the turban of white silk from her head. Her dark hair tumbled down about her shoulders and partly hid her blushes. Actually, she was trembling and tears ran down her face. Like any Eastern bride, whose husband looks on her for the first time, she feared she would find no favor in his eyes. This was the way they enacted the fiction of their "first meeting." As though to bear it out, al-Adil studied her features awhile in silence before saying quietly, "It is well."

Then Yasmin knelt and he laid his hand upon her head as he pronounced the customary words: "O God, bless me in my wife and bless my wife in me. Bestow upon me by her and bestow on her by me. Unite us, as thou hast united, happily, and separate us, when thou separatest, happily!" Then, from the pocket in his belt, he took two identical ruby rings, and placed one on her hand and one on his own. And he kissed her.

Everyone burst into applause; the bride took her place on the divan beside the bridegroom; the musicians played their gayest tunes on pipes and tambourines; the servants rushed in carrying huge silver trays on their heads, heaped with foods—a dozen baked sheep, fowls, chickens and young pigeons, all heaped with cakes of bread and rice. There were also two great piles of sweets carried in by porters with shoulder poles; and all was set down on the floor where the guests sat upon cushions, cross-legged or with one knee raised, with napkins before them. Servitors, with napkins on their arms and carrying ewers and basins, washed the right hands of the company, and a glad murmur filled the room as the customary refrain rose to the lips of all before eating: "In the name of God, the Compassionate, the Merciful."

The wedding ceremony was complete. It would be

hours yet before the last guests rose from their places, murmuring "Praise be to God," politely belching behind their hands, and took their leave. But by custom the bridal pair were the first to withdraw. "May God be well-pleased with you!" cried some, while others more softly murmured, "May the elect of God be exalted to glory!" And turning with a slight smile, the Emir replied, "May our night be blessed!" After that, the principal guests left also, and only the commoners rushed in to finish off the leavings, until they fell asleep and the butter candles guttered in their dishes and the dogs slunk out of their corners to eat the scraps and bones among the sleepers on the floor.

Meanwhile, unmarked by any, the taciturn Abdulla unwound his turban and folded it for a pillow, as he lay across the door of the bridal chamber.

CHAPTER NINE

SALAH-ED-DIN

"The reasons for an attack on Egypt are these: first, the Caliphate in Cairo is sick unto death and the boy Caliph is an idiot; second, the road to Egypt lies open, the Sinai Peninsula is unguarded by the Christians who as usual are quarreling among themselves, and we could easily slip through the desert unseen; third, His Highness, the Sultan, wants Cairo as another conquest to wear in his crown."

The speaker was General Shirkuh, a short, ugly, rotund man with a very red face, whose coarseness revealed his base birth, even by the way he rode in the saddle, with his feet dangling as though he were astride a donkey. But he was a born commander whose men would follow him anywhere.

Despite the universal confidence the General inspired, his nephew, Salah-ed-Din was troubled by his words. They rode side by side upon the desert where the General's troops were holding autumn maneuvers. The plain before Damascus was black with squadrons of men, mounted on swift Arabian horses, shouting their war cries and throwing their spears in the air amid clouds of dust.

"What I mean, uncle," Salah said crossly as they

dismounted, "is—why Egypt? We should be spending our blood on the Christians, not on brother Moslems. This is why the Unbelievers have succeeded in wresting Jerusalem from us and why the Holy Mosque of Omar and the very rock of the Prophet's ascension are in infidel hands. It is all our fault because we have fought one another."

Shirkuh turned toward him—he was blind in one eye and had to look his interlocutor in the face. "Your zeal is commendable, young man," he croaked, "but your intelligence needs sharpening. So long as Islam is divided, we cannot crush the Christians.

"Besides," Skirkuh began animatedly to describe marks with his riding crop in the sand, "Look here—once we are in Cairo, we have the Christians caught in the jaws of a nutcracker. We can launch a fleet from the Egyptian Delta that will blockade all the ports on the Syrian coast. That means no supplies will reach the Christian princes. They depend on men and materials from Europe; they cannot live off the land, as we do. That is their weakness. So we cut their life line from Cairo *like that*, and then we attack overland from Damascus, *like this!*"

Salah began to understand. "Then the Moslems will all be united in the end?" he said.

"Yes." Shirkuh's face darkened, and he glanced sideways at his nephew a little uncertainly. "But we have some unfinished business to do first. We cannot march to Egypt so long as our rear is endangered."

"Endangered by whom?" Salah was also uneasy.

"By your friends, the Ishmaelites. They have great influence, my boy. They are not what you think. They do not seek after riches, or honor, or glory, as we do. If they cannot win all, they will destroy all, completely, utterly. Don't you see what that means? It is the end of the world.

"If we attack Cairo, they will strike our rear, unless we eliminate them first." He paused to look at his nephew. "You are startled, my boy. You must be firm! Nothing must stand in the way of victory for our master, the Sultan—not even friendship!"

Salah's face had darkened into a scowl. He was pacing

up and down like a leopard. "It is not a question of friendship," he spluttered. "I believe there is another way—a better way than slaughter. We can win them to our side."

"Never!" the General faced him squarely. "You can make no pact with the devil! Oh, I know what you would say—he is no devil, this Emir of yours, he is gentle, he is noble, he is wise—I do not deny it. Did I not invite him and his Princess here to see our maneuvers as you wished? But what you do not see is that he may be used by others for their plots, in order to throw dust in our eyes. Let me caution you, therefore, against anything you may say regarding our plans for Egypt—"

"Uncle, whatever you think of my judgment, you know I am loyal."

"And therefore I shall keep nothing from you, not even—See here, my boy, there is something you don't know, something I will show you when we return to our tents. No more now—here are your friends!"

In the distance the Emir al-Adil and the Princess Yasmin, each on horseback, began mounting the knoll where the General and his nephew stood. The newlyweds rode side by side, holding hands and looking into each other's eyes as though they were alone in the midst of this armed camp. They were so engrossed that they did not see Shirkuh waving to them.

"Come up, come up," the Commander boomed, "you'll have the best view up here. What a splendid maneuver that was—did you see how the smaller force, my faithful Ortoquids, split the larger force of Circassians? But then, these white mercenaries are all barbarians." He glanced covertly at his fair-haired guest, but there was no reaction. The Ishmaeli pair appeared charmed with everything they saw—and especially with one another—and they all rode off sociably together.

Later that night in his bedouin tent, Shirkuh sat brooding heavily. How many of these men could he really trust? he wondered. That was the trouble in these accursed times. You did not know if your best friend was one of "them"—

"Stay with me tonight," he muttered softly to Salah. He nodded to his police chief. "Also you, Kashkan." He dismissed the rest with a curt nod.

The Commander kept his dark thoughts to himself for a few minutes before he spoke. "Kashkan, you have brought the file I asked for?"

"I have brought it, O master."

"Then you may read it aloud. I want my nephew to hear."

Impassively, the police chief drew a parchment from the bosom of his jubbeh. He began to read in a toneless voice. "The so-called Emir of the Ishmaelites has been traced to a certain Abdi, a slave merchant in Damascus who sold him one year ago to the Princess of Masyaf for one hundred gold dinars. The said Abdi bought him from the household of the late Governor Ibn ed Daya of Aleppo. He was sold immediately following the Governor's mysterious suicide, and it is thought he may have had something to do with his death. The Governor obtained him as a slave from the prisoner-of-war camp at Moab, directly across the frontier from Nablus. It is believed that he was taken prisoner during a raid on the Frankish Castle of Shechem several years ago, and there was a story told that he was, in fact, the lord of Shechem himself. This story is discounted inasmuch as he was the only prisoner in the raid and it seems highly improbable that the lord alone of all his men should have been captured. His captors probably concocted the story in order to get a good price for him. Another peculiar fact about the prisoner is that he appeared to have suffered amnesia as a result of a fall into the moat, and he steadfastly maintained his ignorance about his past even under torture. Nothing, therefore, has been learned about his antecedents, except that he is indisputably a Frank, probably a spy, now masquerading as an Ishmaeli Emir."

"It is a lie," Salah cried. "I give my body as his surety!"

"Easy, Salah, easy," the Commander said gently. "I did

not say I have accepted the police report. I respect Kashkan's research and reasoning. I listen to what he says. It is always good to listen. Never close your ears to the sound of danger. The young Emir may be innocent. He may really have lost his memory. He may not be an Ishmaeli at all. But don't you see, Salah—he is not one of us! He is an Unbeliever!"

Having given his report, the police chief withdrew, leaving uncle and nephew together. Salah appeared on the verge of tears. He plunged his face in his hands, saying over and over, "I trusted him! I trusted him!"

Shirkuh studied him with the beginning of a smile. "Take heart, boy. We may find a use for him yet. After all, he is the Imam's heir. He has great influence with his people, I am told. Performs miracles and impresses them. But if you could persuade him to hold the Imam's hand, while we attack Egypt—"

Salah looked up. "If Ad'l were Imam—"

The sentence remained suspended in the air while a long thought took shape in both minds. They turned it over in silence. The Commander was the first to find words.

"The trials of Chinese fire are tomorrow. The Emir must be given the seat of honor," Skirkuh said softly. "He may be impressed with its—possibilities."

"The very thing. He has often spoken of the 'science' of war. Perhaps he will find a scientific use for his new weapon—"

"Masyaf could be blown sky high with Chinese fire," Skirkuh added.

"You cannot blow up an idea, of course," Salah was playing the devil's advocate.

"Of course not," the Commander said smoothly. "That's why I have been against a frontal attack on the Imam at Masyaf. He has too many followers outside. But if we were to put the fuse in the hands of the next Imam—"

"Because he himself wants to work with us for the unity of Islam—"

"The difficulty will be to convince the Sultan. His Highness is determined to cradicate the heretics—"

"Unless a new Imam brings his people back to the fold of orthodoxy—"

"You must send the Emir a robe of honor and an invitation to our little demonstration tomorrow. I want to talk to the next Imam of Masyaf." Shirkuh chuckled.

A splendid pavilion had been erected on the height of land overlooking the plain where the maneuvers had been held. Inside the open tent were two royal divans covered with silken rugs, where the Commander, the Emir, his bride, and the other guests sat. The Commander reclined on the lower of the divans while his nephew Salah stood beside him. Salah looked impatient.

Overnight the army had erected a huge stone pyramid nearly fifty feet high. The joints had been sealed with mortar and a large tunnel had been dug underneath. A fuse had been laid in the tunnel leading to a command post some distance away.

When everything was ready, signals were relayed by hand from the command post to the Commander's pavilion. The troops on the plain drew back several hundred yards while an engineer lit a fuse which began to race through the tunnel.

The Commander, looking deceptively relaxed, had kept up a running commentary. "Your Highnessess will observe," he said looking keenly into the faces of his guests, "that the pyramid of stone is thick enough and heavy enough to withstand the heaviest of mangonels. By tunneling under it, and putting a sufficient quantity of black powder in the tunnel we shall be able to destroy this formidable edifice in the twinkling of an eye. With this weapon Islam shall triumph to the ends of the earth!"

A dull explosion ripped up the ground around the pyramid and a tongue of flame shot out of the tunnel, singeing the hands and faces of the men stationed at the command post. But the pyramid still stood. The engineers shouted at one another and rushed up to examine the site of the blast.

The Emir jumped up and strode out on to the field. "Your explosion," he told the Chief Engineer, "will only be effective if it is in a confined space. The tunnel is too large. Let the fuse be encased in reeds and buried in sand. The sand will close up behind it as it burns and when it reaches the chamber the explosion will be completely sealed."

The engineer listened dumbfounded, his reputation at stake. The only possible way to retrieve it was to accept the advice. If it failed again, at least he would not be to blame. He ordered his men to follow the Emir's directions and when the new charge and fuse were laid, the Emir returned to his place in the pavilion.

This time there was a tremendous explosion, ripping the pyramid apart and hurling the stones many feet into the air. Everyone cheered, the officers applauded, and the Commander took al-Adil's hand in his.

"My congratulations, Highness," he said, "Your explosion has carried away the prize. Where did you learn the secrets of Chinese fire?"

"I know no secrets, Commander," replied al-Adil. "I seem to have some instinct for engineering—I don't know where it comes from. But it interests me greatly, this black powder of yours. I see immense possibilities for it."

"I thought you might. It—could be possible to—use it in many places?"

"It is not *where* you use it, that I mean—it's *how* you use it. The explosion you have just achieved is very impressive—but, well, purely static. It relies on the undirected outward thrust of the exploding chemicals. But what if this explosion were to take place in a specially constructed weapon, say, a tube open at one end, just as the first tunnel under the pyramid was open at the front? Thus, the force of the explosion could be directed toward any object at which the tube was pointed. You might shoot projectiles that way . . ."

Though perhaps neither the speaker nor his listener understood the full ramifications of what they were talking about, Shirkuh grasped the general idea. He was overawed, but all he said, after a silence, was: "In the name of God, the Compassionate, the Merciful—are you our friend?"

"I am Salah's friend," answered al-Adil gravely, "and his friends are mine, also."

After another pause, the Commander said thoughtfully, trying not to betray the excitement he felt, "I think your idea may change history. We must try to work together to perfect it.

"And what are you two plotting?" the Princess said gaily, coming up behind them, fluttering her ostrich fan. "Does my husband not remember his promise to talk no business for a full month after our wedding night?"

Salah joined the laughter. "You should put no faith in husbands, Highness. Only bachelors like me are to be trusted."

The Princess tapped his cheek with the fan and glanced at her husband, still conversing with the Commander. "I suppose men must set the world to rights before they remember their women—unless they blow us up first. But, at least, I know where gallantry is to be found," she smiled graciously at him.

Salah bowed and kissed her hand.

Two weeks later, other news came to al-Adil that disturbed him greatly. Several messages from the Jebel Bahra told of increased harassment by the Sultan's forces. One day a street vendor came to the Ishmaeli palace selling oil. He disclosed himself as a dervish who was the last survivor of a mission from the Imam which had been cut to pieces. Masyaf, he said, was now besieged.

The Emir was furious. How could this have happened with no warning from Salah? That night, he paced his apartment, overwhelmed with grief and frustration. A knock at the door brought him an unexpected visitor in the person of Master Sa'di.

The Master of the Dervishes addressed al-Adil with greater than usual reverence. "O Prince," he said, touching his fingers to the floor, "I bring you news of great gladness. I have dreamed!"

"Dreamed, Master Sa'di?"

"A dream, Highness, of such sweetness and potency as no man has dreamed since the night when our Lord Muhammad rose from the earth on his ride through the seven heavens! I have seen—oh, my lord!—I have seen the sign of Him who is to come!"

"What is the sign, Master Sa'di?"

"Let me tell you first how this dream came to me. I was with the dervishes at the noon prayers. When the dancing began, I heard a voice that said to me, very close to my ear, 'Sa'di, today you shall dance again!' 'Lord,' I said—for I knew it was the Most High who spoke—'Lord, I am not able. It is long since I danced. I have not the purity of spirit.' And again the Voice said most terribly, even as It spoke to our Lord Muhammad, when It commanded him to write the Glorious Koran—'Dance!' said the Voice.

"All trembling, I obeyed. And with the first step, I was whirled away into the regions of bliss, among His Chosen Ones, who can do no wrong.

"They were all there, the most holy Imams—Ali, and al Hasan, and al Husayn, and al Zayn, and Muhammad al Bazir, and Jafar, and Ismael,—and after them were seven more whose faces were veiled, being the hidden Imams who remained unknown until the coming of the true Imam. And then again appeared the Imam who is to be, whose face was as bright as the sun, shining all fair and golden, and mounted on a black horse like the Prophet's on his night ride. And as soon as my eyes saw him I knew him and I fell on my face and worshipped him, for I knew the Resurrection had come!"

The Master of the Dervishes, overcome by his revelation, tottered and fell, lying face down and prostrate on the floor. The Emir, bemused, looked silently down on the messenger of God for a long time. At last he said, "You spoke of a sign, Master Sa'di. What sign was this?"

The dervish moaned and addressed the floor. "A sign

not to be mistaken, O Prince. Before my vision faded, I saw the Imam depart, for he rode away through the seventh heaven above me, and a fleck of foam fell from the jaws of his horse at my feet. From this droplet, there sprang a rose."

"You saw this in your dream?" asked al-Adil.

"I saw it in my dream, Highness, and I found it at my feet when I awoke."

"Show me this rose."

The aged dervish lifted himself humbly to his knees, and, reaching into his breast, he drew out a tiny rosebud of purest white and he handed to his master.

"This is not the season of roses, Master Sa'di," said al-Adil gently, taking it in his hand.

"It is not," replied the dervish.

"And why have you given it to me?"

"Because it is yours, O Prince."

"Mine?"

"It sprang from the sweat of your lordship's horse."

"Master Sa'di—I—"

They stared at each other in silence. Then the Emir dropped the rose and plunged his face in his hands.

"I conjure you, Master Sa'di," he said, "to say nothing of this to anyone. Nothing! Not a word!"

"On my head be my lord's commands," said the dervish. Then, almost pleading, he went on, "Let my lord remember that what is revealed by the Most High cannot be hid. The hour of the Resurrection has come. From this moment the will of God is revealed to men through His Most Holy Imam. If the Imam says 'Peace,' there will be peace. If he says 'Destroy', the earth will be destroyed. Legion upon legion of the faithful await your command. Speak, O Prince, and may your utterance be according to the true doctrine, the Doctrine of Love—."

"But, Master Sa'di, the Imam still lives. He is at Masyaf."

The dervish made a gesture of impatience. "The old Imam is superseded by the revelation," he said. "That is why he has been imprisoned at Masyaf. His authority has

been set aside, and his orders may no longer be obeyed.
The era of death is at an end. It is for you to proclaim the
era of everlasting life. Speak, O my Prince; speak and
save your people!"

Abstractedly, al-Adil let him kiss his hand. "Well, well,"
he said, "you have done right to tell me this, Master Sa'di.
Now go and say nothing of this to any man until I bid
you. Go!"

The dervish bowed his head to the ground, and before
he rose, he managed to let fall a small scroll which had
been concealed in his robe. He was nearly to the door before al-Adil noticed it.

"Master Sa'di, wait!" called the Emir. But, with a sur-
prising nimbleness for one of his years, the dervish was
gone.

Al-Adil turned back into the apartment, frowning. He
undid the seals and unrolled the parchment. It bore the
signature of the Imam Rashid Ali and it contained little
more than a list of names, each prefixed by the sign of the
Evil Eye. The list was long, enumerating more than seventy names, among them: The Sultan Nur-ed-Din; the
Crown Prince Ismael; The Commander of the Faithful,
General Shirkuh; his nephew Salah-ed-Din . . .

It was an order of execution. As a rule such orders,
when delivered into the hands of the executioners must be
carried out within forty-eight hours. How many such orders had already been delivered? There was no way to be
sure, but al-Adil knew he must act with speed. Uttering an
oath, he flung himself out the door and awoke Abdulla
outside.

"Go at once to Lieutenant Salah-ed-Din and bid come
here immediately. Lose no time, Abdulla. It is life or
death."

An hour later, Salah-ed-Din, accompanied by Abdulla
entered the Ishmaeli palace by a little-known back way
through the servants' quarters. The hour was past midnight, and in al-Adil's chambers, the coals had burned
low in the fire.

"What is it now, Ad'l," said Salah, smiling, "that will not wait till morning?"

Silently, al-Adil sat by the fire and handed him the parchment. Salah read it without giving any sign of emotion; only the muscle worked quickly in his cheek as he scanned the death list. Then he returned the scroll to his friend.

"How long do we have?" he asked.

"I don't know. This is a master list given me by Master Sa'di. Individual orders are certain to have been issued to every executioner. I saved you before, Salah. This time I can do nothing. Unless—"

"Unless you countermand the order."

"How can I do that, Salah? I am powerless."

"You are the heir—"

"The heir is nothing—"

"Until the crown passes into his hands."

"But the Imam still lives—"

"He is besieged at Masyaf, surrounded by the Sultan's army, and a prisoner cannot act in his own name. When a Prince is incapable of exercising his authority, the authority must devolve upon his heir. That is the law."

"Are you suggesting that I depose the Imam?"

"I suggest that you *are* the Imam!"

It was a moment fraught with fate, and both men seemed to sense this, each in his own way. For Salah it was a matter of reprieve from death, and perhaps for the first time he realized the fragility of human life. He would owe his life not to his own powers but to the will of another.

For al-Adil, the sense of destiny pressed even more heavily. His first thought was to save his friend. But in doing so, he knew he must betray his benefactor, his father-in-law, and his own wife. Involuntarily, he was being swept along by developments far beyond him, leading him toward a role he had no wish to assume, a power almost blasphemous to think about—

"I must speak to Yasmin," he said at last.

Salah looked up, almost as though his verdict had been

given. "Of course," he said. "You will tell the Princess that
no harm will come to her father. I give my word."

"It shall be for her to say."

"Yes, but she will obey, if you command—"

"I will not command. I owe everything to her—"

"So be it. But you will ask?"

"I will ask."

"It is enough."

Through the windows the first light was beginning to
show in the east, and faintly on the morning air the muezzins were sounding the call to prayer: "God is most
great—"

"Listen, Salah," said al-Adil taking him by the arm. "If
I do this thing, I must have your word that the Sultan will
not move against me. Can you give me your assurance—?"

"My uncle will speak to the Sultan. Ad'l, I swear to
you, we mean you no harm."

"Why did you move on Masyaf without telling me?"

"It was by the Sultan's command."

"Then you admit that you cannot speak for the Sultan?"

"He must be convinced!"

"And who will convince him? No, Salah, I will act only
if the Sultan gives me his oath in friendship. No man will
convince the Sultan but myself. You must manage it—"

"It shall be as you say. Wait for a summons from the
Palace. You will not be betrayed."

The two friends embraced quickly and parted.

Immediately afterwards the Emir went straight to the
Princess' apartment. A light was burning inside her door
and the guttering flame flickered through the beaded curtain. When he stepped inside, however, the figure of
Fatima rose up before him.

"No, my lord," she croaked, "you may not come to my
mistress tonight—"

" *May not*, Fatima?"

"It is my mistress' command—"

"Your mistress gives you no such commands for me—"

"In the name of God, master, do not go in!"

Thoroughly alarmed, al-Adil flung himself against the

door of the inner room, when it suddenly opened and the ascetic figure of the dervish appeared, barring the way. Master Sa'di bowed very low, touching the floor with his hands.

"Peace be on my lord, the holy one, the Vice Regent of God—"

"Enough!" cried al-Adil, enraged. "What business have you with my wife?"

"The Princess begs her lord very specifically to excuse her from her duties in attending on him—" Then, as the Emir made a movement to thrust him aside, he shrieked, "Stop, Prince! If you wake her she will die!"

But al-Adil was already in the room. On the large silken mattress, under the vast mosquito net, which had been thrust untidily aside, lay Yasmin, motionless as in a deep sleep, the eyes half open, the pupils turned upward under the lids. Besides the bed stood the hashish pipe, the stem of the pipe still between her fingers. Then, al-Adil understood.

"How long has she been like this?" he asked in a suffocated voice.

"My lord, since the Lieutenant Salah—"

"There must be some reason—what have you told her, old man?"

"She knows everything, Highness,—it was only you who did not know—"

"Know what? Speak or you die!" And in his rage, al-Adil drew his dagger and pressed it to the throat of the dervish.

"That you are Imam!" wailed the old man.

"Then you proclaimed it? Already? Without my permission?" The knife trembled in his hand.

"Aiyee! Spare me, my lord Imam, spare your slave! I had to stop the executions in time. I have sent the order to all dervishes in the country who are under my authority—"

Al-Adil reeled as revelations broke in on him. "Ah, you schemer, Master Sa'di! I see it now. The siege of Masyaf—the dream of the seventh heaven—you and

Salah both knew—you arranged it all! And for what? To make me Imam! Very well, then. I shall be Imam. But listen to me, Master Sa'di, if I am Imam, I shall *be* Imam. I shall be no one's puppet. And when I speak, the earth and all the vile creatures that crawl on it—like yourself, Master Sa'di—shall tremble and obey! Know then, Master Sa'di, it is my will that no harm come to the old man of Masyaf. On your head be it! No more. Go!"

Quaking with fear, the Master of the Dervishes left.

Turning back to the bed, al-Adil sank down beside the sleeping Yasmin. Careful not to wake her, he pressed his lips to her hand, and then, after looking long into her face, he kissed her mouth. There was no response. Yasmin had left him for the efreet. Sadly, he laid his head on her breast. "Yasmin," he murmured, "forgive me!"

Was it imagination or did he feel the touch of her hand upon his hair?

The Palace of the Sultan began to hum like a great hive of bees, when the news spread of the coming of the newly-proclaimed Imam of the Ishmaelites. The gardeners had been at work since early morning planting white lilies in full bloom along the main walks through the Royal gardens. Flag poles ewere erected, each flying the twin flags: black for the Sultan, white for the Imam. The Royal cavalry, mounted on black stallions, lined the triumphal route from the gateway to the audience hall.

Trumpets blew at the gates, announcing the Imam's arrival. The Imam, immaculate in white turban and robes, was met at the gates by a small squad of Royal guards, under the command of Lieutenant Salah-ed-Din. The Lieutenant saluted smartly, and the Imam, smiling faintly, acknowledged his salute with a slight nod. The squad fell in around him, followed by six of the Imam's guards, Master Sa'di and the entire school of dervishes, and last, the somewhat ungainly, peasant figure of Abdulla.

In the audience hall, excitement was feverish, as crowds of onlookers, all wearing the black of orthodoxy, waited for the great confrontation. The secretaries, who had arrived first, managed to have the front positions, standing behind the velvet cords which roped off the central space before the throne. Behind them were the army commanders, the prefect of police and his men, the Grand Cadi and members of the supreme court, the Grand Eunuch and two hundred black eunuchs, and, of course, the one hundred mamelukes who lined the walls with their tall, half-bare bodies covered with iron bracelets, bucklers, shields and scimitars.

The Grand Vizier, Njam-ed-Din Ayub, the father of Salah-ed-Din, and the Commander of the Faithful, General Shirkuh, occupied their appointed stations, the former on the left, the latter on the right of the throne, each accompanied by his secretaries, kneeling beside their *escritoires*. All, including the Sultan himself, Nur-ed-Din the Magnificent, seated cross-legged on the throne of lapis lazuli, rose to their feet when the doors were flung open and the heralds announced: "His Highness, the Most Holy Imam, al-Adil, *styled* the Vice Regent of God."

A thrill of horror at the heretical words went through the room. It was as though the whole splendid edifice had been struck by lightning. A moment later, the two principals faced each other across the room.

Slowly, imperturbably, the Imam approached the throne, followed by the guard commander, Salah-ed-Din, and by Abdulla. The Imam paused a moment at the foot of the dais. Would he, everyone wondered, prostrate himself on the steps, as all ambassadors, vassals and subject kings were bound to do? He made no move to do so. Instead, when the moment grew painful, he turned to Salah and gently removed the black cloak from the lieutenant's shoulders and placed it about his own.

A murmur, then a light applause rose in the hall. Faces began to smile. He was a friend, after all, this new Imam. He would not prostrate himself; the Vice Regent of God could not do that, but he would don the black of orthodoxy in deference to orthodox beliefs. Was this, perhaps, enough?

It was. The Sultan nodded and descended the steps to

meet his guest. This incident of donning the black mantle was long remembered and entered legend as an example of the mysterious powers of attraction exercised by the Ishmaelite Imam. When he did things like that, none could withstand him.

But first, there were intricate courtesies to be observed. Al-Adil was presented to the Grand Vizier and the Commander of the Faithful, both of whom bowed respectfully low. General Shirkuh expressed the hope of a common treaty against the usurper in Cairo, and Shawar, the ex-Vizier of Egypt, a fawning adventurer with huge ears and slobbering lips, was trotted out to pay his respects. Al-Adil observed diplomatically that the usurper in Cairo was not of the House of Ali and therefore had no claim on Ishmaelite loyalty.

The atmosphere began to lighten. Slaves with trays of sherbets passed around refreshments, and conversation became more general. A divan of equal height with throne was brought in and placed on the dais, so the Sultan and his guest could continue their discussion at ease.

"Is your Highness offering us a treaty?" the Sultan asked with an inscrutable look.

"A treaty? Not while your Highness has our territory at Masyaf under siege," al-Adil replied cautiously.

"Ah, yes, Masyaf. I should have thought the siege was not inconvenient to you since your esteemed father-in-law is thereby neutralized. By the way, what is to happen to your father-in-law?"

"By your Highness' leave, Ishmaeli matters are my concern alone."

"You will be returning to your territory, then?"

"As soon as possible. I need only your Highness' word that my people shall be left in peace."

"In the name of God, it is given. And do I have the Imam's word that my person, my ministers and my officers will be spared any further harassment by the descendants of Ishmael?"

"In the name of God, you have my solemn word."

"It is not doubted."

A pause followed, interrupted only by the scratching pens of the secretaries. The first encounter had been concluded successfully, but now the protagonists must narrow the circle, and come to closer grips with one another. Again, the Sultan spoke first.

"Your Highness is to be congratulated on your sudden accession. It is to be inferred that this transfer of power is fully endorsed by your people. Naturally, I do not doubt this, having received the proclamation issued by your ulema of dervishes in Damascus. But all things are committed to God, who sleeps not, and in the morning the proofs of His will are to be seen. What proofs of sovereignty do you show?"

"I have the highest of all proofs—my personal word."

"A word—is this a proof?"

"It is. For when I speak the truth shall be known."

"And how will you make it known?"

"I will reveal my power."

"You make it sound like magic! What will you show me, then—a genie? A tree of Paradise? A garden of beautiful women? Proceed. We are ready."

"What I have to show you is for your eyes alone, Highness. The profane are not worthy of these revelations. You must require the room to be cleared."

"You intrigue me! Very well, it shall be so. Indeed, profane eyes are not deserving of revelations reserved for our sight alone."

To the consternation of everyone, the Sultan told his Chamberlain to command all persons except his own entourage to leave the hall. In a twinkling, behind the clashing swords of the Sultan's guards, the great crowd vanished. But still the Imam demurred.

"You alone, Highness, are worthy of the revelations of highest truth. These, too, must go."

The Sultan's smile became sceptical. But his curiosity was aroused. "Of course," he said, waving toward the Vizier, the Commander, and other high officers of the Court, "leave us!" And, grey with mortification, they left.

Al-Adil smiled apologetically. "Only for your own eyes, Highness—"

Nur-ed-Din's eyes narrowed. "May the Lord of the Daybreak defend us! These are our bodyguard who are left. Never shall we be parted from them!"

"Let them retire with mine," said al-Adil. And at a sign from him, his entire guard, except for Abdulla, retired outside.

The Sultan was nonplussed. He looked at the twelve mamelukes who habitually attended on his safety, and he decided to take the risk. "Very well," he announced, "all of you—except for Reyhan and Kutyet—be gone!" And almost deprecatingly he entreated al-Adil, "These are my most faithful slaves from whom my soul cannot be parted."

After a pause, al-Adil replied, "It is well! Let them remain even as my bodyguard remains. Abdulla would give his life for me. Can you say the same of your bodyguards?"

"Certainly," said the Sultan. He addressed the two mamelukes. "Is it not so?"

The mamelukes bowed to the ground, holding their scimitars above their heads.

Al-Adil held his breath a moment. He could not know if these mamelukes were secret Ishmaelites or not. But the time had come to test the Sign. "Then," he said with authority, "as I am Imam of God the Compassionate, the Merciful, I command you to present your scimitars to me!"

Without a moment's hesitation, the two mamelukes faced about and presented their sword hilts to the Imam. The Sign had come.

The Sultan rose from his throne, rigid with fear. "Turn about!" he hissed to his mamelukes. "Face me, your Sultan, your master!"

"The Imam, the Lord of the World, is our master," they replied.

Nur-ed-Din collapsed, shrinking back among the cushions, like a spider seeking refuge in his web. He was trembling visibly, but the Imam spoke quickly and soothingly.

"Have no fear, Highness. These men are yours to command." And to the mamelukes he gave the order, "Salute your Sultan!" At once, the mamelukes faced about and presented their sword hilts to Nur-ed-Din.

"My kingdom is of the spirit," said al-Adil quietly. "Leave me my kingdom and I shall leave you yours."

The Sultan sat up, displaying a characteristic febrile response to an advantage. He felt relief, gratitude, and a lurking wonder—was it possible?—could this really be the True Imam?

"There is no Deity but God," he said aloud.

"Extolled be His perfection!" answered al-Adil.

"You are a man," continued the Sultan, sizing up his adversary keenly, "a man after my own heart. How comes it we have not met before? I have been badly advised—I should have sought your advice—you see things more clearly than other men—tell me, about this Egyptian campaign—you have heard Shawar—he says it will be very easy—should I attack or not?"

"As God wills," answered al-Adil.

"Yes, but how does He will—?"

"He wills you to be Nur-ed-Din and Shawar to be Shawar. It is in the nature of Shawar to persuade Nur-ed-Din to attack Cairo and restore him to the throne of the Caliphs. It is in the nature of Nur-ed-Din to want to take the throne of the Caliphs for himself. Is it not so? There is a conflict of interest here which is not God's will but yours."

"You advise against it then?"

"I advise against doing God's will in your name."

"And what does God will you to do?"

"To be al-Adil. Yesterday al-Adil was a slave. Today he is Imam. Tomorrow—as God wills!"

Nur-ed-Din became roused by idea. He jumped up and seized al-Adil's arm. "Why should we not act together? I command the greatest army in the world. You have the power of God at your command. Together we could conquer all of the East and all of the West—why, it is unbelievable what we could do! You shall have the precedence!

I will walk behind you in the mosque! Only give the word—"

"What word?"

"Why, the word that we are at one!"

"But we are not one, Highness—we are two. But let us be two brothers, each going our own way, where God calls us, not attacking one another, nor murdering, nor pillaging any longer, but in peace and brotherhood. This is my word. Is it enough?"

The Sultan looked at him shrewdly. "It is enough," he said at last, "until I have conquered Egypt. Perhaps later—?"

"Perhaps."

Suddenly the Sultan was himself again. He clapped his hands and called back the Court. Incredulous, they came trooping in, out of all order and precedence, craning, peering, in their anxiety to learn the outcome of this extraordinary affair. To their amazement they found the Sultan and the Imam standing each with an arm about the other, as though no difference had ever existed between them.

"A pact! A pact!" declared the Sultan. "Let the secretaries set this down at once! Between the Sultan of Damascus and the Princely Imam of the Ishmaelites, there shall be peace and brotherhood. In setting out seals thereto, may each of us ransom the other before God—"

A great cheering drowned out the rest, and the echoes reverberated like widening circles, as the news passed through the corridors, courts and gardens, to the populace in the city. By the time the Sultan had accompanied his guest to the Palace gates, an enormous throng had gathered in the Street Called Straight. With one voice, no longer pent in by fear of proscription, this multitude raised the cry: "Al-Adil! Vice Regent of God!"

Even the Sultan quailed before it, and the Imam softly commanded Master Sa'di to send his dervishes among the crowd to quiet the effusion. But the command had little effect, though a few cries were raised for the Sultan, who did not miss this pacific gesture by his astonishing guest, and he stood looking after him with something approaching awe.

Three days later, everything was ready for the Imam's departure for his kingdom. A caravan of supplies had been assembled in the courtyard of the Ishmaeli Palace, donkeys loaded with arms and equipment, swift horses for the men-at-arms, and a litter for the Princess Yasmin.

Captain Salah-ed-Din, newly-promoted to command a troop of the Sultan's cavalry, was also there to give the Imam a royal escort back to his territory. Meeting amid the turmoil of the departure, the two men grinned at each other, as though they shared a mutual secret.

"I knew you were behind all of this!" said al-Adil.

"You played your part magnificently!" retorted Salah.

But before the caravan master could sound the horn of departure, a horseman arrived from the west, covered in sweat and dust, with a message for the Imam. The Imam Rashid Ali had escaped from Masyaf, and had taken possession of a number of castles in the Jebel Bahra.

CHAPTER TEN

THE ASSASSINS

The small Ishmaeli caravan, surrounded by its cavalry escort, pressed forward across the Syrian desert toward the western mountains. At night, camp was pitched near some deserted oasis, where the horses and mules were watered. The Princess, exhausted by the pace of the journey, slept in her tent, after taking a draught of hashish.

Al-Adil, more wakeful, visited Salah in his tent. They found some difficulty in broaching the subject, but finally Salah came out with it.

"We are going to see this through together, aren't we?"

"Together? But this is my battle now, Salah."

"The devil it is! You have done all this to save my life—"

"And seventy others. No, Salah, it is not even that. I am looking for something—I don't know what it is—the right way, I suppose—"

"The way? What way?"

"God's way."

"You mean you believe that—about Master Sa'di's dream and all the rest? Don't you know he said all that just to make things easier for you—"

213

"I can't speak for Master Sa'di," al-Adil said, a little sternly. "I believe I am Imam. And, as Imam, I shall have to fight for it."

"Well, good! Let us fight together. We are not alone. I can have the entire army down here in three days, if necessary. We could use your explosive experiments to blow this mad dervish off the face of the earth!"

"You forget, Salah—this is what I have become Imam to prevent. These are my people. I am here to save them, not to destroy. And, what's more, the 'mad dervish' as you call him is Yasmin's father. I owe my inheritance to him. I cannot purchase the Imamate with his blood—"

"In the name of God, what will you do then? Do you think you can persuade him, as you persuaded the Sultan? 'Dear father-in-law, you must step down and let me take your place, because you are getting old and foolish and I know better.' He will skewer you on a spear. What do you think you are—a miracle worker?"

"I worked a miracle once," al-Adil said dreamily.

"You mean—oh, Ad'l, don't let this carry you away. They are going to make a sacrifice of you, these dervishes, with all their mystic talk about revelations—"

"I am not carried away, Salah. I told you, I am only looking for the right way—"

"There you go again! The right way for what?"

"For an Imam of God."

"Then you believe—"

"It is not a question of belief. God has made me Imam. He has also made me your friend. Trust me."

Salah looked at him with tears in his eyes. Impulsively, he wrung his friend's hand. "Trust you, Ad'l?" he said. "Till the end of the world!"

In the morning everything was settled. The Imam would proceed into the Jebel alone, accompanied only by his bodyguard Abdulla. Captain Salah-ed-Din would maintain a watch on the plain and stand ready to render assistance if required. Al-Adil took with him a supply of Chinese black powder, in order send up certain agreed signals—white for victory, red for failure.

"But this is only to inform you, Salah," he said, "of what has happened. In no case are you to take any part. It is my battle, from start to finish. To you I leave my wife. Guard her and bring her to me if I should succeed. Care for her if—"

Salah silenced him with an embrace. Never had they felt more at one than in their parting. Both were of the same mold, for all their differences. Each could guess the other's probable action because he himself in like circumstances would do the same, and each could reprove the other, because in himself he detected the same weakness. But, at the moment, it was Salah who felt the keenest admiration, almost envy of a chance so splendid. Of course Ad'l would do it this way! Salah would do no other.

The entire camp turned out to bid the Imam farewell. He walked down the line, acknowledging each salute, stopping to speak to each officer or friend, giving a personal word to each member of his own household guard, and to each of the dervishes. Lastly, he came to Yasmin, standing straight and solemn as a young iris, that has just unfolded its beauty.

They walked together for a while on the stony desert, his arm about her. "Take care, O my lord," she said. And she handed him a dagger, with his name chased in gold on a handle of pearl. He smiled and put it in his belt.

"Trust me," he said, as he had said the night before to his friend.

"Of course," she replied bravely. "Don't you remember, I told you once, your name is one of the ninety-nine names of God."

He started slightly, recovered himself, and, lifting her veil, kissed her passionately on the mouth.

Later, as Abdulla handed him up into the saddle, Master Sa'di came forward and spoke in a low voice, holding the bridle of the horse.

"Highness," he said, "let me come with you. I know what you think of me. Your eyes are terrible and when they look on me they see into my heart, and I cannot bear what your eyes see!" The old man was weeping. "High-

ness, have pity on your servant and save me from myself.
Let me come with you so I may be a witness before the
world that you are He who is to come, the True Imam."

Al-Adil did not reply to him, but turning to a groom he
ordered curtly, "A mount for Master Sa'di!" Without further comment, the three horsemen set out across the plain
for the far distant hills, grey blue against the sky, of the
Jebel Bahra.

The first test came late in the forenoon, as their horses
wended up the narrow trail that criss-crossed the face of
the cliff. Suddenly, they came upon a road block, built of
fallen rock. It was one of the blocks he himself had ordered to be built on his last visit. One of the giant boulders had been levered aside by means of a tall tree trunk,
fastened on an axle, another of his devices. The gate was
open.

As he rode through the passage in the rocks, he saw
that the hills were covered with men, many of them
armed with sling-shots and bows, standing on crags and
boulders, looking down, silent and motionless. He raised
his arm in the familiar salute. "God is great!" he said.

Instantly, there was a shifting of position, as every man
bowed to the ground, and a rasping of guttural voices
echoed among the hills as they replied, "Al-Adil is His
Vice Regent!"

Then they came down, scrambling over the rocks from
which they had watched his approach across the plain all
morning. Now they were pressing against his horse in the
narrow pass in order to salute him. This time he allowed
them to touch him, for now he was Imam, and they
needed him as much as he needed them. Yet they were
quiet and subdued in their respect, this time, with none of
the rejoicing which had met him before.

"There is danger, most holy Imam, danger in the hills."
The grizzled, gnarled faces of the mountaineers pressed
forward to give their warnings.

"The assassins belonging to the former Imam are loose."

"They have taken Rusafa and Ulayqa!"

"They have over-run the villages!"

Al-Adil listened gravely, nodding as though all were quite as he had expected, and he continued on his way. He left orders that all men were to return to their homes, except for a few who were to act as guides over the mountains. They took a route for Rusafa, avoiding the villages. By late afternoon they were on a rise of land overlooking the castle across the valley.

From this position they could clearly see the town, its houses sprawled over the mountainside, the minarets of the mosque. There must be a way to take this town by the power of faith alone, he thought reminding himself again that Rusafa was the scene of his first miracle. Finally, he said, "Someone must go into Rusafa and bid the Sheikh announce my name from the minaret of the mosque at the Evening Prayer." Master Sa'di volunteered, and left with a guide.

As evening fell, the Imam and his guides rode down into the valley. Then, with only Abdulla at his side, al-Adil began the ascent to Rusafa. From the distance, on the clear evening air, he could hear the call of the muezzin: "Come to prayer! Come to prayer! Come to salvation! Come to salvation!" Only now it sounded differently. For the first time he heard his own name from the minaret of a mosque: "I believe there is no God but God! I believe Muhammed is His Prophet! I believe al-Adil is His Vice Regent on earth."

Master Sa'di had done his work. As the last call came from the minaret, al-Adil rode into the square and dismounted. The entire space was filled with people who had overflowed from the mosque into the street. The time had come for the Preacher to mount the minbar. Instead, the Imam strode up and took his place.

"My people," he said, "It is written: 'When thy Lord said to the angels, "Verily, I am about to place one in my stead on earth," the angels asked: 'Wilt Thou place there one who will do ill therein and shed blood?' And God said "Verily, I know what ye know not".' So says the sura.

"Even so you may know your Imam by his works. He who kills by stealth, and sows terror in men's minds, and bows down the hearts of mothers and widows with mourning—such is not a True Imam. By this ye may know him.

"But instead, I bring you peace in this land and in the world. The Sultan has given me his written oath and has signed a pact with me for your security. From this time onward, you are free men, and may hold up your heads in the world without fear on account of your beliefs. By this ye may know me!"

A roar of many voices, rising in waves like an earthquake, gathered force and shook the walls of the mosque and the houses facing the square. The gates of the castle were flung open and the guards of Rashid Ali came out, their hands raised in supplication, and all joined together in the prostrations of the Evening Prayer.

Later that night, after the tall column of white smoke had been sent up on the moonlight air, and the celebrations were over, and the crowds who had come to touch the Imam had gone home, al-Adil prepared for sleep in his room in the castle keep. He called to Abdulla.

"Abdulla," he said, "I have won a great victory this day and I should be glad, yet I am troubled. You know I am not a weak man. Look at my arm, which is nearly twice the girth of yours. Is it not so?"

"It is so, master. Your arm is mighty."

"Then, how is it, Abdulla, that I cannot so much as raise my hand? Whence comes this weakness? Am I bewitched?"

"No, master, you are not bewitched. You have let them touch you that's all."

"Touch me?"

"They touch you to draw your strength, and because they know God will renew you."

Abdulla was right. The next morning, when he awoke, al-Adil was himself again. But thereafter, Abdulla kept the crowds away from his master.

The Imam Rashid Ali was not in Rusafa. He was in the castle of Ulayqa, some forty miles away, with the bulk of his army. This meant Ulayqa, would present a far greater test than any al-Adil had met before.

Still determined not to form a regular army, he set out for Ulayqa at the head of a great crowd of faithful who insisted on following him, by mule and on foot. This slowed his progress, and word of his approach arrived well before he did.

It took two days for the Imam and his followers to come within sight of the towers of Ulayqa. Even from a distance, it was clear that this walled town would be defended with vigor. Road blocks had been set up on the outskirts of town, and the battlements glinted with the black mail and helmets of Rashid Ali's troops.

Al-Adil was extremely concerned. He realized he could be leading his people into a massacre. He pitched camp therefore at a short distance from the town and sent messengers to Captain Salah to have his supplies of arms and armor sent to him. In two more days they arrived.

He distributed the arms among several hundred ablebodied men and he sent away the women and camp followers. Then, before he set out for Ulayqa, he addressed his untrained troops briefly and he instructed them to use their weapons in self-defense only. The Imam, himself, however, carried no arms or armor.

Arriving in the forenoon, the Imam set up his camp among the olive trees on a small plain in front of Ulayqa's gates. He sent forward some of his men to pick up the trunks of the felled olive trees in order to build a defensive wall. They were fired upon from the battlements, and two of them were killed.

These, the first losses of the campaign, saddened the Imam more than anything else could have done. In vain, Abdulla remonstrated with him. "They have given their lives in exchange for Paradise," he told his master. "When the news is brought, their mothers will rejoice and paint their eyes with kohl, and the mothers of those who live will put ashes on their hair!"

Then Master Sa'di came to him. "Highness," he said, "this evil one cannot be overthrown by justice and right alone. For the soldiers of Rashid Ali have not heard of your accession or of my proclamation. But there are many citizens of Ulayqa behind these soldiers who have heard of these things and who believe them. You must give your people a sign; they are all watching and they will set upon the soldiers and slay them."

"A sign, Master Sa'di? I do not know a sign."

"You are the sign, Highness. Do you not recall what I told you about al-Hallaj when he was brought to be crucified? 'If you would recognize God,' he said, 'at least recognize His Sign. I am that Sign.' That is what al-Hallaj said."

"And what sign did al-Hallaj give, Master Sa'di?" asked al-Adil.

"When they brought him to the place of crucifixion, and he saw the cross and the nails," Master Sa'di said with exaltation, "he prayed to God saying, 'Forgive these people, Lord, even though they are about to kill me for Your sake. For if they knew the truth as You have shown it to me, they would not kill me. And if I did not know the truth, as You have hidden it from them, I would not have to die this death. Glory to You, Lord, in all that You do.'"

"Would you have me crucified, Master Sa'di?" asked al-Adil.

"Not unless it is God's will, Highness," replied the dervish.

"His will be done," al-Adil said softly.

The Imam ordered his men to stand to the defensive wall. Then he advanced alone into the open space before the town gates, (Abdulla, at his command, had to be held back by force). There he raised his hand and called in a strong voice to the men on the battlements:

"Tell your master I bring him no harm. I bring only good will to you and to all men. For I am the Imam of peace."

Instantly, at a harsh command, the soldiers let fly their arrows at him. Several dozen feathered darts seemed to whir through the air; many, perhaps purposely, flew wide of the mark; others clattered twanging to the ground around his feet. The Imam faltered a moment, then, raising his arm again, he cried out in a firm voice, "God is great!"

In that moment, everything happened at once. Groaning in despair, the soldiers on the walls threw their bows away; the followers of the Imam stormed the gate; and the citizens of Ulayqa, taking matters into their own hands, overpowered the gate-keepers and rolled up the portcullis. Al-Adil was swept victoriously into the town.

Many soldiers of Rashid Ali rushed for refuge in the keep, but they were cut off by frenzied citizens who hacked them to death in the streets. Others beat a retreat to the far end of town, where they made their escape into the surrounding countryside. Even after a thorough search, no trace was found of Rashid Ali himself.

The Imam seemed unmoved by it all. Tight-lipped, his face drained of all color, he walked slowly toward the castle keep, Abdulla now at his side, keeping all persons away from him. On the steps of the keep he paused, as if intending to say a few words, but instead he tightened his grip on Abdulla's arm and whispered, "Get me within."

At once Abdulla took charge. One would have said he was a major-domo, the way he ordered everyone around until he had safely lodged his master in a large bedroom, and barred the door. Al-Adil collapsed on the bed with a cry, "Save me, Abdulla!"

Abdulla guessed. He sent for water, a burning brazier and an iron. Only then, carefully using his dagger, did he begin to cut away the Imam's robe. Three arrows, fired at close range were so deeply imbedded in his body that their short shafts were lost in the folds of his mantle and robe. The arrow heads had entered fleshy portions of his side and thigh, so that the flesh had completely closed over them, and this staunched the flow of blood.

One by one, Abdulla cut the arrow heads out, stopping the bleeding with the iron which he heated over the fire. After washing the wounds, he bandaged them with strips of the Imam's robe. All this time, al-Adil uttered not a sound. Only once or twice he begged Abdulla not to let him faint, and the bodyguard gave him a drink of wine from his flask.

When the operation was completed, al-Adil attempted to rise but could not. He looked pitifully at Abdulla, and Abdulla responded by saying, "Lie there, master. I know what must be done. I will be your right arm." Al-Adil gratefully succumbed to the waves of faintness that engulfed him.

Abdulla truly was his master's right arm, striking right and left so that men quailed before him. He spread the rumor that the Imam was very angry with his people because they had killed so many soldiers, thereby defiling his triumphal entry into the city. Not until the bodies had been decently buried and the stones washed of blood, and the living purified by ablutions in the mosque, would His Highness show himself.

For a day and night he set the whole town to work and supervised their labors himself, calling for more and more "expiation" of their crimes, until all traces of the butchery. had been removed. He sent up the victory signal, in a mighty column of white smoke over Ulayqa while, behind locked doors, he nursed his master back to health.

After this, there was no question about the Imam's authority. It was no longer founded on the succession, or on Master Sa'di's proclamation, but simply on the Imam's own right. Everywhere he went he was regarded with awe, and men did not want to touch him, but only to follow him. If he so much as looked at them, they cast down their gaze, unable to bear his blue eyes upon them.

This troubled al-Adil and, as usual, in the privacy of his room he applied to Abdulla for the reason.

"It is the miracle, master," answered the bodyguard.

Al-Adil struck him across the face, just as he had once beaten the servants when they stole his bath water. "How dare you say that, Abdulla," he said, "when you, yourself, cut out the arrowheads?"

Abdulla accepted the rebuke submissively, but explained, "It was a miracle because you did not die, master."

Al-Adil drew a long breath, as though light were breaking. "Yes," he said slowly, "I did not die."

Then, suddenly repentant, he gave Abdulla a rough caress, as though to wipe out the indignity he had inflicted on him. But Abdulla felt no indignity. His master could do no wrong.

Now that peace had been restored in the Ishmaeli territory, al-Adil took up his residence at Ulayqa, being the largest town with the most comfortable castle in the Jebel Bahra. He sent for Yasmin, and the Princess arrived in a caravan, accompanied by the Ishmaeli guards, the dervishes and other members of the household.

Their reunion was blissful; he could not hold her long enough in his arms; and he insisted on carrying her up the castle steps. It was with immense surprise, therefore, on going to her bed that night, that he found himself refused. He sat down beside her and, taking her hand gently in his, asked the reason.

Yasmin looked at him with wide, dark eyes. "I am carrying your child, my lord," she said.

Impulsively, he kissed her; then he asked, "How long have you known?"

"For several months—three, nearly four," she replied. "That is why I have been so often ill."

"And did not tell me—why?"

"Because you were busy—because of the troubles—" But that was not all. Eventually it came out. "I thought you would not want an heir. It would displace you in the succession."

"I had not thought of that," he said, frowning. "Anyway, the Imamate is mine now. Of course I am glad! You must take good care of yourself. I will send for a doctor from Damascus—"

"That is not all. Salah says I am to tell you he has intelligence that my father has returned to Masyaf and the siege is to begin again."

"The devil he has! Well, let him stay there. I shall stay here. And you, my darling, shall bear me an heir!"

Al-Adil went to enormous lengths to make his wife

happy. He refurbished the entire castle, always thinking up
new things for her pleasure. At one time, he decided to install a bath, and for weeks men were employed laying tiles
and fittings under his direction. Then he conceived the
idea of a roof garden, and more men were set to work
transplanting trees and shrubs to the top of the battlements. He gave the muleteers no rest, fetching all sorts of
luxuries from Damascus; he even sent Mesroor to buy
four strong eunuchs to carry her litter up and down stairs.

In spite of everything, Yasmin did not thrive. A sadness
seemed to weigh on her, as though she knew more than
she could tell. She did not sleep at night, unless she took
the hashish, which she did with greater frequency. When
al-Adil found out about this, he said nothing to Yasmin,
but he took her old nurse, Fatima, aside and forbade her
to give her mistress the hashish. But when he had gone,
Fatima shrugged. "I know my mistress better than he
does," she confided to Mesroor.

Another cause for Yasmin's uneasiness were al-Adil's
increasing absences from home. As long as the Imam
was in his territory, he was expected to hold Court and
this forced him to go to each of the villages, hearing cases
along the way.

The Imam's justice was prized because, although his
sentences were acknowledged to be severe, he took great
trouble to find out the truth about a matter. If a man believed in the rightness of his case, he was ready to risk
the Imam's judgment. Women, too, were dealt with con-
siderately in his courts, and no woman who came before
him was ever beaten or suffocated. This was a scandal to
some in a land where it was taken for granted that women
were the source of all evil and merited heavier punishment. The Imam's unfailing courtesy toward women was
a puzzle to be accepted but not explained.

In many towns where he set up his tent, the sheikhs, or
headmen, brought him their marriageable daughters.
Every virgin in the Imamate was looked upon as the
property of the Imam. In practice, no virgin was allowed
to retain her virginity after the age of sixteen, but it was

considered especially auspicious if the Imam broke the maidenhead himself. Besides, it was expected of him as a form of patronage—it raised the girl's brideprice!

Al-Adil accepted his maiden tributes with great gentleness, and sent them back to their fathers untouched. But he always entertained them in his tent, feeding them candied fruits and telling them stories—for they were no more than children—so that appearances were preserved.

This gave rise to another legend, that of his insatiable appetite for virginity, which was salaciously reported to Yasmin. She never confronted him with his "infidelities" —would any woman make allowance, even under such temptations, for the weakness of man's flesh?—and she gave him no chance for denial. Instead she turned to her pillow in grief.

More often than ever, Fatima brought the pipe, and in the loneliness of her darkened room the efreet became a regular visitor. Sometimes he comforted her and she knew a fleeting peace of mind, but more often he played upon her guilty fears so that she was afraid ever to look at her husband's face. Then, in June, the killings began again. It was reported that several headmen, who had offered bread and salt to the new Imam had been killed. They died in the way familiar to the Assassins—with a dagger in their hearts and the sign of the Evil Eye on the hilt.

No one was ever found who had seen the murderers, or who could give the kadi any information whatever. All over the territory, the silence of fear descended. Even when the Imam himself appeared and asked men and women to come forward and speak, they hung back, their eyes filled with tears, and they said, "Do not ask us, Highness. We cannot refuse you. Take pity on us and do not ask!"

In July, a message came from Salah. An attempt had been made on the life of General Shirkuh and the assassin, who died in the attempt, proved to be a hashishi from Masyaf. "The Sultan has ordered the siege of Masyaf to be prosecuted with great vigor, and I, myself, am sent there immediately," wrote Salah. "In any case," he concluded laconically, "I have no choice but to fight. Another assassin was caught in my tent last night."

Al-Adil was beside himself. Everything he had built up, the peace between the heretics and the Orthodox of Islam, the cessation of the Sultan's persecution, the end of the assassinations—all was lost. The old days of suspicion and fanaticism would return. And there was nothing he could do, because against the fanatic there is no defense. He cannot be controlled. He must be destroyed.

Evidently, Masyaf was honeycombed with secret tunnels and exits which were used by the assassins to come and go on their deadly errands. Of what use was a siege? An army might remain encamped before it for a year and effect nothing. Masyaf was impregnable. Only the initiates knew the way in or out—and among these must be the Master of his dervishes.

The Imam sent for Master Sa'di. The old man had aged much since these events began and he had lost, perhaps forever, the thing he had waited for all his life; the leap into union with God. But he was fond of his protegé (he still liked to regard him as his disciple), and was immensely grateful that the Imam had let him prove his loyalty. They lived together in an attitude of mutual toleration, a little unsure how much the other believed, or what, or why.

"Highness," said Master Sa'di, "there is only one way into Masyaf. It is in the heart of the mountain, and it can be reached by tunnels in the rock from all directions. But once you arrive at the central point, there is but one way up—by rope. The shaft is many hundreds of feet high— the ropes work in shifts, each suspended from a separate platform and worked by a separate pulley. At a signal from above, all these pulleys can be cut and the platforms destroyed. No one can reach the top, even if he knows the way, unless he is bidden."

The two were walking through the great hall of the castle, and al-Adil paused before a window. He watched a woodsman, who was plodding behind his donkey piled with faggots, under the walls. "Yes, Master Sa'di," he said,

"I see that an army cannot enter Masyaf. But a single man might do so, might he not—if, as you say, he was bidden?"

"Of course, Highness. But what sort of man is this man who enters Masyaf alone—an assassin?"

"Myself."

"You!" The old man looked horrified. "You do not mean to be—yourself—a hashishi?"

"Not exactly. As you know, I have never taken the hashish. I hope, for what I have to do, I do not need it. But I must talk with the Imam Rashid Ali—I must come to terms with him."

"Never!" asserted the dervish emphatically. "Never will you make terms with this man. He is not your sort. You speak a different language. You will not understand each other—"

"What sort of man is he, Master Sa'di?"

"He is a jinn."

"You mean he is not a Believer?"

"He believes nothing."

After a pause, al-Adil asked, "Why, then, did you serve him, Master Sa'di?"

The dervish looked down. "It is my weakness, Highness. I thought I could be an influence on him. I believed I could help create a new kind of community, a community of love, in which all men would be brothers, serving one another instead of seeking the rewards of cruelty and ambition and desire. The Imam Rashid Ali said this could only be done when we had destroyed the power of this world, and I believed him. He said it could be done very easily because the world had no defense against us, and I believed that, too. He said *we* are the world, and *they* are the shadow, and this I wished to believe most of all. But I was mistaken."

Al-Adil watched the woodsman disappear around the castle walls.

"Rashid Ali will listen to me because he loves his daughter," he said suddenly.

"And how will this love make him listen?"

"She bears my child—his heir."

"You will hold the child hostage?"

"The child shall be the next Imam!"

He left Master Sa'di nonplussed, and, calling for his bodyguard, sent him posthaste for the woodsman. A short time later Abdulla brought back the donkey, and the woodsman's entire clothing, which he had purchased for a purse of silver.

Next, al-Adil had to break his intention to Yasmin. She listened with horror and then abruptly rose from her bed. She would not contradict him or even attempt to persuade him against his will. Such was her sense of honor. She demanded only one right—a wife's right at all times. She would accompany him.

This presented a new problem, but she could not be stopped. Abdulla had more errands to do at the hut of the woodsman, paying a high price for rags. Late that night, while the town slept, three peasants left Ulayqa, a woodsman and his helper, driving a donkey, on which rode a peasant woman big with child. They took a mountain trail over the hills in the direction of Masyaf, more than sixty miles to the south east.

The journey took almost a week. From the first, Yasmin was deathly sick, and she had to rest frequently. Time and again, al-Adil made up his mind to send her back in the care of Abdulla, but she would not hear of it. Who else could guide him into the mysterious fortress? Who would advise him how to negotiate with her terrible father? Who, in the final instance, would protect him with her body? Her only thought was of him. In the face of such devotion, even his habit of absolute command (for the exercise of unlimited power had made him somewhat absolute) failed him. He nursed her tenderly, sent Abdulla to the villages for water and herbs, and they struggled on.

Masyaf stood on the eastern massif of the Jebel Bahra, rising two thousand feet from the plain below, up a sheer rock face, unapproachable from any side. There were no roads to Masyaf and no army had ever captured it.

The route taken by the three travellers led along a stream. Both sides of the enbankments were so steep that they had to walk for some distance in the stream itself. Suddenly, Yasmin, who had been lying inert across the back of the donkey, sat up. She pointed to a decayed tree whose trunk lay half across the stream.

At this point, the water gurgling into a deep cavern, seemed to disappear into the ground. But behind the gnarled roots of the tree, another passageway opened out between the rocks. Obviously, this was where the river had run before it was diverted. The small party fought their way through the tangled underbrush and emerged in a narrow siq that had been the bed of the river and was now a dry, stony path, leading down into the bowels of the earth. The rocks almost closed together over their heads; the sunlight was shut out; and they advanced into a twilight gloom.

Endless twists and turns followed; sometimes the siq would open out into little glades, green with mosses and hanging stalactites; then other times the walls would close in on either side so that the travellers could scarcely squeeze through in single file.

Without warning, their goal loomed up before them— the entrance to the castle, the pilasters, the architrave, the pediment, all carved in the living rock. Not a soul was to be seen, here in the underground gloom, lit only by the crevices in the cliffs, hundreds of feet above.

They tethered the mule and went inside. Behind the entrance lay a long narrow tunnel leading into the interior of the mountain. After several minutes' walk, however, they could see lights ahead.

Overhead was a tremendous open shaft, rising straight into the castle. This was the entry Master Sa'di had described. There, far above them, was the wooden platform, hoisted by two stout ropes with a counter-weight capable of lifting perhaps a dozen men at a time. But there was no one around. Yasmin went to the wall and pulled on a hanging rope. A bell tolled faintly, far above them.

It was a long time before there was any answer, but fi-

nally, the platform above them began to descend. On it
was a dwarf who looked at them uncertainly as the platform came to rest on the ground. Then, with sudden recognition, he bowed to Yasmin.

"Peace be unto you, Princess," he said.

"We must go up," she replied.

"You, Princess, may do so. Not these, until I have orders."

"Then go at once and tell my father that I have brought
with me my husband and his servant and we demand entry together."

The dwarf bowed and without another word hauled
himself up the shaft. A little while later, the platform returned and took the three visitors, stage by stage, changing
platforms every hundred feet or so, to the top of the
mountain. The dwarf flung open a door on the uppermost
level and they stepped out into blazing sunlight.

The sight before them was worthy of the Thousand and
One Nights: a forecourt, bounded on three sides by the
cliff's edge, and on the fourth by a castle cut into the face
of the mountaintop. The open space was filled with orange
trees and flowering shrubs, with an airy pavilion in the
center with carpets, cushions, and musical instruments
scattered around in profusion. Splendid, handsome
white-clad guards walked around in pairs. They had been
recruited by Rashid Ali in the villages, brought up on
hashish, and fed on tales of Paradise which, they believed,
lay upon the top of the mountain whose rocky summit
rose directly above them.

Yasmin, leaning on al-Adil's arm, led the way up the
steps and into the castle. They went into a big room, the
great hall, with walls of rough-hewn rock, a scattering of
divans, and, in an arched recess at the back, the Imam's
throne.

Rashid Ali was sitting there, his sardonic, dark face, his
beak-like nose and glittering eyes, under an immense turban, half-hidden by the recess. He was quite alone.

"I thought it better to receive you without witnesses,"

he said, "since any business we may have together is purely a family matter."

Then he saw that Yasmin was fainting in her husband's arms. At once, he jumped up. "You are ill, my darling! What has happened? Guards! Ho!"

He clapped his hands and instantly half a dozen servants appeared, who, at his command, carried his daughter to a chamber above. He ran up the stairs after them calling out directions and advice. Later he returned, looking shaken and dismayed.

"Why did you not tell me was ill?" he asked querulously.

"She is with child," al-Adil replied.

The old man sucked in his breath. "At last!" he said. "An heir!"

"That depends."

"Depends on what?"

"On whether it is your heir or mine."

"I am Imam," Rashid Ali said haughtily.

Al-Adil let this pass. "The child is Yasmin's," he said. "Perhaps we should let her decide—"

They were standing in the midst of the room, talking in whispers. Abdulla lurked in the doorway. Suddenly, Abdulla said, "Master—one comes!"

A guard in white was mounting the steps of the castle two at a time. "Highness!" he called. "News! The army of the Sultan is sighted on the plain below. There are tens of thousands of men, horses, flying catapults, all coming from the east!"

Rashid Ali took the news with calm, even with scorn. "They have tried before. They may try again. Never will they scale this mountain—unless," he turned to al-Adil, "someone has shown them the way?"

"I came unknown to any," he replied coldly.

Rashid Ali studied his son-in-law a moment, then decided to accept his word. "That's what I always liked about you," he said. "You speak the truth. We must talk later. We have much to say to each other. Meanwhile I must give directions to my captains on how to pick off these gnats who come to trouble our peace!" And, striding off, over the hills, his robes flying in the wind, he disappeared from view.

In the evening, Rashid Ali liked to sit in the pavilion in the forecourt of the castle. The pavilion faced east, and from this extraordinary height, it was possible to see the faraway cities of Homs and Hama and even sometimes Aleppo, glittering across the desert. Then as the sun went down, these fabulous cities vanished, too, like a mirage on the sands. All the world became blue, and the stars began to shine.

That evening, Rashid Ali sat on his silken rugs in the pavilion, smoking his pipe of hashish, alone with al-Adil, who was newly clothed in a fresh white robe. The motionless shadow of Abdulla lay on the steps outside the pavilion. In the distance, five guards paced resolutely up and down, two pairs and one alone, along the brink of the precipice. It made al-Adil shudder to see how close they marched to the brink, for there was no wall.

"What is your proposal, after all," Rashid Ali was saying, "except an attempt to blackmail me into giving up the Imamate to your son. And that I shall never do while I have life and breath. Oh, I know what you think. You think that, because you hold a few castles and villages, and people bow and kiss your feet and bring you their daughters, that you are Imam. You are wrong. You have blundered into something you don't in the least understand. Your claim is based on loyalty, on respect, on 'love' as Master Sa'di would say. You should not have listened to him for he has seriously misled you.

"The Imamate is founded on power. What do you know of power? Do you think it is a matter of horsemen and infantry and catapults such as the Sultan has mustered against me? I assure you I have more power in my little finger than the Sultan has in his whole realm."

Al-Adil shifted impatiently. "What good is your power?" he asked. "You are a prisoner here in Masyaf. You may never be free again."

Rashid Ali laughed delightedly. "You think that? I assure you, men tremble before my power at this moment as far away as Mecca and Medina. In Baghdad, the Caliph fears to proscribe my honors in the mosque. Even in Paris—ah ha! You start!—my hashishin leave their warnings upon my enemies."

"Ah, my lord, but that is fear. The jackal is feared but he is not the king of beasts."

"Wrong again, my son!" The old man was working himself up to a pitch of pleasure. "I'll tell you what power is—it is will. Tell me—have you ever sent a man to his death?"

Al-Adil felt a shadow creep over him. "I have killed men in fight," he murmured.

"Not that! Have you never spoken the word—die!"

"I have given the sentence of death in my courts in accordance with the law."

"Still more than that. Have you never coolly, calmly, casually, extinguished a life for no reason at all?"

"Never."

"Then you do not understand power. Let me show you what I mean."

The old man of the mountain clapped his hands. Instantly, the five guards, standing across the forecourt, turned in his direction. He looked from one to the other, almost benignly, as though weighing their youth, their beauty, their virility, in the scales against his power to extinguish so much. Then, selecting two of the guards with a gay and benevolent nod, he raised his hand above his head and waved it in a gesture of farewell.

Without a moment's hesitation, both the guards joined hands and, with a glad cry of "Ali!," jumped over the cliff.

Al-Adil froze with horror. It was some moments before he could utter the words, "You are mad! Mad!"

"Mad, eh?" The old man's voice was heavy with sarcasm. "I have mastered the riddle of the universe and you call me mad! That is because you understand nothing, nothing at all. You think power works by fear, but that is not so. It is driven by will, the primal will in all creation.

What binds my followers to me is the unity of will, so that they have made their will my will."

He clapped his hands, and again the remaining guards looked toward him expectantly. He signalled to two of them. "See the joy in their faces," he continued, "for I bring them the greatest fulfillment they can have, the enactment of my supreme will!" And, with another gesture, he waved them over the cliff's edge. Their cries rent the soft evening air until they were far below. Then, they suddenly ceased.

"Stop!" Al-Adil jumped up. He was trembling violently. "I don't know how you have done this, what charms or enchantments you use, but you shall do no more evil in my sight!"

"Evil? Is it evil that we should all be united at last? Isn't that what you want? You want us both to abdicate the Imamate. Very well, let us prove our good faith to one another. I will give you the life of my last servant as proof of my honor." He indicated the lone guard left in the forecourt. "Will you give me the life of your servant?"

Abdulla's eyes glinted in the shadows.

"His life is not mine to give," al-Adil replied slowly.

"How?" ejaculated the old man. "Would your own bodyguard not die for you?"

"He would die, if need be, but of his own free will."

"Then let us put it to the test! Let these young men join hands and jump together into eternity that our wills may be one." And with an imperious gesture he summoned the last guard who ran forward and knelt on the step beside Abdulla.

"No, no!" cried al-Adil. "What you ask is impossible, terrible! I will never permit such a thing!"

"Ah, well, then," said Rashid Ali with mock resignation. "We shall not agree—and this young man's sacrifice shall not be required after all. What a pity!"

Impetuously the young guard knelt at his feet. "Master!" he cried, "let me die! Only say I am worthy!"

The old man smiled. "Do as you will," he said kindly.

With a grateful murmur of thanks, the young guard

kissed the ground before him, and running, flung himself off the cliff. Abdulla had not moved from the step outside.

The moon rose in the east, filling the empty courtyard with a deathly, cold light, and the two cross-legged figures in the pavilion looked like statues modelled in porcelain. The old man drew occasionally on his hashish pipe, then put the stem aside.

"Of course, I could kill you," he said reflectively, "but I will not do that for Yasmin's sake. She is all I love in the world and her happiness is all I care for. You have reckoned on that. But you shall never take your wife from this place again. And the heir—if it is a son—shall be mine!"

At this moment, a servant emerged from the shadowy castle and hurried to the old man's side, whispering in his ear.

"What!" Rashid Ali ejaculated. "Already? Yasmin has been brought to bed with her child!"

The labor was very long. Yasmin lay in a small, stuffy room, whose single window faced east. Under the fierce summer sun, the stone wall became like a furnace, radiating heat. The evenings were still, and no other window drew the breeze.

For three days, al-Adil sat by the bedside, patiently ringing out cloths in cold water and placing them on his wife's forehead. After the first onset of the pains, there was a long period of delay, and during this time Yasmin was quite herself, talking and smiling. But later she grew feverish and she did not seem to know anyone. She called for Fatima, but Fatima was not there, and realizing the reason for the call, al-Adil sent for the hashish.

He gave it to her in small doses, every few hours, but still she called to Fatima for more and al-Adil was at his wits' end. He did not know what limits there were to the dosage, but he could not bear to see her suffering. Finally, he fed it to her in large spoonfuls.

When she came out of her trance, it was daylight of the fourth day, and the labor began again. This time it was very severe. There was an old woman in attendance, who worked in the kitchens and laid some claim to midwifery. She came armed with a rusty knife, a basin of asses' milk and some powdered camel dung. But she had little idea how to hasten the birth, and al-Adil sent her away until she was needed.

Hour after hour, Yasmin cried out, until her voice failed her, but towards evening she became calm again and, opening her eyes, she smiled at her husband.

"Ad'l," she said, taking his hand, "I love you. I have always loved you from the first time I held your head in my lap. God has been very good to me to give me a place in your favor. Because you see, my dearest, I have always known you did not love me in the same way. Wait! Don't protest! I know what you would say. Of course you have loved me. But not in the same way. Your real love is reserved for another kind of woman than I, your own kind, with whom you would be—oh, so much more free. Princess as I am, I have only been a slave girl to you. That's why you had to have others—oh, I knew about them all, Jullenar and the daughters of the headmen—there were so many of them, and it was so like you, Ad'l, to be generous. I am not blaming you. Why should you not enjoy your rights? Do not think me a jealous woman. I have given you everything I have and I expected nothing in return but your smile. Oh, you have smiled on me, you have been all goodness to your bond slave, my dearest lord. But—should you ever want to—to be free, to come into your own, do not let me be a burden to you. Only let me love you from afar, and do not remember me with annoyance or scorn."

This strange little speech made a deep impression on al-Adil and, try as he would with protests and kisses to deny what she had told him, her words found a mark. For, even though the infidelities she laid up to him were imaginary, he felt in himself the stirring of another man and another life. But against this perception, there arose such a passion of love for his wife, which perhaps he had neglected to show her, that he smothered her with kisses until she cried for mercy.

When the pains began again, he cared for her himself, bathing her with hot and cold cloths, and feeding her the hashish. After taking the drug, she became incoherent, but she still held his hand and several times indicated to him that she wished to speak again. At last, with a supreme effort, she overcame the effects of the drug, and, reaching up, took his face in her hands.

"Ad'l," she said, "there is something I must tell you—I have deceived you—only say you will forgive me, or I cannot speak—"

Al-Adil soothed her with kisses. "You can do no wrong in my sight, beloved," he told her. "If it was the slavery, that is all forgotten—"

But she became more distraught. "No, no, not only the slavery—something much worse—I enslaved your soul—I kept the truth about yourself hidden from you, so I could have you to myself—oh, my dearest lord, punish me, punish me, but say you will forgive me—"

"You are forgiven, no matter what it is, beloved," he answered her, "only do not tire yourself. Do not speak of such things—"

"But I must speak. I shall burn forever if I do not speak! It is your name. I must tell you your name—only the efreet will not let me—the efreet is tearing out my tongue—oh, save me, save me from the efreet!"

And, to his horror, she actually seemed to be flung about the bed by a superhuman force, as though she was in the hands of a genie. She looked at him piteously, gasping for breath, under the blows and buffetings of the unseen hands.

Al-Adil felt the hair on his scalp rise with dread, but he remembered he was Imam, he remembered the "dead" child at Rusafa and later the arrows that did not kill—and, by a supreme effort, perhaps the greatest he had ever made in his life, he surmounted his doubt. Laying his hand on her, he said in a commanding voice, "O spirit of the shetani, spawn of Iblis the devil, come out of this woman, in the name of God, the Compassionate, the Merciful!"

Her eyes were starting out with terror—she saw her

husband cast the spirit out of her—and her body fell slack on the bed, exhausted and still. After a moment, she looked at him trustfully. "You are the True Imam, beloved," she said.

"Then," he replied, "if I am the True Imam, that is my true name. You are never to speak of another name to me again!"

She smiled faintly. "On my head be my lord's commands."

Toward dawn of the fifth day, the child was born. It was a boy. Al-Adil took the good news outside to his father-in-law, who at once went in to his daughter, for she was calling for him. The old man spent a long time alone with her and what they said was never known to al-Adil. Sometime later, however, Rashid Ali came out of the bed chamber, reeling like a drunken man, and made his way downstairs to the great hall, where al-Adil lay asleep.

For a long time, the old man sat motionless on the floor, staring into space. At last he moved nearer to where his son-in-law was sleeping and shook him by the arm.

"Ad'l," he said piteously. "Wake up. I can't bear to be alone any longer. Take pity on me. She is gone. She is dead!"

The shock overwhelmed him. He had left his wife resting peacefully, the efreet exorcised. What had happened? No one seemed to know. The midwife said the birth had been premature; there had been a great loss of blood; the mother had probably been injured on the journey. Then, on leaving, she mentioned the hashish—"always fatal in childbirth."

Horrified, al-Adil went up to the death chamber. There he saw the pot of hashish, half-consumed, by the bed. Of course! It was retribution for his presumption in supposing himself to be God's Chosen Instrument! He had cast the devil out of his wife, but instead he had killed her himself! The thought drove him literally out of his mind. He threw himself about the room, beating his head against the walls 'till the blood ran, but he found no relief from his self-accusation.

Then he came to a standstill beside the hashish pot. Almost automatically, he lifted it to his mouth and began to eat. He continued swallowing the raw hashish, without dilution, until the remainder of the pot was consumed. Then he lay down on the floor. It was not long before unconsciousness came.

Stars.

Mountains and valleys of space.

A long corridor of light, leading to the sun. In the foreground, very large and black, silhouetted against the light, the efreet, holding Yasmin in his arms. He was carrying her away to his bed forever. "Ad'l, I love you—I love you—I love you!" She was gone.

Fireballs, flying everywhere.

The muezzin atop the minaret falling, the minaret splitting, breaking into segments like a soft candle, the muezzin still chanting, "God is most great! I believe there is no God but God! I believe Muhammad is His Prophet!" Nothing left. No mosque. No minaret. No muezzin.

World's end.

Time stops.

Eternity begins again.

A giant tree trunk, with a single cross bar, standing on a rocky headland. The sky dark and lowering, the wind blowing. A man, bloody, nailed to the tree, his head crowned, his lips parched. He is crying out, "Why have you forsaken me?"

Trumpets.

The jousting ring, filled with spectators.

Two knights in armor, mounted on chargers, visors down, jousting sticks at the ready. Thunder of hooves. Spectators roar. One knight is unhorsed, he falls upon the ground, his helmet torn off, his blond hair dragging on the ground, his blue eyes glazed in death. The second knight dismounts, raises his visor, crosses himself. It is Guy of Vienne! He has slain al-Adil!

Abdulla found him and carried him out of the death chamber, half-dragging the inert body down the stairs into the great hall. He propped him against the wall, and bathed the dried blood from his face. Then he sat down beside him to watch for his awakening.

It was high noon when the bodyguard, whose eyes never left his master's face, saw the eyelids flutter, and the color slowly return to the waxen features.

"Master," he said, shaking him, "are you all right?" Guy of Vienne opened his eyes in a strange world. It was as though he saw with double vision. He recognized Abdulla perfectly. He knew his wife was dead. But he also knew he was no longer al-Adil.

"Yes, Abdulla," he answered. "I'm all right. But I have this night descended into Hell and returned a changed man." A shadow of pain crossed his eyes. "What have they done with my wife?"

"The servants have laid her out for burial. They are digging the grave now on the hills."

"And my son?"

"He lives. A fine boy. His hair is fair, master," Abdulla added shyly.

"Abdulla, listen! I am not what you think. I am no longer your master. I must leave here now and go far away and be seen no more by my people. Will you stay and serve my son? Someday he shall be Imam. I want him to remember me."

And taking off the blood red marriage ring on his finger, he handed it to the bodyguard. "When he is old enough, give him this. And speak to him of me."

"Master, I will."

"Enough!"

Guy rose, a little unsteadily, and made his way back to the room where Yasmin lay wrapped in a shroud, ready to be taken out on the hillside. As he had expected, his father-in-law was standing beside the bed.

In a single night the old man had aged to the point where he resembled a death's head. The cords stood out in his neck and his eyes were like burning coals. He neither turned nor looked at Guy. But he said, "Can you pray?"

"Can you not?" asked Guy.

"I—do not believe in God," answered the old man in a low voice. "I never have. It was all a fraud from the beginning."

"Then I will say the prayers over the grave," answered Guy coldly. "After that I shall go. You will never see me again."

The old man looked at him almost regretfully. "And your son?"

"—is Imam!"

"So be it!"

"I shall make peace with the Sultan and ask him to appoint a regent."

"So be it!"

"You shall keep Masyaf, but your power is at an end."

"So be it!"

"Then swear to this on the body of your daughter!"

"I have already sworn everything you wished while she was still in life—before she died!" said the old man.

Guy looked at him strangely, then lowered his eyes to the body of Yasmin between them. "Yasmin!" he breathed. "It was your victory after all!"

It was sunset when they buried her. Two grave diggers had dug the ground in a small cleft among the rocks where a lone thorn tree grew. Guy read the burial prayer, and then the two gravediggers prepared to lift the planks on which the body rested and lower them into the grave. But Guy stopped them.

Leaning over, he uncovered the face, while the gravediggers looked decently aside. Yasmin was as she had always been, perfectly composed, her eyes closed as though looking down demurely before her husband's gaze the night she was presented to him, her tiny mouth pursed, as it were, for his kiss. He kissed her. Then from her hand, already stiff with *rigor mortis*, he drew the marriage ring he had given her, the mate for his own, and he slipped it on his smallest finger.

He waited until the last spadeful of earth had been

heaped on the mound before he turned away. Followed by
Abdulla, he went down to the Castle, changed into his
woodsman's guise, and prepared to take his leave.

He gave Abdulla several letters: one for the Sultan, re-
establishing the peace; one for Salah-ed-Din asking him to
act as regent for his son; one for his people, enjoining
them to obedience to his son, to be read in the mosque.
All the letters he signed, (but not without a long moment's
hesitation), as "Al-Adil, Vice Regent of God," and sealed
with the seal of the Imam.

Abdulla was near tears.

"Abdulla, my friend," said Guy, "you have served me
well."

"Master, you gave me life. If you had commanded, that
night, I would have jumped!"

Guy's eyes were wet as he embraced him.

"And what shall I tell your people, master? Shall they
expect you again?"

"Never. I am no longer Imam. I am no longer al-Adil. I
have gone to another life."

Abdulla kissed his hand. "I will serve you, master, in
your son," he said.

Long after Guy had gone, the stars came out, and high
on the lonely top of the mountain where, in the imagination of many, the Courts of Paradise once existed, an old
man lay face down on the new heaped earth of the grave,
weeping.

MOUNT SINAI

CHAPTER ELEVEN

HOMECOMING

In November the oak leaves were brown and withered, but still clung to the boughs, in the way of oaks, waiting for the first winter gales to tear them free. The whole Vale of Shechem was robed in oak forests, below the line of the escarpment of Mount Gerizim, that reared its stony mass heavenward, as though shaking free of the trammels of earth, to commune alone with God.

In the woods, a hazy sun filtered through the shrivelled leaves and filled innumerable small glades with pools of light, catching the yellow plumage of the golden oriole as he darted from bush to bush in search of summer's last fruits, or highlighting the antlers of the wild deer as they grazed on fallen acorns.

No one in these woods would notice a solitary man with a donkey, following the barely perceptible trail of the woodcutters, that led onto the heights above Castle Shechem. He paused, to hitch his donkey to the branch of an oak. He could have passed for a woodcutter himself, weary at the end of a day of chopping and cording, and glad of a moment just to sit and stare.

The twilight scene before the stranger summoned up far

more than a lost summer. In his beggarly guise, wearing
an Arab kaffiyeh swathed around his head that entirely
concealed his features, he would not necessarily inspire
confidence. The Castle dogs had already been set upon
him. They drove him away from the gatehouse, where the
guards of the King's Constable took their ease. In the village at the tavern and at the synagogue, people had
thrown stones after this suspicious figure, when he came
begging for scraps. The countryside was filled with these
wandering vagabonds, and had been ever since the King
had disenfranchised many of the late Queen's knights and
their serfs, taking their lands for himself. Robbery and
murder stalked behind the hedgerows in the most peaceful
villages.

With the fast fading twilight came a chill that nipped
the bones on these Judean hills. The wanderer cracked
open some acorns and picked out the pulpy stuff, but it
was green and he made a face on swallowing it. He would
have been glad of a flint to light a fire and eat his acorns
roasted, but that would not have been safe—someone
would have undoubtedly spied the flame.

Then, from just below the rise of land where he sat, he
saw a wisp of smoke curl up on the evening air. Even in
this lonely spot, some cotter must have his cot, some
housewife must be firing the oven for the evening meal.
He drew near the edge of the hill and found himself looking down into a small farmstead, a house built of logs in
the Norman fashion set against the side of the hill, and before it a yard, fenced in with a stone wall.

A single man was at work herding his swine, perhaps
twenty or more, into the yard from the hillside. When the
last one was inside, he closed and barred the gate and began driving his grunting charges toward a pool in the
yard. Carefully, the swineherd forced each pig into the
pool, sloshing it clean with a stiff brush before it was allowed to scramble into the pen for the night. Strange! The
wanderer had never seen such care lavished on a pig since
he was a boy on his own father's estate.

Unhitching the donkey, the man in the Arab kaffiyeh

made his way down the hillside and leaned upon the stone wall of the swinery. After some minutes, when the last pig had been dealt with, he called respectfully to the swineherd.

"Might a beggar sleep with your swine for the night, sir?"

Night had almost fallen, and the swineherd came forward to look intently at his would-be guest.

"Where are you from, stranger?" he inquired. "What country?"

"A refugee from the lands of the Paynim."

"Paynim or not, by Jesu, I know that voice!"

"And I yours. Is it—Hugh?"

"Master!"

The gate was flung open; the men embraced. When the donkey had been brought in and safely bedded down for the night in a shed against the wall of the house, Hugh turned to his former master with a trace of embarrassment.

"Will you spend the night with us, sir? We are poor folk now—we have no bed to offer you—"

"You and—"

"Me and Esmeralda. I have married. A native girl—you know how it is, sir—a man gets lonely."

"Let me sleep with the donkey in the shed. With a bit of hay I shall be well enough."

"Anyway, you must come in and eat. Plain grub—but you look as though you could do with it."

Later, they sat across the fire from each other in the plain one-room cot, while the silent Esmeralda waited on them, moving noiselessly on the hard, mud floor. Guy saw that Hugh was older and tireder; the heart had gone out of him somehow. He must have had a bloody time—Good God! He had made a gentleman of him. He shouldn't be herding swine! He wondered how many of his men were left.

"I suppose we are all scattered?" he said aloud.

"We?"

"The troop from Vienne."

"Ah. I don't know how many are left. Sergeant Berthold died, of course, the night you disappeared. He went after you and so did Messer Adhemar. They had a tremendous fight of it and killed a giant as big as Goliath, but in the end they were overpowered. They both died fighting."

"I forbade them to do it!" Then Guy crossed himself, and added, "May they rest in peace." A profound sadness overcame him as he realized he had brought only death and ill-luck to these men. They had come with him at his bidding and he had deserted them all. He said aloud, "But you held out?"

"Yes, thank God! The enemy broke into the gate-house, but we held the keep against them. I don't remember how, exactly,—it's a long time ago." Startled, Hugh thought, he can know nothing, after all, or he never would have come. It was strange to think his master as a beggar. Somehow with his long hair and his beard, he looked more like some kind of a heathen king. Hugh was astonished that he hadn't asked about *her*.

"And the others?" pursued Guy.

"Of us? I couldn't say, exactly. We're all scattered. You've been to the Castle?"

"I paid a brief visit this afternoon. The Constable has unfriendly dogs."

"Then you know. It wasn't so bad while the old Queen was alive. She was a grand old lady, she was. When she handed over the crown to old rotten guts, King Baldwin, she kept Shechem as her fief. She became a nun, you know, and she used to come and see me and patted my hand like she was my own mother—I forgot to say, sir, that Mother died. A knight brought me the news last year. You remember how fond she was of you—we both of us had her milk together. That's when I lost my wish ever to go home—and so Esmeralda and me got married. I hope you like her, sir. She's good to me, Esmeralda!" And he gave her a pat on the rump as she passed by.

With an effort, Guy said, "You've done well, Hugh. My congratulations." To himself he thought that everything was lost. His foster *maman* was dead, too! God, how could he bear any more? He dared not ask—surely Hugh would tell him if—

"Yes, we're all gone on our ways," Hugh rambled on, "there's none of us left here now but me. You see, sir, I got my freedom. It was the Queen's doing, really. She made me castellan—until your return, of course. So I put a bit of money by—you know, sir, you never really squeezed the peasants the way you could have. Some of these farmers are rich as lords! Anyway, I kept my sock hidden and when the Queen died, I hopped. First Baldwin was King, then Amaury, his brother. The new Constable, Amalric—may he rot in hell!—got the fief from King Amaury and he sold all the men. Put them up for auction to the highest bidder! He's always hard up—that's how I was able to buy my freedom from him. It's not a bad life, sir, but it's lonely and I miss the old days."

"Would you like to get out?" asked Guy.

"Would I?" Hugh was affirmative. "I'd go like that!" And he snapped his fingers.

"Where? Back home?"

"No. I'd like—you'll pardon me, sir, you'll likely not understand—but I'd like to do a bit of freebooting, like—just in a small way, you know—working on the Moslem caravan trade in the valley. All I need is some arms and a few men to work for me—"

"I'm sorry, Hugh," smiled Guy, "I'm not in a position to help you—"

"Of course not, sir. You look in a bit of a bad way yourself. Was it hard—over there?"

"I was a slave for many years. Then I had certain—opportunities."

"You were always a clever one, sir. Did you really twist the heathen Paynim?"

"I suppose you might say that. They were very good to me."

"Imagine that! Made you a free man again?"

"A king."

"Sir!" Hugh was overwhelmed. He had guessed right after all. To win a Paynim crown. Who but his master could do such a thing! And then he lost it again. That was just like him, too. There must have been a woman in it somewhere. He was too soft, the master was. Clever, but soft, 'specially where the women were concerned. Like in the case of—but there was no use mentioning it. Obviously, he had forgotten everything that had happened that night. Best to let it be forgotten. He need never know. "You should quit these parts, sir, if I were you," said Hugh aloud.

"I detect a certain hostility in the air at Castle Shechem," replied Guy. "But unluckily, I have nowhere to go. I'm at the end of my rope."

"Then you shall stay here as long as you like." Hugh's latent loyalty rose to the surface. Still, it was inconvenient to have the master on the premises. Someone from the Castle was bound to notice it. Then he would have them all down on him like a swarm of angry bees. He said, "Lay low, though, master. You are not among friends here."

"Thank you for that advice, Hugh," Guy smiled a little wanly. He had no friends left in the world, not even the one person in the world he had hoped for the most. But the past was dead and he must begin all over again.

He bedded down easily that night in the donkey's shed and, although the night was cold and he had to cover himself with the hay, he slept soundly.

After a few weeks, Guy settled down to a routine. He helped Hugh with the pigs each day, taking them up to pasture in the woods, where they feasted on acorns, keeping an eye on them throughout the day, and then bringing them back at evening. Somehow, he felt that Hugh liked it best this way—it kept him out of sight. It was not as though he were unwelcome but—what does an honest yeoman do with a beggared king in the house? Guy knew he must move on. But where, he did not know.

One morning, early in December, Hugh and Esmeralda took the fattest pigs to market in Nablus, in time for the

Christmas sale. They left before dawn, and Guy remained in sole possession of the cot under the hill. After breakfast, he went out in the yard, bent on a task he had long decided upon. First, he sharpened his dagger to a razor edge on a whet-stone. Then he stripped to the waist and knelt down at the edge of the pool, soaping his face and splashing it in the water. A moment later, he was shaving off his beard.

It is curious how much an act like that means to a man—almost as though he were cutting away a part of his personality. And it is true that Guy looked very different when the clean, square lines of his face appeared again. No longer was he the oriental despot, resplendent in his hirsute majesty. But what was he now? He looked into the pool, puzzled. He did not know himself.

A moment later, another face appeared in the brackish, sunlit water. It was a girl, standing behind him, her hair piled high on her head with a comb, a yoke across her shoulders from which hung two pails, one on each side. She was very still, and her features were all in shades of green like the water, so that she might have been a water nymph herself.

Guy stared, transfixed, unmoving. The water nymph made the first move. She reached up and took the comb out of her hair, so that the rich shower fell down about her face, obscuring her features, and reached nearly to her waist. The spell was broken. Guy turned and stood up, slightly embarrassed to be found this way—and then he knew her.

"Alice." The name dropped from his lips almost without volition.

She seemed unable to speak and for a long moment they stared at each other. Then she began to gather her wits together. "You've come back."

Mutely Guy nodded and started to pull on his shirt but she stopped him. "It's all right," she said shyly. "I never saw a man shave before. Don't stop." She sat down on a stone, unfastening the yoke and putting the buckets on the ground.

With growing surprise, Guy observed the simplicity of her manner. He remembered her haughtiness, especially toward *him*, and now she seemed to put no distance between them. But did that mean she cared any more—or not at all? He glanced quickly at her hand. There was no ring.

He returned to his shaving, but his hand trembled and he cut himself. "It looks most dangerous," she commented. "Wouldn't you like me to try for you?"

"Of course not," he said, laughing. "Shaving's not a woman's business. You'd skin me alive."

"Not any worse than you're doing to yourself," she observed.

He felt he wasn't doing very well, so he explained, "It's the first time I have shaved in years. They don't shave— over there."

"So you've been a regular dervish all this time?"

He started. "How did you know?"

"I mean—you look so wild, with your long hair and all—just as though you were going to do one of those whirling dances."

"Then I'd better cut it, too," he interrupted. "Perhaps you could do that better than I could—" He handed her the dagger.

"Indeed I could." With quick, deft strokes, she trimmed him to a neat semblance of what he had once been like in time gone by. "There," she said, "now you can put your shirt on. You look quite yourself again."

He did look himself, she thought. Quite as handsome as ever. But he had lost something, too. What was it? Happiness? What did a man want most of all? He had lost it. Of course, he was older now. There was a trace of grey in his hair, and a sadness about the eyes. Youth, and the dreams of youth, faded in the light of day, just as hers had faded—Oh, God. What must she look like to him? She should never have come. But perhaps it no longer mattered now—

"Thank you," he said with his grave courtesy.

"I must go," she floundered. "I only came down to borrow a little water from Hugh. Our well has gone dry."

"*Our* well?"

"Oh, the wild creatures—we still inhabit the tower. I guess I'll never change—"

"Really?" He was delighted to hear it. Something was still in its place. The whole world might dissolve in the flames of the Apocalypse, but Alice would still be in her tower on the hill with all her wild creatures about her. But how on earth had she managed? That tower had been burned to a shell years ago! "Let me fill your buckets for you."

He took them to the stream outside the yard where the water was fresh and brought them back brimming. She had hardly moved from her place on the stone. But when she bent to pick up the yoke and put it on her shoulders, he gently took it from her and placed it on his own.

"But I can manage perfectly," she said. Then she smiled. "That's what I said to you the first time we met, wasn't it? I always seem to be refusing your kindness. I used to think it was masculine despotism. But I know better now. I don't think you're a despot. "You're," she hesitated, "You're the kindest man I ever knew."

They set out up the hill. It did not take many paces before Guy could see that something was wrong. Alice barely kept up with him, her left leg was dragging and she seemed out of breath. He felt an acute pain at her distress and quickly decided to face it then and there.

"You've hurt yourself, Alice."

"It's my leg," she panted. "It's fine if you don't go so fast."

"An accident?"

"The night of the fire—it's really all right, if you'll let me take your arm."

The advantage of the yoke was that he had an arm free to give her. The fact that she had asked for it cheered him more than anything, and in fact, walking together, they climbed the hill with ease. They both felt better and were panting and laughing when they came to the top.

What a sad sight it was, though, to see Alice's tower tumbled into ruin, shored up with crude wooden buttresses—fence poles she had begged from the farmers—and the roof fallen in, to be replaced by mere thatch, draining inside the blackened walls, and out a gutter in the mud floor! Only the ground floor was left, with her bed and a few possessions huddled around the fire.

Guy rubbed his freshly-shaved chin ruefully and set down the buckets. "Alice," he said, "your tower. It needs rebuilding. I would do it if you'd let me."

"Oh, Guy," she said, "your generosity is always—no—I'm not worth it, anymore."

He could not clearly see, the way her hair was hanging down, but he knew she was crying.

He knew he must face it. "I must tell you something. You haven't asked because, I suppose, you want to spare my feelings. I have nowhere to go. Even Hugh doesn't want me around because they're on the lookout at the Castle. If you'll let me move up here, I'll put up a workman's shed for myself and I'll have your tower rebuilt before the snow flies."

She was standing in the midst of the floor, looking down, her shoulders shaking. She gave him her hand, still with head averted. "Oh, Guy," she managed. "I guess you knew. Somehow you must have known. I couldn't get through another winter alone. If you need a place to hide, it's yours. But—but there's one thing you must understand. The past is over. We're living new lives now—just like two old friends. And—I'm very, very glad you've come."

And so it came about that Alice acquired a handyman, who scoured the woods for fallen branches, hauled them to the tower, and chopped them into lengths to fit the circular shape of the roof. He ran up a ladder of pegs in the outer wall, up which he carried the new beams and fitted them into the groin, close together, across the top. Lacking most tools, he used thongs to bind the logs in place, and skins to cover them. As he had promised, the roof was finished before the first black skies overhung Gerizim with the foreboding of snow.

All the while, the two outcasts lived side by side in perfect amity, as though their mutual plight had eliminated all differences between them. All differences? If Alice felt any embarrassment at having a man on the premises—and this man, of all men—she went out of her way not to make him feel it. She brought his food to him, washed for him, made him new shirts since he had only cast-offs of Hugh's to wear.

For his part, he respected her wishes meticulously, and never intruded himself upon her. He lived in the little work-shed he had built, as though it were his own home, rarely coming to the door of the tower and never entering it. When the roof was finished, he spent much of his time with the animals, reinforcing their shelters and occasionally mending an injured paw or a broken wing.

A mutual trust grew up, casting a new light on their relations, that seemed to overlay and altogether replace the former tension that had existed between them. This is not to say that each was not acutely aware of the other. But if, at times, she found him masterful—and he had grown, she found, more masterful—she told herself it was his maleness and not his fault. And this characteristic, formerly so repellent to her, was now compensated by his new consideration and above all by his kindly gift of silence—on the subject she feared the most.

Guy was alone in the woods.

It was good to be alone all day, sharpening the arrows for the new bow he had made, or just sitting on this fallen log, staring into space. After leaf fall, the woods were empty. You could see into the heart of things.

Fighting was like that—during the heat of battle there was no time nor disposition, to understand its meaning. Only when the flags had fallen and the field was deserted, was it possible to assess the reasons, the mistakes, the failures, the lessons.

The past was dead. He would never be able to deny that it had made a wound in him as deep and raw as if some wild beast had torn open his body. He had staunched the wound outwardly, but inwardly he was bleeding to death. The wound was Yasmin.

Ah, Yasmin! Now that he could see you whole, now that he remembered the night in the cart on the way up to Jerusalem, the night in the Tower of David, how much more he was able to understand. This was the key which explained everything, the key which you had kept hidden from him, lest he should unlock the door of the past and seek his freedom.

No, Yasmin, this was not the freedom he wanted—freedom from you—no, no—he would have remained your slave forever, if only you had not hidden him from himself. That day in the slave market, when he felt your eyes on him in his nakedness and shame—if he had only known they were the eyes of love, and not the eyes of Potifar's wife, buying him for her bed.

The wanton kiss, that day in the empty audience hall—how beautiful it was; he felt the surprise of it, the warm succulence of your beautiful mouth against his, the demand which was in reality not a demand at all but a restatement of an act of love made long ago in the Tower of David—had he but known it.

He had come to accept these things and still to love you, Yasmin! How could you doubt that? Did you not remember the Night of Destiny, when the angels of the Lord came down with blessings on your bed, the sweet intermingling of his flesh with yours, the perfect oneness of your happiness? And, in the morning, how you rubbed his feet 'till he was awake—and how many times afterward you did that!

But you doubted him because he would be free—you feared his freedom—you interpreted his freedom as indifference. You even believed him guilty of massive infidelities with all the daughters of the headmen! Oh, Yasmin. He was only a man; he was far from you; he was tempted once or twice—but unfaithful? Never. And you died believing it.

That was why you turned to the efreet, you gave him your body, you stole away from your husband's bed into the cold, dark bed of earth, and now you will never know how much you were loved by him you loved, how lonely he is for you, how his life, too, has ended with yours!

Guy drove the dagger he was holding deep into the trunk of the tree, so that it stood there, vibrating. It was strange how life-like it looked, quivering as if it had a being of its own! Then he remembered how Yasmin had given it to him the day he left for the Jebel Bahra. It was all he had left of her—except the ring. Should he use it now?

Suddenly he seized the handle, overwhelmed by his impulse, but it would not come free. He stood, pressing his foot against the tree trunk, pulling with all his might. The blade stuck fast. He desisted a moment, and a look of awe came over his face, as he studied the shining hilt. Perhaps, after all, there were signs for him still—?

"Yasmin," he said aloud, "the weapon is yours. If you forbid me, I will not use it against myself. May I have it back, please?"

Again he took hold of the hilt and it came away quite easily in his hand. Trembling slightly, he put the blade in its scabbard, collected his arrows, and turned for home. But in later days his footsteps often found their way back to the same spot in the wood. He would sit on the fallen tree and stare at the place in the trunk where the dagger had held fast.

It was almost as though he were listening for something. Was it a bird, singing somewhere above his head? Was it a voice, with once-loved human accents, calling him? He could not be sure. But his thoughts took a new turn. He looked into the past and sought there the answers to his own arguments. And the words came easily to him, as he apostrophised himself.

Guy, Guy, you were wrong to reproach her. She did not deceive you. You deceived yourself. How could she have restored your memory just by telling you who you were? That would only have destroyed you, destroyed the person you had become. But you need not reproach yourself either. She loved you as you are. Your misunderstanding of her, your forgetfulness at times, your "unfaithfulness" mattered not at all. She forgave everything, even your "infidelities."

After all, she was an eastern wife. She would never expect you to be faithful in such circumstances. Why should you be, with so many pretty maidens awaiting your pleasure? But you wanted to "prove" your faithfulness as a token of your love. And you did prove it, in the only way a man can prove it—by loving her.

And she did not desert you for the efreet. She saw you as Saint George slaying the dragon even as his fiery breath burned her flesh. And when you cast him forth, he descended to the depths of hell, never to rise again. She is free of him now, just as she would make you free of the past. She wants you to live your own life now, your true life; to be free, truly free, and to be yourself, just as you once were when you rode up to Jerusalem many years ago. She wants you to begin again.

So Guy reasoned with himself, and a strange lightness came over his spirits, as though the words that entered his mind were not his words at all but hers. With a sudden halloo, he spied a deer among the trees and, taking his aim, he felled it with a single arrow from his bow. He carried the carcass back at twilight, skinned it, dressed it and hung up the meat. Food was short now and, although Alice did not like to kill the wild creatures, he must put by their winter store.

The snow came the day before New Year's and made further excursions into the country impractical for the time being. The landscape glistened whitely; in the woods there were enormous groanings and crackings, as mighty branches came down under the weight of the snow; and on the open heights the tracks of the fox and the antelope could be clearly seen, as they sought their lairs.

It was very cold. Guy busied himself all day with the farmyard chores, feeding the animals and building a windbreak to protect their pens. When he came to the door of the tower at dusk to receive his supper in a steaming porringer, his fingers were stiff and blue.

Alice saw it at once and begged him to come in and eat by the fire. He shuffled and demurred, but finally gave way to her entreaties, bringing in some extra logs. Now that there was no second story in the tower, the smoke from the hearth rose straight up and out a flue he had made in the roof, so the air inside was clear and bright. Alice spread some rugs by the fire and they sat together, eating out of the same bowl, as the wind howled outside.

After supper, he lay on his back and she put a pillow under his head. He watched her moving about, cleaning up the dishes and setting them in a shining row on a hanging shelf he had built for her along the wall. Then she lit an oil lamp, shaped like a small boat, with an opening for the oil at the top and a straw wick at the front that she suspended from a bracket in the wall beside the fire; after that, placing the only chair beneath it, she sat down with a book.

Alice had a strange collection of books which she had obtained from the nuns at the convent in Nablus. Queen Melisende had brought them with her from Jerusalem when she took the veil, and there were many the good nuns looked at askance, with their illuminated scripts often containing lewd pictures of pagan lore—Virgil's *Aeneid* in Latin and the *Odyssey* of Homer in Greek. They sent them to Alice with much shaking of heads and warnings against the snares of the devil.

Guy's eye fell on the Greek script in her hand and he took it from her, studying it curiously.

"Where did you learn Greek, Alice?" he asked.

"I had a Greek tutor when I was young. A Byzantine, actually. He taught me Greek, Latin, Syriac, theology, cosmology and mathematics. So you see I am very learned. Much good it has done me."

"Heavens. I won't know how to talk to you any more," he laughed. "My conversation must seem very dull."

Guy turned the pages of the *Odyssey* and she told him the story. Especially, he wanted to hear about the return of Odysseus to his native land, the faithful swineherd who hid him in his hut, the goddess Athene who appeared to him in the guise of a beautiful woman and armed him against his enemies.

He insisted that she read the stories to him, translating from the Greek. He would stop her many times, asking for an explanation here, an opinion there. It seemed clear that Alice did not think much of Odysseus, his wiles, his masculine insouciance toward the women he loved, his selfishness toward the men he led to the world's end. But she welcomed the curiosity of her listener.

What a strange and lovely creature she was, Guy thought as he watched her read. How unusual for a woman to read Greek! And she did it so simply, so naturally; it seemed almost a part of her. She was Athene, she was Penelope.

Once again he found himself admiring the fine, high-boned features of her face, the noble brow, partly obscured by the shower of tawny hair that habitually fell down the left side of her face; the clear, wide, startling lamps of her eyes. She was a goddess, he thought, and he had no business falling in love with a goddess, especially since he was now a beggar. Besides, she had forbidden it. The past was dead. Yet he felt rising in him unbidden the unmistakable signs of desire.

She had reached the passage where Penelope tells Odysseus how she fended off the suitors during his absence, by the making of the web, which she wove every day and undid every night, saying she would not marry again until it was finished.

"How did you keep him away?" Guy suddenly asked. "He wanted you, you know. He planned to have you for himself."

"Who?" she asked, not raising her eyes.

"Amalric."

She was silent awhile. Then she said, "He had no power over me. The land, you see, and the tower were mine. You remember, you sold me the deeds."

He took it in. Of course! Those deeds she had forced

him to sell her had saved her life in the end. She had been right all along to depend on herself and not on him. The thought made him a little sad.

"Did you live in the Castle then?" he asked.

"I did at first. Hugh was castellan. He let me have my old room and the men were always respectful and honorable to me because—," she became confused, "well, because of you. They all expected you to come back, to escape, or ransom yourself somehow. But after the Queen died, the fief reverted to the Royal Treasury. The King awarded it to Amalric and we were all evicted. Amalric himself came down with his men-at-arms and took possession of everything, castle, lands, serfs—and me. He was going to marry me, he said, by *droit de seigneur*."

"*Droit de seigneur!*" Guy was indignant. "As though such a thing existed in this day and age! Why, I could never have—" He stopped himself, but she took it up.

"Yes, you could. It's on the statute books. Amalric showed me a copy of it. You could have forced me, when you were *seigneur*—"

"What nonsense we're talking, Alice. As though I would have done such a thing." Privately, he thought it might have been better if he had; then none of this would have happened. Instead, he pressed the question. "But how did you get out of it?"

"I shocked him. I frightened him. I reduced him to jelly," replied Alice grimly. She seemed to be steeling herself to some resolution, the prospect of which terrified her and yet which she could not avoid. She advanced into it with all the heroism of a great soul facing its own destruction.

Guy felt the danger and tried to avert it. "You showed him he was no match for you," he said.

"I showed him I was no match for *him!*" she enunciated distinctly. "He sent for me to dine in the Great Hall. All the great ones were there from the Court in Jerusalem. The barons, the knights, the King's courtiers and their ladies, all had come down to bask in his good fortune. The hall was decorated as for a Royal fête, with mirrors and candles everywhere, servitors all in uniform, trumpeters at the entrance, and two thrones at the high table for—_us!_"

She got up and began to pace the floor, acting it out in memory. "I dressed with especial care that night. He had bought me an expensive dress; I put it on; I loaded myself with all the jewels I could lay my hands on. I descended the tower stairs from the balcony, where he met me, and I placed my arm in his. I walked with him up the aisle to the head table, between the ranks of bowing courtiers."

She had retreated to the old blackened, disused stairs of the tower, advancing into the room as she talked, re-enacting the bows, the hand on the imaginary arm, until she had arrived at the center of the floor under the light of the lamp. Then she said, "I showed myself to them as I really am!"

And on these words, she flung back her magnificent, tawny hair with a sweeping gesture of her left arm, holding it taut behind her head, and looking down at Guy with her left profile fully exposed to the light. He saw at once that the left side of her face had been badly scarred from the temple to the lower jaw, where the skin had been burned away and had healed in ugly weals. Seen like this, in lurid profile, she was hideously disfigured—yet a moment before, no one would have guessed it.

Guy leaped to his feet. "Alice! Dear Alice!" he cried, holding out his hands to her. But she only tottered a moment, and fell to her knees, burying her face in her hands, her hair hanging forward onto the floor. "Now you know! You know!" she sobbed.

Quickly, he knelt beside her, his arm about her waist. But she turned herself away from him, refusing his comfort, stopping her ears to his endearments.

"Listen to me, Alice," he pleaded. "I am not Amalric. I am Guy, your own true knight. You are more to me than all other women in the world. I swear it to you! By Christ's blood, I swear it! This—this _accident_ has only brought us closer together. Remember—it was I who carried you out of the tower—I put the fire out in your hair with my own hands—"

He held her now, his strong hands around her waist; she felt their warmth under her breasts and she trembled with a strange fear—no, it was not fear of him, but fear of his kindness, his pity. It came to the same thing—she must refuse him. With a sob, she turned to him.

"No, no, it is impossible," she said. "I am not for you—I am a witch!"

His face bent close above hers. "Sweet witch," he murmured, "you can't refuse me now. It was you who bewitched me!" His lips brushed hers. She must refuse—she must—she must. The struggle filled her whole soul, so that she wept streaming tears, which ran down her cheeks and he tasted their bitter salt on her mouth. But she could not prevent him.

Once their lips were joined, the physical struggle was over. There was no denying their love; it filled them both with awe at its tumult. Guy drew her down on the rug beside the fire; he covered her with kisses, on her mouth, her ears, her neck, her whole face including the injured part, saying no word. Alice yielded to his impetuousness; the musk of his desire was overwhelming, her head swam with it. She could not resist him, but still she must save herself—or was it him she wanted to save?—by throwing herself on his mercy.

"Guy, dear Guy," she pleaded, "let me go now."

He was surprised at the gentleness, the sweetness of her tone. This was a new Alice, *his* Alice. Yet still he had not fathomed the inner mystery, the secret she would not yield up to any man. Not even to the man she loved? Ah, not to him above all! How could she explain that she was fated to live and die as pure as any Vestal of ancient Rome? Surely that was the meaning of the brand upon her face—the seal of her virginity.

"You can do what you like with me," she went on, "only please, please do not force me—"

Guy smiled down at her. She was lying with her head resting on his arm, looking up at him. With his other hand he caressed her body through the taut wool of her dress. "Of course not, beloved," he replied. "But that will not stop me from kissing you!" He matched the action to the word, and yet it chilled him, this kiss, with the freezing fires of the temple of Vesta. Even in his arms, she must always remain beyond his reach.

The wind howled long that night around the tower on the hill, and Guy never went back to his bed of straw in the yard outside. But neither did he sleep in hers. Instead, he lay by the fire, wrapped in the hearth rug, his head on the pillow she had given him.

Alice was more wakeful and several times she rose from her pallet of straw by the wall and tiptoed to the hearth to put on another log. Then she would pause and look down on him as he slept.

"I will die for you," she whispered, "only let me remain a virgin 'til I die, please let me, dear Guy."

And on returning to her lowly bed, she offered up a prayer to the Blessed Virgin in heaven that it might be so.

A few days later, the thaw set in. Guy left the tower early for a day's hunting in the woods. A short while afterwards, Alice, having given no word of warning, set out on a visit to Nablus. She arranged for a lift along the way in a drover's cart, and she arrived in the forenoon before the gates of the Convent she had left many years before.

She felt a pang as she entered once again the quiet, brown stone cloisters beside the old belltower, topped with snow. There, in the center of the courtyard, was the garden she had tended formerly with such care, its roses now banked for the winter. The cypresses beside the doorway drooped their heads under the weight of wet snow. Somewhat like a ghostly revenant, she rang the bell.

The sister who answered knew her at once. "Why, Sister Alice!" she cried, "—that is, I suppose I should say Mistress Alice now! Or are you married yet? Well, come in out of the cold."

"Thank you, Sister Agatha," replied Alice, as they walked down the corridor together toward the parlor. "I have really come to see Mother Superior. Is she well?"

"Of course, quite well. But older, you know. We are

none of us getting any younger, are we? But you look so fresh still. I sometimes think you did the right thing, going back to the world. For you, that is. For me, well, there never was anything—I'll get Mother now, if I can. She is working in the leprosarium. You may wait here by the fire." And the sister fluttered away like a tired, white moth.

The Abbess Joveta was not particularly pleased to hear that Alice was waiting for her. She had never known how to handle her as a refractory novice and had been heartily glad when she left. Afterwards, she had regretted this, done penance for it, and now it seemed, the good Lord was giving her a chance to make amends. So it was with a sigh that she rose from the bedside where she was reading to a patient, and passed into the parlor.

"Welcome to Christ's house, dear daughter!" She held out her hands from the folds of her ample white habit. Alice knelt to kiss them both.

"Mother, I know you must wonder at me, coming back like this, after such long absence. I have never forgotten you. I have treasured the books you sent—you were always so good to me—and I so unworthy—" She began to stammer and her voice trembled a little, as she continued kneeling on the parlor floor.

Mother Joveta gathered her erstwhile daughter up into her arms and kissed her on both cheeks. "Come and sit down, Alice," she said, "tell me all about yourself. You must have so much news. We hear little nowadays; since the great Queen died, God rest her soul, no one from the big world comes to our door any more."

"I am not from the big world, Mother," said Alice, sitting on a small stool beside the Abbess's chair. "I am only a very small mouse in the wainscotting. And, of late, the mouse has been caught in a trap. She needs your clever fingers to free her!"

"You—caught in a trap! I shall never believe it, after all the little creatures you have saved, yourself, from those wicked toils the farmers put about—so cruel with all the sharpened stakes and what not and just to get their skins

to sell for gold—ah, well, I suppose they all must live, too!
But never mind my talk; say what you have come to say."

Alice paused and then came out with it. "Mother, I
want to return to the religious life."

The Abbess took this in, steeled herself against recrimi-
nation, but decided on caution. "I suspected it, daughter,
when Sister Agatha told me you were here. I hope you
have thought well this time, so that there will be no need
to go over the old ground. We must never go back. We always go on."

"Yes, Mother. I am no longer proud. Even if you tell
me to kiss the floor, I shall no longer rebel, as I did before. See—!" And she knelt to kiss the cold stones at their
feet.

"Stop. Get up at once, child," cried the Abbess. "No
one has asked you to do such a thing. It is unseemly to
put on a show of self-abasement. That, in itself, is a form
of inverted pride. Now, sit down, and tell me what has
brought you to this decision."

"I see now that I am not fitted to live a life in the
world—to be a married woman."

The Abbess struggled with her rising wrath. "And are
you any more fitted to be a nun—*as the bride of Christ?*"

Alice acknowledged her mistake. "He will, perhaps, not
ask so much of me."

"On the contrary, the Lord asks us for the last ounce of
blood we have to give in His service, and only by His
grace have we the strength to perform His labors. You
have been among us; you know the hours of prayer, the
duties in the scullery, in the leprosarium, in the school, in
the fields, at the altar—how can you say this is a life for
the weak and the unfit?"

Alice saw that she would get nowhere with the Abbess
unless she threw herself on her mercy. "Dear Mother," she
said gently, "help me, please help me. I am entangled in
the snares of the world. If you do not release me, only
death will set me free."

The Abbess waited for more and, as there was none,

she commented more gently, "Well, daughter, what are you escaping from this time—a man again?"

"A man—yes."

"And is he as bad as all the others?"

"He is not bad—I never said he was bad."

"Good then?"

"Very good."

"Daughter, you speak in riddles." The Abbess was impatient, but curious. "What is your objection to this man who, you say, is driving you to your death?"

"I have no objection—he is not driving me—oh, how can I explain it to you? If only you knew him you would understand—yes, Mother, you would see at once the goodness in him—"

"In brief, daughter," the Abbess cut her short, "you are in love."

After a pause, "Yes, Mother."

"And does he love you?"

Another pause. "Yes, Mother—that is, I think so. He told me so once long ago, and I refused him. But since he has come back he has—indicated it—"

"Indicated? How?"

"By his advances."

"And you resisted him?"

"I did, but he is very masterful—"

The Abbess studied her quizzically. Strange girl, she thought. She really does need protection from the world, she understands so little and she feels so much. "Well, you must not blame him for that."

"Oh, I don't blame him for anything—"

"I see. You blame yourself. Why?"

"Because, you see, I am not worthy of him. Since— since he first knew me, I had this terrible accident, the night of the fire, and I became horribly, horribly ugly. He cannot love me anymore. It is impossible, out of the question."

"Surely that is a matter for him to decide," said the Abbess quietly.

"I can't let him," cried Alice, bowing her head.

The elderly nun put her hand on her arm. "I believe you are telling me the truth, daughter. You did very well, to bring it all out like this. You have not told me one thing—does he know?"

Alice barely whispered, "I showed him."

The Abbess looked at her with a new attention. "You are a brave girl,—yes, very brave. I'm proud of you. I hope he is a very good man. He will need to be to deserve you. Very well, let's face it. What did he say?"

"He said nothing."

"Nothing?"

"He—he kissed me."

"I see," the Abbess had to grope her way. "Was it a pure kiss, daughter?"

"It was not."

"Well—then you are answered, child."

"You mean by the very impurity—?"

"I mean," said the Abbess severely, "that he has told you he loves you the best way he can, in order to make you believe it. What more do you want?"

"I want—I want—"

"Well?" The question grew grim.

"I want not to burden him—I want to spare him the shame of—of an ugly wife."

"And who is this man who is so much too good for you? Is he so very great, then?"

"He is not great. He has lost everything in the world."

The Abbess got up and began to pace the floor. Truly, this was a girl to try the patience of a saint. Never satisfied, she must always be seeking some ideal beyond the attainment of ordinary life. Having refused all suitors because she did not love them, she was now refusing one because she did. As though love of that kind mattered so much. She came to stop in front of Alice.

"So this is why you choose the religious life, once again—because you cannot accept the tasks God has given you? We are not here in this world just to satisfy our wishes, daughter. We are here to do the Lord's work. Make no mistake—we are not born at random—we are

not here that we may go to bed at night and get up in the
morning, eat and drink and laugh and talk, sin when we
feel like it, and repent when we are tired of sinning. The
Lord sees every one of us. He creates every soul. He
plants it in our body, one by one, for a purpose. He needs,
yes I dare to say it to you, daughter, He needs every one
of us.

"What has physical love to do with this? Nothing. Yet
through our bodies we may still serve Christ, if He so calls
upon us. If you love this man and he loves you, it may be
your work to help him, to strengthen him, to bear his children. The country needs strong men to defend it against
the cruel infidels. You may yet serve the Lord through
him."

Alice looked at her with the wide eyes of surprise. "You
mean—the Lord has called me to marry him?"

The Abbess went over to the window, looking out
through the louvred shutters at the snow. "I don't know,
my daughter, do I? It depends if his intentions are good.
You have not even told me his name."

Alice hung her head. She was ashamed to pronounce it,
after all the gossip about them in years gone by. "I expect
you have heard how the former lord of Shechem wooed
me. On the night he disappeared he gave me his ring. Now
he—he has come back."

The Abbess whirled about. "The lord of—the same
whom the Queen—why did you not say so at once, you
foolish girl?"

She seemed tense, pacing about, clutching her rosary in
one hand, holding the other to her head. At last she
seemed to get hold of herself and sat down again in her
chair by the fire. "Alice, my dear," she pursued, "you must
be very sensible. This young man has returned from the
land of the Saracens, you say, he is penniless, he has lost
everything, he needs your help.

"Now, I must tell you something of the greatest importance to you and to him. The late Queen was, as I suppose
you know, very fond of this young man, and she also
knew of his affection for you. When she lay dying of a fe-

ver here, she told me her wish concerning you both. If he were to return and claim you in marriage, she wished you to have a dowry that was worthy of him. She did not want him to marry a beggarmaid, she said. That was when she entrusted me with the jewels—her personal jewels which were kept in a casket under the stones of this very convent. They are Royal gems, my dear—a Queen's fortune. And they are to be yours—if he marries you."

Alice took it in extremely slowly. "I don't understand—she never liked me—"

"My foolish dear! They are not for you, they are for him."

"But only if he marries me?"

"Yes."

"I see. I suppose she felt it was the only way he would accept them. She must have loved him very much."

"Naturally, I have told no one of this. It would not do to let idle tongues talk about a fortune under our floors! I was to keep it hidden for seven years, and if he did not claim you, I was to turn it over to the Church—"

"But he has not claimed me yet!"

"What? Did you not say you were betrothed?"

"But I never wore his ring," wailed Alice.

The Abbess held her sides. "Oh, you wretched girl—is there no end to your foolishness? Where is this ring?"

Alice took it out of her bosom, suspended on a neck chain, which she unclasped. The Abbess took the ring briefly in her hand and commented, "A man's ring! Not quite suitable for you—still if he gave it to you, it is your duty to wear it for him." And she slipped it on Alice's finger.

They both rose, facing one another in the silent, stone-walled parlor, under the tall, Norman vaulting of the ceiling.

"But, Mother," stammered Alice, "I cannot be any man's wife—look at my face—" She lifted her hair.

The Abbess went to the wall and pulled a bell cord. Sister Agatha came in instantly. "Sister," said the Abbess, "fetch us that damask cloth in the late Queen's chests, and also bring some gossamer veils and a set of clean linen head cloths." Agatha sped on her errand.

"You," said the Abbess, with a certain amused asperity, "are going to become a woman at last. You should never have been allowed to wander about as you have, dressed like a wild thing, in bare feet and rags, with no care for yourself at all. Fortunately, you are beautiful enough that it did not spoil you, but now you must learn to make the most of yourself."

As the articles sent for arrived, the Abbess set about fitting them on Alice. "Don't talk to me about your face! What are coifs and wimples for? Now if you wore a proper headband, like this, and passed the linen under your chin and over the sides of your face, like this, tied it on the top and covered it with a gossamer veil, like that—you would have a very splendid headdress in the highest fashion—and no mark to be seen on your face at all!"

Alice herself began to feel the excitement of it—almost as though she were being dressed for her wedding. Was it really true that, coiffed and wimpled, no trace was to be seen of her disfigurement? "Could I—look in a glass, please?" she begged.

"We have no looking glasses in this house," replied the Abbess a little severely. "You will have to take our word for it. You are exceptionally beautiful, without a flaw. Any man would be proud to have you on his arm. Now you may take the damask and make what you can of it for a dress."

"I think, perhaps," she went on, leading Alice toward the door, "it would be better for you to move in here for a while, when we make your trousseau. You can have one of the late Queen's rooms. Of course, your young man can call on you anytime he likes, provided you meet in the parlor. I am very anxious to see him—"

"Oh, thank you, Mother," cried Alice, kissing her impetuously at the door. "Thank you! You have been so good to me. Is it really possible that anyone can be so happy, after all?"

"All things are possible with God, my daughter," replied the Abbess. She stood looking after her as the girl ran, clutching her bundle, to the gateway where the drover's cart stood waiting patiently to take her back home. And to think this beggarmaid, barefoot in the snow, was heiress to a Queen's fortune! The Abbess shook her head, and went back to her lepers.

When Alice reached the tower on the hill, as the early winter twilight closed in, she knew at once that something was wrong. Hugh was standing in the front yard, idly waiting for her.

"I wanted to be here when you arrived," he explained. "It's about the master. They've taken him away."

"Taken him? Who?" Fear gripped her heart.

"The Constable's men. They arrested him for poaching. The woods here belong to the Castle. I warned him not to hunt on the Constable's property—"

"It's Guy's property—you know that!" Alice blazed at him. "They are all thieves!"

"Well," Hugh temporized, "they caught him, anyway, red-handed with a pheasant he had shot—"

"Did they know him?"

Hugh hesitated. "Yes. I think the poaching charge is only an excuse. Because, you see, they have taken him in chains up to Jerusalem."

CHAPTER TWELVE

THE PRISONER OF THE TEMPLE

"Well, young man, come in, come in! These are not the happiest circumstances in which we meet again—but there it is, we are all tied to Dame Fortune's wheel—one day we're up, one day we're down. Sit down, there is no need to stand, we shall just have an informal talk together—a flagon of wine?"

Manasses of Hierges, seated behind his desk in the Citadel of Jerusalem, was ill at ease. He had no liking for his present role as Governor of Jerusalem—a mighty fall from his former estate as Constable of the realm—and particularly so, on this morning in February, when he was called upon to examine his new prisoner, the erstwhile lord of Shechem. He had never cared for this young man in the days when he was the Queen's favorite—but he was distinctly pained to see him now standing before him, loaded with chains on wrist and ankle.

Guy sat down carefully, his chains rattling in the ornate chair, and accepted the flagon of wine. It was all he had had except bread and water for several weeks since his incarceration. "Thank you, my lord," he said, "Dame Fortune is kind enough to put me in your hands!"

273

"Oh, in my hands!" Manasses puffed, blowing out his cheeks, "My hands are tied. I, too, have had my tumble. I made my peace with Amalric after the surrender of the city, and I take his orders now. But it does not come easy to a man who is used to command." He looked quizzically at his prisoner. "You would have done well to make your peace, also," he continued. "He is your liege lord, is he not?"

"I am vassal to his father, the Count of Poitou," Guy answered. "But he has no right to my fief of Shechem, which was a royal grant. He has no right to my men whom he sold like butcher's meat on the nail. He has no right to arrest me for poaching on my own estates."

"Rights! Rights! There are no rights in this world unless we can enforce them. Besides, you abandoned your estates at Shechem, did you not?"

"Is it abandonment to be taken prisoner in combat with the enemy?"

"It is abandonment if you are living in complicity with the enemy." He looked hard at the prisoner for some moments, then got up and placed his hand on the younger man's shoulder. "I like your spirit—but I doubt if you realize the peril you are in. The Constable Amalric has put certain facts before me. It is my duty to examine you on these facts. Believe me, I do not like this any better than you do. Here—have some more wine." He filled the flagon, cleared his throat a few times and sat on the edge of the desk, swinging his leg. At length he came out with it. "When did you begin this treason; was it before or after you went over to the enemy?"

"Manasses!" Guy looked him in the eyes. "You don't mean that! You can't think me a traitor?"

The Governor dropped his eyes. "We know," he said, "what we know. There is no use blustering it out. My dear Guy—if I may call you that—let me advise you for your own good. I cannot do much for you. But I will treat you as a gentleman, for I believe you are one. Now, let us begin at the beginning. Who were your accomplices?"

Guy was trembling inwardly, but determined not to

show a tremor. "You astound me, Manasses!" he said. "I did not think you could be bought like this. You know perfectly well that I have no accomplices."

"Does the name al-Adil mean nothing to you?"

So they knew! The trembling inside became nearly unbearable. Still, he would see it through. There was nothing in his record of which he need be ashamed. Unless they were to use it against his friends, his people, his son—! He decided to disown the past which, after all, he had shed the day his memory had been restored. This, surely, was the only honorable course.

"Nothing," said Guy.

Manasses sucked his teeth, blew out his breath and sighed. "It is not so simple as that, young man. One cannot just dismiss the facts as though they were not there. I suggest that you do know al-Adil very well. Let me recall him to you—tall, blond, very impressive in his white robes and white turban, a blood red ruby on his finger—" He glanced down at the ring Guy was wearing.

Guy followed the glance and for the first time felt the breath of fear. How did they know so much? It was uncanny. He was not sure if he was equal to a battle of wits such as this, for he was grappling with a darkness, an unknown enemy. Yet he persisted. "I never met him," he replied.

"Better than that! I suggest you know him as well as you know yourself—his most intimate thoughts, his overweening ambition, his diabolic sorceries, his assumption of the prerogatives of God—"

"This man," interrupted Guy, "you are talking about—who is he, anyway, that I should know him?"

"An enemy—a most foul enemy of the Kingdom of Jerusalem," Manasses replied distinctly.

"Then I deny emphatically that I know any such man!"

Manasses got up and retired to his magisterial chair behind the desk. "I believe you read and write Arabic?" he remarked, apparently at random.

"I know something of it."

The Governor picked up an object from the desk which

he proceeded to study with some attention. It was Guy's pearl-handled dagger, chased in gold with the name of al-Adil on the hilt, which had been taken from him on his admission to the Citadel. He felt a momentary wave of relief—so that was how they had obtained the name.

"I, too, have studied the Saracen script," remarked the Governor, turning the blade over in his hand. "It lends itself to much flowery expression—like this, for example, Al-Adil, the True Imam, Vice Regent of God on Earth. Very pretty. It is yours, I think?"

"A gift—I had it as a gift." Guy continued to struggle.

"Ah! Then you did know him?"

"Why is it so important if I know this man?"

"If he is our enemy—"

"And if he is not—"

"That will be for the Court to decide."

"The Court—?"

Manasses leaned across the desk, in an access of genuine sympathy. "My dear boy," he said, "let me advise you as if I were your own father. You are a fine young man. I have watched you fight; you have a strong right arm. You are, I think, honest and intelligent. But you are out of your depth in all this. Your puerile defense today confirms it.

"Later, you will come before very able judges, who will know how to lay your mind bare, so that you can keep nothing back, so you will have nowhere to hide your thoughts, so you will appear as transparent as a child. You have neither the wit nor the resource to fight these men. You must also remember that they will have ready all the necessary means to make you talk fully, explicitly, copiously, in fact to make you even eager and anxious to tell them everything they wish. Theirs are arguments flesh and blood cannot withstand.

"Think, then; think carefully before you resist these men. They already know everything about you. The Constable has been in communication for many years with his agents among the infidels, and in particular with the Master of the Ishmaeli sect of the Assassins—why do you start? Surely, you realize that in war everything cannot be left to the hazards of battle? We have always relied on our friends inside the enemy camp to help us; or at least we have used them for our own ends, with the avowed intention of destroying them later. It follows that these friends have been able to supply us with valuable information on enemy positions, weaknesses, intentions, and so on. They have also informed us of any counter-agents who were working against us for the enemy.

"Consequently, we have had full documentation on the said al-Adil, who served the anti-Christian forces in Damascus in a spectacular fashion, posing as a false prophet, infiltrating the Ishmaeli camp, neutralizing its campaign of sabotage, and even replacing the Master of the Assassins himself. He is a dangerous and wicked enemy, this false prophet, who has helped to unite our enemies against us. The Christian Kingdom has always been outnumbered by its enemies and we have had to survive by keeping them disunited. With the forces united under their new leader, Saladin, the infidels have marched on Cairo and seized the Fatimid Caliphate. We are surrounded.

"Our best chance is to infiltrate the enemy camp and to sow divisions in Syria while their army is away in Egypt. This is where you may be able to help us. If you offer, of your own accord, to undertake this role, and to give information which will help to destroy the work of the accursed al-Adil, you may be spared by your judges. But this is the only way to save yourself—throw yourself on the mercy of the Court, humble yourself before the Lord Constable, kiss his feet—"

"Never!" Guy suddenly came to life and stood up amid a clanking of chains. "Never! Let them tear me limb from limb—"

The Governor blew out his breath. He had talked in vain. Who would have thought the young man had so much stuff in him? He remembered him as the Queen's favorite, a handsome sapling then, who had won his advancement by love-looks and pretty ways. Now he had grown into an oak. His eyes ran over the tall, erect figure,

the clean limbs, the straight look—and he sighed again.
What a pity, what a pity! Thank God, he did not have to
see it.

He dismissed the prisoner to his cell.

The prisoner was to be examined *in extremis*—a point
insisted on by the Lord Constable, and the Court was convened in a large chamber of the dungeon beneath the Citadel. The room was damp, seepage ran down the slimy
walls, and the light from the few, high, barred windows
was so dim that the judges had to have tapers burning on
their long table at the end of the room. A Royal Inquisitor
and two assistants sat quietly at the other end of the
chamber in front of a heavy leather curtain that stretched
across the width of the room. In the center, was a chair
for the prisoner, flanked on either side by two prison
guards with pikes. The witnesses against the accused, the
clerk of the Court, and a number of friends of the Lord
Constable sat on benches against the side walls.

The Lord Constable, himself, insisted on conducting the
examination. Amalric was thoroughly enjoying himself. He
had grown immensely fat and rolled about in his seat,
swathed in costly silks, bemedalled and bejewelled, and
darting little side glances at his friends on the benches, as
he made his witty sallies. He savored the telling of the
prisoner's history, his former dereliction of duty to his
liege lord, his insolence to his superiors, his deception in
the matter of curing the leper prince, his subversive con-
tacts with the Moslems in the city, and his subsequent
flight into the enemy camp, and he missed no opportunity
to complete the humiliation of his former vassal, now his
victim.

At last came the delicious moment for which he had
been preparing. With a flourish he produced the pearl-handled dagger, and pointed it at the prisoner.

"And does the prisoner recognize this lethal Saracen
blade?" he asked.

"I do," Guy replied in a low voice.

"To whom does it belong?"

"It is mine."

"And whose name does it bear?"

"The name of al-Adil."

"The Imam of the Assassins." The Constable looked about in triumph. "Now, is it not a curious thing that the prisoner, who denies any complicity with the enemy, should have in his possession the personal dagger of the Master of the Assassins? Especially so, when we understand that the Imam al-Adil was a false Imam, who deposed the True Imam, our ally Rashid Ali. Next, let us consider who this al-Adil really was. I have here a letter written to us by the Imam Rashid Ali in the summer of last year, clearly stating that his power had been seized by an agent of the Sultan, with the help of the Sultan's lieutenant, Saladin. The agent's name is given as al-Adil. And here is the most important information he gives us. 'It may interest you to know,' writes Rashid Ali, 'that the said al-Adil is a former Frank, once the lord of Shechem, by the name of Guy of Vienne.' "

The sensation produced in the court was savored by Amalric. If they had been told that the devil himself was in their midst, they could not have looked with greater horror and fascination at the man in the prisoner's chair.

After enjoying his triumph, the Constable put the question to Guy, "Do you admit or deny the evidence that you and al-Adil are the same person?"

"I admit it," replied Guy.

"Excellent!" rejoined the Constable. "We shall get along splendidly now. Perhaps you will tell the Court how you came to play this infamous double role."

Guy stood up before the judges. His words were quite unprepared. He spoke in a low voice and made no attempt at eloquence. What he said was merely a statement of fact: the fight before the castle at Shechem—the fall into the fosse—the loss of his memory—his service under Ibn-ed-Daya—his purchase by the house of Rashid Ali—his marriage to the Imam's daughter—the dream of Master Sa'di—his proclamation as Imam—the pacification of the Jebel Bahra—his journey to Masyaf and reconciliation with Rashid Ali—the death of his wife and the restoration of his memory.

The Court listened spellbound. The very quietness of the recital lent it an added verisimilitude, so that the listeners appeared to be assisting at a real-life tale from the Thousand and One Nights. They groaned at the account of the battle for Ulayqa, and held their breath at the miracles of the dead child and the arrows. When the speaker ended, there was a murmur, almost of approbation, from the large crowd that had gathered in the chamber.

This was not to the taste of the Lord Constable. Amalric saw his prize slipping from his hands and he made a prompt move to reverse the tide of opinion.

"A most interesting tale," he said sarcastically. "If I believed one word of it, I should put my soul in mortal danger! What has the prisoner told us except that he has acted as a minion of the Devil, the father of lies? He proclaimed himself the instrument of God! Is this not blasphemy? He took his power from the God of the Unbelievers, the Devil-worshippers, the spawn of Hell! Is he not, therefore, a devil himself? He laid claim to miracles! Is he not condemned out of his own mouth as a sorcerer?"

His words had the desired effect. The hall became hushed, almost as though a chill of the supernatural had descended on the spectators. Amalric pressed his advantage.

"Let us put the story to the test," he continued, his relish returning. "Master Inquisitor, you have, I believe, your instruments ready. Will you display these instruments to the prisoner and explain them to him, so that he may have an opportunity to think better of his testimony while there is yet time."

The Inquisitor stood up and bowed to the Court. He was a quiet man, with an impassive face, large-boned and very nearly handsome except for a broken nose. He was dressed in spotless, white linen and tight-fitting, black tunic and breeches. At a sign from him, his assistants drew aside the leather curtains and displayed an array of instruments of torture at the far end of the chamber.

The Inquisitor turned politely to Guy. "If the gentleman will step this way, I will do my best to explain everything to him as the Lord Constable has directed."

Guy did as he was bidden. The Inquisitor gently took his arm and led him toward a table, strewn with metal objects of various sizes and curious shapes.

"I suppose you are unfamiliar with most of these tools, sir?" Guy nodded. "Quite so, they would not come within the ordinary experience of a gentleman like yourself. Many of these, in fact, are seldom used, unless especially called for by the Court of Inquiry. The iron mask—the spiked collar—these are corrective instruments; that is to say they correct a man's thinking, but they are not normally employed to loosen his tongue. For questioning, we usually employ one of the simpler instruments—the thumb screw or the rack."

He indicated first a small device like a clamp attached to the table, consisting of two iron bars, upper and nether, operated by a small winch. "The thumb screw works the fastest. As a rule it takes only a few turns to make a man talk. Of course, it depends on his constitution. He might hold out for fifteen minutes, but hardly any longer. The pressure, you see, is unremitting and gradually increased. Of course, the bone cracks after a certain point is reached, and then the instrument is useless. In your case, sir, I would suggest we begin with your left thumb, so as to spare your sword hand. Then, if you respond well, it would be unnecessary to damage both hands. Do you have any questions, sir?"

Guy felt physically sick; his knees were weak under him, and the scene dark before his eyes. Dumbly, he shook his head. Gently, the Inquisitor directed him toward the rack, a large frame standing against the rear wall, in which were suspended a number of ropes and pulleys, worked by a large wheel.

"Sometimes the Court may direct us to employ the rack," the Inquisitor went on smoothly. "In your case, sir, I should say the rack was quite suitable. You are well-built and young and in good health. If you will permit me to feel your joints—"

He passed his hands expertly over Guy's limbs, feeling the knees, ankles, elbows and wrists. "You will do very well on the rack, sir," he said. "Your joints are supple and can withstand tension for as long as half an hour at a time without disjointing. At the same time, if I may say so, sir, your flesh is soft and you are unused to pain so you will talk sooner. It would take longer, now, with a tanner or a mason. But with a well-bred young gentleman like yourself, I think I can safely promise that you will answer all questions satisfactorily within the half hour before any serious damage is done. Of course, if the Court desires a longer statement or formal deposition—" The Inquisitor paused significantly.

"The Court does so desire," Amalric interjected.

"Then, in that case, the ordeal will be longer." Turning to the prisoner, he continued blandly, "Depositions take more time because you will be required to supply proofs of guilt, implicating as many other persons as possible and exposing the entire plot. This will probably require several hours, because a young gentleman of your type often has difficult scruples and little points of honor which have to be overcome. But with my help you can overcome them quite easily. Rely on me, my young sir, as your very good friend. Trust yourself to me entirely and I will see you through. I know every turn of the wheel by heart, so I can give you just the help you need to unburden your mind, but not more than your limbs can bear. If you cooperate, we shall get on splendidly together, you and I, and I dare say—with a little luck—we shall produce a satisfactory document before the Court rises today."

The Inquisitor finished his discourse and bowed politely to Guy and more profoundly to the Court. "May I have the Court's direction?" he asked.

Amalric was inflamed. "Well, Sir Guy," he said, "you have heard our Master Inquisitor. Are you ready to put the truth of your statements to the test?"

"I have spoken the truth," Guy replied, almost inaudibly. "I can say no other, no matter what you do to me."

"Master Inquisitor, the prisoner appears obdurate. What do you recommend?"

The impassive man replied, "I think, my Lord Constable, that I would like to rack this gentleman. He would be an excellent test for my skill. May I have the Court's permission to proceed?"

"You have it," Amalric replied thickly.

The Inquisitor turned courteously to Guy. "I must ask you to remove your clothing, sir. My man, Hervé, will oil your body to make it more supple—" He paused and looked around. There was a movement in the crowd as a gentleman in the robes of a Templar pushed his way to the front. It was Gerard of Ridfort.

"My Lord Constable," he announced, "I have watched these proceedings with interest and I must inform you that this Court has no jurisdiction to try a case of heresy. All such cases, by Royal statute, fall under the ecclesiastical courts and are to be brought before the Order of the Temple."

Amalric jumped to his feet. "Outrageous, Master Gerard!" he blustered. "This prisoner is mine. I am proceeding under military law on a charge of treason."

"Not so, my lord," answered Gerard. "You have introduced the charge of heresy, specifying diabolism and sorcery, and you read it into the record yourself. In the Kingdom, heresy takes precedence over all other charges. You must surrender the prisoner to me."

Pandemonium broke out in the chamber, but the upshot was that Guy was marched out under an escort of Templar knights waiting at the door. Amalric stormed out to complain to the King. The Master Inquisitor regretfully passed his hands over the ropes muttering, "What a pity! I should have liked to rack this gentleman!"

It was May before the ecclesiastical court received the necessary authority from Rome to proceed with the charge of heresy against Guy. Throughout this time, he remained in a lightless cell in the Temple prison, below the foundations of the Temple of Solomon. But at least his fetters had been struck off, he was provided with good food, and he received many visits from the Master of the Temple himself.

"My dear Guy," said Gerard of Ridfort one day, after a particularly stormy interview, "you would not be in the cell at all, if you were the least bit cooperative. I would have lodged you in one of our guest rooms and treated you as a visiting prince. It is your own refusal to enter a reasonable defense, and your inexplicable reluctance to pledge your honor not to escape that forces me to these measures." He paced up and down the cell. Guy sat mute upon his cot. "Of course, I know your reasons are impeccable. You are going to tell the truth, the whole truth, nothing but the truth. Well, you saw what that gained you in the Constable's Court. The King's Inquisitor would have left you without the use of your arms and legs for the rest of your life and you would have denied your truth in the end anyway. Fortunately, the ecclesiastical courts do not proceed with the use of torture. That day may come—indeed, heresy is springing up all over Europe and the princes are calling for the right to use their inquisitors to put it down, but personally, I hope I never live to see it happen. In the contest between the flesh and the spirit, the spirit may triumph, but what is a soul without a body?"

Guy answered good humoredly, "You don't give me the benefit of much strength of purpose, if you think I would have denied the truth to the King's Inquisitor. I might have weakened under his wheel, but I would have recanted afterward."

"Truly, you are a magnificent idiot," said the Templar. "I hope you do not behave like this before the ecclesiastical court or you will burn at the stake. All I want is your agreement to enter a plea of guilty due to loss of memory, which will earn you a nominal sentence. Is that so hard for you?"

"Yes, because it is not true. I am no heretic. I have

served One God only, whether as a Moslem or a Christian—"

Master Gerard held his ears. "Stop! You'll be the death of me, if you do not kill yourself first. You simply are not fit to appear before the court. I will have the session postponed because of illness—"

"Master Gerard, I am sorry. I don't know why you trouble yourself about me—"

"Yes, why do I indeed?" The Master sat down beside him. "Because you are an extraordinary person, to have done what you have done, and become what you have become, and come through unscathed. It argues great genius, or great simplicity. I have felt a kinship with you, an answer to some want in myself. I am a lonely man—Master of the Temple, the right arm of God, yet I do not know where to find Him. I thought perhaps you could tell me—"

"No, Master Gerard," Guy answered, "I do not know that. But there is a bird that sings sometimes just above my head, when I am about to do the true, right thing. I don't know how to describe it—but I listen for the bird."

Master Garard placed a hand on Guy's shoulder. "Will you listen then, and tell me if you cannot appear in Court tomorrow and sit silent, only letting me speak for you to the judges, who are all kindly men and who will, on my recommendation, discharge you of any major fault. Please, Guy, will you refuse me this?"

"Of course," Guy said simply, "if that is all you want, I will do it."

Master Gerard went away relieved, bemused and a little puzzled. "A bird that sings—" he repeated to himself several times, shaking his head.

At the preliminary hearing, Master Gerard's plan went smoothly into action. Under the soaring marble arches and shining dome of the Temple, the ecclesiastical commission of the Kingdom met *in camera*; all spectators were turned away, and only the principal witnesses, including the Constable Amalric, were admitted.

The Court was presided over by the Archbishop of

Tyre, now extremely old and a little wandering in his attention, but very well-disposed toward his former protégé. To induce the Archbishop to head the commission had been not the least of Master Gerard's triumphs, and when Guy made his submission to kiss the Archbishop's ring, the old man patted his cheek and smiled a little, as if to say "We know there is no harm in you, my boy."

In deference to Master Gerard's submission concerning the precarious health of the prisoner, Guy was bidden to sit throughout the proceedings, and all questions were directed to his custodian. Thus, the Master of the Temple was able to present his prisoner's case as that of a man grievously injured, suffering from loss of memory, who was imposed upon by the enemy to play a role as leader of the sect of Assassins without his own understanding. As proof of this, he argued the prisoner had proved his good faith by voluntarily returning as soon as his memory had been restored.

The first witness, Amalric, tore this argument to shreds. Submitting the dagger, with its blasphemous inscription, as evidence of the prisoner's guilt on the charge of heresy, he produced the prisoner's own testimony concerning his heretical beliefs. The account, read by the clerk of the court, was profoundly shocking to all the listeners. That a Christian, suffering from loss of memory or not, should lay claim to such titles and powers, was difficult for any ecclesiastical court to accept.

"Does the prisoner admit these statements?" the Archbishop asked a little anxiously.

"He does, Archbishop," replied Master Gerard, "subject to the defense of loss of memory at the time of the offense."

"Loss of memory cannot be submitted as a defense against diabolic acts," interjected one of the judges.

Master Gerard was on his feet at once. "If the prisoner had no memory of his Christian teaching, he would be unable to withstand the blandishments of the Devil and would not, therefore, be responsible for his acts."

But the judges were not satisfied. If a man were not a Christian, but still worshipped the God of the infidels, he would nevertheless be a Devil worshiper. If he claimed to act in the name of the Devil, he would be a false prophet. And if he performed miracles, he would be a magician.

"Does the prisoner have anything to say to these charges?" asked the Archbishop.

Promptly, Master Gerard told the Court, "The prisoner is not a theologian. He was not capable of judging his beliefs or acts as the Court judges them. Before a man is enlightened by divine knowledge, he walks in darkness. His thoughts are thoughts of darkness; his acts are acts of darkness. Until he receives the light of Grace, therefore, he is not responsible for his thoughts or his acts."

The Constable Amalric intervened to demand proof that the prisoner had lost his memory. "We have only his word for this, the word of a self-admitted Devil-worshipper. No reliance can be placed on such evidence. I am in a position to provide the Court with complete evidence, amounting to an admission of guilt on all counts—heresy, magic and treason, with a list of all his accomplices and co-conspirators. All I ask is to have the prisoner delivered into my hands for three hours."

Again Gerard was on his feet to advise the Court that this was tantamount to condoning the use of torture, which was inadmissible in an ecclesiastical court, and the Constable's demand was rejected.

The Constable sighed in mock regret, "Very well, if this Court is determined to acquit on the charge of heresy—so be it. The sooner you are about it, the sooner the prisoner can be released into my hands, to face the grave military charges against him. Because, believe me, gentlemen, this man, for all his seeming innocence, has a tale to tell so dark and foul and filled with danger for the survival of this Kingdom, that you will blanch to hear it."

But the Master was ready for him. "Not so," he told the Court. "We do not seek an acquittal. We seek a verdict of guilty on a reduced charge of involuntary heresy. Such a verdict will carry with it a penalty of imprisonment at the

discretion of the Master of the Temple. In other words, I
ask you to deliver the prisoner into my hands."

The prisoner was asked to stand and say if he considered this judgment fair. Guy did so and professed himself
ready to throw himself on the mercy of the Court. The
Archbishop pronounced judgment. "Guy of Vienne, you
are found guilty on a charge of involuntary heresy, and
you are deemed deserving of a sentence of imprisonment
at the pleasure of the Master of the Temple. May God
have mercy on your soul." Then, to Gerard he added, "I
charge you, Master Gerard, to treat this young man well. I
have known him as a promising youth and now he has
grown to be an exceptional man, I should not want any
harm to come to him."

After the Court adjourned, Guy found himself alone
with Master Gerard, on the steps of the Temple prison, to
which they had brought him. "Well, Master Gerard," he
said, "you have me now in your power. Will you set me
free?"

The Master smiled his thin, bitter smile. "Yes, I have
you in my power. I said one day you would come to me.
Now you have come. Let us go inside."

Spring passed into summer, and summer into autumn,
yet Guy knew none of these things in his cell under the
Temple of Solomon. His solitude was intense. No other
prisoners inhabited this area of the vast prison, and he
lived alone as a castaway on a desert island. Except that
here he saw nothing but four stone walls, lit by a single
candle, the bounds of his present kingdom.

He was well looked after; the cell was dry; he was
provided with decent clothes and clean linen; his food was
plentiful. He had, however, nothing to read. He was
deprived of all recreation except his own thoughts and
fancies. Two warders came in twice a day to supply his
needs and both were mute. So it came about that the
greatest event in Guy's life, and the one he found himself
inevitably looking forward to, with almost palpitating in-

tensity, was the weekly visit he received from the Master of the Temple.

One day, he was sitting on his cot, his head between his hands, when Master Gerard entered his cell.

"Why are you doing this to me?" he said, without looking up. "I have done you no hurt. You do not believe me guilty of any crime. Even the Court directed you not to treat me ill. Yet you are punishing me in the most inhuman fashion possible. Why, Master Gerard, why?"

"What do you complain about, my dear boy? Have I not saved you from the rack and the stake?" Gerard spoke lightly.

"No, Master Gerard, you have not saved me. You are my Inquisitor. Your methods are the same. You say to me: 'Let me be your very good friend. Trust yourself entirely to me. I will see you through.' And you turn the wheel just enough so I will scream a little, and then you relax it so I will love you for your kindness. I do not understand this kind of friendship."

Gerard, standing beside him, looking down, lightly ran his fingers over the prisoner's bowed head. "My dear boy," he said, "I would not touch a hair of your head, except in kindness. It was to spare you the tortures you speak of that I have, so to speak, sequestered you from the world. The next step is one you alone can take. I want you to have all the time you need to think about it and to see your own true, right way, as you say."

"In the first place," replied Guy, "I am no longer a boy. I am a man and I have been a king of men. In the second place, you are not helping me to see *my* way; you want me to see only *your* way. And you think that by this refined torture, this loneliness, this darkness, this living death, you can drive me to you. But you cannot."

Master Gerard sighed and sat down beside him. "Very well, my dear man, my dear friend, I must ask you to look at my position. I, too, in a sense, am a king of men. The Order of the Temple is a world-wide army with chapters and divisions in every land. It is the army of God. What we have begun here is just the first battle of a mighty struggle for the souls of all mankind. Only when this struggle is ended will the Kingdom of God come on earth. The strength of this Order is founded on obedience. Each man surrenders himself whole and entire to the Order, taking nothing for himself, giving all to the glory of God. And, under God, there is only one commander—The Master. I am that man.

"You speak of your loneliness, here in your little cell. Think of my loneliness, whom all men in the Order obey, but none befriend, none love. You are alone with yourself within these four walls, cut off from all mankind, without any human contact to solace and assuage your heart from the terror of the dark. I, too, am alone, utterly alone, with the immensity of the universe, the great, dark, empty night spaces that haunt me with their oppressive nothingness. Is this not a living death?"

"What do you want of me, then?"

"I want you, your very self!" The Master turned his dark, magnetic gaze upon the younger man. "You are what I once thought I could become, the other half of my own self, the truer, finer part. Yet you are lacking one thing: the strength of purpose to turn your finest qualities to good account. I have that strength of purpose. I will set you on the road to a greatness, which will make all you have achieved, your most dizzy flights of eminence, seem like the first flutter of an eaglet from the nest. When you enter the Order of the Temple, it will be as my adjutant, my deputy, my other self. In time you will be Master, carrying on the work I have begun, and crowning it, yes, crowning it with a pure nature, free from the dross, the sludge of common ambition. Is it wrong of me to wish this for you?"

A silence fell between them. In the little cell the candle on the table threw the shadows of the two men, face to face, in grotesque enlargement upon the wall. Guy saw himself back in the courtyard of the Ishmaeli Palace, under the torchlight, the night the Imam proclaimed him his heir. "But I do not wish it for myself," he said at last.

On other occasions, however, the two men, gaoler and

prisoner, got along very well together. As the months went by, Guy did, in fact, become dependent on these visits for his sanity. He saved up his thoughts, scratched them upon the wall, and would hold forth quite eloquently to his captor on his arrival.

The Master liked to make him talk about his experiences with the Saracens. He was fascinated about the stories of the 'miracles'. Did Guy really believe in these miracles himself? Could he perform them by his own volition? Or did they just happen to him?

Guy was not sure himself. "You see," he said, "there was always another possible explanation for them. At first, I took these other explanations as the true ones. It was, I think, the insistence of the people to accept them as genuine miracles which made it difficult for me. But later, I came to accept them. I began to see them as signs, to tell me to proceed on the course on which I was embarked; they were encouragements to me and to those with me, without which I might never have accomplished anything."

"Did you then believe yourself to be the True Imam?"

"I did, once I became convinced of the rightness of the action I had to take."

"Even after you questioned the genuineness of Master Sa'di's dream?"

"Even then. Because, you see, it did not matter whether the dream was genuine, so long as it set in motion a chain of events which were essentially necessary and right."

"So that even a false sign could lead to a true result?"

"Yes."

"You know, you are a casuist who could put some of our doctors of theology to shame! But when did you cease to believe you were the True Imam?"

"From the moment I knew who I really was. It was possible for al-Adil to be Vice Regent of God, but not for Guy of Vienne."

"Why not?" Master Gerard took this idea up delightedly. "As Master of the Temple one day, you will have more power than ever you would have had as Master of the Assassins. No man shall stand above you, neither kings nor emperors, save the Pope—and even the Pope shall tremble when the Master of the Temple speaks. Is this not the true, right thing?"

But at this, Guy lost his pleasure in the dialogue. "It is not true or right," he said, "because God does not wish it."

"Oh, so he speaks for God now, does he?" retorted the Master sarcastically. "I suppose you think you are already Master of the Temple?"

"I do not speak for God at all," Guy replied in a low voice. "I only know when He is blasphemed."

Master Gerard struck him a glancing blow on the cheek and was immediately sorry, begging his 'friend's' pardon a thousand times, and offering to make any reparation.

"Only let me go—only let me out of your sight!" groaned Guy.

But as winter came, with no end to his solitary ordeal, Guy's health began to break. The cell was bone-cold underfoot, even though a carpet was laid on the floor for him. He stopped eating, and no threats from Master Gerard had any effect. He spent a great deal of time in prayer, he wept much, and collapsed several times from weakness.

It seemed to him that he was alone with God, as every man is alone when he comes into the world and goes out of it. And this aloneness made him feel the uniqueness of God who speaks in each heart directly, differently. That was why Master Gerard was wrong, because he took upon himself the right to speak for God and he made all men close their ears to any voice but his. It was the sin of Lucifer and his temptation was the greatest of all temptations.

At last, one day when the Master of the Temple called; he had begun rather anxiously to visit his prisoner daily, he found Guy lying on his back on the floor. "Master Gerard," Guy said, not getting up, "will you kill me?"

"My dear man, I shall do no such thing!"

"Please, Master Gerard, I want to die."

"But why, when you have such a splendid opportunity before you?"

"You have turned the wheel too tight, Master Gerard. You have broken something in me."

"But let me only take you out of here and we'll have you back like your old self again in no time, I promise you!" And he stooped to help the younger man to his feet.

"Can I go then?" asked Guy unbelievingly. "Can I walk out that door?"

"Of course you can. See, I'll help you do it. Let me put my arm about you. From now on, you're going to trust yourself to me, aren't you?"

"Yes, Master Gerard," said Guy faintly.

And the two men, arm in arm, followed by the two mute warders, made their way up the stairs from the dungeon into the light of day.

The preparation for the ceremony of initiation into the Order of the Temple required about one month. During this time, the new postulant received his instruction from the Master alone. He also slept apart from the other postulants, for he was under medical care and lay a part of the time with bandages over his eyes, because his sight had been weakened by the long period spent in darkness. He soon picked up strength and regained a little color, but he remained silent and uncommunicative.

The Master became worried about him and asked whether he had the strength to go through the ordeal of the initiation. But Guy professed himself quite able. His only pleasure seemed to be in taking practice in the exercise yard, and he was proud of his ability to outfence the others or throw them in wrestling.

The day of the ceremony was bitterly cold and a dozen initiates shivered and danced around a brazier in the exercise yard, while the master sergeant called them out, one at a time, to undergo their tests. From a window in the tower, the Master of the Order looked down, and his presence was not unmarked by Guy. In fencing and wrestling, Guy held his own, and although his guard had slipped from lack of practice, he was never put down.

Each man was then required to sever a block of wood

with a single stroke of the sword. A couple were disqualified by failure, but Guy placed the two blocks, one on top of the other, rolled up his sleeve to the shoulder, and wielding the sword in his massive right arm, he severed both completely.

In the ordeal of the fire, all the remaining initiates were ranged in a line about three paces apart and given a red-hot, iron bar to pass from hand to hand without dropping it. Again, two men failed the test, but Guy, who stood last in line, carried the bar all the way back to the brazier without turning a hair. It seemed as though he was determined to prove to the man in the tower that he could not be broken, after all.

After the evening meal, the remaining postulants, wearing their new, white robes, were led to the Consistory. Guy surveyed this room with special interest. He had not seen it since the night he inadvertently spied upon the secret ceremony from the opening in the coffered ceiling. Then, he had been able to see only a part of the room—the dais at the far end, with its altar of stone, its lighted candles, and the grossly large, obscene image of the cat.

Now the whole room fell into perspective: he saw that the motif of the cat was carried out in innumerable designs upon the ceiling and the walls. The cat, with arched back and erect tail, looked down from every niche, every angle, and was even woven into the carpet on the floor. A sense of unease immediately seized him; once again, he knew he had ventured onto unknown territory. The kingdom of the cat was vertiginous—it turned nature on its head and made the natural unnatural, the unnatural natural.

For this cat represented both the male and female principles in one—the arched, feline body was provided with distended teats, lactating, maternal. It was also phallic—thick, distended with lust, bearing within it the seed of all mankind.

So this was the mystery of the Order—it united the male and female principles into one; it was both father and mother, and its members were men-women. That was why it was so esoteric, exclusive and powerful. Self-renewing, and independent of all other resource, it was bound, in the end, to overcome the world.

Guy took this in slowly, as the full meaning of the ceremony dawned on him. In swearing allegiance to the Order, members were required to renounce all other beliefs, to make a mockery of them and deny their validity, thereby binding them ever more closely to the one "true" principle.

To this end, the natural order was inverted and, in the place of the Cross, the altar was adorned with the hermaphroditic cat. Instead of the mass, the solemn rites celebrated the sacred mysteries of the Order, to which all obedience was pledged. And, most terrible of all, upon another altar at the rear of the consistory, the symbols of orthodox belief were displayed upside down—the crucifix, the chalice and the pyx—in token of the Black Mass.

At once, Guy's eye sought out the Master, who stood, throughout the ceremony, on the dais facing the consistory. Master Gerard returned the look with an intensity which bespoke his own unease. It was a threatening look too, as if to say, you are in my power now, remember there is no turning back, you have yielded to me, you have no choice left—and at the same time pleading—as if to beg for understanding, suggesting that these signs and symbols are for ordinary men but not for us, who are above the common herd and can see the ultimate goals. "Even a false sign can lead to a right result," Guy had said. The Master's look reminded him of this.

The postulants stood facing the Master in a group in the center of the consistory. Across the back of the room were ranged two rows of Templar knights with swords drawn, as though to bar the exit of any faint-hearted postulant. And indeed, it was generally believed that no person who participated in these mysteries ever left without being admitted to the Order, and none who were admitted ever spoke of what he had done.

It was these knights who chanted the mournful litany that occupied the preliminary moments of the ceremony:

"You must entirely renounce your will
And entirely submit to that of another
You must fast when you are hungry
And keep watch when you are weary
Thirst when you would drink."

The first postulant, a rude, ignorant Swabian knight, was called forward and bidden to kneel at the foot of the dais. The Master addressed him in his gentle but vibrant voice: "Do you still wish, Adelbert Wittold, all the days of your life, to be the servant of this Order?"

Adelbert Wittold replied, "Yes, sir, if God please."

"Learn then to obey, by doing as you are bidden," commanded the Master.

At a sign from him, two knights at the back of the room took down the great crucifix, which was suspended upside down upon the nether altar, and dragged it forward to a position below the dais and directly in front of the postulant.

Adelbert Wittold stared at the crucifix before him in stark terror. On either side of him knights, with drawn swords, whispered in his ear, "Place your hand on the crucifix and deny Christ three times!" And Adelbert Wittold repeated three times, "I deny Him!"

Again the knights whispered to him, "Now spit upon the cross!" And Adelbert Wittold spat.

Then the Master spoke again in gentle tones, "Has this man passed the tests?"

The knights replied hoarsely, "Sir, he has."

"Come then, Adelbert Wittold," the Master said softly, "and receive from me the kiss of peace."

Descending the steps of the dais, he raised the near-fainting knight to his feet and kissed him upon the mouth. Burying his face in his hands, Adelbert Wittold staggered to the door and was allowed to leave the room.

Seven times the ceremony was repeated, and although the atmosphere of the consistory fairly reeked with pity and terror, no man reneged on his vow. Of course, the vow was made first, and the act of apostasy came after.

Thus the postulant, having vowed total obedience, would not refuse to obey any command. Having then obeyed, he had put himself forever beyond the pale of Christian society and was thenceforth a tool of the Order till his death.

Guy remained to the last. The Master had planned it this way, so that for him the ceremony might be curtailed. When Guy's name was called by the Master, he came forward and said, "Master Gerard, I beg you to receive me in private."

At a nod from the Master, the knights withdrew and the two men faced each other alone.

"Guy of Vienne," said the Master softly, his voice trembling a little over the words, "will you receive from me the kiss of peace?"

For answer, Guy mounted the steps of the dais and confronted his tormentor. He stared at him a moment, as he might have stared at a toad or a basilisk; then he spat full in Master Gerard's face.

The Master winced perceptibly and turned very white. Slowly, he wiped the spittle off his cheek with the sleeve of his gown. "I was afraid it would come to this," he said, hoarsely. "Of course, you don't know what you are doing. There would have been no need for you—oh, Guy, Guy, why do you torment me like this?"

"I, torment you—?" asked Guy astounded.

"Yes, you! You have tormented me from the first moment I set eyes on you. I loved you for yourself. Why could you not return my love? We are alike, you and I; we both see the great truth which the world cannot see, that there is a Kingdom beyond the present Kingdom. I want to sweep away the present Kingdom, all the filth and corruption and bestiality, and establish that pure Kingdom which you and I have both seen. I cannot do this with men as they are; that's why I need a new kind of men who will renounce everything, even the good of their souls, for the sake of the Kingdom. You are that kind of man. Why will you not see it?"

"No, I'm not your kind of man," said Guy quietly. "I know your kind. You would be pure and you wallow in filth. You would be just, and you trample on human life as you would on a dung-heap. You love and you torture what you love.

"I could kill you now."

"But you won't."

"Why not?"

"Because it would kill you to do it."

"Very well, what shall I do with you then?"

"You will let me go."

"Never! Do you think you are still a miracle worker? That you can mock our mysteries and spit on me, the Master of the Temple, and go free? No. For once, you are wrong, Sir Guy. I have you and I am going to keep you. You shall be mine forever!"

For the third time, the darkness of the tomb closed over Guy, when he returned to his cell under the Temple of Solomon, where neither night nor day, nor the changes of the seasons were marked in any way upon the passage of time. Only now there were no visits from the Master of the Temple. No visitor ever entered the cell's four walls, except the two mute warders; no voice ever broke the silence of the grave.

THIRTEEN

SISTER ALICE

"Sister Alice! Sister Alice!" In the infirmary of the Convent at Nablus, the cry went up all day, and often through the night. "Sister Alice will change the bandages!" "Sister Alice will cauterize the wounds!" "Sister Alice will bring the towels and compresses!"

As she hurried in her novice's habit, from ward to ward, and bed to bed, one would have thought that this young woman carried in her reticule the recovery and salvation of the entire hospital. Were the floors clean? If not she would scrub them herself. Did the lamps need oil? She would fill them. Did the bed patients lack clean linen? She would wash and iron for them.

Mother Superior, looking after her, as she flew on her errands, shook her head and sighed. It was all very well that the poor girl should occupy herself this way. It was a work of mercy and an example to others which attested to the purity of her soul. At the same time, she was wearing herself to death and all so that she might not think of—.

The Abbess well knew the source of this martyrdom. At first, she had resisted the girl's desire to return to the religious life. Alice, she had argued, had chosen her vocation, not because she loved Christ, but because she was grieved in an earthly love. In the end, the Abbess yielded to the importunity, solely to help save Alice's sanity.

In the early days after Guy's arrest, Alice lived in daily terror of what she would hear. The first news was terrifying. He had been imprisoned; he had been tried for treason; he had been put to the torture!

When Alice heard these things, she nearly lost her mind. She arrived at the Convent in a fainting condition, and the nuns despaired of her life. Later came the subsequent news of his incarceration in the prison of the Temple, from which no man was known to return to the world. Thereupon, Alice rose from her bed and announced her intention of re-entering the sisterhood.

As the Abbess watched her novice fill the Convent with her labor and her light, the thought came slowly to her that love is all one, and that the love of a woman for a man might find its expression as well in a sick ward as in a marriage bed, and that such love when given to the least of these, His children, is acceptable to Christ.

Spring of another year broke upon the Holy Land with all its flowered splendor in meadow and desert, and no word came from the silence of the grave. But there was other news to set tongues wagging: King Amaury had died unexpectedly of a fever. His fancy Byzantine Queen was barren and so the heir proved to be the son of his repudiated wife, Lady Agnes of Courtney. He was Baldwin, the leper prince.

Soon after this, Hugh paid his weekly visit to market in Nablus and stopped by the Convent to speak with Sister Alice. She came into the parlor, smiling and wiping her hands on a towel.

"How is it today, Hugh?" she asked brightly. "Will you be selling more pigs for the feasting on the King's coronation?"

"I have sold a brace of spring piglets today, Sister, but I am saving my best for Easter, when they'll fetch a better price."

"Always canny, Hugh. What other news do you have?"

"That's what I want to talk to you about, Sister. It's about the King. He's a leper, you know—"

"I know. It's so sad, isn't it, and such a fine young man, they say—"

"And he was once a very good friend of—"

"A friend of whom, Hugh?"

"The master."

It was the first time Guy had been mentioned between them in almost a year. Alice sat down suddenly, giving her mind to this piece of information. Hugh helped her out.

"You see, when master was with the Queen, she had the little prince in the house. He was sickly then, and the master used to take him on rides in the country, and he even brought in a wizard to cure him, and he did, but it didn't last. They swore some kind of oath together—"

"An oath, Hugh?"

"Well, one of those blood-bonds, you know, that the gentry make—"

"Are you telling me that the King and Guy—"

"Yes, Sister, that's it, and what I'm getting at is that somebody's got to tell the King."

"Oh, Hugh, you must hurry—hurry to Jerusalem—don't lose a moment—"

"Sister Alice, that's all very well to say, but I'm a plain man, don't you see, I'm—well, I'm a serf. It was well enough when the master was here; I could come and go as I pleased and live with the best of them, but now—I wouldn't get past the gate. Besides, I hear the King is very sick, and no one gets to see him."

"Hugh, what are we going to do?"

"Well, the way I hear it is—the only way to the King is through his mother, the Lady Agnes. She has the power, now that her son is king, and she hates the lot of them, the Lord Constable especially. They say he was her lover once and he left her—"

"Oh, never mind all that! We've got to do something at once—"

"But, if you'll pardon me, 'all that' is important. Amal-

ric will stop anyone seeing the King. But if you could talk
to Lady Agnes—"

"I? Why I?"

"Because there's no one else, Sister. You're the master's
only chance."

"But—I'm a nun!"

"Are you, Sister—still?"

The news struck Alice almost like a physical blow. She
staggered under it, as though her present equilibrium had
been destroyed. And, of course, it had. If Guy were alive,
if he could be rescued—what was to become of her? But
she had no time to think of that now. She must act at
once.

With the permission of the Abbess, she hired a carriage
and horses in Nablus to take her to Jerusalem the next
day. "Don't worry about the expense," the Abbess told
her. "In a case like this, I shall without hesitation sell
some of the Queen's jewels. They were all for him anyway." She also wrote a letter to the Mother Superior of
the Sisters of Zion in Jerusalem, introducing Sister Alice
and asking shelter for her.

On a fine Spring day in April, Alice dismounted at the
convent on the Way of the Cross. With the tremendous
resourcefulness that was hers when she was laboring for
others, she quickly located the whereabouts of the Lady
Agnes at the Citadel. She was a stranger to Jerusalem; the
streets frightened her with their constant traffic; and the
guards at the Citadel turned their pikes toward all comers.

But a holy sister could pass where none other might go,
and long before twilight came, she was patiently waiting in
the gallery of the Great Hall outside the door of the royal
apartments. At last a head looked out.

"Are you the sister come for the Lady Agnes?"

"I am."

"Then come."

The room in which Alice found herself was small and
close, divided in half by a curtain, presumably shutting off
a bedroom area, while in the main part of the room, fur-

niture, luggage and kitchenware were all tumbled about in the utmost confusion. A serving maid in the corner was sitting on her haunches cooking up some smelly dish on a small brazier; another maid was unpacking boxes, and a third was combing out the hair of a lady seated by the table, studying herself in a mirror.

The Lady Agnes of Courtney was a slatternly, middle-aged woman who had led a reckless, dissipated existence, and looked it. In this raddled face was a long history of insatiate loves and abandonments, years of poverty and shame, and lastly an unexpected stroke of glory. She was living in the palace as though she were still in a hovel, with beds and kitchen all in the same room.

Never a Queen, she had been repudiated before her husband's coronation and had been forced into ignominious retirement. She had not even been allowed to bring up her own children. Her son, Baldwin, had been given into the care of the Archbishop of Tyre, and her daughter, Sibylla, to the sisters of the convent at Bethany. The world had used her hardly, yet she never gave up her dreams of romance. With man after man she had sought the ideal—even with Amalric—only to be disillusioned. Yet such tribulation had not embittered her; rather it had inclined her to pathos and kindness.

"Come inside, sister, don't mind all this confusion. We are hardly at home here yet. They have not aired out the Palace to get rid of the maggots from my late husband's corpse. I don't care for royal residences anyway. I had rather put up in a prison among friends, than sup in a palace with my enemies. But never mind an old woman's complaints! To your business!"

Alice curtsied to her and bent to kiss the grimy, be-ringed hand. But the Lady Agnes withdrew it. "Your lips are for holy things, sister. I am a sinner, not worthy of your kiss. I have repented, but the past cannot be undone—pray for me, sister." A tall, very beautiful girl of about sixteen, with long, blonde hair and a supercilious expression, came out from behind the curtain. "This is my daughter, the Princess Sibylla," went on the Lady Agnes.

"The holy sister has come on some special errand—is it alms, my dear? I simply haven't any money at all. I don't know where to turn until we put the squeeze on the Constable—"

"Mother," said the Princess, "I don't think the sister wants any money. I think she is unwell—"

And indeed, Alice felt very faint. Either it was the closeness of the room, the smoke from the fire, or the terrible burden on her mind, but a moment later she fell to the floor. Smelling salts were brought at once; water was fetched; the Lady Agnes herself laid a cushion under the head of her mysterious visitor. All attention was focused on Alice when she opened her eyes.

"You must be quick," she said at once. They've buried him alive—"

"Whom are you talking about, my dear?" The Lady Agnes was kneeling beside her.

"Guy," answered Alice faintly. "Guy of Vienne. Oh, please save him!"

"And who is this Guy you speak of? Your brother perhaps?"

It was a long time before Alice answered, but at last she said, "He was my betrothed."

"Ah!" The Lady Agnes took it in. It was a love drama and that was something she understood. "Where is this man now, sister?"

"In the prison of the Temple."

"Ah," the lady replied again, in a lower key. "Then it is a matter for the Templars; there is nothing we can do about it."

"And who is Guy of Vienne?" A man's figure was standing in the opening of the curtain from the bedroom area. He was a very fair, pale, young man, with a striking resemblance to the Princess Sibylla, except that his face bore the unmistakable signs of the disease which was eating him away. A portion of his jaw and nether lip was wound with a bandage.

"Answer, child," said the Lady Agnes. "This is my son, the King."

"He is a good man," Alice answered, her eyes still closed. "The kindest in the world to me—"

"But is this man," said the King, "—was he—the lord of Shechem?"

"Yes—yes—"

"God have mercy!" The young man turned to a page and said sharply, "Fetch the Governor Manasses at once!"

When the Governor came, and Alice was better able to tell a coherent story, the truth was brought out in all its grim detail. Manasses assured Alice that Guy had not been put to the torture—"though he was only a hair's breadth away from it"—to her immense relief. Manasses explained that he had been condemned on a charge of heresy arising from his life among the Paynim—"So that's what became of him!" murmured the King—and turned over to the Templars. But in the prison of the Temple he was outside the Royal jurisdiction.

The King's mind was alert. "Under whose authority was he condemned?" he asked.

"Under a papal commission," replied Manasses.

"Who presided?"

"The Archbishop of Tyre—of course, sir!—your old friend!" Manasses now warmed to the scent.

"Find the Archbishop and ask him to sign an order of *habeas corpus*," ordered the King. "Take it to the prison and fetch the prisoner here. About it, man!"

Manasses bowed and withdrew.

"Don't worry, sister," the King smiled. "Your Guy—our Guy—if he is alive, will be here tonight."

The hours crept by slowly and Manasses did not return. By midnight a little company still sat waiting up in the Great Hall. The King on one side of the fire was playing a game of draughts with the Seneschal, Miles of Plancy. The Lady Agnes, attended by her maids and Alice, dozed in a chair on the other side.

Suddenly, they all gave a gasp as the Royal guards arrived in the Hall. The King jumped to his feet, upsetting the draughts. Lady Agnes awoke and reached for Alice's hand. Manasses came forward, leading a man with a bandage across his eyes.

Alice alone knew him. She stood, clutching her crucifix in her hand, her heart pounding. He was back, back from the dead, he was whole, he was walking, only his eyes were covered—but he must not see her like this, in her nun's habit. She drew back in confusion.

Manasses addressed the King. "I apologize, sir, for the delay. It was not an easy matter. Master Gerard is a hard man. But he had to acknowledge the authority of the Papal commission. The Archbishop ordered him to release the prisoner and—here he is!"

The King stared hard at the man with the bandages; then he said, "Master Guy!"

Guy replied without hesitation, "Master Baldwin!"

The King lurched forward—he could not walk unaided—and grasped Guy's hand. "A good guess, Master Guy, after all these years! No, no, you mustn't take the bandage from your eyes—"

But Guy was tearing it off already. "It's all right," he said. Then, covering his face with his hands, he added, "Only take the torches away. I cannot bear the light yet. Where am I? Is it the old Citadel again?"

"Yes, Master Guy," said the King. "This is my house now. Times have changed. You see, I'm King."

Guy was staggered. "King! Oh, I should not have spoken as I did! I should have called you sir."

"You shall call me Master Baldwin till the day you die." answered the King with a laugh. And he added, "Let me present you to my mother, the Lady Agnes, and my sister the Princess Sibylla, and—the Sister, there, I think you know."

Guy knelt to kiss the hands of the two Royal ladies, and then he looked up into the face of Sister Alice. He saw, first of all, that she was very beautiful in her starched white coif and wimple; he saw that, although she was smiling, her face was wet; and he saw that she was a nun. He rose and approached her.

Alice retreated, confused—he followed, taking her by

the waist in his possessive way. But before his impatient kiss was given, she put her hand over his mouth. "No, no, please, Guy," she stammered, "—don't you see!"

"I see you, Alice—what else should I see?"

He seemed again about to embrace her, but the Lady Agnes intervened. She placed her arms protectively around Alice's shoulders, saying, "Sir, apparently you have not seen yet that the lady is a holy sister—"

Guy stood still. He took it in at last. Once again, she had eluded him. A holy sister: What must she think of him importuning her this way? "Alice," he said after a pause, "I wish you well." And, with steel in his heart, he turned back to the others at the fire.

Although the hour was late, a chair was found for Guy; food and drink were brought; and the talk burgeoned. There was much ground to be covered that night. The King was beginning to consolidate his power and the Governor, Manasses of Hierges, and the Seneschal, Miles of Plancy, had placed their forces at his command. But due to the King's physical incapacity, much of the actual power would rest with the Constable, Amalric of Lusignan, who had the support of the barons of the realm. This was deeply resented by the others, and they voiced their opinion hotly.

"He has half the Kingdom in pawn already," exploded Manasses; "within another year he'll be wearing the crown jewels on his own fat paunch!"

"There's no getting him out now," grumbled Miles, another veteran of the wars, "there's too many would lose their pawn tickets! The only thing to do is to divide the command. That's the solution: divide and rule."

"With whom should it be divided, Miles?" asked the King. "With you—with Manasses?"

"Not me!" said Miles.

"No, sir," echoed Manasses, "I'm too old a horse, and so is Miles here, to put our necks in the traces. It needs someone younger—someone who can outstep the mulish bastard—"

"Someone like Guy here?" asked the King.

"Why not?" answered Miles. "Wasn't he lord of Shechem?"

"And didn't he lose the fief to Amalric?" chimed in Manasses.

"We must get it back for you, Guy," said the King. "By what authority was the transfer made?"

"Oh no authority, sir," replied Manasses. "Amalric declared the fief vacant due to the absence of the lord and he took it for himself. Now the lord is back, he'll have to vacate, that's all."

"You mean—I shall have the fief again?" Guy asked, astonished at the turn of fortune.

"You have it now," said the King. "See that the order is prepared for me to sign, Manasses. And more than that. I want to talk to you seriously about a joint command in the army—"

While the men talked, the Lady Agnes quietly studied Alice, who sat by the fire in silence. Here was a story she could understand; though perhaps she misconstrued the details, she grasped the grand outline. All her life she had pursued the winged cupid and he had eluded her. Still she longed to capture him in flight.

"Tell me, my dear," she said, pressing Alice's hand, "are your vows complete?"

"Not yet," Alice said in a low voice, "but complete enough."

"But I thought you were betrothed to this young man?"

"That's an old story, my lady. He doesn't need me now—"

"Not need? Not need? He loves you, child. Can't you read a man's eyes? The way he looked at you—"

"It is too late, my lady. I am bound to chastity."

"I see." The Lady Agnes didn't see at all how this was possible but she was bound to get to the bottom of this strange story. "And how long have you known this young man? Tell me the story, child."

Alice told it, as well as she could, doing full justice to Guy, and less than enough to herself, but closing the door on the past. Lady Agnes puzzled it out. The girl was in love with him, of that she was sure. What, then, was her objection? Was it the vow of chastity? That could be dealt with, surely. Or was it something else?

"But, my dear, you will want to talk to him alone, to explain matters and perhaps to reach an understanding—"

"Oh, no, my lady," Alice said quickly, "but I wish you to say to him that I am glad he is well and free."

Lady Agnes looked across the fire at Guy, who was now telling of his adventures in the land of the Paynim. A strange tale, too. Her mind went back to her own lovers, Reynald of Marash, Hugh of Ibelin, Reynald of Sidon, all swashbuckling adventurers, but none with the air of absolute command of this astonishing young man. Perhaps that was it—was she afraid of him?

Suddenly, she took Alice's hand and advanced toward the men's group. "Sir Guy," she said, "the young lady with me, whom you know well, has something to say to you. Speak up, girl."

Alice burned with shame. She replied in a firm voice, however, "I only wished to say, I am glad you are safe and you have come back to us. I'm very, very glad, Guy. Now, with your permission, I must go—" She turned aside with a little convulsive movement.

Guy was at her side instantly. "Alice," he said quietly, "are you staying in Jerusalem?"

"With the Sisters of Zion," she said breathlessly.

"I know the place. Will someone give me a sword? I'll see this young lady home."

"Gladly," said Manasses, handing over his own. "Take torches and a guard with you also. It is late. We will talk in the morning."

The Lady Agnes looked after the departing couple and smiled enigmatically. Something might be done yet, she reflected, to stay the flight of the winged cupid. But, ah, if she had only been younger herself—

But in the morning, when Guy returned to the Convent on the Way of the Cross, Alice had already left. He cursed himself then for letting her slip through his fingers. He had so far respected her reticence the night before that he had not even pressed her for any explanation. The nun's habit put a new barrier between them, that he did not know how to bridge. But, having found her and lost her twice over, he could not reconcile himself to losing her forever.

The barons of the realm and their retinues were gathering in Jerusalem. Each day their numbers grew in the Great Hall of the Citadel, shouting to see the King. A new occupant of the throne meant a new struggle for power among the nobility of the Kingdom, each seeking to enlist the Royal support for their dynastic rivalries and petty quarrels.

Baldwin IV was a popular king. His youth, his infirmity, and his courage engaged the loyalty of everyone and he kept it to the last. Nor was he a weak ruler; he had an active intelligence and knew how to make himself obeyed. But he was not equal to the physical demands of his office.

Even a few minutes on his feet each day was an agony to him. Much of his time was spent in bed, reading correspondence and signing documents. He had lost the use of his toes and most of the fingers of his hands. He had to have the bandages changed on his face several times a day. Yet he never complained, and when the barons shouted for him in the great hall, he got up, and greeted them from the balcony, addressing them by name with a special word or jest for each.

On these occasions, there was a new figure by his side—Guy of Vienne—Lord Protector of the realm. When a quarrel needed settlement, or an injury required redress, Guy was the one to see about it. Even the great princes and counts soon found it politic to recognize the new power behind the throne. His skill in government, which had been exercised in the rule of his little kingdom in the Jebel Bahra, now commanded the great Kingdom of Jerusalem.

This, of course, brought Guy into direct conflict with the Lord Constable. Amalric was incensed at Guy's sudden elevation. He attempted to revive the old charge of treason, but this came to nothing in the face of the King's unquestioning confidence in his boyhood friend. Eventually, it became necessary for Amalric to trim his sails to the prevailing wind and he asked for an interview with Guy.

Guy received him in the small office in the Tower of David, where he dispatched the King's business each morning. Amalric arrived, accompanied by his younger brother, Guy of Lusignan, newly come to the Holy Land. The introductions were cold, but punctilious.

"I have come," said Amalric expansively, "to make amends. During your enforced absence in the hands of our enemies, I undertook the care of your estates. Since your fortunate return, I have taken steps to restore them to you. Castle Shechem is now at your disposition."

"You are most generous," replied Guy, who was perfectly aware of the King's order. "But I think there is more to settle than that. It has come to my knowledge that in my absence you sold my entire garrison, which was composed of men of Vienne."

"As you say," Amalric temporized, "the garrison had to be disposed of. I can make you compensation, allowing for a certain depreciation in value since—"

"I am not speaking about compensation, Lord Constable. I am speaking about men—flesh and blood—who lived on my estates in Vienne. These men are my serfs, and under the law of King Henry of England, whose writ runs in Vienne, they cannot be sold like cattle. Men, Amalric, men. Where are they?"

"You are right," blustered Amalric, "they must be found. The difficulty is that I have kept no record of their whereabouts. There were ten, I think, not counting that swineherd who purchased his freedom—"

"Ten men, Amalric, and I want them back. I don't care if you have to call out the army to find them. I want them back."

"As you say, Guy, as you say. Let us be friends. After all, as liege-lord and vassal, we should be on terms of trust—"

"Your father, the Count of Poitou, is my liege-lord,

Amalric, not you, and I do not look forward to the day you ever succeed in his place."

"Well, you needn't worry on that score. I've decided not to go home. There's no room there for younger sons. That's why my brother, Guy, has come out here, too. We're both planning to settle down. And that brings me to a request I have for you. Now that we're friends again, I wonder if you would put in a good word for my brother Guy here, with the King?"

Brother Guy of Lusignan, who was a simpering and idiotic-looking young man, although passably good looking, smiled foolishly. "You see," Amalric went on blandly, "my brother is awfully taken with the Princess Sibylla, aren't you, Guy?"

"Oh awfully taken," simpered Guy of Lusignan.

"They have met a few times at the Coronation dances, and the Princess has given my brother every encouragement, hasn't she, Guy?"

"Oh, every encouragement."

"But you must put in a word for him to the King."

"Why must I, Amalric? Would it be because the Princess Sibylla happens to be the heir to the throne?"

"Not at all! It's just that since we three here are all from the County of Poitou, we should stick together, shouldn't we?"

"All right, Amalric, when every last man of mine is back under my roof—*then* I'll think about asking the King to grant your brother courting rights."

Guy got his men. Within a few weeks every one had returned to Castle Shechem: Yves, Robert, Bertrand, Balian, Hugh the Miller and Hugh the Farrier, Peter the Tall, and Peter Short, were repurchased by Amalric's agents: Geoffrey and Jean simply ran away from their present masters when they heard the news of their lord's return.

Even Hugh came up to the Castle, looking sheepish, as soon as Guy arrived. "I reckon, master," he said, "I didn't have the right to buy my freedom from the Lord Constable, after all. Only you can give me that. So here I am."

"Do you really want to be free, Hugh?"

"Yes, master—any man likes to be free, doesn't he?"

"What would you do with your freedom?"

"Well, I've got the swinery, and I have plans for—"

"—a little freebooting, I know, I know. I'll tell you how it is Hugh. I don't need you for a groom any more. But I do need a good castellan. Now if you do that job all right and run this place properly for me, as soon as I can spare you I'll give you a free charter for your land in Vienne forever. Will that suit you?"

"It will suit me gloriously, master."

Guy's return to Shechem was also the occasion for much soul-searching in the village. Times had been bad in Shechem since he left: the Saracen raid had destroyed their property; the extortions of Amalric had driven many of the peasants to starvation and ruin; and the blight had wiped out the greater part of their herds.

It was hoped a good ruler would bring the good days back. But they were also fearful. No lord, argued the villagers, could be expected to let rebellion go unpunished, and they predicted terrible exactions made on every household. The women at the washing pool, who were always well-disposed to the lord in the Castle, took the more pleasant view that he would content himself with having the mukhtars flogged.

A village council decided, however, that it would be wisest to take the initiative and throw themselves on his mercy. A soft word turneth away wrath, the Chief Priest reminded them. And so, early one evening, soon after Guy's return, the entire village of Shechem marched to the Castle gate in a solemn procession. At the head came the new Haccohen Hagadol—for the old man had died, and had been succeeded by his son, a circumstance which made reparation easier to make—followed by the three mukhtars, the men, the women, and the children. The crowd filled the courtyard and overflowed out the gate and down the hillside.

Guy received the delegation of village elders at the top of the Castle steps. He had expected a demonstration of welcome, but he was met instead by a ceremony of penance. The Haccohen Hagadol first, followed closely by the three mukhtars, knelt on the top steps, while two acolytes served them with an urn of ashes. Each dignitary dipped his hand in the urn and sprinkled himself with ashes, on his splendid high-crowned turban, his robes, his face. After that, they chanted a psalm of lamentation and lowered their heads to the ground.

Guy knew the role he was expected to play and, as always, he found the right way to erase the past and bind his people to him again. Raising both arms, he said, "I forgive you all!" Then, sensing that something more was hoped for, he added, "It has been a hard time for both of us, you and me. Tithes will be remitted for the remainder of the year."

This was cause for great rejoicing. The Castle doors were thrown open and everyone was allowed in to gape and gawk and slurp up the lord's ale.

"That's the master for you," Hugh grumbled, with secret benevolence, to Yves and Geoffrey, while they dipped their flagons into a golden vat of ale. "Too soft and too giving. He should have tithed them double. Who's going to pay for all this? He hasn't a groat. God help us all!"

"Maybe so," said Yves, "but I wouldn't have another master, an' I had a choice!"

"Nor I," echoed Geoffrey.

That night, Guy had his bed moved back to the old room that looked out on the hill. The view on this soft, spring night, was just as he remembered it. He had put his life back together again in a way he wouldn't have believed possible. But the tower on the hill was dark and empty. He wondered, sadly, where he had gone wrong.

Each time Guy journeyed from Jerusalem to Shechem and back, he stopped in Nablus. Alice might put up barriers, but he would ignore them. He had the excuse that his calls at the Convent were purely social and no one could find fault with that. He brought down presents from

Jerusalem, yards of bandages, blankets, candles, fruit, flowers. The grateful Abbess told him she didn't know how she had ever managed without him.

His visits occasioned a tremendous stir. To begin with, he now travelled with an escort of at least twelve horsemen, attached to the person of the Lord Protector. Men and horses created an uproar in the Convent yard, so that Guy attempted to turn them all out into the street, but the nuns were so delighted to be able to bring out cakes and wine for the visitors that he let it pass.

But, from the first, Guy was not content with a general visit. He had, he said, come to see Sister Alice and he was taken to the parlor, where Sister Alice was brought to him. They sat, according to visitors' regulations, on the benches across from each other, against opposite walls, and Sister Agatha, or one of the other sisters, was delegated to stand at the door as a chaperone.

"Well, Alice," Guy would begin, sitting on his hands and smiling across at her, "how are all your wards today?"

"We are all well enough, thank you," she would reply. "And how are your wards?" This was how they referred to the animals at Shechem, which Guy had now moved to the Castle yard, and taken under his own care.

"All well, except Blanche," he would reply. "Blanche is still pining away. I think her mate came to the edge of the wood and called to her the other evening. Don't you think we should let her go free?"

"But her leg is not strong enough! She'll never run like the other deer and someday she'll get caught—"

"Wouldn't she rather take the chance, perhaps—"

So the discussion would run on. They never seemed the least bit self-conscious; they were old friends meeting again across the interstices of the years and the chasms which time had opened up in their lives; they were good-natured mariners, signalling to one another from the bridges of their ships, bound on different courses.

The sisters in the Convent thought differently. Guy appeared to them in only one light—he was the wronged lover, whose patience and charm deserved their reward,

which had been snatched from him by a cruel fate. Sister
Agatha would make every excuse to absent herself from
the parlor during these interviews, but there was never the
least sign that he took advantage of it. Nor did Sister Alice ever drop the smallest suggestion that she had not
given him up forever.

The Abbess Joveta looked upon these meetings with a
more penetrating eye. In her view, the Lord Protector was
a great man. That he should humble himself to sit in her
parlor on the visitors' bench each week, talking to Alice,
without the least hope of personal gain—that was, for her,
a sign from God. Which is not to say she was blind to his
faults and, in fact, she had decided to take him to task
one day.

But first, she had to have things out with Alice. "Sister
Alice," she said at the end of a summer day, while the
nuns took their evening walk in the garden, "walk with
me. I need your help."

"Of course, Mother. What help can I give you?"

The Abbess studied her aslant, as they walked. "You
like to help, don't you child?"

"I—I hope I am useful."

"More than that—you are invaluable. But I do not want
my need for you to alter your own decision."

"What decision, Mother? My vows are taken. The last
step comes soon—oh, I cannot wait!"

The Abbess smiled. "Do not be impatient. Life is long.
But perhaps there is some other work you would be doing
—some other field—"

Alice stopped walking. Falteringly, she asked: "Are you
sending me away? Have I offended—"

"Of course not, dear child. I want you only to search
your conscience and see if there is no other way in which
you think your helping hands can glorify the Lord through
service to others."

"But what could there be?" asked Alice, troubled, as
they resumed their walk. "I have always cared for the
wild creatures—I learned their haunts, their habits, by
heart; I gained their confidence so that even the timid

ones would eat from my hand. Oh, I loved them so, Mother, the mongoose that I used to let sleep in my bed, and my dear Adèle, the gazelle who died in the fire, was like a sister to me; we kissed every morning on awakening, and every evening on going to bed—"

"But then you found that we poor human beings needed your help also—the lepers, the motherless children, the sick—did you not feel them also tugging at your heart?"

"Oh yes! You know, Mother, the first time I went in the ward—it was the leper ward, I remember—I felt sick, really sick; it was the smell, I think, the sweet, decaying smell of death. But later, I got to know them all by name, and I learned each one was different. I had to be a different kind of help to each, so that I felt I was stretched out in a hundred directions; there simply wasn't enough of me. Is this love, Mother?"

The Abbess put her hand through Alice's arm. "Yes, child, this is love. It is the love the Lord asks of us for all His creation, so that, by loving the things He has created, we are loving Him. But sometimes He asks harder things of us than that."

"Harder?" Alice was surprised.

"Much harder. It is easier far to give our love to those who beg for our help, to receive the gratitude of those we have helped, than it is to love simply for the sake of love, asking no return. For when we love where we are needed, we are great in the eyes of our beloved. But true love wants not itself, is not puffed up. Have you that kind of love?"

"To love where I am not needed? No, I never thought of such a love. But why would the Lord ask it of me?"

"Because the Lord wants your love for all His creation, the great as well as the small. It is easy to admire a violet,—but can you love a thunderstorm?"

"I think I know what you mean," replied Alice. "When I was a child at Shechem, I used to be terrified of thunderstorms. We have so many in the valley. I used to hide in my bed and cover up my head. Then I remember very well one day when I was out alone on the hills and I was caught by the storm. The lightning fell all round me, and the cracks of thunder threw me on my face. I thought I would die and I ran for home through the rain, soaked to the skin, but I was laughing when I arrived at the door."

"So you see—?"

"I think I see—But how can I use this kind of love?"

"Only by not hiding and covering up your head. You must seek the Lord in the great world, Sister, not just in our little corner of it. You must learn not to fear the thunderstorm."

"Then, you *are* sending me away, Mother?"

They stopped by the cloister gate. The Abbess smiled her encouragement. "Not a bit of it. I want you only to *think* before you take an irrevocable step—"

"If you mean think about *him*—I have no more thoughts to give. I am quite decided. He does not need me now."

"We all need you, daughter; we all need one another. Let us not, then, shut our hearts to anyone. For remember, no matter what you do, the Apostle says, though you bestow your goods to feed the poor, though you give your body to be burned, and you have not love, it profits nothing."

She began to move through the gate, but Alice detained her. "One moment more, Mother—do you mean I do not have love, true love of Christ?"

"Only you know that, child. I believe you are my faithful daughter in Christ, and may His peace be with you." And she passed inside.

The next time Guy called at the convent, the Abbess told Sister Agatha to watch for his departure from the parlor, and beg him to step into her office. She received him graciously, fetching him a chair of honor, and offering him cakes and wine. Still she felt a little timorous before his steady gaze, because she had things to say which are not usually said to a Lord Protector of the realm.

"My lord," she began, "you have been too good to us—too good altogether. I beg you to stem this flow of generosity. Our larders are filled to bursting!"

"I hope this does not mean you are closing your doors to me?" he said quietly.

"Far from it. Our sisters live all week in anticipation of your visits. Especially Sister Alice, of course."

"Does she?" He looked at her, suddenly serious. "I mean—does she really?"

"My lord," said the Abbess, equally serious, "I know, perhaps better than anyone, how much Sister Alice thinks of you. You are her great friend, her true friend."

Guy swallowed. "Is that all?" he asked.

"Ah, how much men ask! Is it not enough that this dear sister of ours, whose whole life is dedicated to our work of mercy, should keep you a place of honor in her heart?"

"I was not thinking of honor—"

"Of what, then?"

He dropped his eyes. "Of love, perhaps."

"My Lord Protector, you should not come here speaking of love. This is a Holy Order—"

He acknowledged his error. "Forgive me, lady Abbess. A man cannot help his feelings. But, believe me, I have never transgressed—"

She softened toward him. "No, indeed. Sister Agatha has told me you have been at all times correct. But, my dear lord, surely you did not expect, after all this time, that our Sister Alice—"

"I expected nothing. You see, I have known Alice a long time. I believe I understand her, too. She is far above me in character, talents and merit of every kind. She reads Latin and Greek—I feel I am an oaf beside her! She is incomparable, unattainable. And yet I hoped. I will tell you something, lady Abbess, that no one knows. The night I saved Alice from the fire, when she was badly hurt, and delirious with the pain, I held her in my arms and she confessed that she loved me. I believed it and I gave her my ring. Of course, I had no right to expect that after all these years—"

"No, my lord, you had no right to expect anything." The Abbess spoke severely. "If we must speak of love—

your kind of love—you are the last person to whom a girl like Alice could have given herself."

"The last person—?" Guy was taken aback.

"She would have chosen a weakling rather, or even a bad man to be reformed, rather than yourself. What room have you made for her in your life? Alice is strong—did you ever ask for her strength? She is able—did you ever ask for her ability? She is generous—did you ever ask for her generosity? Oh, I know, you have been kind, you have given her every consideration, you are a very great gentleman. There! I do you justice!

"But you are too strong, too self-reliant, too masterful for her. There is no way in which she can help you. Alice has always given herself to the helpless, the weak—see how she cared for the wild things nobody else cared about—and now it is the same with our poor patients here in these sick wards. She works herself to the bone for them. That is how the good Lord uses her for His purposes. She says you do not need her—"

"Oh, but I do!" Guy burst out. "My lady Abbess, what you say is very true. I do not deserve her. I am a proud man, I think too much of my task, my mission—whatever you may call it—I have followed it into far places and done strange and terrible things on account of it. But, in my own way, I have tried to use my life for God's purpose, too. I have looked for the way, without finding it. I, too, need help—"

"Then you must learn to ask for it!"

"You mean—it is not too late?"

"It is already much too late to be talking of such things!" the Abbess said with some asperity. "Sister Alice is vowed to chastity and obedience. These vows cannot be loosed unless she asks for dispensation before the final vows are taken."

"She will not ask." Guy was dejected.

The Abbess leaned forward with a sudden maternal solicitude. Men were so helpless, really, she thought,—even the powerful ones, the conquerors, like this Lord Protector—so strong, so gallant, so helpless before women! Why could Alice not see that? Well, she would help him after all. "You have my permission to speak to Sister Alice once more about this, if you wish," she said, adding with a smile, "Sister Agatha will not be present. I think you will do better by yourself. There are certain things you should know, my lord, which I tell you in confidence. Alice has kept your ring. She even persuaded herself to wear it before your incarceration. It was entirely her doing that you were released, for she went to the King herself. She also has a large dowry, left her by the Queen, which she wished to bring you. But, you see, *then* you were in need. Now—"

"Now I am still in need!" Guy said emphatically, standing before the Abbess, his steady gaze fixed on her, so that she quailed before his terrible sincerity. "It is Alice I need. No dowry! Nothing else, only Alice! Oh, Mother, thank you. You will save me yet!"

After he left, she looked out the window musingly, and saw him mount his horse at a single leap, his spirits restored and soaring as he rode away. "Foolish girl," she sighed to herself.

It was later this same summer that the storm, so long in gathering, burst over the Holy Land with the fury of a hurricane. The great Sultan 'Saladin', as he was called by the Crusaders, had marched out of Egypt. In Jerusalem, a conclave of barons lasted for three days, meeting in the open courtyard of the Citadel, while inside the Great Hall, the King's councillors, the Constable Amalric of Lusignan, the Lord Protector, Guy of Vienne, the Seneschal, Miles of Plancy, the Masters of the Order of the Hospital and the Order of the Temple, debated the issue.

At last, a proclamation was made by the King, read from the steps of the Tower of David, to which all the barons shouted assent. The King, at the head of the entire army of the Kingdom, would advance into Egypt to meet the Sultan. The crowd called for the King and he came out, very fair and pale, wearing the usual bandages, but vigorous in his movements and stirring in his words. The barons loved him and insisted that he should accompany the army so that orders for a special litter were issued at once. A message was also sent to the Patriarch Heraclius, requiring that the True Cross should be yielded up to the King's commanders and borne into the field.

There was grumbling, too, among the leaders coming out of the assembly in the Great Hall. Few were satisfied with the arrangements under which the command of the army had been divided between two men: the Constable and the Lord Protector. The King had insisted on this, as a check on the ambitious Constable; and, since the King would be present with the army and the last word would rest with him, the assembly agreed. But Amalric stormed out, surrounded by his knights, in righteous fury. Other voices were raised against the campaign as well. The Master of the Hospital supported it, but the Master of the Temple withdrew all his forces from the expedition. The altercation between the two Masters and their followers filled the courtyard with recriminations.

The Lord Protector left the Citadel quietly, accompanied by his usual cortege of horsemen, and made several private calls. First, he stopped in a shop in the Street of Jewellers and made some purchases. Then he called at the Archbishop's Palace, and asked to see William of Tyre. The old man talked with him in the garden for a long time, while the men and horses waited patiently outside; documents were sent for, duly drawn up, signed and sealed; and Guy took his leave. Then the whole body of horsemen took off at a gallop for the road to Shechem.

It was late afternoon when they drew up in the courtyard of the Convent at Nablus. The unexpected arrival of so many men, all in mail, threw the sisters into confusion. The Abbess herself came out to meet them, and Guy, dismounting, kissed her hand.

"There is no cause for alarm, Mother," he said. "We have this day voted for war against the Sultan and we leave for Egypt in three days. You should secure your Convent gates. There may be diversionary raids across the border. I will try to give you some protection. Meanwhile, I must speak with Sister Alice."

"Oh, my lord," cried the Abbess, tears springing to her eyes, "may God protect you. I'll send her to you at once."

Guy and Alice met as usual in the little parlor. If Alice noticed that Sister Agatha was absent on this occasion, she gave no sign. She must also have guessed that something momentous was in the air from Guy's appearance itself, his hauberk in place, his face and hair caked with summer dust and sweat. But he seated himself, as usual, on the bench across from her and made no untoward move.

"Alice," he said quietly, "I have something to say to you and I beg you to hear me out. In three days I leave for the wars in Egypt. I can't go away again and leave you like this. We have been doing this for too long, you and I—meeting and passing, needing one another and missing one another, loving and losing.

"I want to marry you, Alice. I shall die there, simply die in Egypt, unless I can come back to you, as my wife. It has been too much for me, Alice, all alone. I want you to take over Castle Shechem. All my men, except Hugh, must go with me to Egypt. You must raise a levy of men in the village and taken command. The Saracens will raid the frontier and I'll lose Shechem unless you save it for me. I'll need money, too, for my men—you must find some way to raise it—perhaps you can sell off part of my fief. But come to Shechem with me, and let us be together in the end."

Alice did not know whether to laugh or cry. "What an extraordinary proposal!" she said. "You need a bailiff to look after your finances, and a commander-in-chief to man the walls. Might I also double as a castellan, jailer and laundress?"

It was a brave last-ditch stand for Alice. But it crumpled before his next assault. He quite simply looked at her, his eyes never wavering, and said, "No, Alice. I want to marry *you!*" It must have been unintentional, but his voice did not obey him; the sound died in his throat, leaving only his lips to make the shape of the words.

Suddenly she realized how much, behind the masculine assurance, he was really suffering—because of her. In an instant, all resistance to him was gone; it melted away like winter snows before the warm spring rains. Suddenly, her face was wet with tears, and here she was, sitting on her bench, and he on his, as though they were talking about the price of tea in China!

She tried to be practical. "But I should have to ask for a dispensation," she said.

"I have brought the papers down with me for you to sign," he replied, reaching into his tunic.

She wondered at him. "But it will take time for the approval to be granted—"

"I have brought the approval with me."

She wondered more. "You did all that, before you even asked me? You were so sure?"

"No, Alice," he replied, "I was desperate. I just prayed—"

She smiled at him.

She was his now; he knew it. "How long will it take you to be ready?" he demanded.

"But Guy, it will take days and days and days—"

"I'm going in three days! Alice, be honest with me—is there any reason why you can't marry me now?"

"Now?"

"Right now." He reached into his pocket again. "I brought the ring."

She stared at him, overwhelmed. And, almost without thinking, she replied in a small voice, "No, Guy, no reason."

Then, and only then, did they come together, and she went out a moment later, her face and habit all smeared with his dust, to call the Abbess.

Of course, matters simply could not be managed like this, thought the Abbess, as she received the couple in her office. She must make them see reason. Alice was in her sister's habit and hadn't a dress to wear. Her trousseau had not even been begun. The banns had not been read in church. There wasn't a priest at hand.

But the Abbess Joveta had not yet taken the full measure of Guy of Vienne. He was quiet; he was polite; he would keep his men waiting indefinitely. But he would be married. She conceded that there might be justice in his determination—he had lost Alice too often before to risk it again. Besides, he *was* Lord Protector.

A messenger was dispatched to fetch the priest. Within the hour, some of the sisters had remade a habit into a splendid white wedding dress, with coif and wimple in the style of the Court ladies. All that remained was to find the jewels to go with it, and for this the Abbess brought out the Queen's casket. Alice gave the casket to Guy, who chose the stones she was to wear. She was, in fact, the most beautiful woman in the Kingdom, at that moment.

The priest came; the whole sisterhood, the Lord's horsemen, and as many of the patients in the sick wards as could walk, crowded into the chapel; the Abbess gave the bride away; and Guy kissed her in the sight of all. Moments later, he lifted her onto his horse, sitting side-saddle before him, and he rode away, followed by his troop, holla-ing and huzza-ing. The Convent bells rang, bringing startled heads to Nablus windows—the Lord Protector had married Sister Alice.

Along the road to Shechem, Guy felt Alice tremble a little and he slowed his horse to a walk, putting one arm about her. She looked up at him a little ruefully and laid her head against his chest.

"Oh, Guy," she said, "be gentle with me, please. I just need a little time to get used to it."

He looked down at her protectively and a little puzzled, but made no reply. Moments later, they clattered into the courtyard of Castle Shechem.

Every torch in the Castle was lit that night in honor of the lord's wedding night, and many were placed on the battlements to carry the news far and wide. A dozen sheep were slaughtered and roasted on spits and the feasting went on far into the night. The seigneurial bed was brought back from the small tower room to the master's

bedroom at the front of the keep. The bride and groom
retired early.

Guy was gentle, but their time had come. He took her
that night, and she knew then that she had wanted to be
taken all along; she cried a little, but she loved him the
more for it; and he saw in this night a sign that he was
still on the way to the right, true goal.

CHAPTER FOURTEEN

THE BURNING BUSH

Ascalon sat by the sea like a great sleeping cat, curled up, its mighty paws before it. The bastions of the city faced landward in a huge semi-circle, each of the two central projecting towers a striking claw. Seaward, its approaches were protected by a long mole, like a tail, to keep out hostile ships. Lapping its brown-white walls: water and sand —and beyond that: Egypt. Ascalon was the last outpost of the Kingdom.

The khamsin began to blow. The Great Hall of the Citadel was sealed up with leather curtains across all the windows, but still the wind blew in, filling the air with a cloud of fine sand. The tapers flared in their sockets, and men went about in semi-darkness, cursing the grit in their eyes, their teeth, their hair. Even at noon, the sun was obscured.

At the long table in the center of the Hall, the commanders sat and talked, studying the maps in the hope of gaining some light. But there was little light.

"What do we know?" asked Amalric, looking testily around. "Just that an army is approaching out of Egypt. No one knows what kind of an army, how many men,

how many horses, and so forth. Bedouins report that this
army left Cairo ten days ago. If it were bound this way, it
should be here by now. Chances are that it will by-pass us
and cross the Sinai peninsula to Damascus."

Guy sat at the other end of the table, toying with his
dagger, without looking at the speaker. "What makes you
think that, my Lord Constable?" he asked.

"Because, my Lord Protector, I have good intelligence
reports on the Sultan Saladin." Amalric enjoyed a reputation for omniscience. "Let me remind you of the facts.
Some years ago, the said Saladin went to Egypt with his
uncle General Shirkuh, to reinstate the Grand Vizier
Shawar. No sooner was Shawar back in power than Saladin began to undermine him. In fact, it was not long before he cut off the Grand Vizier's head and declared himself Sultan of Egypt. That is the kind of man we are
dealing with.

"Now, when the Sultan Nur-ed-Din of Damascus died,
this Saladin began to cast his eyes on the throne of
Damascus which is at present held by a mere boy. The
faithless Saladin has no doubt planned to attack Damascus
and seize the throne from the son of his former master.
That's how all infidels are—perfidious, treacherous and
base. You may rest easy on that score, gentlemen."

"No!" cried Guy, driving his dagger into the table top.
"Not perfidious, not treacherous, not base! You do not
know this man as I do. He is faithful—but to his own beliefs. He is loyal—but to his own friends. He is noble—but
not with the nobility of birth. His aim is not personal
power. It is the unity of Islam. And why does he want to
unite his people? I will tell you why. Because he believes
in an ideal—so lofty an ideal that you, with your petty
brawls for money and loot, appear to him as midges, as
flies eating off dead carrion, as vermin to be stamped out
from the face of the earth. And that's what he aims to
do—to destroy you all, to sweep you into the sea, and to
restore the land to the people he calls 'the people of
God.'"

"Well!" replied Amalric with heavy scorn. "At least, we

know where your sympathies lie. Indeed, we have always known; and, if we had had our way, you would be locked up now as a self-confessed traitor in the Citadel of Jerusalem!"

Guy snatched the dagger from the table and advanced on Amalric. "I challenge you to repeat those words before the King."

Hands restrained him. But Amalric replied haughtily, "I wish the King were here to hear you call the infidel the 'people of God!' "

"Liar! I did not call them that. Each of us, Moslem and Christian, yes and Jew, believes ourselves to be God's chosen people. But if we take that name, we must be worthy of it. And I tell you, gentlemen, we shall have to fight this man you call Saladin; we shall not escape because of his greed or his ambition; he will face us out—if not today, then tomorrow—if not this year, then next—but our reckoning will come, and in that hour, if we are not prepared to stand before the judgment of God, we shall be lost!"

Shortly, as if to underscore his words, another messenger arrived with news from the desert. He was a ragged bedu who dismounted from a camel and asked to see the King. Although Baldwin was scarcely able to walk, he came into the Hall, supported by two aides, and faced the man of the desert. The bedu knelt to kiss the King's hand and asked for gold. A purse was thrown to him. Then he said, "The Sultan is at El Arish."

He could not have caused a greater sensation. El Arish was but one day's march away and well north of the route to Damascus. The hour had come and they were unprepared. Quickly the maps were consulted.

"How long before our allies come from Tripoli and Antioch?" demanded the King, who now took the chair.

"At least two weeks, sir, perhaps three," answered Guy.

"How many knights do we have now?"

"Counting the garrison at Ascalon, not more than five hundred, with their men."

"What about the towers and castles around?"

"Every castle and tower has been stripped of its defenders. The country up to Jerusalem is defenseless."

"Then we must stand fast." In a crisis, with his back to the wall, the leper King showed a good fighting spirit, which infected all his commanders, so they shouted, "Stand fast! Stand fast!"

"But where shall we stand?" asked the King. "If we are besieged in Ascalon, we shall be caught like rats in a trap and the enemy will burn the countryside. We must keep our freedom of maneuver. I tell you what we shall do. We shall go out to meet this Sultan, with all our five hundred knights, and take the True Cross with us. All in favor, say 'ay!' "

"Ay!" shouted the commanders.

In the silence that followed, only Amalric was heard clearing his throat. "Sir," he said, "to whom have you given the command?"

"To you, Lord Constable—and to the Lord Protector jointly," replied Baldwin.

"With due respect, sir," pursued Amalric, "I cannot serve with that traitor."

"Withdraw that word!" Guy was on his feet again.

"Gentlemen," implored the King, "this is no time for unseemly quarrels. I have decided on a joint command and this is how it must be."

"Never!" Amalric shouted, growing heated. "I cannot bow my neck to a double yoke!"

"Nor I," Guy said firmly. "We shall agree on nothing if we command together."

The King looked anguished and the Seneschal spoke up. "Sir," he said, "will you not let the command be on alternate days, so one shall have full command today and another tomorrow?"

"Yes, yes, it will be better so!" Baldwin grasped at the solution. "We shall march out before first light tomorrow. Lord Constable, you shall command the first day; Lord Protector, you the next. Tell the Bishop of Bethlehem to take horse also, and command the Royal guards to provide an escort for the Cross. And may God defend the right!"

The sun glared like a fiery red ball through the clouds of blowing sand that darkened the sky at morning. It rose behind them as they rode down the coast road to El Arish, mailed men on mailed horses, but the khamsin came out of Egypt directly into their faces. Many knights wore their Arab kaffiyehs over their helmets, swathing their faces so that only a slit appeared for the eyes, but still the sand drove in, inflaming the eyelids.

They rode in silence, between the sea on the right and the desert on the left, neither talking nor laughing, but only listening for the sounds of the approaching army, hidden in the blowing curtains of sand. In the silence, each man was alone with his thoughts, remembering his own green valley at home, the pleasures and wenches he had left behind, and he cursed his luck that brought him to this evil hour.

Riding with the main body of knights, beside the King's litter, Guy was preoccupied with his own misgivings. "Oh, Salah," he thought, "why could we not have continued to be friends, each in his own way, opposed yet not opposing, unlike yet liking, divided yet not dividing? I would not have raised my hand against you. I would have offered you a peace, had you given me time, as I did once before when I stood before the Sultan and the mamelukes gave up their swords to me. And there would have been peace in this land we both call Holy—a peace only you and I could make. Why did you not wait for me? Oh, Salah, why is it too late, even before we have begun?"

About noon, scouts returned down the coast road at the gallop. The Saracen force had been sighted less than a mile ahead. Of its size and composition, the scouts had nothing to tell, except that it was 'numerous'; the sand storm obscured all else. The Sultan had set his standard on a small hill commanding the road. Such was the meager intelligence.

Amalric, taking command, reformed the small Crusader force. In the center he placed the Royal knights, with

their retainers, surrounding the King's litter and the True
Cross. This division consisted of perhaps two hundred
knights and their men. On each flank, he deployed a division of vassal knights and their men, while mounted archers fanned out across the front. When the sergeants had
completed the re-formation, Amalric raised his baton, in
signal for the advance to continue.

Still, the sky was filled with sand, descending in curtains
of black, brown and yellow, like rain squalls obscuring the
view, then lifting here and there to let in the sunlight in
lurid shafts, like some phantasmagoric landscape of hell. It
was one of these shafts of sun that picked out the standard of the Sultan on his hill. The whole top of the hill
and its sides were covered with motionless horsemen,
armed with bows, swords and lances. Like an antique
frieze, they stood still and watched.

"Look! The Paynim Saladin!" cried Amalric, pointing
ahead. About five hundred yards separated the two armies. As soon as the Crusader forward archers came
within range, they loosed their arrows, and the frieze
came to life. The Saracen horsemen, screaming and charg-
ing down the hill, returned the fire, racing toward the
Crusader army, firing from the saddle, then wheeling away
and continuing to shoot Parthian shots backwards as they
retired. These sallies confused the advance but did not halt
it.

Meanwhile, the Crusader archers had been sent foward
on either flank to cover the advance. It was clear that
Amalric intended to assault the hill with a heavy cavalry
charge, but this could not be done until the hilltop was
within range of his own archers. The moments of waiting
grew tense, as wave after wave of Saracen archers har-
assed the advance with their shafts. Crusader knights in
the solid mailed wall were falling from their horses, mor-
tally wounded. The cries of the dying rose from under the
trampling feet of the horses. And Amalric grew impatient.

Suddenly, he saw his chance. The Sultan's standard was
struck. Incredibly, the Saracen force on the hill wavered
and retreated. *"Deus Vult!"* cried the Constable, giving the

signal for the battle charge. And, with a lowering of spears, the entire Crusader army charged up the hill. The weight of these armed men, all in heavy mail, mounted on their enormous chargers, also fully-mailed, was like a typhoon unleased on the more lightly-armed Saracens.

The enemy line broke, retreating in the center, though holding tenaciously on the flanks. This meant that the Royal knights, with Amalric at their head, gained the advantage, while the vassal knights were able to make little headway along the sides. With the Sultan in flight, there was no holding Amalric. Leaving his vassals in the rear, he charged forward and gained the height of land.

The victorious Crusaders formed an armed circle atop the hill; in the center they raised the True Cross, its rugged shape held together by bolts and strips of iron, towering above the men and horses; the Royal standard was unfurled; the King descended from his litter and took the salute. All was confusion, joy, sweating and cheering. Then the curtains of blowing sand lifted again and they saw the vista before them.

To the south and west, behind the hill, as far as the eye could see, the desert was black with men. In their thousands, the Saracen army seemed like some migration of locusts which had eaten up the country to the bone. There in the distance was the Sultan's base camp, surrounded by the tents of his emirs, each with their mounted mamelukes, retainers, bowmen and troopers. All these horsemen were marshalled in regular formations, like teeming colonies, waiting to be loosed on their enemies. Amalric, viewing the scene, exclaimed, "By Jesu, it is not an army—it is an infernal horde!"

Then the counter-attack began. Swinging around the hill in two great arcs, the Saracen mounted archers swept down on the Crusader vassal knights in the rear, putting them to flight all the way to Ascalon. The whole plain was swarming with savage whoops and yells, as the victorious Saracen horsemen thundered and wheeled, throwing their spears in the air and catching them, kicking up clouds of sand which whitened their armor. On the hilltop, the small contingent of Royal knights took the measure of their isolation and their doom.

So the sun went down, and with it died the khamsin wind which had concealed the face of the earth and its horrors throughout the day. Now the stars began to shine; the whole plain winked with little fires, as the Saracen horde brought up their supplies and food and cooked supper amid general rejoicing; the sound of their voices, with laughter and belching, came extraordinarily clear on the evening air, and also the cries of the hyenas, skulking about in search of corpses among the dunes.

The band of knights on the hilltop lay by their horses, talking little, thinking much, and altogether dispirited. The King, supported by his aides, went from group to group with words of cheer. By morning, he said, the force from Ascalon would return with help. The allies would soon arrive. The Templars would come. But, though they saluted him gravely, and admired his spirit, none believed him.

Amalric, veering from overconfidence to craven fear, counselled surrender. But this was abhorrent to all. With the True Cross in their midst—the origin, the meaning of the Crusade—surrender was unthinkable. Better they should die and spatter its fragments with their blood! And yet, in such a hopeless cause, none had any taste for death.

The King turned to Guy. "Do you not remember, Master Guy, how once I had a dream in which I stood on this very hill—and the True Cross stood there—and you stood here—and I called to you to be my eyes, and my ears, and my tongue, so we might be saved? What hope have we, Master Guy?"

"No hope," answered Guy. "But, if you will empower me, I will talk to this man."

"Yes, yes!" the others eagerly assented. "Save us!"

"Save the True Cross!"

"Save Jerusalem!"

"What can be saved," replied Guy, "may be no more than our own souls, but I will carry out your commands.

Make a flag of truce. Let a trumpeter accompany me. I will go to the Sultan's tent!"

Before the third hour of the night, a small party, consisting of Guy, two of his men and the King's trumpeter, left the hilltop and descended to the plain, riding their horses slowly, and carrying their weapons reversed. Almost as though they had been expected, they were met by Kurdish horsemen of the Sultan's personal bodyguard, who conducted them courteously, through the rows upon rows of staring faces, lit by the lurid campfires, into the heart of the Saracen camp.

The curtain of the tent was lifted by two black Nubian slaves. Inside all was brightness, as dozens of torches lit the vast high enclosure, the den of the lion. Guy walked across the skins of animals stretched on the sand, his eyes dazzled by the lights and smarting from the smoke of a fire in the midst of the tent. He was met by the rising of the emirs from their cushions on the ground—scores upon scores, in the leopard skins of Nubia, in the short tunics of the Turcomen, in the kaftans of Mongolia—the whole horde was here, the gathering of the people of God.

"Salaam! Salaam!" The emirs bowed to the ground as he passed, which puzzled him more than a little, for it was not the custom thus to greet the emissary of a defeated enemy.

Beyond the smoke of the fire, in the far reaches of the tent, surrounded by half a hundred mamelukes, all in yellow tunics and armed with unsheathed scimitars, he saw the master of the horde, seated atop a pile of mattresses covered with cloth of gold, but clad himself in a plain, black woolen mantle, the Sultan Salah-ed-Din.

He approached to the foot of the dais and prepared to prostrate himself according to the Eastern fashion, but, with a sudden leap, the Sultan landed on the ground before him and prevented the obeisance. Raising him with both hands, the royal host kissed his guest on the cheeks and said in a low, intimate voice, "Peace be unto you, al-Adil."

"Peace be unto you, Salah," replied Guy, using the same undertone.

Then, turning him about to face the throng, the Sultan announced, "I present to you, emirs, tawashis and qaraghulams, the emissary of the Unbelievers, one who is also a great prince among us and a true friend of our own, His Highness the Imam al-Adil!"

"Salaam! Salaam!" they murmured, bowing low.

"Look on his face well, O emirs, tawashis and qaraghulams," continued the Sultan, "for this man comes as a friend and not as a foe, and whatever may come of our meeting, whether it is God's will that we should make war or peace, no man shall do him harm."

"On our heads be your commands," replied the assembly.

Then, with a curt nod, he dismissed everyone in the tent, except for a few of his favorite mamelukes. Leading Guy with an arm about his shoulders, he approached the fire, for the night was cold, and he offered him a steaming cup. But Guy shook his head.

"Salah, I have men outside," he said, "who are as thirsty as I. Let them drink first."

"I know not these men," replied Salah. "Let them return whence they came. They shall have no succor from me."

Surprised at his friend's new, hard tone, Guy took the cup and, going to the tent door, called his men and offered it to them. When the men had drunk, the Sultan called out, "Remember that it is he who gave you this cup, not I."

Guy turned about, dismayed. "Does this mean that you do not give these men the protection of the tent?"

"Let them go and no harm shall come to them. You alone are my guest."

Guy dismissed the men, telling them to return to the Crusader camp without him.

"Ad'l," said Salah, as he refilled the cup for him, "you are always the same. It would be better for you to think of yourself now."

"If you took your own advice, I should not be here, Salah. I am a thorn in your side. I come to talk peace, not war. And you should remember to call me Guy."

"Guy—Guy—" Salah sounded the name several times and smiled. "It does not sit right on my tongue. In this tent you shall be Ad'l."

He called to his mamelukes, and bade them relieve Guy of his heavy mail, substituting a soft Arab farajeyeh. "It is better, so we can talk at our ease," he said, as they sat on the ground before the fire. He went on, shaking his head, "I had rather you were anywhere but on that hill, Ad'l. It was a mistake, a serious mistake. How could you forget our tactics? Your forces are heavy on the ground. We are light. We must give before the weight of your cavalry charge, but yielding only in center, our horsemen swelling back on the flanks, scattering your rear and swallowing you up. Besides, you should not have attacked before your archers had covered your flanks; that was elementary, elementary. You will forgive me for teaching you this lesson?"

Guy smiled wanly. "I did not command today. We are in joint command, Amalric and I. He commanded today, I tomorrow."

Salah looked at him wonderingly. "You are extraordinary, you Roumis, perfectly extraordinary! It is wonderful that you accomplish anything! And now what can be done? You are lost!"

"We can fight."

"But to what end?"

"We have allies; all the Kings of Europe will come to our aid."

"Too late, too late. Better to end it now, Ad'l."

"We cannot—not while we have the True Cross with us."

"Ah, the True Cross! And for this you must die?"

"Yes."

Salah fell into a reverie, gazing into the fire, as if he expected to see the answer to the mystery of the Roumis in the twisting flames. A strange people, truly! Faithless, treachous, cruel, avaricious, barbarian—yet they would die for a piece of rotten wood that some trickster had foisted on them as the cross of Jesus. At last, he said, "What, then, do you ask of me?"

Guy then realized the enormity of what he had to ask—to require this enormous horde to stop was like asking the sun not to rise on the morrow. Instead, he reverted to an episode in the past. "Will you not let me come to you, Salah, as I came to the people of Ulayqa, with my hands empty and my heart full, quite simply as the Imam of peace?"

"But they shot you full of arrows at Ulayqa for your temerity, did they not?"

"Shoot me then, Salah," said Guy, smiling; "I did not die at Ulayqa and I will not die here."

"Never will I raise a hand against you, as you well know, Ad'l. But neither will I talk peace. At Ulayqa you were among your own people, the Ishmaelites. Here you are among the host of Islam. I have raised this host, I, Salah-ed-Din, the son of a poor Kurdish horseman; I have made myself General of all this assembly of nations; I have crowned myself Sultan and Commander of the Faithful; I have done all this, not for poor Salah-ed-Din, who will one day go to his death wearing nothing but a rag for a shroud—No, I have done it for the glory of God! In His name I shall conquer, and no man—not even my friend al-Adil—can stand in my way, for there is none greater than God, Whose name be exalted and Whose perfection be extolled!"

At this, Guy fell silent, for he saw that there was no making peace with this man, dearly as he loved him. Then he said sadly, "Well, Salah, then I see that I must die, because I cannot desert my dear Lord and Savior."

"Stop!" exclaimed Salah. "We shall not talk of life and death until we have eaten. You are my guest. You must sit in the place of honor. You must eat of the best food!" He clapped his hands and the mamelukes called in the slaves, who were ready and waiting with trays of delicacies on their heads; the smell of hot roasted mutton filled the air, together with aromatic spices of India and China; fruits packed in ice from Mount Hermon tumbled in profusion on the low, round table at their feet; and many sweet wines from the mountains of Armenia stood in amphoras with deep, conical bottoms driven into the sand.

"In the name of God!" said Salah, waiting for his guest to plunge in his right hand.

"In the name of God," answered Guy, choosing the first morsel.

So began an evening of good talk, tender memories, and fanciful speculation, such as they had not enjoyed since the nights long ago in the Golden Cockerel—and such as, each knew, they would never enjoy again. For a few hours, Guy forgot the knights' vigil on the lonely hill; he was back with his friend Salah in the land of the Paynim.

"And what have you to tell me of my son?" enquired Guy, between morsels.

"He is well—I saw him but three months ago—a fine boy, strong and handsome. He is very fair—I thought you would like to know that."

"What have they named him?"

"Al-Adil, of course, after his father the Imam. They have removed him to Ulayqa where Fatima dotes on him like his own mother."

"And you are still regent?"

"Yes, but I have appointed Abdulla Governor. Does it please you?"

"Of course, but why Abdulla?"

"He understands the people well, but more important, because he knew you well. You should see him! He has modelled himself on you to the life! He conducts the courts exactly as you did—stern with the men and overgentle with the women. But still, he is not Imam, and the people are sad because there is no one to whom they can bring their daughters—until your son is a man!"

"And Master Sa'di?"

"He is still busy opening houses of propaganda up and down the land, but, since they are not seditious, I do not interfere. He has told the people you ascended to Heaven from Masyaf on your black horse, like the Prophet, Whose name be exalted! And they believe it! Perhaps he believes it! After all—no one did see you leave—"

"What nonsense, Salah! You should put a stop to it!"

"Why? The people want it this way. You brought them in touch with God; let them honor you for it."

"And does the Old Man still live?"

"At Masyaf. He is a recluse now; no one ever sees him, and they say he is very mad. Sometimes he does a little murdering, when the fit is on him, but most of his followers have deserted him for the True Imam."

"The True Imam?"

"Your son."

Guy's eyes filled. "Remember me to him, Salah. Someday, when he is old enough, talk to him as I would talk; let him know something of me beside the foolish legends; bid him not be proud because the Imamate came to him as an inheritance; bid him be kind to my people; bid him remember that he is the servant of the Most High and not God Himself."

Salah promised all these things. Then their conversation turned to the curious revolutions of fortune, which brought some men high and others low, and how the hand of God was to be discerned in all this, yet how it was impossible for any to know God, because His nature was unknowable, and how the greatest mistake any man can make is to think he knows what is in the mind of God. On all these things they were agreed.

And after a while Guy fell silent, for he was thinking again of the knights' vigil on the windy hill, and Salah said, "Well, Ad'l, what, after all, is it that I am to do for you this night? Because, you know that I am bound in honor to give you a life in exchange for my own."

"For yours?"

"The time you saved me from the death list—you remember? A life for a life is the code of Islam."

"Ah," said Guy, remembering. Then he came out with

something else, again. "I think what must happen is that you will give me the King's life."

"The King's life!"

"You said I may have a life, didn't you? It is very necessary that the King should live and return to lead the Kingdom, no matter in what adversity—"

"Wait, wait, Ad'l. Are you bargaining with me for the life of another—not your own?"

Guy looked aggrieved. "Surely I may ask for what life I choose, mine or another?"

Salah was outraged. "And who is this King that his life should be worth more than yours?"

"Very young, very brave, very sick and like to die—but very much a King. And there is one thing more. The Cross. Grant me the True Cross, Salah, I beg you—"

"Stop, Ad'l. I will not have you beg in this tent. I am only doing you justice. It shall be as you say. Now, listen to me carefully. At dawn, when there is just light enough to tell a white thread from a black, for the space of one hour, there shall be a truce. The lines of my soldiers shall open. The King, with the Cross, and a dozen of his knights may leave on the road to Ascalon. You will be among them. There! Does that suit you?"

"But I cannot go."

"Cannot go?"

"You forget—I am commander tomorrow."

"Do you mean to say that, no matter what I do, I cannot save your life?"

Salah's anger knew no bounds. He raged about the tent, roaring at Guy, throwing the cushions around, striking any mameluke that came in his way, so that none dared to enter the tent and none dared to leave. Guy only sat on his heels by the fire, silent and unmoved by it all.

Then Salah came to him and knelt down at his feet, pleading with him humbly, "Ad'l, listen to me, please listen. There is no need for us to fight. After the King has left, I will give the order to strike camp and resume the march. We will simply ignore you, as we would bypass a fortress we had no need to capture. Will this not be enough to satisfy your honor?"

Guy considered it. "But then, you see, Salah, I should be obliged to attack your rear, and I could make short work of your baggage train, so that you would be cut off in our territory without supplies."

Salah looked into the candid, blue eyes of his friend and said softly, "Truly, God must love you, Ad'l, to have made you such a fool, and to have watched over you as He has. Of all the proofs of His omnipotence, you are one of the most profound, for, by all the logic of this world, you should have destroyed yourself long ago. Now, commit your affair unto God, and may He open to you some other way. I can do no more for you."

Guy rose. "You have done everything and more that I could have asked. Oh, Salah, you have been my best friend to the very end. And if, as I think likely, you will win the day in the Holy Land, I would ask you to do as I would have done—deal hardly with the men, but spare the women and children and set a new example the world will remember. And now, goodbye."

The men embraced, and Guy exchanged his farajeyeh for his hauberk, and quickly left the tent to be escorted by the Sultan's guard as far as the edge of the Crusader camp. It was still about three hours to dawn. Watching him go, Salah-ed-Din turned to his battle marshal outside the tent and said, "Mark that man's face well. If he is found among the slain this day, you shall be crucified and your body thrown to dogs!"

At precisely the hour when the cocks crow in the peaceful homestead, the muezzin throws his raucous cries on the morning air and the impartial dawn rose on a lonely hill in Sinai, a party of knights, carrying the True Cross in their midst, set out on the desert road to Ascalon. Among them rode the King and with him a picked band of a dozen men.

No sooner had they left, however, than bitter strife broke out among the remainder of the knights' division.

Some, led by Amalric, held that they should all have taken advantage of the truce to escape, even though the safe conduct was given only to the King's party. Others maintained they should surrender, as there was no point in resisting, now that the King and the True Cross had escaped.

Guy, as commander of the day, riding about the inner circle of mounted knights, addressed them sternly. "Soldiers of Christ! Remember your vows. You came not to save your lives; you came to save God's Kingdom. We are a handful of men against a mighty host, but if we stand fast this day, the Kingdom shall be saved. By the grace of God, the King will raise another army to defend the Holy City; the holy places will not be desecrated and the True Cross will not be defiled. Only you must stand fast. You must delay the pursuit and gain time for the defense. A single stone may throw a rider, and here on this rock today, we shall break the fury of Islam. Stand fast and God be with us!"

Glumly, the knights heard him out. He marshalled them in three ranks, one commanded by Amalric, one by the Seneschal, and one by himself in the front facing the Sultan's camp. Around the knights, he drew up the mounted archers, covering the approaches to the hilltop. The silence grew intense, broken only by the snuffling and pawing of the horses, and an occasional curt command.

The Saracen lines were beginning to stir; tents were struck and loaded onto pack animals; the fires were put out; and men looked to their accoutrements. Still the hour of the truce was not run out and the gap in the Saracen lines in the direction of Ascalon remained open to a distance of perhaps a hundred yards.

It was too much for Amalric. Suddenly, after a whispered colloquy and a surreptitious signal, he and his men bolted down the hill and through the gap. Guy detected the move; instantly, he ordered the trumpets to sound the battle call; but it was too late—the defectors had got away.

The Saracen trumpets answered and at once the infidels

formed up in battle order, their mounted archers in the
forefront, the knights in their black armor, holding their
lances at the vertical, in the rear. The enemy formations
began to circle the hill, passing to the eastward, without
attempting to engage the defenders. Guy divined the intention, and ordered his archers to intercept the Saracens
from bypassing their position.

The fire was returned, but the enemy had to shoot
uphill, and many of their shafts went astray. Their lightly
armed archers, on lean Arab horses, rode in closer, raid-
ing the front rank of the Crusaders, attempting to draw
them out, but Guy held his knights in rigid formation.

From their vantage point on the hill, the Crusader archers had effectually interdicted the coastal road; the enemy
were swarming about like angry wasps; and a party of
Saracen knights moved up to the assault. With lances lowered, the Crusaders withstood the charge, throwing many
of the infidels to the ground, or killing them in the saddle
with their battle axes.

But the unequal struggle could not go on. The Saracen
marshals began to throw wave after wave upon the hill,
and the small band of Crusaders gradually dwindled; gaps
began to appear in the line as knights and horses fell, and
there were none to take their place.

In the forefront, Guy felt the emptiness around him.
An enemy horseman, armed with a small round shield, a
lance and a club, advanced, swerved and passed on his
left. Another came and passed on his right. Save for his
own troop from Vienne, he was alone.

"Master!" One of his men, Yves, rode up to him with
tears running in the muck on his face. "Master, they have
all gone!"

Guy turned and saw an extraordinary thing. The gap in
the Saracen lines in the direction of Ascalon was still
open. One by one, the knights had saved themselves.

He looked at Yves, and at the blanched, fearful faces of
his men, Robert, Bertrand, Balian, Geoffrey, Jean—these
alone were left. "Then save yourselves!" he commanded in

a hoarse voice. "There's nothing left to fight for this day." And without a word they fled.

It was then Guy saw the mameluke in front of him. He was a large fellow, with the slanting eyes of the Circassian, all in black mail and mounted on an Arab stallion. He carried a short, Arab lance in his hand and a scimitar in his belt. But the mameluke made no attempt to accost him.

Too close in to use his long lance, Guy lunged at him with his sword; the mameluke swerved aside and, using his shorter lance with the point *reversed,* thrust Guy from the saddle. He fell to the ground with a ringing clangor of steel. On his feet at once, Guy thrust again with his sword, but the mameluke passed on. Unable to recover his horse, Guy sought to dismount one after another of the Saracen horsemen who were swarming over the hill, but none seemed to see him; they all swerved aside, leaving him alone.

Then, stunned by a glancing blow from a kicking stallion, he fell under the trampling horses. He was unable to rise; he lay inert, waiting for the end. But still the end did not come. The thundering hooves passed over his head, the sand was churned up into an impenetrable cloud which hung heavy in the sky long after the hooves were gone. The khamsin had risen again.

When he arose, he was alone in the desert. The sky was the color of sulphur and the sand drove into his face no matter which way he turned. The sand devils eddied and swirled about him, so that he lost all sense of direction and began staggering blindly in search of the road to Ascalon.

Night fell, and he took shelter in the lee of a giant dune, and the hyenas came and smelled his feet but, finding him still warm, postponed their meal for another day. The next morning, he struggled on. Somewhere, he was sure, he must come out at the sea, but it always eluded him. He was growing weak from thirst now, and covered very few miles in a day.

After three days, the wind dropped, but he was unable to get his bearings. The sea was no longer in sight. Now the sun burned the sand to a radiant heat, reflecting into his eyes, so that a hundred suns danced before them. Toward noon he collapsed and lay on his back, with blackened lips and lolling tongue, unable to move. The sun burned through his lids, and when he awoke he did not know whether his eyes were open or shut.

Toward evening, he got up and walked on into a blood red sky that gradually turned black. But when he looked up to read his bearings in the constellations, there were none to see. It was cold at night and this helped him to go on, but always now in a velvet blackness, so that he stumbled often and at last sprained his ankle in a desert water hole.

The next day was worse, since he could only crawl, but this he did in order not to stiffen and die for the slavering hyenas which patiently trotted after him. And now he saw nothing—nothing at all. Only when he lifted his face to the sky, a redness flooded his vision, and a pulsing roar filled his ears, as though he were drowning in a sea of blood.

How long he lay inert on the sand he never knew; but the hands that lifted him were kindly, to the accompaniment of the soft voices of the desert, the grumbling of camels, and the tinkling of the bedouin caravan bells. He lay in the howdah on the camel's back, the curtains closed to screen him from the light, and several times a day he was given asses' milk to drink. And always the rhythmic jerking of the camel made its way into his dreams, like the rowing of the Sun boat of ancient Egypt, as it carried Osiris to the nether world.

At last, the camel groaned and shuddered and lay down. He was helped from the howdah and stood unsteadily on the sand.

"Welcome, my son," said a deep, booming voice, in the Greek tongue.

"Where am I?" asked Guy.

"Can you not see?" enquired the voice, switching to Arabic.

"I can see nothing at all."

"Well, then, this is Mount Sinai. You are a guest of the Holy Monastery of the Burning Bush. Let me help you in."

Helping hands aided him on all sides, men with voluminous, rustling robes and deep, quiet voices, speaking to one another in Greek. They led him through a gateway, across a courtyard, where the sun's hot rays seemed to be filtered by some overhanging vines, then through a low doorway—so low that he grazed his head—in the thickness of the fortress wall. They were in the monastery itself. He could tell by the sudden coolness, the intense quiet, the smell of water and wells and ground corn and animals in stables.

There were many passages, twisting this way and that, now upstairs, now down, sometimes under roof, sometimes in the open again. Then they climbed an external wooden stairway clamped to a whitewashed wall, up three flights onto a verandah that connected rows of little cells. The helping hands stopped at a door and opened it.

"Kala?" said a deep voice. Then slipping into Arabic again, "Will you be all right here? Let me help you lie down."

He lay on a stone bench, covered with straw. The gentle buzz of voices faded. Someone gave him water, and later a little dish of meal, and he slept.

He awoke to the sound of a bell, first three notes, low-pitched, then three more, louder. It was very cold and felt like nighttime, about the hour before dawn. From somewhere below the verandah, possibly in the basilica, came the sound of chanting. "Kyrie eleison, kyrie eleison," the intoning, the responses, hour after hour. He fell asleep again.

After breakfast, which was brought him by a bedouin boy—his name was Hassan, he said—the Father Superior came to see him. His voice was old and friendly and Guy visualized a craggy face, muffled in a crinkly white beard.

"I am Father Porphyrios," said the voice. "You are looking better today and I have no doubt we shall have

you well in no time. No broken bones, eh? You are fortunate my bedouins found you. They come back here for
half the year to work in granaries at harvest time. They
have brought you far from home, I fear. Mount Sinai is at
the end of the known world. There it is, just outside your
door. It was in this place the Lord said to Moses, 'I am
the God of thy fathers, the God of Abraham, the God of
Isaac. I am He who is the God of Jacob.' This house is
the door of God. You will find peace here."

There was peace, it seemed, but not for him. As the
days passed, he grew strong enough to get up and sit on
the floor of the verandah in the warmth of the sun, facing
into the wind off Sinai. Later, he was allowed to come
down into the courtyard, where the monks sat under the
vine leaves, sifting grain at long tables. He learned to do
the work quite easily, separating the fine from the coarse,
and gathering it into baskets to be taken to the bake-oven.

At other times, Hassan took him for walks. They left by
the courtyard gate and walked under the cliff for some
minutes until they reached the beginning of the steps.
There were seven thousand steps, Hassan said, cut into the
side of Mount Sinai, leading to the top. Sometimes they
climbed a little way. It grew colder up there and the wind
was stronger, and always there was the smell of water. At
the lower levels, it was the water of springs, dripping
among the vines and mosses of the caves. Higher up it
was water from the melting snows. "Not so high, master!"
Hassan would caution after a while, and they would go
back. But still no one seemed to notice his trouble.

"Kyrie eleison. Kyrie eleison." Sometimes, when the
sound of chanting came from the basilica, he would find
his way there, feeling along the twisting corridors, following the sound of the rising and falling voices. It was always bone cold in the basilica, kneeling on the rough stone
floor, in a corner of the choir stalls and the cold, clammy,
sweet scent of incense hung heavy on the air. The litany
of the saints and martyrs was always very long, as the
Sacristan went about from eikon to eikon, lighting the
candles before each and swinging the thurible, which emit-

ted clouds of the sweet-smelling incense. From the distance the Father Superior, in his chair by the altar, chanted his office and the monks repeated the endless responses, "Kyrie eleison, kyrie eleison." But still, there seemed no help for him here.

And one night, when he felt more than ever oppressed by the great darkness in which he now lived, he made his way alone out the gate, under the cliff, and up the rock-hewn steps of the mountain. For a long time he climbed on hands and knees, till his flesh was scraped and torn on the rough stone, for the steps twisted this way and that, and there was no railing to indicate the direction of the turns. He had once asked Hassan what was at the top.

"Wind and snow, master," the boy had replied.

"And does the mountain fall away on the sides very steeply?"

"Very steeply."

"And could a man stop there for long?"

"He would die."

They found him the next day, lying on a ledge about fifteen feet below a twist in the stairs, where he had missed the turn and tumbled down the face of the precipice. Hassan, with a curious prescience, had led them to the spot as soon as he was missed. He was delirious and raving from his night on the mountain and struggled with his rescuers, so that they had to tie his hands and feet with rope. Back in his cell at the monastery, they gave him opium and he fell into a deep and dreamless sleep.

Father Porphyrios came to see him again and sat on the stone slab at his feet. "God has touched you, my son," he said.

"Is He an Inquisitor, then, who puts me on his rack like a very good friend?"

"He is a Teacher. He teaches us to turn our evil into good. *'Omnia convertantur in bonam.'* The suffering you are undergoing is not desired by God. But the learning is desired. You are learning now how to overcome evil, so that it may serve God's purpose. You are being carved and cut and polished, so you, too, may be a stone in the building of the heavenly Kingdom."

"But why must I lose my sight, Father? Must a builder not see what he is building?"

"God sees all. You see only in part. You must learn to let Him see for you, by uniting yourself to Him. It is a hard thing to unite oneself to God. Many have tried it by false means, and have failed. Uniting ourselves to God means, in every case, leaving ourselves, dying partially to what we love. *Oportet illum crescere me autem minui.* To grow in God, we must diminish in ourselves."

"But, Father, how can I grow in God, if I am less of a man?"

"God must make room for Himself in you, is it not so? He must hollow you out, if He is to penetrate into you. Perhaps you have been too much yourself, too much your own master. Now, perhaps, you will divert your activity onto other paths, which, though still of this world, may be more propitious. After all, that is what happened to Job, whose final happiness was greater than his first. His evil became his good. That is the greatest miracle."

"Father, tell me how to work this miracle."

"By faith, my son. By faith and nothing else is the world explained, so that evil is transformed into good, chaos is resolved into order, suffering becomes the caress of God. But if we lack faith, if we put faith in ourselves rather, in our own omnipotence, then the waters of life which Moses struck from the rock remain dry, the Voice in the Burning Bush falls silent, and we are alone in an empty universe."

"And if it is empty, after all—?"

"If it were empty, we should all have failed long ago; our weakness, our predilection for evil would have dragged us under; our own foolishness would have destroyed us. Despite ourselves, we are borne up on angels' wings. Have you not felt it—this immense saving grace which brought you to this very door, which saved you in the desert and on the mountain, which leads you through the valley of the shadow of death, so you need fear no evil—?"

"Do you mean, Father, that I may have my sight again?"

"Wait and see. The important thing is that your suffering is transfigured into a saving grace. That is why, and for no other reason, my dear son, God has touched you."

After that, Guy grew calmer and consented to be led about quietly, so that he took part in the daily life of the monastery, sweeping out his cell like the other monks, taking his turn to clean the courtyard, the kitchens, the latrines, working in the granaries, sifting and winnowing, eating in the refectory while one of the brethren read the scripture in Greek.

But he often had little conversations with Father Porphyrios. Once, when they were passing one of the granary buildings, the old man stopped and told his blind follower to put out his hand. Guy did so, and his fingers closed on a thorny creeper, like a rose, nailed to the wall. "That," said Father Porphyrios, "is the Burning Bush itself—or a graft from the same, made by our monks when they first came here in the reign of Justinian. It was from this Bush that God spoke."

"Will He speak to me?"

"But He does—and to all men who listen."

"To Christian and to Moslem both?"

"He draws all men to Him."

"Why, then, does He say different things to each, one thing to Christians, another thing to Moslems, so that we make war on each other and kill each other, and all in His name?"

"We are all growing in God. We rise upward on our prayers, on our efforts, even on our mistakes. God uses all things for good. *Necessarium est ut scandala eveniant.* We cannot avoid these shocks and scandals, because we are not yet perfect, and will not be perfect until His Kingdom comes. We can only do what each of us believes to be right, even in discord, and leave the ultimate harmony to God."

Another time, Guy, who had meditated these words

long in the silence and darkness of his present world, asked the Father Superior the simple question around which his life had revolved. "Father, when will His Kingdom come?"

The old man did not answer for a long time. Then he sighed and rustled his robe a little. "Not now," he said at last. "Not for a long time. We must not be impatient. It will not be consummated with swords, with laws, with revelations—only if we desire it—through the accumulation of our desires—There now, the bell is ringing for matins—shall we go?"

Not long after this, Hassan announced that the bedouins were returning to the land of Jordan for the spring grazing. The whole tribe would make the journey, with all their flocks, and families, the men riding the camels, the women and children in howdahs on the camels' backs, stopping at watering holes along the way, and setting up their crooked, black tents in the desert. It would take many weeks. Would the stranger like to come?

He accepted. So, from the dark underworld of Egypt, he returned to the upper world of Judea, now equally dark to him. But he treasured certain words Father Porphyrios had spoken to him. He would be patient. He would *wait and see.*

CHAPTER FIFTEEN

THE LETTER

Suddenly, all along the eastern frontier, from Nablus to Beersheba, the Kingdom was swarming with Saracens. Alice noticed it first at Shechem when she took her morning walk on the hills. The smoke of burning villages to the north could be clearly seen from the heights of Gerizim.

At once, she returned to the Castle and sent for Hugh. Alone, of all Guy's men, he had been left at her command. "The Saracens are coming," she said. "Sound the alarm in the village and bring in the women and children. Also, ride to the Convent in Nablus and ask Mother Superior if the nuns will take shelter here."

Hugh obeyed. In the days since Guy's departure, Alice had been preparing for this emergency. With Hugh at her side, she had comandeered all stocks of grain in the village; she had purchased stores of oil and pitch; she had enlisted twenty able-bodied youths for the defense of the Castle. Now the crisis had come.

She went to her room. In the closet hung the suit of mail Guy had left her—an old hauberk he had worn before he outgrew it. She buckled it on over her dress, lacing the joins tightly to her tall, spare figure, gathering her auburn hair under the chain helmet, encasing her long slender hands in the heavy steel gauntlets. She looked at herself momentarily in the glass. "Now we are one, you and I," she said.

The villagers swarmed into the Castle, filling the yard and overflowing into the guard room and even into the Great Hall. The Mother Superior sent word that the nuns could not leave their patients in the leprosarium, and anyway, God's work had to be done, Saracens or no. Then the Castle gates were shut, barred and bolted.

The next day, the Saracens came. They were not regular soldiers but a rabble belonging to the emir of Moab across the Jordan, who thought to take advantage of the absence of the regular garrisons. They burned the village and set fire to the long grass of the mountain, so that the smoke hung in a pall over Gerizim for several days.

Later, came the soldiers of the Sultan of Damascus, who set up regular siege engines about the Castle of Shechem. They were quiet and methodical, digging trenches and building walls for defense against the fire from the Castle walls. They gathered large supplies of stones to fire from the mechanical balistas which were stationed on the road. Once the bombardment began, it never let up, as relays of engineers brought up the missiles in carts, loaded and fired.

Alice kept her watch on the battlements, pacing back and forth all day, and even having a pallet set up for her there at night. For a while, she directed the fire on the attackers. She was expert with the long bow and took pride in her accuracy. But soon the supplies of arrows dwindled, and there seemed nothing to do but wait.

After a week, the outer gates began to crumble. There was a rush among the villagers in the courtyard to take refuge in the keep, and pallets of straw were set up for them in the Great Hall. The yard was abandoned and the portcullis lowered in the keep.

Once the Saracens had broken into the courtyard, they began mining operations under the wall of the keep. Several charges of black powder were laid and the explosions shook the whole building with fearful tremors. Now Alice had the cauldrons and fires brought up to the battlements, and she and Hugh together boiled the oil and pitch, and poured it through improvised funnels on to the besiegers below.

But another specter soon arose against which Alice had no defense. Supplies of food ran low, and even with the strictest rationing, she could not feed so many. Whenever she came downstairs, the village women and their babies cried and clutched at her hauberk. With misery in her heart she gave her pet animals to be killed, but the hungry mouths were still there.

The day came when she went out with a flag of truce to speak with the Saracen commander. He was a dissipated young Kurd, full of exaggerated courtesy and vastly intrigued to ascertain that the "boy" commander on the walls was actually a woman. He determined now to press the siege and to make an addition to his harem. When she asked for a safe-conduct for the civilians in the keep, he told her, "I give you their blood, if you give me your body!" She left without a word. Looking at her as she walked away, he told himself he would enjoy a rape better anyway.

Then, one day, Hugh came to her as she sat in her room, staring at the gaunt, hollow-eyed reflection in the glass. "My lady," he said, "I have very bad news. There is no water."

"No water?"

"The well is dry."

"Then—this is the end?"

"Yes, my lady."

She was appalled. "But in such a case—what am I supposed to do?"

"You can ask for terms."

"I know his terms, this lecherous young Kurd!"

"Then, it is up to you, my lady."

All day she thought about it, and at evening she sent for Hugh again. "Very well," she said, "prepare another flag of truce. I will surrender." Her voice was near breaking.

She tried very hard not to think of Guy, but she could not help it. After all, had she the right to dispose of her own body like this, without his knowledge?

"Hugh," she said, catching his hand before he left the room, "you have been close to my husband for many years; you know him better than I. In this case—would he surrender?"

"No, my lady."

"Then why did you not say so! Tell me at once, what would he do?"

"But I don't know, my lady. He is a lord. I am only a common serf. I don't know how the lords think. I just know he would not surrender."

She was alive again with hope. "Think, Hugh, think! Have you never been in a situation like this before with your master? What has he ever done that we can do?"

Hugh thought. "There was one time we were besieged in Jerusalem. We climbed out through the sewers—"

"The sewers! Do we have sewers?"

"We have the drains—" A light began to illuminate Hugh's face. "That's it! The drain from the latrine in the guard room empties into the fosse!"

"You could get away to Jerusalem. Manasses would send enough men to raise the siege!"

Hugh hesitated. "But I could not do that, my lady. The master told me I was to stay with you."

"But in a case like this, Hugh, surely—"

"He said, 'stay with your mistress,' that's what he said."

"Then it is I who must go to Jerusalem."

Hugh's agony was worse. "Still I must follow!"

"But why, Hugh?"

"You don't understand, my lady. He's master. I'm man. I must obey if I die for it!"

Alice pitied his dilemma. "Consider it this way, Hugh. If your master were here in this room, what would he tell you to do?"

Hugh considered it. At last he said, painfully, "He would say, 'Hugh, you go to Jerusalem!'"

And so it came about. Alice, on the battlements with a

dozen of her village youths, began a diversion by shooting at the Saracen sentries on the eastern side of the Castle, while Hugh slid down the drainpipe and into the fosse on the west side. The night was dark and the weather favoring, for the Valley shuddered under one of its habitual thunderstorms, facilitating the escape.

When Hugh got to Jerusalem, he found himself caught up in a wild, popular celebration. The King had returned at the head of his troops following a "miraculous" victory over the Sultan Saladin at Montgisard. Citizens, who had feared the worst for weeks, laughed and wept in each other's arms. Church bells tolled, the True Cross was paraded through the streets, and the crowds outside the Citadel called again and again for the King.

In his office in the Tower of David, Manasses received Hugh gravely. "You have done well to come here, my man, very well. I will send a hundred men to Shechem at once. Tell your mistress there has been a great victory and the worst is over for now. Tell her to hold on and not to give up hope. You see—" he blew out his cheeks and coughed—"you see, your master has not come back. We are hoping, still hoping. Tell her to hope also."

Hugh was stunned. Even after he had returned with the task force to Shechem and the Castle had been liberated, he hesitated to approach Alice. But he had to do it. He found her eyes following him about the Castle everywhere he went, as though waiting for him to speak. But, in the end, it was she who spoke first.

"Guy is missing?" she said.

Dumbly, he nodded.

The first signs of spring were in the air. The warm wind of the south blew into Shechem, scattering the blossoms on the fruit trees, drying the roads after the winter rains. Somehow, in this tortured valley, life was resuming its ancient rhythm. The shepherds had retrieved what they could of their scattered flocks; the women folk were in the fields sowing the crop; the men who took to the hills were back at work, putting the roofs on their blackened homes.

In fact, Alice had commandeered fifty men from the village to rebuild the Castle gates. They grumbled and complained but she was obdurate. The work must be finished by *his* return. One by one the men of Vienne found their way home—Yves, Robert, Bertrand, Balian, Geoffrey, Jean—those who survived. Each time one of them came to the gate, Alice felt a constriction in her heart. Why him, and not—? But she smiled at each one and simply said, "You are welcome." After all, if they could come, perhaps—.

One soft spring evening, when the sun was already off the mountain, they brought word that there was a stranger at the gate. He was a bedu, they said, and came on a camel, attended by a young boy. Her heart almost stopped as she ran down the stairs and into the dark courtyard. The stranger was standing there beside the camel, his face muffled in the folds of his checkered kaffeyeh, his large form wrapped in a black burnous, too tall for an Arab. He heard her step but did not turn his head.

"Alice?" he said.

"Guy!"

They embraced there in the courtyard, among all the soldiers and kitchen maids and clucking chickens, and everyone knew the master was home. They came forward to kiss his hand, and he smiled and patted the head of each as they knelt to him, but he seemed restrained, and begged leave to talk to them another day.

Turning to Alice, he said, "The camel boy here must have a purse of gold; see that he gets it. And now I am very tired. You must help me to my room." And leaning heavily on her arm, he slowly mounted the stairs to the bedroom. She called for tapers but he cut her short. "Not tonight," he said. And wonderingly in the dark, she helped him to undress and laid him on the bed.

"Oh, my love," she breathed, as she held him in her arms that night, "have you really come back to me? Is it really you that I have again? Because without you I am simply not myself any more. Come back to me, dearest love, so I can be whole again!"

And in the dark, he loved her, so that she knew it was really he, and none other, who could give her such joy. Yes, he had come back to her again!

He slept late in the morning and when he awoke, the sun was streaming in the room across the bed. She stood at the foot of the bed, holding the post in her hands, and gazing down at him, as she had done when he slept in her tower on the hill.

"Will you get up now?" she asked as he stirred. "It is a glorious day and everyone wants to see you."

"I shall see no one," he murmured.

"Are you still tired? Then you need only stay at home and let them come to you. Let me wrap you in a robe and put your favorite chair here, and you can sit in the sun."

After a pause, he said, "Where is the sun?"

Then she knew he was blind. It came to her as though she had known it all along, and had only desperately pushed the thought from her. But here he was telling her, because he wanted her to know it, to accept it, to help him with it.

"Oh, my dearest!" she said and went to him. And the memory came back again of the night in the tower, when she had shown him her scars, and of how he had said nothing, only kissed her and forced her to believe he loved her, even as she was. So be it. She would say nothing; she would simply accept him and love him as he was, so that he should know he was loved beyond any other earthly love.

"Oh, my dearest," she said again, kissing him.

It passed off easily enough, when it came time to make public the news. Guy gave over to his wife all the powers of government at Shechem. Hers was the final authority in all things. For himself, he reserved only a consultative role, like that of the family councilor, who had, however, no final responsibility.

Alice was nervous about accepting this state of things, until she realized that he really wanted it this way, and was happiest when he did not have to shoulder a burden he could not bear. He liked to walk in the woods, with one of the Castle dogs, and he became very adept at finding his way about without help. He was always cheerful, and seemed quite himself, only a little quieter.

He continued to ride, always with Hugh at his side, visiting his lands regularly, remembering the names of every peasant family, and often giving sound advice in the matter of building new additions, barns, and pens for animals. As usual, the peasants complained they had no money for these things, but they liked to talk with him, and they long remembered what he said.

One difficulty arose in the matter of the law courts. While Alice had won the respect of everyone for her defense of Shechem, no one would have a woman sit in judgment. This was also a thing Guy did so well that his judgments were a by-word in the countryside. Therefore, Guy heard all cases in the village and the Castle, and was as meticulous as ever at cross-examination, only complaining now and then, "If only I could see his eyes, I'd know if he's telling the truth."

Once a week, he rode to the Convent in Nablus and brought some present for the sisters. The Abbess outgrew her feeling of pity (when she first saw him blind, she wept), and she came to lean on him for advice in her most difficult problems. Like two old soldiers, they sat by the fire, and he told her about his adventures in the lands of the Paynim, and she recounted how she had held the Saracens at bay in her own Convent, by tending their wounds, and showing them the little Arab children in her hospital beds.

The King, who owed his escape at Ascalon to Guy's extraordinary intervention, wrote, begging him to come up to Jerusalem, where new honors awaited him. "If illness did not prevent me, by the grace of God, from conquering the Sultan, no more should it prevent you from giving me your counsel," said the letter. "I shall send Manasses down to you soon to persuade you to come."

But Guy, when the letter was read to him, only sighed and said it was too late. Alice caressed him and told him he was well enough as he was; but silently her heart was breaking, to see his great powers wasted, his mighty sword arm idle, his sure, true look unseeing. And yet there was about him, she felt, a new seeing, a quiet acceptance of God's purpose, that gave him, and all who knew him, a sort of peace.

Manasses came in early summer. They received him in the Great Hall, amid the new hangings, carpets and furnishings which Alice had been buying with her dowry money. She had completely refurbished the Castle, in an effort to make it comfortable, since Guy spent so much of his time at home now.

The old man looked around, raised his eyebrows, slapped Guy on the shoulder and proposed a walk on the hills. When the two were alone together, he accosted Guy about these expenditures. "You shouldn't put your money in all these fripperies, my boy," he said reprovingly. "This peace isn't going to last. It's true we had a lucky victory. By Jesu, I wouldn't have believed it possible! The way the King tells it, it was all due to you. After he got away with the True Cross to Ascalon, he was besieged for weeks. But the Sultan grew careless. He ravaged the country right up to Jerusalem. Then the King broke out of Ascalon, joined up with the forces from Tripoli and Antioch and surprised the Sultan in the pass at Montgisard. The Saracen force was cut to ribbons; only the mamelukes saved the Sultan himself from capture. But still, I tell you, my boy, it can't last. They were like the sands of the desert, these infidels, and the Sultan himself is a veritable jinn—he will blow up a storm that will bury us all someday."

When they returned to the Castle, dinner was served in the Great Hall, and they listened to a troupe of musicians with a minstrel perform parts of the Song of Roland, a favorite of Guy's. The minstrel was a leathery, weather-beaten troubadour, dressed in the faded finery of several European courts where he had plied his trade, travelling ever eastward to the land of Outremer. His rough, grating voice, nevertheless, carried a thrilling realism as he sang of the death of Roland and Oliver, facing the Saracens

alone in the pass at Roncesvalles. And then he reached the
lines—

> "There Roland sits unconscious on his horse,
>   And Oliver who wounded is to death,
>   So much has bled, his eyes grow dark to him,
>   Nor far nor near can see so clear
>   As to recognize any mortal man ...' "

The assembled guests stirred uneasily, and Alice, finding
the words too apt, thought to dismiss the troubadour by
throwing him a purse. But Guy would not let him go. "Do
you now remember the lines, minstrel, where Roland
buries his sword Durendal and turns his face to Spain—?"

The Minstrel took him up, tuning his harp and nodding
to the musicians (there might be more pay yet tonight).
And he sang:

> " 'Count Roland throws himself beneath a pine
>   And toward Spain has turned his face away.
>   Of many things he called the memory back,
>   Of many lands that he, the brave, had conquered,
>   Of gentle France, the men of his lineage,
>   Of Charlemagne his lord, who nurtured him;
>   He cannot help but weep and sigh for these ...' "

When the song ended, the audience applauded and another purse was thrown, but Guy remained abstracted,
staring before him at nothing.

"He thinks he is in the pass at Roncesvalles!" whispered
Manasses to Alice. Poor devil! he thought; he will not stop
the Saracen again. Later, when the entertainment was
over, and the three friends sat alone beside the fire,
Manasses cleared his throat.

"My lord of Shechem," he said with mock formality,
"There is a matter on which I have waited till now to inform you. A letter has lately come to the King's Court,
addressed to you from Poitou. Due to the wars in France,

it has been delayed, as it was brought out on an English ship. The date, I fear, is already a year old."

"What do you say?" asked Guy, aghast. " 'The wars in France'—are we at war, then?"

"King Henry of England and King Louis of France are fighting in the Aquitaine. Your manor, I believe, is in the English sovereignty?"

"We are King Henry's loyal subjects," answered Guy, his anxiety rising. "What has happened? Are we invaded?"

"Perhaps you had better read your letter." And Manasses took from his tunic a worn and battered document. It was from Guy's mother.

"Read it to me," Guy asked Alice.

Alice read: " 'Beloved son, I write in small hope that such a private letter as this will ever reach you, except by the mercy of God, but we think of you and pray the Blessed Virgin for your safety on our knees—I and all your servants, your freedmen and your serfs in your manor lands. For I must tell you, beloved son, that all the lands and people are now yours. Your brother Henry died a year ago of a fall from his horse. You are now our master, and we look, in fear and trembling, for your safe return, for without you, we shall be lost. We are fallen on evil times and ruin faces us every day. The land has been plundered by the King of France and we have lost many flocks and herds carried off and buildings burned, but, by God's mercy, the manor is still intact and we are all still safe.

" 'Another dreadful blow has fallen on us for our sins. King Henry has had a quarrel with our great Archbishop of Canterbury, Thomas à Becket, and the blessed man has been murdered at his very altar. It is said the blood on the stones will not dry and none can wash it away. His Holiness the Pope has placed all King Henry's lands under interdict, no Mass has been said for a year here, we are all excommunicate, and your brother Henry died in his sins. God help us all!

" 'When you have conquered the wicked Sultan and put the heathen to flight, we hope you will remember us and come back to save us from ruin. May it be soon, beloved

son, and may the Blessed Virgin and all the saints protect
you and spare your life. Pray for us at the tomb of the
Savior.

" 'Let me not forget to tell you that you are released
from your oaths to the Count of Poitou. King Henry has
banished all the Lusignans for base rebellion and our liege
is now the gracious Queen of England, Elinor of Aquitaine. Your loving mother.' "

A silence followed this reading, as the group slowly
took it in. It was as though they had felt the earth move
under them. Nothing in this world was sure—all things
shifted and changed—the future was known to God alone.
So their thoughts ran. But Guy came out with his decision.
"I must go home," he said.

He was the master of his life again. In that moment,
he shed the inactivity, the helplessness of the past months,
and he gathered his powers together, just as though there
were no disability to hinder him.

"My wife," said Guy to Manasses, "has never been out
of Outremer. I want her to see the Aquitaine—the forests,
oh, the gigantic forests, teeming with game—and the
cities, Poitiers, Angers, Tours, bursting with life, people,
markets, minstrelsy, miracle plays! Perhaps we shall go to
England and stay in London, a right, rich city—they say
the streets of London are all paved with stones, and the
gardens are the fairest-smelling in the world. I have an idea,
too, that I would like to go to Canterbury, to pray at the
Archbishop's grave—perhaps others will come, and we
shall make a pilgrim company—

So he rambled on, and Alice's heart lifted, for she knew
her husband was himself again.

"So, you are going away, Master Guy," called out the
young King gaily. He was sitting up in bed in his tower
room in the Citadel in Jerusalem. It was a beautiful summer day; the hot sun made the white walls and green cypresses shimmer in a noonday dream; and the window
overlooked the winding road to Jaffa and the sea.

"Who told you that, Master Baldwin?" Guy asked, coming into the room and sitting unceremoniously on the bed.

"Well, it's written all over you." Baldwin said. "I did not know you favored these fashions, with tight breeches, and soft leather boots, and such quantities of fine linen. Just look at that travelling cloak now, fastened with a jewelled ring, too—and you ask how I know you are going abroad!"

Guy smiled, a trifle embarrassed. "It is my wife's doing. She inherited a rich dower from your grandmother, the Queen. Her own jewels, in fact."

"So, that's where they went! I was always afraid Amalric had got hold of them somehow. Well, they look very handsome on your back! But you must leave your wife something, you know—a poor girl's dower is her last resort!"

"Oh, she manages my money for me—and spends it all on me, I'm afraid. But that doesn't tell me how you knew—"

"Manasses told me you want to go home. I think it is a splendid idea. Just the thing for you to do. Be sure and tell them at the court of England that we need more help if we are to hold on out here—"

"Master Baldwin, I can't leave you like this—"

"But I'm all right—as long as I last. The only trouble is I don't seem to have much lasting left in me. I'm dying, Master Guy, every day. Do you remember the wizard you brought to see me once? You know, I really thought he had cured me. Why did it fail—was he a fraud, a mountebank, or something?"

"Yes, he was a mountebank, one of the greatest that ever lived. I did not know it at the time, of course, but I met him later in the land of the Paynim and he told me the truth. He made believe he was God."

"Then how was it he seemed to cure me? Was it the devil's work?"

"I do not believe the devil fools any but his own. I think you *were* cured, Master Baldwin, for that moment, just as we all have our moments of knowledge, and moments of joy, and moments of peace. They come from

God, these moments, and He does not mind what shabby human means He uses to give them to us. But they do not last, because they are not meant to last. They are glimpses of the other side—His Kingdom, you know."

"Have you had such glimpses?"

"Often."

Baldwin hesitated. He was terribly anxious to ask something very hard, and at last he dared. "Master Guy, do you *see* anything like that, when you are blind?"

"See anything on the other side, you mean? No, nothing like that. But I do find that not looking at everyday things makes room for other signs—"

"Signs? You mean signals?"

"Something like that. I have inklings."

"Inklings of the future? Oh, can you tell my fortune? May I know it?"

"Nothing at all like that," Guy laughed. "Call it a hunch, rather. But I don't think you are going to die. Not right away anyway. You have a big job to do, and there's no one else to do it."

"There's Sibylla. She wants to marry that other Guy, Amalric's brother. Then he'll be king someday."

"Don't let him, Master Baldwin. These Lusignan brothers will be the ruin of the Kingdom. They have been chased out of Poitou by our King Henry and I am free of my oath to them, thank God. Now they are settling on this country to pick it clean. Beware of them, Master Baldwin. That's what my hunch tells me."

"But what can I do? My mother manages everything while I lie here in bed all day. They keep everything from me. All I hear is whispering and plotting behind the curtains, and if I ask any questions, it's 'There's nothing to worry about, dear.' "

"Then you must not stay in bed. You shall get up and govern this Kingdom, Master Baldwin!"

"But I can't, I haven't the strength any more."

"You had it at Montgisard! You have it when you are in the army with the men, and away from these women's intrigues at Court. Proclaim yourself Commander-in-

Chief. The barons, the knights, the men would all love you for it. Live in the field, eat the rough fare, sleep in a camp. If you can't walk and can't ride, they'll carry you. Be a King, Master Baldwin!"

Baldwin looked at him curiously. "Are you curing me, Master Guy?" he asked. "The way—what was his name?—Master Barac did, by spells and enchantments?"

"I don't know my breviary well enough to say it forwards, let alone backwards." Guy laughed, "And as for adders' tongues and mandrake root, I don't have the recipe." He jumped up and stood in the middle of the room, his arms outstretched to Baldwin. "I just say to you, no matter what it costs, get up and walk to me!"

Baldwin seemed to be under an influence stronger than himself. Though he had not walked alone for years, though his feet were no more than stumps on which he rocked in danger of crashing to the floor, he stood up and advanced slowly to Guy—one, two, three, four, five, six paces—and fell forward into his arms. "For you, Master Guy," he panted, "I can do anything. But if you leave me—"

Guy helped him to a chair, then sat on the arm of it beside him. "You'll go on and save us all! You mustn't lean on me. It's your own guardian angel you need, Master Baldwin. Find him and he'll see you through."

Baldwin was shaken by the unaccustomed effort, but his eyes were bright. "By God's blood, Master Guy," he said, "you are a magician!"

"Not a magician," smiled Guy, "just your sworn friend."

"But do you believe it possible that I may save God's Kingdom?"

"Of course, the true Kingdom of God cannot be lost. But this Kingdom is within you and me and everyone of us. Whether you can save the Kingdom of Jerusalem is another matter. But it is worth a try."

"And can you do this for me when—when you have lost your own sight? How do you explain that?"

"I don't explain anything, Master Baldwin. There is a good deal too much explaining done, most of which is

misleading and mistaken. I accept things as they are and
do what I can with them, and try to leave an opening,
that's all."

"What do you mean by an opening?"

"A chink—a loophole—for the light to shine through,
don't you know."

"I see. From the other side."

"Something like that."

Baldwin considered it. And then his mind turned to
something else. "Do you think, Master Guy," he said, "I
could ever ride again? You remember our old rides—do
you think—"

"Let's try it. Come with me to the stables."

And together Guy and the King made their way, the
halt leading the blind, past astonished courtiers and servants, down the stairs, through the courtyard and into the
stables. It did not take Guy long to improvise a simple
harness to secure the lame youth in the saddle, so that he
could guide the reins with his wrists and hold on with his
knees, and still ride free.

They left the Citadel, mounted on two of Guy's best
horses, which were accustomed now to trot without
guidance, followed at a distance by their respective
grooms. They took the Jaffa road.

"And what will become of Shechem when you go?"
asked Baldwin, as they ambled side by side.

"It is a Royal fief. It reverts to you, I suppose."

"Have you no wish, how I should dispose of it?"

"Yes, Master Baldwin, I have a wish, if you will be
good enough to grant it to me."

"I, good enough! I'm not in it. The question is—what's
good enough for you?"

"Well, it's a long story. If you'll give me leave, I'll tell
it to you—"

And so they rode on, down the Jaffa road.

Before autumn, the preparations for departure from
Shechem were nearly complete. A survey had been made

of all the Castle lands to confirm the title deeds granted to each peasant for his property. The Cohanim sat in prolonged session debating the lord's proposals for an agreed system of taxation, hired labor and co-operative marketing. Agreement was reached on all points, except his proposal to abolish the whipping post. That, the elders felt, was too great a break with tradition. Let the lord retain it at his discretion.

Hugh was indefatigable in implementing these developments, riding out every day to make surveys, take inventories and talk to the village elders. His private feelings were inscrutable, for, as a serf himself, he felt keenly the need for social reforms, and yet, as the lord's agent, he felt resentment at the loss of so many privileges by his master.

One day, when they were walking on the hill together, for Hugh always accompanied his master on his morning walk, Guy asked his castellan about himself. "What do you want for yourself, Hugh?"

"Why, it's as you say, master," replied Hugh.

"You will not return home?"

"Only if you bid me."

"Then where?"

"I'd like to stay, if I may, as I am."

"Castellan? For another master?"

"Ah, that would depend—"

"For yourself—your own master?"

"How might that be, now?"

"You have served me well, Hugh. You have saved Castle Shechem for me. I would like you to keep it—as lord."

"As lord!" Hugh's eyes widened at such an impossibility. He must have misunderstood. "But, master, I am a serf!"

"We're coming to that." Guy reached into his tunic and drew out a document which he passed to his castellan. "Some time ago you asked for your freedom. This document makes you a free man and gives you freehold for your lands in Vienne. If you want to transfer your freehold in Vienne to me in exchange for Castle Shechem, I will execute the deed for you."

"Castle Shechem!" It was still too much for him. "But, master, I am a plain man—I cannot read nor write—I could not become a lord—"

"There are many lords who cannot read nor write, Hugh, and some who have less claim to their titles than you."

"But still, even a freedman cannot become a lord—"

"He can if the King gives him the title."

"Title?"

"King Baldwin will grant you a knighthood if you will accept it."

To this Hugh had no reply. He merely gazed at his master in a sort of dumb wonder. This man was going to turn the whole world upside down to suit himself. When peasants became lords—! And yet, why not? Long ago, Guy's ancestors, the great, blond giants of the North, had come to Hugh's land and taken it for themselves. Now, perhaps, the time had come for some restitution. But slowly! It would not do to go so fast! The thought came out in Hugh's words, "How would me and Esmeralda look at Court?"

"As well as any lord and lady by the King's favor," replied Guy. "Is your answer 'yes'?"

"Do you wish it, master?"

"I wish it very much, Hugh."

"Then I will do as you say, master."

The farewells were as endearing and sorrowful as anyone would wish. Guy and Alice, with Hugh at their side, visited every house in the village and exchanged good wishes and tokens of esteem. The village was regretful at Guy's departure and a little apprehensive at the prospect of a serf-made-lord in his stead, but they relied on their new charters to protect them.

At the Convent in Nablus, the nuns fairly wept to see them go. Alice had long outlived the suspicion in which she had once been held. She was remembered now only as the indefatigable worker and the light of the infirmary ward. Yet, even though they lost her, everyone was glad she had married Guy.

The Abbess had a few words with Guy in the parlor, as Alice revisited the wards. "You have been good for her, Guy," she said, squeezing his arm with approval. "We are grateful for what you have done for us, but most of all for what you have done for her."

"She is good for me, Mother," replied Guy, "without her, I would have come to nothing. And I begin to see how much I owe to you. It was your doing, dear Mother—you taught me to be humble. And now, I have had to learn to be very humble indeed—" He passed his hand over his eyes.

The Abbess looked at him with compassion tearing her heart. "The end is not yet," she said. "God's ways are wonderful. Believe!"

"I do," replied Guy, smiling.

The King, to everyone's astonishment, was now up and about. On a new pair of crutches, he walked unaided and received all ambassadors, petitioners and guests himself. He convened a special Court to bid goodbye to the Lord Protector, who handed back his seals of office. And he publicly knighted Hugh and saluted him, to the latter's vast embarrassment, with a kiss on either cheek.

He would, in fact, have ridden to Acre with Guy and Alice, but Guy refused the courtesy. Instead, they parted from one another alone in the Tower of David. And what they said no one knew, but all remarked that the King was like a new man, and even though he grew more frail, his determination to see things through never failed him.

Guy's six men-at-arms—all that remained of the twelve who left Vienne many years ago—travelled down to Acre with him. Even though Guy gave them a choice of remaining behind, all, without exception, voted to return home. Suddenly, their senses were filled with anticipation of the lost sights and sounds and beloved faces of Aquitaine. And with them, at least as far as the shipside, came Sir Hugh of Shechem, followed, according to Syrian custom at a respectful five paces, by the Lady Esmeralda.

Acre bustled as usual with all the commerce of East and West. To the delight of his men, Guy had chosen a passage on a Genoese passenger ship, instead of one of the wallowing pilgrim ships in which they had come out. This meant that they would reach Marseilles in only three weeks, and proceed overland to the Aquitaine by private carriage. For this, and for many such blessings, Alice's dower provided.

Hugh had only one last thing on his mind, as they stood by the rail of the ship, before saying goodbye. "Master," he said, "I have figured it out and I find by my calculation that at Shechem, when the taxes you have set are collected, and the expenses for administration are paid, there will be little left over for Esmeralda and me. You see, under your plan, there isn't any more profit in being a lord. And so, I was wondering if it would be all right with you if I went back to my original plan—"

"You mean you want to be a brigand, Hugh?"

"Just as a sideline, master—"

"Hugh, I appreciate your consulting me, but you must remember I am not your master now."

"Yes, master—I mean—"

"This is a matter for your own conscience. I would not want you to break the laws of the Kingdom, or to bring shame on the King's knighthood."

"But there's no shame in robbing a few infidel merchants on their way to Damascus, is there? I mean— they're not human beings like the rest of us, are they?"

"Hugh—I leave it to you. Do as you think best in everything!"

"Oh, thank you, master! I mean—oh, dammit, God bless you master!"

The ship's bell rang; the wind stood fair for France. But before throwing off the ropes, there was a last minute stay. A mounted messenger arrived, wearing the Royal crest, and he was accompanied by a trumpeter, whose shrill notes arrested all activity and brought silence down on the tumultous crowd. He handed over a despatch box for Guy from the King. Wonderingly, Guy opened it, surrounded by all the curious eyes, there on the open deck.

"What is it, Alice," he said, flushed. "I don't find anything, except a block of wood—"

It was a piece of the True Cross.

EPILOGUE

VIENNE, SEVERAL YEARS LATER

Alice came down the stairs and into the Hall with a startled surprise, tossing back the white veil of her head-dress with one hand, the other smoothing out the rich velvet of her dress. She need not have been concerned. Her appearance, like that of her house, was faultless in every respect, even for the Lord Chancellor of England.

"My Lord," she said, sweeping him a low curtsey, "your humble servant."

William Longchamps looked at her with an admiring eye. Rough, gnarled, squat as a hobgoblin himself, he knew how to appreciate a fine woman. They told him at the Court of Poitou, "You must not pass Vienne without a look at the manor—and the mistress, too." But that, of course, was not why—not exactly why—he had come.

"My lady," he smiled, "in my visit to His Majesty's territories in the Aquitaine, I have been advised to seek the counsel of your husband. About the Crusade, of course. I hope I shall find him at home?"

"Of course! He is just below on the greensward by the river, shooting the longbow with our son, I believe." And picking up a shawl from the back of one of the chairs by the fire, she led him out onto the terrace overlooking the valley. It was a perfect autumn afternoon.

They descended the steps and crossed the grass, which had been neatly nibbled by droves of wooly sheep. The Lord Chancellor did not fail to note the perfect order and peace of this house, the massed flowers, the well-drained river banks, the peasants' cottages, clean, neat and prosperous, outside the manor wall.

At the edge of the river, a target was set up and father and son were rivalling one another in the accuracy of their shots at a hundred paces. Two teen-age village youths ran back and forth retrieving the arrows. "Hooray!" they shouted, when young Perceval, who was their own age, scored in the center ring. But "Hooray!" they were obliged to shout again a moment later, when his father struck the bullseye.

"My dear," said Alice, coming up, "we have been honored by the Lord Chancellor."

The two men bowed and clasped hands. Longchamps studied his host with a penetrating eye. A noble man, the lord of Vienne, he thought, still straight as an oak, despite his silver hair, and worthy of the legends men told of him. How extraordinary that a man like that would busy himself in such a quiet place.

'You are a prize shot, I see," he remarked. Guy accepted the compliment modestly. "It is a long time since I shot in earnest," he said, "but I'm glad I have not lost my sharpness."

"Indeed, you have not." the Chancellor pursued the theme. "Yet I have heard it said—the Seneschal told me at Poitou—that you once did lose your eyesight when you were across the seas. Is that so?"

"It is a long story. I can tell you sometime, if you desire it. Meanwhile, shall we go up to the house and take a glass of wine? I have some Malmsey just arrived from Spain."

They crossed the green, talking easily of country matters. The Chancellor expressed a desire first to see the peasants' cottages, because "I can see your people are prosperous," he said; and so he and his host took horses and made the rounds of the village. The visitor was struck by the modernity of the farms and houses; each had a croft growing a self-sufficiency of vegetables before the door; the walls were of timber, with thatched roofs and smoking chimneys. Everywhere they were given friendly greetings as cottars came back from the fields, carrying scythes and shears, and housewives left their cheese-press or kneading trough to cluster at the garden gate.

"Whence comes all your prosperity?" inquired the Chancellor.

"Since the death of King Henry and the end of the wars in France, we have enjoyed peace hereabouts. I guess we are just making the most of it," Guy said.

"But how do you manage to give your serfs so much luxury?"

"I do not have to give. They are no longer serfs. Each man in the village is now a freedman and pays me taxes for his land. He works his own field and makes it prosperous. That way he grows rich. Is it not so, Yves?"

"Ay, master," replied an old peasant in a smock, raising his cap. "But then, you raise the taxes, too."

"And did I not build you a road last year, and a new mill the year before?" demanded Guy. "So we all benefit!"

The Chancellor was intrigued. He said to Guy as they rode away, "Would you believe, my lord, that my grandfather was a run-away serf from these parts—perhaps from your very land! And today I am Lord Chancellor of England. What do you think of that, now?"

"I think we are moving on," replied Guy, "moving on— The world is becoming a better place. So we may build Jerusalem in this green and fruitful land!"

The Chancellor looked at him quizzically and said nothing.

Soon, they were all seated in the Hall around the wall-fireplace, which had been lighted, for the late afternoon was cool. An extravagance of Guy's this, an idea he brought back from Saracen lands, to place the fire in the wall, with flues to conduct the smoke outside instead of filling the room with soot. The Chancellor was vastly pleased with it, "But it would never do in England, you know," he said, "—too much heat would be lost up the chimney!"

He looked about and took in the calm beauty of the room: the fine, woven tapestries to keep out the cold, the woolen rugs on the stone floor, instead of rushes, the bright gleaming crockery set out on the fine-wrought dressers. No warrior's house this, he thought, but a center of peace—peace without, and peace within. Yet surely this could not be preserved without struggle and strife. Jerusalem would not be built except by the sword.

The group was joined by the family's two daughters, both beautiful young girls like their mother. And the visitor's eyes then fell on Perceval, the son, whose fair, blue-eyed freshness carried the unmistakable stamp of his father. Would he, too, fight for the Cross?

But he didn't ask. Instead, he said, "I believe you promised to tell me the story of how you recovered your sight."

Guy disposed of it briefly. "It is, I must suppose, a miracle," he said. "Not long after our return from the East, Alice and I went on a pilgrimage to Canterbury, to visit the tomb of our holy, blissful martyr. He had not been dead long then, and the miracles were just beginning. Oddly enough, the very first miracle happened to a man who had had both his eyes torn out—a serf, I believe, who had been convicted of some crime. In place of his eyes, two small pupils grew in the empty sockets in his head, and he could see as plainly as you or I.

"But to return to myself. Great crowds of pilgrims were flocking to Canterbury, and the miracles were attested by many thousands. I, myself, had little thought of such an eventuality. I went to offer the monks of Canterbury a piece of the True Cross which I had brought back from the Holy Land, and to touch the holy stones where the blessed Thomas fell. In those days, I was almost wholly blind—not quite, for there were glimmers of light before my eyes, but no definite shapes of any kind.

"We left the Cathedral at evening, and returned to the

pilgrim hostel where we slept, and we went to bed expecting nothing and even talking happily to one another with no such thought in our minds. I had, I remember, a refreshing night's sleep. And in the morning, when I awoke, I saw as plainly as ever I did and as I have done ever since. Call it a miracle, if you will."

"Indeed, indeed!" said the Lord Chancellor, "and with such circumstantial evidence, as we all know, there has never been such a miracle worker as our blessed Thomas à Becket! And to think he was once my predecessor in office as Chancellor of England. I would I could perform such miracles with my Exchequer."

They all laughed at this, and the talk turned to the prospects of King Richard's new crusade. The Chancellor had turned the country inside out to find the means to fit the ships and equip the men. "His Majesty would sell the city of London, if he could, to recover the Kingdom of Jerusalem," said Longchamps.

How shameful, how terrible it was to think of the Holy Land, and the True Cross itself, in the hands of the infidels. They spoke with sadness of the death of the leper King, the accession of the foolish King Guy of Lusignan, and the foolhardiness of his brother, Amalric, who led the army of the Kingdom to defeat. All, all was lost.

"But not forever!" asserted William Longchamps. "Never has an army been raised like King Richard's. You should have seen them at Vézelay this summer! They came from every side, as thick as drops of rain. I tell you, tears were flowing in the streets, as men, signed with the cross, broke from the embraces of the women-folk, and set their faces to Jerusalem. Every soldier, says the King, is now a soldier of God. *Deus Vult.* And, if we each play our part, we shall conquer!"

And again his eye fell on the fair, eager face of the boy Perceval, looking today every bit the same as his father had looked when he took the Cross many years before. Guy followed the glance. "We have done all we can," he said, a shade defensively. "We have paid the Saladin tithe in full."

And a tenth of the revenues of this manor would amount to a pretty penny to help defeat the Paynim Sultan, thought the Chancellor. But it was not enough. Surely the lord of Vienne knew that. The test of faith must be made in flesh and blood—flesh of my flesh and blood of my blood. He turned to Perceval. "And what do you say, young man? Have you no friends who are taking the Cross?"

Perceval looked him in the eyes with a steady glance the Chancellor had already seen elsewhere. "My best friend, Gawayne of Poitiers, is vowed to go. But I have not a knighthood, sir," he replied.

"And if I told you that Queen Elinor, as your liege-lady, will give you a knighthood when she makes her visit to Poitou which I am here to prepare—what then?"

"Then I—I will obey my father's wishes," said the boy flushing.

The Chancellor smiled. "Your father will wish you to be no less of a man than he is, I am sure."

Later that evening, when William Longchamps was gone, father and son sat alone in the Hall together, beside the fire. Alice had gone to bed, leaving two lighted tapers on the dresser, to give them light up the stairs.

It was not long before Perceval put his request to his father, who fully expected it, and gave his consent. "You must do what is right for you, my son," he said. "It is a great step you are taking. There are many pitfalls, many wrong turnings. Only listen for this voice that tells you the turning you must take. And remember—Jerusalem, the true Kingdom, is not here, or there, or anywhere in particular. It is all around us."

They talked long and earnestly, and Guy gave his son much detailed information and advice about the Holy Land. He also made him a present of the curious ring he had always worn—a blood red ruby in an Arabic setting. "Wear it," he said, "to bring you luck. And if you should ever meet another man, wearing the same ring, spare his life for my sake."

Perceval, who had long sensed his father's reluctance to

part with him, was overwhelmed with joy. "I must go at once and tell Gawayne!" he cried, and rushed from the Hall, leaving the doors wide open.

A moment later, Alice came down the stairs in her nightdress, divining the event. "You have let him go?" she asked, a tremble in her voice.

"I have let him do what is—for him—the right, true thing," he answered.

"Oh, my dear!" she gasped and laid her head on his breast. He placed his arms about her in his familiar, possessive embrace.

The night wind rose, banging the doors and blowing out the tapers. They kissed in the dark.

THE BIG BESTSELLERS
ARE AVON BOOKS!

The Kingdom L. W. Henderson	18978	$1.75
To Die in California Newton Thornburg	18622	$1.50
The Last of the Southern Girls Willie Morris	18614	$1.50
The Hungarian Game Roy Hayes	18986	$1.75
The Wolf and the Dove Kathleen E. Woodiwiss	18457	$1.75
The Golden Soak Hammond Innes	18465	$1.50
The Priest Ralph McInerny	18192	$1.75
Emerald Station Daoma Winston	18200	$1.50
Sweet Savage Love Rosemary Rogers	17988	$1.75
How I Found Freedom *In An Unfree World* Harry Browne	17772	$1.95
I'm OK—You're OK Thomas A. Harris, M.D.	14662	$1.95
Jonathan Livingston Seagull Richard Bach	14316	$1.50
Open Marriage George and Nena O'Neill	14084	$1.95

Where better paperbacks are sold, or directly from the publisher. Include 15¢ per copy for mailing; allow three weeks for delivery.

Avon Books, Mail Order Dept., 250 West 55th Street, New York, N.Y. 10019